## COMING HOME FOR CHRISTMAS

Julia Williams has always made up stories in her head, and until recently she thought everyone else did too. She grew up in London, one of eight children, including a twin sister. She was a children's editor at Scholastic for several years before going freelance after the birth of her second child. It was then she decided to try her hand at writing. The result, her debut novel, *Pastures New*, was a bestseller and has sold across Europe.

To find out more about Julia go to her website at www.juliawilliamsauthor.com or follow Julia on Twitter @JCCWilliams.

By the same author:

*Pastures New*
*Strictly Love*
*Last Christmas*
*The Bridesmaid Pact*
*The Summer Season*
*A Merry Little Christmas*
*Midsummer Magic*

# Coming Home For
# Christmas

## JULIA WILLIAMS

AVON

To Ann Moffatt, my wonderful mother. With love.

AVON
A division of HarperCollins*Publishers*
77–85 Fulham Palace Road,
London W6 8JB

www.harpercollins.co.uk

A Paperback Original 2014

1

Copyright © Julia Williams 2014

Julia Williams asserts the moral right to
be identified as the author of this work

A catalogue record for this book is
available from the British Library

ISBN-13: 978-1-84756-358-3

Set in Minion by Palimpsest Book Production Limited,
Falkirk, Stirlingshire

Printed and bound in Great Britain by
Clays Ltd, St Ives plc

**MIX**
Paper from
responsible sources

**FSC**
www.fsc.org
**FSC® C007454**

# *Prologue*

Cat Tinsall was standing by the window, stirring the Christmas pudding, looking out as dark clouds rolled over the hills, threatening a cold and rainy night. The kids would be in from school soon, and her granddaughter Lou Lou was upstairs having a nap. She was glad to be in her cosy warm kitchen, with a cup of tea, and her husband, Noel, who was working from home today, sitting at the table on his laptop.

'Bugger!' Noel was angrily staring at his computer screen as if by some miracle it could tell him some happier news.

'Problem?' Cat asked.

'Not sure,' said Noel. 'But it looks like we've been gazumped again on some land to the north of Shrewsbury Ralph and I have been looking at. We were planning to build affordable starter homes, but this firm, LK Holdings, seems to have got in there first. That's the second time in the last few months. They're acquiring a hell of a lot of land in the area. We'll have to look for somewhere else. Damn. That was such a good spot, and so needed.'

Cat smiled fondly at her husband, his fair hair might be greying now, but his eyes were the same dazzling blue, and thanks to a strict gym regime, Noel was still as attractive to her as the day they met. And bless him, he was always

1

saying the same about her, though her figure wasn't quite as trim as it once was, and her own fair hair was going to need some help from the hairdresser soon.

She wandered over, still mixing her pudding, to see what had fired him up now. Noel was at his most passionate when talking about sustainable development, a subject he cared about deeply. And so much happier here in the picturesque village of Hope Christmas, working for Ralph Nicholas, a local landowner who ran a small family business, than when he'd worked for a big engineering firm in London and felt all his principles being compromised on a daily basis. One of the many good things about making a home, here, was the new lease of life Noel had gained from the move.

'Never mind,' she reassured him, 'I'm sure you'll find something else.'

'It's not just that,' said Noel, looking pensive. 'I've heard a rumour that LK Holdings are sniffing around Hope Christmas. They're big in the leisure business, and want to build a luxury development here.'

'Really?' said Cat surprised. Hope Christmas was the kind of place that supported upmarket B&Bs, rather than big hotels: the last of which had long been sold for a nursing home.

'Really,' said Noel. 'There are one or two large bits of land on the market at the moment. I'd say they're ripe for the picking. I believe Blackstock Farm has been for sale for several months. I know it's been empty for a while.'

'Isn't that the one opposite Marianne and Gabriel?' said Cat. Marianne was one of her best friends in Hope Christmas, and partly the reason they'd come here. She'd entered a magazine competition that Cat had run to find the perfect Nativity, when she was still a magazine editor in London. Cat had ended up not just finding that, but when she came up to meet Marianne, she'd also found the perfect place to bring her growing family, and hadn't had a day's regret since. 'They can't build there, it would be a travesty.'

'Wouldn't it just?' said Noel. 'I think I'd better contact Ralph. He's already gone away for Christmas, but he'll want to know about this.'

Cat stared out at the darkening sky, towards the hills of the town she loved. She hoped that Noel was wrong. Hope Christmas was perfect the way it was: small enough to have a really strong community, big enough that you weren't living in anyone else's pockets. The last thing it needed was a major development, and she and Noel would do anything to protect the place they loved so much.

A chill wind blew down the valley, as Marianne North struggled up the lane from the village with the double buggy. Her three-year-old twins, Harry and Daisy, were perfectly capable of walking, but they were jacking up today, and it seemed easier to push them. As a few icy raindrops started to fall from a dark, angry sky, she was glad she'd wrapped them up warm. Pausing to tighten her coat against the wind and tucking her dark curls under her hat, Marianne swore crossly at a big dark car driving too fast past her, spraying a cold and dirty puddle up her legs. Thoughtless idiot. Couldn't be a local, no one drove up here that fast. She wondered where the car was going; once you got past Pippa and Dan's farm at the end of the road, there was nowhere else to go. She only understood when she saw the car stop and pull in on the right verge, by the gate of Blackstock Farm, which had stood empty for months. A woman Marianne vaguely recognised as a local estate agent leapt out of the passenger door, and fumbled with a key at the gate. Aah, that explained it. Dark car driver must be a potential buyer. She hoped whoever it was showed more sensitivities to the locals, if they did decide to buy.

By the time she reached the gate, there was no one in sight. Just a badly parked shiny black BMW which had churned up the mud going into the farm. In the distance, she could see two figures – a man and a woman it looked like – wandering down towards the woods. She shivered. The rain was starting to come down in sheets, now. She didn't envy them. It was cold and wet out, and it was a bit of a schlep to the woods.

'Come on, kids, let's get you home,' she said. She cast one last look back at the fields. She wondered who was planning to buy Blackstock Farm, and if they would be keeping it as farmland. There had been a lot of developers sniffing around Hope Christmas of late, and even talk of building on the lower slopes of the hills Marianne loved so much. Whoever was looking around Blackstock Farm, clearly wasn't a farmer. She shivered again. For some reason, she had a bad feeling about this . . .

Pippa Holliday walked slowly up to the back field, where she knew that Dan was working on repairing some fencing that had blown down in recent storms, rehearsing what she was going to say. A sharp shrill wind was blowing down the valley, and she felt cold to the bone, despite the layers of warm clothing – stupidly she hadn't worn her hat, and her ginger curls were damp and wild. 'Hi Dan.' She ran over in her head what she might say. 'You know Christmas Day was supposed to be about us . . .' – no that wasn't right, it wasn't about them anymore, it was about the kids . . . 'Dan, would you mind awfully,' – god no, she sounded like

4

something out of a seventies sitcom. Best come clean. 'Dan, I have a problem . . .'

She found him sitting down on a log, taking a break, with a flask of tea beside him, staring down the valley, into the fields below. It was a gloomy dark day, with storm clouds rolling over the hills in the distance, making them look threatening and hostile.

He looked startled to see her, as if he'd been thinking about something else entirely.

'Hi,' he said, running his fingers through his dark hair, his blue eyes brooding and sad – as they seemed to have been ever since the catastrophic accident nearly two years ago, when Dan had fallen from a tree and suffered a terrible head injury which had changed their lives forever. Dan wasn't the same person anymore, and though much better than he'd been, still suffered from blind rages and occasional depression. Pippa had thought she could live with that, Dan hadn't wanted her to and moved out.

Pippa felt absurdly awkward. A year on from their separation, and it still felt no easier. This was ridiculous, he was the father of her children and she was going in a new direction with someone else – it was time she got over Dan.

'Hi,' she said. 'Dan, there's something I need to run by you, about Christmas . . .'

'Fire away,' said Dan, still staring intently towards the fields below.

'It's about Richard,' Pippa said. She was always loath to bring up her new partner's name in front of Dan, but she had no choice, so, hesitatingly, she told him how Richard's plans had changed and he had nowhere to go, '. . . so I know it's not ideal, but would it be ok if he was there on Christmas Day?'

'Sorry, what?' Dan looked up at her, as if really noticing

5

for the first time she was there. 'What do you think they're doing out on Blackstock Farm?'

He hadn't been listening at all. Pippa looked where he was pointing. She could see two small figures trudging back from the woods below them, up towards the farmhouse, which had been empty for some months. She could make out a car parked in the farmyard.

'Do you think someone's buying at last?' she said, all thoughts about Richard temporarily forgotten. She, Dan and Gabriel whose farms all bordered their neighbour's, had been fretting about what would happen to Blackstock Farm for several months. If a farmer didn't buy, there was plenty of room for development which could have a huge impact on all of them.

'Could be,' said Dan. 'I've been watching them for about half an hour. They've looked over the whole site really thoroughly.'

'You never know,' said Pippa brightly, 'maybe it's being bought by a farmer.'

'You know Old Joe let it go to rack and ruin,' said Dan. 'I doubt anyone in their right mind would touch it as a farm. There's too much to do.'

The rain was starting to come down in sheets now. It was too cold and wet to be up here. Pippa watched as the two figures made their way back up the field. They didn't look like farmers.

'We'll just have to wait and see, I suppose,' she said, trying to stay cheerful, but her heart wasn't in it. Something rotten was coming to Hope Christmas. She could feel it in her bones.

'The farmhouse itself needs a lot of work,' Jenny Ingles was explaining to her client, as she opened the gate to Blackstock

Farm. He was a rather good-looking city type, with fair hair and a charming smile. He clearly wasn't used to the country though, and was inappropriately dressed in a thin suit, a barely warm winter coat, and smart shiny shoes, which were likely to skitter all over the icy courtyard. Unlike Jenny, who had tucked her red hair into a warm woolly hat, and was muffled in a puffer jacket, scarf, long skirt, woolly tights and fur-lined boots.

Her potential customer didn't seem all that interested in the farm, focussing on something apparently more vital on his iPhone. 'And as you can see,' Jenny continued, 'there are lots of outbuildings, and plenty of space and a great view of the woods and hillside, part of which belong to the farm. Let me show you inside, it's freezing out here.'

'That won't be necessary. I'm more interested in the land. But I suppose the main building can stay. It might make a decent welcome lodge,' said her companion, finally looking up from his phone. Really, so very rude, Jenny thought. She wondered why he'd come. He hardly looked the farming type, but no one had shown an interest in Blackstock Farm in months, and she could do with a sale before Christmas. She and her boyfriend, Tom, were planning a skiing trip over the festive season; a bonus would come in handy. 'Can we walk down to the woods from here?'

'Yes, of course,' said Jenny, grateful that she'd had the sense to dress up warmly, 'but are you sure? It's likely to be cold and muddy.'

Dark storm clouds were rolling over the hills and the temperature felt like it had dropped a couple of degrees. A few streaks of sharp cold rain fell, making Jenny shiver.

Flashing a devastatingly winning smile, her client said, 'I'll manage. I'm sure it will be fine.'

Jenny led him to a gate in the furthest corner of the yard.

It was a good ten minutes' hike down to the top part of the woods, and despite her boots, her feet were like blocks of ice when they got there, and her skirt was soaked through at the bottom where it had trailed in the wet grass. Keen as she was for this sale, as the rain started to fall in earnest, Jenny cursed her enthusiastic companion (who apparently didn't notice the cold) for dragging her down here. On a sunny day in June it would have been lovely . . .

'This is perfect,' he was saying. 'We could do so much with this.'

'Oh?' she asked. She'd assumed he was a townie looking for an escape to the country, but now she was intrigued. 'What did you have in mind?'

'I'm afraid I can't reveal that,' he said, 'but I can tell you that my company will be very *very* interested, indeed. This is just what we've been waiting for.'

He smiled that dazzling smile at her again, and she felt herself go weak at the knees. If she didn't have a boyfriend . . .

'Right, I think I've seen all I need to see,' her client, and, she hoped, now prospective buyer, said, 'thank you so much for your time and trouble.'

'My pleasure,' she said, and hoping she wasn't being too pushy added, 'I take it you feel you'll be able to move forward with this, maybe before Christmas?'

'We'll have to see,' another flash of that winning smile. 'I have a few calls to make first.'

As they walked back towards the farmhouse, Jenny wondered what his company was planning. This was a lovely part of the world, and she could see the attraction of living on a farm like this. Perhaps they'd be putting starter homes up here. Hell, if she and Tom had the money . . .

Jenny showed her client round the farmhouse briefly but

could tell he wasn't really interested. Maybe she'd got it wrong; maybe he wasn't going to bite. She didn't *usually* get it wrong.

But then, he said those magic words: 'I think my boss will be *very* interested to hear about this property and land. I'll get back to you as soon as possible.'

*Result*. That Christmas bonus was looking much more likely. Jenny thanked him and agreed to call him early the following week. As she walked through the icy winter rain to the car, Jenny was delighted to hear him on the phone, presumably to his boss, saying, 'Felix? Luke Nicholas here, I think we've found our location.'

# Christmas Day

'Are we *ever* going to have lunch?' Cat's thirteen-year-old daughter, Paige, prised herself away from her brand new iPhone for five minutes and came wandering into the kitchen looking hungry, as if she hadn't been fed in months.

'Sorry, darling,' said Cat, Santa hat slipping, boiling hot and uncharacteristically fraught in her gleaming stainless steel kitchen; normally her favourite place in the house. But today, as she fiddled with the knobs on the cooker, she felt like hitting something. Preferably the cooker. Brand new, when they'd moved in just over seven years ago, it hadn't stood the test of time. 'It's this sodding oven. It's playing up again.'

It was the one spanner in the works, in what had been so far a perfect Christmas morning. Having teenagers in the house meant that no one got up too early, apart from her beautiful one-year-old granddaughter Lou Lou. Luckily her eldest daughter, Mel, had done the decent thing and got up with the baby. Later, they'd sat around opening presents, enjoying watching Lou Lou surrounded by boxes, revelling in ripping wrapping paper to shreds and clapping her hands in delight. Having prepared the vegetables the day before, Cat had been quite relaxed about the turkey, until she'd realised the oven wasn't working.

'I *knew* we should have got a new one before Christmas,' said Noel, laughing at her, as he came in the kitchen bringing her the glass of Prosecco he'd promised several hours earlier.

'Shut up, know it all,' said Cat, throwing a tea towel at him with an affectionate grin, 'you said nothing of the sort. Anyway, Paige, despite the cooker having a tantrum, it *is* nearly ready. So can you tell your brother and sisters, and ask Mel to make sure Lou Lou is settled.'

Paige, whose hair seemed to have changed colour overnight for the second time in as many weeks, vanished like greased lightning now that food was in the offing, and she could be heard shouting, 'Everyone, it's nearly time to eat, at last!' It wasn't as if they hadn't been eating chocolate all morning.

'Right, ready to carve?' she asked Noel, putting her oven gloves on and opening the oven door. The turkey dish was very heavy, and also extremely hot. Oven gloves were also on her must buy list, she realised ruefully; these were wearing through.

'Can I do anything to help?' Angela, her mother-in-law wandered in at that moment, with impeccable timing, always making sure she did something to put Cat's teeth slightly on edge. She meant well, but it was hard sometimes not to feel like she was criticising Cat's every move.

'No, we're fine, thanks, Angela,' said Cat, just as she lifted the turkey dish out, and then dropped it slightly, realising there was a hole in her glove and she'd burnt her finger. 'Oh sod!' she added as the dish slipped out of her hands and fell on the open oven door and turkey fat accidentally spilt on the floor. Gingerly she picked up the turkey dish, and put it on top of the oven, shut the oven door, and went to fetch a cloth, only to find Angela delightedly rushing forward, at last finding an opportunity to be helpful.

11

'Careful!' shouted Cat, too late as her mother-in-law slipped on the turkey fat and slid gracefully across the grey flagstone floor, landing with a rather undignified thump on her backside. Cat stood transfixed in horror, not sure quite what to do, till Noel broke her stupor as he raced to his mum's side.

'Mum, are you ok?' he asked.

'I'm fine, don't fuss so,' said Angela, but she was clearly shaken and was breathing very hard and in a rather laboured way.

'Slowly does it,' said Cat, helping her mother-in-law sit up, and fetching her a glass of water. 'Get your breath back, before you try and stand up.'

She shot Noel an anxious glance and he grimaced back at her. Angela was generally fit and healthy, but she'd gone down with a hell of a thump.

They waited about ten minutes, till Angela was breathing more comfortably, but try as they might, they couldn't get her up.

'It's my hip,' she kept saying, 'it's rather painful.'

She was looking very pale and shaking slightly. What if she'd broken it? Cat felt her anxiety levels rising,

'Do you think we should ring an ambulance?' Cat asked, looking at Noel worriedly.

'You can't, not on Christmas Day,' said Angela, in a very determined manner. 'I'll be fine.'

'Well you can't stay down there,' Cat pointed out.

In the event, after another ten minutes, Noel and Cat were able to help Angela up onto one of the kitchen chairs. By now the children had all come in, agog to know what was happening.

'Granny's had a bit of a fall, I think it's probably best if we take her to hospital just to get things checked. It might take hours for an ambulance to come out today. Angela, do you think you could manage to get to the car? We'll take you to casualty.'

'I don't want to ruin things,' said Angela, but she looked faint and not very well, and was clearly very far from being fine. 'What about Christmas lunch?'

Lucky she hadn't had that glass of Prosecco yet, Cat thought with a pang, but Christmas lunch was going to have to go on hold. 'It can wait. Sorry, guys, you'll have to have sandwiches for now,' said Cat. 'Mel, can you take charge till we're back?'

'Sure,' said Mel, who was bouncing Lou Lou up and down in her arms.

Paige pulled a face. 'Does she have to be in charge?' she said, 'Mel's so bossy,' but Cat silenced her with a look.

Then together with Noel and their son James, they walked slowly out of the kitchen, down the oak beamed hallway, and out of the house, awkwardly manoeuvring Angela along the snowy path and into the family car.

It was a twenty minute drive to the hospital, but fortunately, it being Christmas Day, they were seen very quickly, and the cheery doctor pronounced Angela to be suffering from bruises and shock. In light of her age, and there actually being room on the wards, he wanted to keep her in for observation overnight, so within a couple of hours, as Angela insisted they get back to continue Christmas with the children, Cat and Noel found themselves on their way home.

'That didn't go quite as expected did it?' said Noel with a wry grin. He looked pale and shaken, as well he might. Noel hadn't always got on with his mother, but Cat knew how deeply he loved her.

'You can say that again,' Cat agreed. 'Honestly, why does

it always happen to us? It was the perfect Christmas till then.'

'You don't think—?' Noel started, looking sombre as he pulled into the drive.

'What?' Cat asked, but she had a feeling she knew what he was thinking.

'That this – might be, you know, the start of something? I mean Mum is in her seventies now.'

Cat squeezed her husband's arm. She knew how he felt. When her mum had started her long slow decline into Alzheimer's, it had been little things that had gone awry at first. Cat knew at first hand how hard it was to see a much-loved parent going downhill. She hated the thought of Noel having to go through that too.

'Don't fret,' she said, trying to remain positive. 'You heard the doctor, Angela will be fine by tomorrow.'

'And if she isn't?'

'We'll cross that bridge when we come to it,' said Cat.

Pippa stood in her kitchen, sipping a glass of wine, staring into the garden, as the last embers of the setting sun leached away, setting the snow-filled hills alight with flaming reds and golds and casting a gold, warm light across her battered kitchen table and Welsh dresser. This was the bit of Christmas Day she'd always liked best when the children were younger: lunch eaten, presents unwrapped, everyone sprawling around the lounge either watching TV, or playing games, and most certainly gorging themselves on chocolates they really didn't want. In the past she'd have relaxed with them all, letting Dan take over the clearing up, but not this year; this year everything was different. Everyone was being so polite and friendly, she'd wanted to scream. So as they all settled down to late afternoon boozing in front of the telly, Pippa had escaped out here, claiming tidying up duties, to avoid the feelings of suffocation which threatened to oppress her.

It had seemed like the best thing to do – the *grown-up* thing to do – a year on from her split with Dan to have a family Christmas as they'd done in the past. While *she* might have been able to cope with another Christmas without Dan, she couldn't let the kids down, they'd been through too much already. They'd all begged her individually if Dad, Grandpa and Grandma could come like they used to.

'It wasn't the same last year,' Nathan her oldest son had said a little mournfully.

'I want things the way they were,' added George, though at thirteen, he was old enough to know that couldn't be the case.

Her lovely boys had coped so well and maturely with the events of the previous twelve months – Nathan in particular, who'd tried to become the man of the house, would have been enough to sway her. But as ever, it was her wheelchair bound twelve-year-old daughter Lucy, whose cerebral palsy gave her enough to deal with, who made the decision for her. Lucy had been stoical about her dad moving out, though she missed Dan keenly. So when one night she typed on the computer which allowed them to communicate, 'Can Daddy be with us for Christmas, *please*,' Pippa felt any resolve she may have had dissipate.

One of them, Pippa could have resisted, but all three? And so it had been agreed that Dan, his mother and father would come for Christmas Day.

And it probably *would* have been fine, if Richard's plans for Christmas hadn't gone catastrophically awry. Richard normally stayed with his mum and sister and visited his daughter, apparently, but his sister had suddenly announced she was going skiing with her new partner, which led his mum to declare that she was spending Christmas with an aunt whom Richard detested. This was all new to Pippa, last Christmas she'd only just met Richard, while organising a Christmas Ball to fundraise for Lucy's respite care, and their relationship was still at a fairly tentative stage. She hadn't factored in him coming for Christmas Day.

But what could she do? Without thinking about it, Pippa had said, 'Well of course you must come here,' ignoring the black looks from Lucy and the unasked what the—? questions from the boys. Richard was still new enough for her not to be sure about letting him into her home territory; still new enough for the children to be wary of him, especially Lucy. In an ideal world she would have never invited him, but in for a penny, in for a pound, she decided it would be make or break.

After all, in the last difficult year, when Pippa had finally had to accept that Dan was lost to her, Richard had been a bright ray of hope, giving her comfort that life could move on, and she could be happy once more. Never intrusive, but kind and supportive, Richard had been a rock of empathy to her during the most difficult period of her life. He made her laugh, and was thoughtful and sweet, as well as being very attractive. In the last few weeks, their relationship appeared to have gone onto a more permanent footing, and though Pippa was still not sure where they were headed, she'd decided she owed it to Richard to give things a go. Dan wasn't coming back, that was clear, and Pippa decided for her sanity's sake she couldn't sit moping about forever. Second chances didn't come every day. Maybe Christmas Day was the day to accept this one.

Luckily, she'd invited her cousin, Gabriel, his wife and

her best friend, Marianne, and the twins over too, thinking there was safety in numbers. In such a potentially awkward situation, she was grateful she had done. Marianne was tact itself, and she liked Richard, and could happily be relied on to entertain him if necessary.

As it was, everyone was on their best behaviour and it was only Harriet, her ex mother-in-law who seemed to find it difficult, despite the fact that Pippa had made it clear that Richard was sleeping on the sofa. Their relationship, if it even *was* a relationship was still at a very tentative stage. Harriet came sobbing into the kitchen early in the day, after one too many glasses of sherry, hiccupping that she was so sorry about what had happened.

'Harriet, I'm sorry too,' said Pippa, fighting back tears of her own, 'but Dan left me, remember. I am *allowed* to move on.'

Except, was she moving on? Could she, when she had spent the whole day watching Dan, so natural with his daughter, who loved being with her dad, comparing him to Richard, so ill at ease, yet making an effort. Seeing the pair of them in the same room had sent her into total turmoil. What did she really want?

Was it Richard, who was so kind to her, and had gently reintroduced her to the idea that she might still be attractive, or was it Dan, who even now felt like a part of her that she would never get over losing?

'Maybe I'm rushing things,' she said aloud as she stared out of the window. She sighed, and sipped her wine, as she pottered around, tidying in the kitchen. Her two closest friends, Cat and Marianne, didn't think so, pointing out that she and Dan had been living apart for over a year now and that he'd made his feelings perfectly clear. But part of Pippa felt guilty for finding someone new so soon. Even though it was illogical. As she'd reminded her mother-in-law, Dan was the one who had left.

'Need any help in here?' Pippa turned round with a start to see Dan standing in the doorway. Her heart pounded that bit harder. Should she still be having this reaction to him, when she had Richard? Guilt tightened across her stomach once more. 'I rather think that's my job, isn't it?'

Not anymore, she felt like saying, but didn't.

'Go on, sit down, Pippa,' said Dan. 'If I know you, you've been on the go since six this morning.'

And that of course was the point. Dan *did* know her. And understood her, and *got* her. Did Richard? It was too soon to say. And unfair to consider, she scolded herself. She was just getting to know Richard. They both needed time.

But it was nice to be bossed about by Dan, so Pippa let herself be persuaded to sit at the table with a glass of red wine, while he loaded the dishwasher, dealt with the remains of the turkey, and even cleaned out the roasting dish, which she'd left to soak, intending to do it in the morning. Pippa wondered if Richard would ever do that if they stayed together – then felt guilty again for making the comparison. Richard brought different things to the table. She shouldn't dismiss him for not being like Dan.

It was then that Dan dropped his bombshell, quite casually as he wiped fat away from the roasting dish, just as Pippa was beginning to feel mellow for the first time that day. For a second it felt like old times, and if she shut her eyes, she could imagine that things were as they'd always been, Dan in the kitchen by her side.

Before Dan said the words she'd never wanted to hear.

'You and Richard look good together,' he said. 'I'm pleased for you.'

'Oh,' said Pippa who had been worried about his reaction.

It had taken all her courage to ring Dan to tell him that Richard was coming for Christmas lunch, after her first aborted attempt. 'You're sure you don't mind? I mean, I wouldn't have had him over this Christmas, under normal circumstances, it's a bit soon . . .' her voice trailed off. How soon, was too soon, when your husband had rejected you?

Dan put the tray on the rack, and then turned to her, in such a familiar gesture it made her throat catch.

'You had to move on sometime,' he said. 'I've been expecting it.'

'Oh,' said Pippa again. Her palms were sweating. Where was he going with this?

After a long and pregnant pause, Dan eventually said, 'I think you should give it a go.'

'But—' Pippa wasn't quite sure how to react. Whatever she'd been expecting, it wasn't such calm acceptance of the situation. It really was over. She'd have to face it now.

'We're still married?' said Dan. 'I know. And I've been thinking. We can't go on as we are, working the farm together as if nothing's changed. Pip, I'm holding you back.'

Don't say it, she begged him silently, please don't say it. The words she'd been hoping never to hear, since he first suggested separating a year before. If he didn't say them, there was still hope.

'Pippa, I think it's time we sorted this out properly,' Dan said. 'I think we should file for divorce.'

Marianne picked herself up reluctantly from the very comfortable spot where she had been sitting in Pippa's cosy lounge. The twins, who had behaved impeccably well all day, were getting into hyper mode. It was only a matter of time before they lost the plot totally. She was so grateful Pippa had invited them for Christmas lunch, as December had been frantic this year, and she was glad to pass up the opportunity to cook on Christmas Day, particularly as her thirteen-year-old stepson, Steven, was going to spend Christmas with his mum, Eve. Gabriel was always moody the years when Steven wasn't with them, as Eve had been a flaky mum at best, so it was good he had a distraction. Plus Marianne knew it would help Pippa (she and Gabe were closer as cousins than a lot of siblings, Marianne knew) to have more people there to minimise the awkwardness of the first post-separation Christmas together with Dan and his family. When they'd arrived and realised that Richard was there too, Marianne had worried the day was going to be more difficult than she'd imagined. But thanks to superhuman efforts from both Pippa and Dan, there had been no histrionics, and everyone had had a lovely day.

Marianne started to gather coats, bags and presents together with a sigh. It was so warm and mellow inside, she wasn't looking forward to braving the east wind whistling off the hills.

'Oi, lazybones,' she said, gently giving Gabriel a kick. He was sitting sleepily by the fire, having uncharacteristically for him, tucked into the port after lunch. Gabriel's parents, David and Jean, had opted for a quiet Christmas this year, and David had volunteered to do the evening shift on the farm, so for once Gabriel could relax. Marianne was pleased that he'd been able to enjoy himself, but he looked firmly ensconced where he was, and she had a feeling it was going to be hard work prising him out.

'Come on, Gabe, it's time to go,' she said, as she'd had no response to her first foray.

'Oh do we have to?' said Gabriel, looking at his half full glass longingly. 'It's still early yet.'

'The twins?' said Marianne pointedly, trying not to feel

irritated. Gabriel didn't often do this to her, but she didn't really want to go home on her own. 'It's nearly their bed time.'

'Ten more minutes,' pleaded Gabriel.

A further ten minutes elapsed, and Marianne was going to suggest they left again, particularly as Harry and Daisy erupted into a squabble, which was threatening to turn into all-out war. She glanced over to Gabriel, and saw he was deep in what looked like an important conversation with Dan, who'd emerged from the kitchen where he and Pippa had been closeted quite a while, looking rather gloomy. Marianne didn't feel like she could disrupt them, and neither did she want to. Gabriel and Dan were good mates, and since his accident two years ago, she knew Dan needed to offload from time to time. Marianne hoped Pippa was all right. She'd followed Dan in five minutes later, looking a little bright-eyed, but, being Pippa, was now laughing and joking as if she didn't have a care in the world. Marianne settled back to give it another half an hour, by which time the children were climbing the walls.

'I really think I'd better take the twins home,' said Marianne, hoping Gabriel would take the hint. Which he didn't. I'm your *wife*, she wanted to say, and it's Christmas. Was it too much to ask to cuddle up with her husband, while the children were in bed, and watch cosy Christmas telly, drinking wine and counting their blessings? Clearly Gabriel wasn't even thinking about it.

So, with simmering resentment, Marianne took two over-excited and overfed three-year-olds home alone. They were so hyped up they refused either bath or bed for a whole fractious hour, before Harry shouted 'I feel sick,' and promptly threw up on the lounge floor. Followed five minutes later by a wail from his sister who had followed suit. Marianne had just about cleaned up and was about to pour herself a glass of wine, and sit down grumpily in front of the TV waiting for Gabriel to come home, when the phone rang. The instant she answered it, she heard Steven's panic on the other end, and everything else was forgotten.

'Marianne,' he said. 'It's Mum. She's really not very well. She's locked herself in the bathroom and I don't know what to do.'

*Part One*

*It's Been Too Long*

# My Broken Brain

I don't even know why I'm doing this. I'm not the sort to bare my soul. I've never ever written anything down about the way I feel. Except a letter to Pippa once, a long long time ago. This is just not me. But then I don't know who me is anymore . . .

The old me was calm and patient, and easy going. The new me – is impatient, depressed and angry . . . So very angry at what's happened to destroy my family, my life.

Which is why Jo said it might help to write stuff down. (Jo's my counsellor.) Christ. I can't believe I wrote that. But then, I can't believe I have a counsellor either.

*Five minutes later*
I keep sitting looking at the screen. What am I going to write? It's not as if I have anything interesting to say. My life is pretty fucked up at present. That's all I know.

I knew this wouldn't help.

*Half an hour later*
I've had a cup of tea. Come back, sat here staring some more. I'd give up now, but Jo will want to know that I've written *something* down.

Where do I even begin?

Jo says, at the beginning . . . that sounds like some kind of lame story we had to write at school. I was never much good at that. I was never much good at anything apart from tending to animals, and ploughing the land. And now I'm not much good at that.

So . . . the beginning.

I used to be happy once. I had a family, a lovely wife, a farm we ran together. I didn't know it then, but life was pretty damned perfect.

Then, two years ago, I had an horrific accident which caused me brain damage. And nothing's been the same since . . .

# 20 Years Ago

## First Christmas

'You're here! Already?' Pippa looked stricken as she walked across the snowy yard, delightfully scruffy in an old raincoat, thick woolly jumpy, jeans, wellies, her auburn curls tied up in a loose ponytail. 'Just look at me, I haven't even changed yet.'

'That doesn't matter,' said Dan, his heart singing. Pippa could have been wearing a brown paper bag and she'd still have been gorgeous. He resisted the urge to pick her up and swing her in his arms, just in case her parents were looking out of the farmhouse window. He'd only met them again once, since he and Pippa had got together at the Farmer's Ball, though of course he remembered them from when he and Pippa had been at school together, a lifetime ago. Pippa's parents had been nothing but friendly and welcoming, but he didn't want to get in their bad books this early on in his relationship with their daughter.

'You did say, Christmas Eve, your place, 7pm, didn't you?' said Dan, puzzled. 'We are still going to the Hopesay Arms, aren't we?' They'd made the arrangement earlier in the week, but what with it being Christmas week, he'd been flat out helping his own parents on their farm, and presumably Pippa had been doing the same.

'Oh!' said Pippa, her face dropping. 'I thought we said eight. Mum and Dad like going to the early Christmas service at church, so they can be up early for the cows on Christmas Day. I offered to take charge of milking tonight for them. One of the farm hands was supposed to be coming up to help me, but he's just rung to say he's down and out with flu. I'm so sorry, but I'm not going to be ready for hours.'

'I can help,' said Dan, who didn't care where he spent time with Pippa, so long as they were together. Ever since their first date, he'd been pinching himself that she was interested in him. Pippa North, the girl every guy in his year at school had fancied. And now she was his. Permanently, he hoped.

'Would you really?' Pippa looked like she might burst into tears.

'Of course,' said Dan with a grin. 'Where do you want me?' Luckily, he hadn't dressed up too much for their date, and he didn't mind if he got his clothes dirty. He'd do anything for Pippa, he realised, anything at all. Every time he met her, she astonished him more. How many other girls her age in Hope Christmas would be milking the cows instead of heading for the pub on Christmas Eve?

'You're amazing,' said Pippa, throwing her arms around him in an embrace which he wanted to last for ever. 'Let me find you some overalls to wear.'

Which is how Dan found himself half an hour later, sitting in the milking shed, listening to Christmas carols on Pippa's old cassette deck over the hum of the machines and the cows bellowing, laughing at the way the evening had turned out.

'And there was me planning to show you a wild night in Hope Christmas,' he said, grinning. 'At this rate we're going to be too knackered to do anything.'

'That would be difficult,' said Pippa, smiling as she expertly removed a cow from the stalls and cleaned it up before patting it on its rump and sending it out to the yard. 'Hope Christmas is hardly a hub of night life. I am sorry I've kept you from the pub though.'

He loved that about her, the way she was always so positive and kind.

'Don't be,' said Dan. 'I don't care where I am so long as I'm with you.'

She looked at him shyly, and blushed.

'Me too,' she said, and he was hit by a sudden revelation.

'I love you, Pippa,' he said. It was the first time he'd ever said that to any girl, ever.

'Oh Dan,' she said, her eyes shining, 'I love you too.'

He wanted to kiss her there and then, but there was a cow between them, and work to be done. But as Dan watched her, focussed completely on the task in hand, totally at one with the animals she was dealing with, he was hit by a second revelation. Come what may, Pippa North was the girl he was going to marry.

*This Year*

*January*

# Chapter One

Marianne walked down the lane, feeling gloomy. It was a crisp clear January morning, but the Christmas snows had melted, leaving patches of forlorn looking but lethal ice. The twins had just gone back to nursery after Christmas. After a hassle to get them out of the door, they had readily raced down the lane, reminding her of the way Steven, and Pippa's boys had run the same way when she'd first met them.

Now Steven, Nathan and George were turning into strapping young teenagers, their childhoods almost a distant memory. She should hold onto these moments with the twins. They would be over in the blink of an eye. Time seemed to be moving faster than she'd like. It seemed like only yesterday that she'd first moved to Hope Christmas, newly in love with stunningly good-looking Luke Nicholas, who'd promptly broken her heart. She'd nearly fled back to London then, but the lure of the beautiful countryside had been too strong. And then of course, there'd been Gabriel . . .

Even now, Marianne still found it hard to believe she could have been lucky enough to find Gabriel. He too had been left heartbroken when his wife Eve, who suffered badly from depression, left him, and slowly they had built something new together. And now, seven years on, Marianne was married, with a stepson and two lovely children of her own. Life couldn't be better. And yet, and yet . . .

Marianne tried to shake off her feelings of melancholy, but she felt unsettled and as if she'd lost her sense of purpose. Another year and a bit, and the twins were going to be at school. Although Gabriel wasn't putting her under pressure, Marianne felt she should be thinking about what she was going to do next. There was plenty to do on the farm, and Gabriel could always use extra help. But while Marianne loved being a farmer's wife, she wasn't born to it like Pippa. And although she also loved looking after the twins, she missed work.

'I don't know,' she said out loud to a passing crow, 'should I stick at being a farmer's wife, or is it time I went back to teaching?' She looked across at the fields bordering her home. It was lovely being out here, and she enjoyed working outside with Gabe, particularly in lambing season, but she missed being in front of a class. Not that she'd want to go back to Hope Christmas Primary, where the current head teacher had made her feel worse than useless. But if not there, where? And how? Marianne felt unfocussed, muzzy. Maybe when the twins were older, and maybe to another school . . .

Besides, work wasn't the total reason for her discontent. Not really. She sighed, as she walked up the garden path and let herself into the home where she had been so happy for the past seven years. Where she still *was* happy, she corrected herself. It was just that Gabriel seemed a bit distant at the moment.

When questioned about it, all she got was a curt, 'I'm fine,' but he had admitted to being shaken by Pippa and Dan's divorce. 'I still can't believe they've split up,' he told

Marianne, 'they seemed so right, so solid. It makes you think, doesn't it?'

'Not too much I hope,' Marianne joked, but Gabriel hadn't responded, just taken himself off to the fields, retreating into a taciturn silence at home.

It had been like that since Christmas. Marianne tried to be supportive. This was the start of Gabriel's busiest time of year, and he often came in late from lambing, usually too late to see the children. Which was a pity, because the only thing that seemed to cheer him up was the twins. He always came to life when they jumped on him as he walked through the door, or at the weekends when Steven was home from school. But the rest of the time, Gabriel seemed to brood. Marianne knew that brooding look of old – it was the way he'd looked when she'd first met him. Unhappy, sad, lost. Marianne had hoped never to see that look again, and she had a feeling she knew what was causing it.

Eve. Gabriel's ex. Since that frantic phone call on Christmas Day, things had gone from bad to worse with Eve. Marianne and Gabriel had dropped everything and gone to rescue Steven, kids in tow. They had been greeted with sobbing hysterics, and while Gabe had worked his magic (born of years of practice), calmed her down and persuaded her to take her medication, it had only been a temporary fix.

A day or so later, she'd been on the phone telling Marianne that she was being spied on, and nothing Marianne could say could calm her down. And after that they'd endured a week of late night phone calls, of worsening degrees, till eventually one morning they had a call from a neighbour to say Eve was outside her house, dressed only in a nightie.

Gabriel and Marianne had dropped the twins with Pippa

and rushed over straight away, to find Eve, looking lost and bewildered, sitting sobbing in her neighbour's kitchen, her feet bleeding, where she'd cut them on the garden path.

'We have to call an ambulance,' Marianne said as Gabe tried unsuccessfully to coax her back home.

'I can't go there,' Eve said anxiously, gripping hold of Gabe's arm, 'they'll find me.'

'Who?' asked Gabe with patience acquired from years of experience. 'Eve, there's no one here but us, and we won't hurt you.'

'Them,' said Eve stubbornly. 'Can't you hear them? They're whispering about me all the time.'

Marianne, Gabriel and the neighbour exchanged helpless glances, and when Gabe questioned her further it transpired Eve had stopped taking her medication altogether. By now Gabe had got onto Eve's mum, Joan.

'She's the worst I've seen her in a long time,' Gabe said. 'I really think she needs to go to hospital.'

In the end, on the advice of the doctor who came out, to Gabriel's evident distress, Eve had to be sectioned for her own safety, as she clearly couldn't be left alone. It was an upsetting business, Eve screaming that they couldn't make her go, the doctor saying she had to. In the end after Gabriel made numerous promises that he and Steven would come and see Eve as soon as they could, she was persuaded to get into an ambulance by the kind paramedics.

'I wish there was another way,' Gabriel said desperately to Marianne as they followed Eve to the hospital. 'I'm never convinced hospital helps her.' He was really shaken up by the whole thing, clearly reminded of the time when Eve was living with him and had done similar.

'It makes me feel so helpless,' he said to Marianne. 'Even now, after all this time, I want to help her, and I can't.'

It was really sad, Marianne could see that, and she felt particularly for Steven, who was very distressed by his mum's relapse.

'It was really scary, Marianne,' he confided in her. 'I didn't know what to do.'

She was glad that he'd gone back to school, where he could be distracted from worrying about his mum. And at least now Eve was safe and being looked after.

'She's not your responsibility anymore,' were the words she longed to say to Gabe, but she knew that he would always feel responsible for Eve, come what may. It was something she'd taken on when she married him, but back then Eve had been well. Marianne hadn't factored in this, or the impact it would have on her marriage.

Normally Marianne wouldn't have minded, but now it made her uneasy. She'd always accepted Eve for Steven's sake, but since Eve had split up from her ex, Darren, a year ago, she'd become more and more needy. And from where Marianne was sitting, it seemed like the person she needed most was Gabriel.


'Peekaboo!' Cat was lying on the floor on her tummy, face to face with her granddaughter, whose nose was pressed up so close to her own, Cat was surprised she could still breathe. 'Peekaboo' was always guaranteed to make Lou Lou giggle, which it did now.

'Boo! GaGa! Boo!' Lou Lou gurgled, clapping her hands in delight. Cat loved the fact that her granddaughter was trying to say her name already. It gave her a warm glowing feeling all over. In fact, considering her inauspicious beginning, literally born in a barn to her 16-year-old single mother, Mel, Cat still couldn't believe how happy Lou Lou made her. An unexpected blessing, despite the uproar it had caused in all their lives, especially coming so soon after Cat had lost her beloved mum, Louise, after whom Lou Lou was named. Now Lou Lou was part of the family, and it was as if she always had been. And Cat couldn't help a sneaking feeling of gratitude that she had this second chance baby, to replace the one she'd lost around the time Mel had got herself pregnant.

'Peekaboo,' said Cat again, and Lou Lou giggled as if it were the funniest thing in the world. Cat giggled too. She'd forgotten how much babies laughed, and it made her realise she didn't laugh enough. Sometimes it felt as though the years of responsibility, looking after the children, and her mother who had developed Alzheimer's frighteningly young, had taken their toll. Lou Lou was teaching her how to laugh spontaneously again, which was an added and unexpected bonus of being a granny.

Mind you, it was hard to remember to laugh sometimes, when you were working till late to make up for the chores lost due to time spent playing with your grandchild. Luckily Cat who had developed a somewhat unexpected career as a TV chef since coming to Hope Christmas, was in between TV series at the moment, as she seemed to be doing more than her fair share of childcare, since Mel had gone back to sixth form college to start AS Levels in the autumn. When she got the green light for the new programmes she was planning: *A Shropshire Christmas*, a programme devoted to local recipes and traditions from Shropshire's past, things were going to get a bit more tricky.

'We'll have to cross that bridge when we come to it, Lou Lou, won't we?' Cat said, tickling her granddaughter.

It wasn't Mel's fault – for the first few months of Lou Lou's life, she'd been great. Accepting her loss of freedom without complaint, dropping out of school for a year to care for her daughter, allowing Cat the time to continue with her working life relatively uninterrupted. And when sixth form college was first mooted, Mel had protested, saying 'Lou Lou's my responsibility, Mum, I can't hand her over to you.'

Never had Cat been prouder of her daughter, or loved her more, despite the difficulties involved in trying to support her. But there was no way that she and Noel were going to let their beloved daughter miss out on her education. So when Lou Lou was eight months old, Mel went back to college, Lou Lou went to nursery part time, and Cat found herself suddenly being far more of a hands-on granny than she'd quite intended.

The results had been worth it. Cat loved the time she was spending with Lou Lou, and Mel who was working really hard for her exams was predicted good grades. She wanted to go into journalism, and had found a course she was interested in at Birmingham so she could study and live at home. Which was wonderful, but Cat felt with some degree of certainty, that Granny was going to be called on even more often than before.

And that was fine, of course it was.

'Don't be so negative,' Cat chided herself, it was just that at a time in her life when she'd hoped to have a lessening of responsibilities, she felt that she was getting bogged down in even more. And it was hard not to feel a little resentful. Was life never going to get easy?

Since Christmas, Angela, who up until now had always been very independent, seemed to need more of their help, which was worrying. It only seemed like five minutes since Cat's own mum had been ill, and Angela had quietly stepped into the breach and been immensely supportive. Cat wasn't ready to lose her too.

'Banish that thought from your head, right now, Cat,' she muttered, concentrating instead on trying to make Lou Lou laugh some more, which was much more cheering. 'And on the bright side, your clever mummy has been earning some money,' she added.

'Mama, mama,' agreed Lou Lou, giggling as Cat tickled her tummy.

Mel had managed to get herself a book deal via her anonymous blog, *Mum Too Young*. She'd written a quirky, funny take on life as a teenage mum, complete with cartoons, which she'd self-published. It had been a great hit, and Mel had since been taken on by a publisher. She'd retained her anonymity, 'I just don't want to start sixth form college with baggage,' she'd said, 'I want to be the same as everyone else,' – which made Cat want to weep for her daughter. She had given up so much by having Lou Lou so young, and coped so well with it. But Cat did wonder if it was a good idea for Mel to keep her two lives secret.

The phone rang, reminding her that she was supposed to be working today as well as looking after Lou Lou. She'd been waiting for a call from her agent, Anna, re her proposed new Christmas book and series. She'd been a bit distracted with babysitting of late, and hadn't been as assiduous about chasing it up as she'd intended.

'Catherine, honey, how are you?' Anna was the only person who ever called Cat, Catherine.

'Fine,' she said, propping the phone in one hand, while tickling Lou Lou with the other. 'Sorry, I'm a bit tied up today, I've got Lou Lou.'

'I'm very sorry to be the bearer of bad news,' said Anna, who tended to be blunter than Cat's original agent, Jenny, who'd retired some years back, 'but they're not interested in the new series. They feel *A Shropshire Christmas* is a bit too retro.'

'What?' Cat was staggered. 'But it was their idea.'

'I know, I know,' said Anna, 'but you know what these TV companies are like. They want to freshen things up a bit, bring in a different cook. They're talking about Sienna Woodall, she's the latest thing, apparently.'

And ten years younger. The words lay unspoken between them. Cat should have seen this coming. She'd had a lot of jokey comments from the crew during her last series about fading to grey, and needing to botox, now she'd passed 45, and there had been several nasty swipes in the press about middle-aged spread – 'A greying corpulent whale' as one reviewer had not so kindly put it. It was true, she couldn't shift the weight as easily as she once had, but she was hardly obese. It was so unfair. No one complained about Jamie Oliver putting on weight.

'I'm sure something else will turn up,' continued Anna, in a not terribly convincing manner. 'You're still in great demand.'

'It's fine,' said Cat, with an optimism she didn't feel. 'I always knew it would happen one day.'

And it was true she had always known it deep down. Faces went out of fashion all the time, why had she thought she would be any different? She'd been lucky to get the gig at all, and TV was a fickle world. She was no more special than anyone else.

Pippa was baking, partly to relax, partly to supply the community café and shop in the village run by Vera and Albert Campion. Several years ago when the post office Vera had singlehandedly run was under threat, the whole of Hope Christmas had come together to save it and the shop and café was the result. Pippa baked for them most weeks but more frequently when she was under stress. Today was definitely such a day.

Dan had swiftly acted on his Christmas decision, and the first week of January had seen a letter arrive from his lawyer, which Pippa had promptly shoved in a drawer in the dresser. She had been ignoring it ever since, pleading busyness, when Dan mentioned it. So far he hadn't been nagging, but Richard had started to – stupidly, she'd opened the drawer and he'd asked what it was.

Pippa had considered not telling him. Part of her wanted to say 'It's none of your business.' But she had to recognise it *was* his business. Gradually, over the last few months, Richard had become a necessary part of her life. If she was to have a future with him, then divorcing Dan was the next logical step. So why was she delaying?

Richard had proved himself kind, thoughtful and supportive; understanding that Lucy in particular was struggling with the new situation and not pushing himself forward. He had been tact itself on Christmas Day, so that the day had gone off with no dramatics. Pippa owed it to Richard to make a clean break with Dan.

She kept telling herself that Dan had made his intentions perfectly clear, so she was free to move on. And, on that basis, when Richard asked where they stood, she'd promised to give it a go with him, 'But slowly, Richard,' she said, 'I need time to sort myself out.'

'You're worth waiting for, Pippa,' Richard had said simply, which made her want to hug him, and yet at the same time she felt terribly guilty.

For the truth was, Pippa had always secretly hoped Dan would change his mind. She fretted she might be leading Richard on. Perhaps it was too soon for a new relationship.

But when was too soon? And Dan clearly didn't want her. As she explained to Marianne, 'I just need time to process that. It's such a huge change in my life.'

Dan was the love of her life. Pippa had never imagined she would have another. And now here was Richard, attractive, charming Richard, whose company she enjoyed, and who liked her too. Dan was giving her an opt out and she needed to make a decision towards her future, rather than hanging onto her past, but equally she wasn't quite ready to let Dan go (will you ever be? the voice said. It really was annoyingly persistent), or get serious with anyone else.

And Richard was nothing if not determined.

'It's private,' Pippa had said, snatching the letter from him, feeling absurdly defensive.

'Ooh, touchy,' joked Richard, then seeing the look on her face, he stopped immediately. 'What's wrong?'

Instant empathy was something Richard was very good at. It was one of the reasons it had been so easy to let him into her life. His ready understanding of the situation she was in meant she didn't feel the need to explain.

Pippa sighed and sat down, feeling a little wobbly.

'You may as well know,' she said, trying to keep the tears out of her voice. 'It's from Dan's solicitor. He wants a divorce.'

'Oh Pippa.' Richard sat down too and took her hand in his. 'I'm sorry, truly I am. But you knew this would happen one day.'

She squeezed his hand and looked out of the window, at the hills bordering the farm. She'd always sat here at this table looking at those hills with Dan. No longer. She blinked away her tears. Richard didn't need to see them.

'I know it seems final,' Richard said. 'Don't forget, I've

been there too. But it's been over a year, Pippa. Perhaps it is time for a fresh start.'

Pippa knew he was right, and she knew what he was saying, but she couldn't bring herself to say that this was what she wanted. What she really wanted was to wipe out the past two years; for Dan never to have fallen out of a tree, for him not to have suffered brain damage; for her to still be sitting here with him. Which of course wasn't going to happen. She should take the opportunity Dan was giving her to make a clean break. She'd been immensely lucky to have hit the jackpot first time around. Some people never got that. And she had the chance of happiness again. If only she'd let it in. So why did it feel like second best?

'You're right,' said Pippa. 'I'll sign it and post it tomorrow. I should have done it straight away.'

'You'll feel better when you do,' said Richard. 'I know I did when my divorce finally came through. Time to get the ball rolling.'

They'd talked no more about it, but Pippa had gone to bed with a heavy heart and hardly slept a wink. She'd been up early to feed the cows in the barn, and sent the kids off to school. Walking back down the frost sharpened lane, to wave Lucy's bus off, she'd bumped into Dan, which hadn't helped. Her heart lurched. His six foot frame towered over her, and she wanted to throw her arms around his strong lean torso. But he gave her a sad smile and she felt paralysed. Never had he seemed more desirable to her, nor more distant. She felt guilty about Richard, but she couldn't help herself. Dan still made her heart leap.

'I'm just sending this to your lawyer,' the words had been on her lips, but she found she couldn't say them. Instead she told him that the cows were fed, and he asked how Lucy had been that morning, idle meaningless chitchat, to put off the big things hovering over them. They said goodbye at the front gate, while Dan went off to milk the cows and Pippa shoved the letter back in her pocket and went home to bake out her misery.

She'd post the letter tomorrow, she thought as she battered a cake viciously. There was no rush. Tomorrow would do.

# Chapter Two

'So what are you going to do?' Marianne asked.

Cat was having a consolatory cup of hot chocolate in the village café with Marianne and Pippa. They'd all been busy since Christmas, and it was the first time they'd had a chance to get together. The café was the perfect spot to meet, cosy and warm, the windows steamed up from the busy mums and pensioners all enjoying a mid-morning break.

'Dunno,' said Cat, who was still trying to get her head around the idea that *A Shropshire Christmas* wasn't going ahead as planned. 'I'd got so used to there always going to be another series, I'd not really thought about what happened when the work dried up. Stupid of me really, I should have planned it out better.'

'There's always *I'm a Celebrity*,' joshed Marianne.

'Oh please,' said Cat, rolling her eyes. 'I might be desperate, but I'm not that desperate.'

'Sorry,' said Marianne, looking stricken, 'it was only a joke.'

'Don't worry,' said Cat. 'I'm sure that's exactly what Paige and Ruby will be demanding I do next, they're obsessed with celebrity tv shows.' She paused and sighed heavily. 'Maybe it was meant to be, I do seem to be spending more

46

and more of my time with munchkin here, so maybe it's a good thing the work's dried up a bit. I don't think I'd have time anyway.'

Munchkin, who was sitting in her buggy drinking milk, obligingly smiled revealing a milk-splattered nose. Cat automatically wiped it with a tissue, which elicited a cheering giggle. There was nothing like a baby's laugh to cut through your gloom.

'You can't mean that surely?' said Pippa.

'No, I don't,' grinned Cat ruefully. 'I just feel like suddenly, I've become old overnight. Since my miscarriage, I'm finding it harder and harder to lose weight, I feel like I'm sagging in the middle, lacking the energy I had. Plus I keep finding grey hairs on a daily basis. I get much ruder comments on the internet than I used to. *And* to add insult to injury, I've just found out I need reading glasses. I look at Sienna Woodall, and I can see why they want her. She's sexy, voluptuous, and *younger* than me. Hell, *I'd* pick her over me. Looking at her, and looking at me, I feel, I don't know – *invisible.*'

Lou Lou gurgled happily in the buggy. She had a toy rabbit which she dropped on the floor, for the dozenth time, and Cat absentmindedly picked it up.

'But can she cook?' asked Pippa.

'Who knows?' said Cat. 'And who cares? The TV bods probably don't, and neither do the public. Maybe I'll take a leaf out of Delia's book and start doing my own stuff online. And maybe I won't.'

With a determined shake of her head, Cat pulled herself out of her gloom. She turned to her two friends. 'It's not all about me. How's life treating you two?'

Marianne looked away when Cat asked, and she felt like she might have said the wrong thing, but if there was something awry, Marianne clearly didn't want to talk about it. Cat suspected it might have something to do with Gabriel's ex, Eve. Marianne had hinted there had been a few problems since Christmas, when Eve had been taken ill and eventually sectioned. There was a pause, then Pippa smiled a deliberately cheerful smile, 'Fine,' said Pippa, 'everything's just fine.'

'That sounded convincing,' said Cat, anything but convinced. 'What's up?'

'Only this divorce business,' sighed Pippa. She took a battered envelope out of her pocket. 'I keep meaning to post this, but somehow, I can never bring myself to . . .'

'Pippa!' exclaimed Marianne, clearly shocked, 'you said you'd done it last week.'

'I know, I know,' said Pippa, looking thoroughly miserable. 'I just can't seem to do it. I know I have to, eventually.'

'But not today?' said Cat with sympathy. Pippa had had a rotten time of it over the last year, sorting out her divorce was probably the last thing she wanted to do.

Pippa looked embarrassed. 'It's really stupid, I know,' she said. 'I know I'm not facing up to things. But once I post this, it's so – final. That'll be me and Dan done and dusted. And nothing will ever be the same again.'

'Oh Pippa,' said Cat and squeezed her hand, and Marianne gave her a hug. 'And here's me harping on about a stupid TV programme.'

Cat looked down at Lou Lou who was still playing happily with her rabbit, kicking her toes in the air without a care in the world. Cat might have lost a job, but she still had her family and her husband. And that was worth all the lost jobs in the world.

\* \* \*

48

Marianne walked back home, feeling bereft. She'd enjoyed the break with Cat and Pippa, enjoyed sitting in the warmth, sipping hot chocolate and chewing the fat. It was one of the best things about coming to live in Hope Christmas. Here she had solid, reliable, decent friends, so unlike flaky Carly and Anna her so called mates in London. She knew she could trust Cat and Pippa to help her whenever she needed. It was a very comforting feeling.

But much as she'd love to, she couldn't stay in the café all day; the twins had a long day at nursery today and there was plenty to do at home, she should make the most of their absence to give the house a good spring clean for starters. It was just that . . . She didn't particularly feel like doing any of it. Perhaps she should go and help Gabriel in the fields. At least it would get her outside, and on a fresh clear day like this, it was much better than being indoors doing housework.

She felt cheered by the thought – before the twins were born, when she wasn't working, she'd often helped Gabriel out, but since their arrival, there was simply never enough time. Marianne didn't have much time today either, but she could do *something*. Anything was better than tidying the lounge, cleaning the kitchen, and sorting out the toy room for no particular purpose as it would be trashed again once the kids got back.

But when she got home, Gabriel was already indoors, sitting by the fire feeding a new born lamb.

'The mum died,' he explained. 'I found this one in the back of the barn, baaing beside the body.'

'Oh, I'm sorry,' said Marianne. Gabriel always took the deaths of his ewes personally. Sometimes she thought he was far too sentimental for a farmer.

'Can I help?' One job she never tired of was feeding new

born lambs. Something about their lovely wriggliness made her feel cosy and warm.

'The twins will be thrilled to pieces,' she said.

'Won't they just?' Gabriel smiled the smile which always made Marianne go tingly all over, even now, when they'd been married all this time. With his shock of dark hair, soulful brown eyes, and lovely wide open grin, it always made Marianne feel blessed that he was hers. It felt like ages since she'd seen him smile like that. Maybe that's what happened when you'd been married a few years, and had an awkward ex hovering in the background. You forgot to smile at each other.

They shared a cosy half hour till the lamb was settled, and then, finishing off his tea, Gabriel got up to go out again.

'I'd love to stay all day,' he said, 'but needs must . . .'

'Can I help?' asked Marianne. 'It's either that or slit my wrists over the state of the playroom.'

'Sure,' said Gabriel, his face lighting up. 'It's been ages since you've come out on the fields with me. It would be great to have some company. I was just going back out to check on the pregnant ewes, and make sure they've got enough feed.'

'It will do me good to get some fresh air,' said Marianne. 'I mustn't forget to pick the twins up, though.' She grabbed a coat, hat and scarf, and went to the boot room to pick up her wellies. Just as well she'd never been one for glamour – being a farmer's wife gave you precious few opportunities to spruce yourself up. You *chose* this, remember, she said to herself, as she followed Gabriel down the lane, to the gate at the end which led to their fields. The pregnant ewes were in a barn at the end of it, Gabriel always liking to keep them in till they'd had their babies, although it made for a lot of hard work keeping it clean, but the alternative was scouring the hills looking for lost ewes, which still also happened occasionally.

As they climbed over the foot stile towards their lower fields, where the pregnant ewes were wintering, Marianne noticed some activity in the field next to them, which belonged to Blackstock Farm, on the other side of the lane. It was the same field where she'd seen an estate agent showing someone round just before Christmas.

'I see there are people back in Blackstock Farm again,' said Gabriel.

Blackstock Farm had lain empty for some months, since Old Joe (the farmer who'd owned it) had died at the grand old age of ninety. Rumours abounded in the village about what would happen to the land; Old Joe having no family that anyone could remember.

'What do you think they're doing?' said Marianne.

'No idea,' said Gabriel. 'With any luck it's going to go for auction and we'll find ourselves a new neighbour.'

'With any luck,' said Marianne. But as she looked back down the field, she saw several men, unsuitably dressed in office garb and smart shoes, and wondered. They were taking photographs, and making notes, and seemed very animated. She remembered her feeling of foreboding from a few months earlier. She had a nasty feeling they hadn't heard the last of Old Joe's farm.

*How's your day been? :-)*
Pippa looked at Richard's text and sighed. How to explain her day so far? After coffee with the girls (the highlight), she'd got home to discover another letter from Dan's solicitor, gently reminding her she hadn't responded to the first. She decided Richard didn't need to know about that.

*Fine. Yours?* she responded, and instantly a text pinged back.

*Boring. Missing you xxx*

Oh. Richard often added little comments like that to his texts. She wished he wouldn't. It made her feel panicky, as if he were forcing an intimacy she wasn't quite ready for. *Me too x* Pippa texted, feeling it was required. The truth was she still didn't know how she felt where Richard was concerned, and felt guilty about leading him on. But it was nice to have someone kind and gentle who seemed to care for her. Perhaps she should just accept that for now. She felt she was going round in circles, and could never get her head straight about what was the best thing to do.

Pippa sighed. She really ought to deal with this letter; every time she didn't, it cost Dan (and them) money. She should get on with it. And she would. *Later.* For now she needed to look through the accounts. The tax year was nearly up and she'd been neglecting them, much to the irritation of their accountant, John, who was practically having a nervous breakdown. The trouble was, everything was in such a mess.

Since Dan's accident they'd had to scale back the workload, he simply couldn't do as much as he had done, and even with help from both their dads and the boys at the weekend, it wasn't enough. In order to manage they'd cut back on the amount of cattle they were rearing, which of course ate into profits. At one stage they'd been able to afford extra help, but after the year they'd just had, coupled with the abysmally low price of milk and the high price of animal feed, hiring any help this year was out of the question. It was an ever increasing downward spiral of financial misery, and she wasn't entirely sure what she was going to do about it. The trouble was, that for both her and Dan, the farm was a way of life, and not something either of them could give up easily. Hence Dan's still hanging around to help run it with her, even though he'd moved out.

Pippa felt a familiar feeling of sickness in the pit of her stomach as she looked through the figures again, willing them to be better. She had started having sleepless nights about money, and for the first time since she and Dan had taken over the farm from her parents fifteen years earlier, she was really worried that they might not make a go of things. They'd weathered storms before, but this, this felt different. And she was more and more overwhelmed by the bills which kept coming. She knew she needed to face up to it, but at the moment it all felt too much.

And of course, now that Dan wanted a divorce, they'd have to look at what to do about the farm properly. Which was complicated, as in order to make improvements over the years, they'd borrowed from Pippa's parents who were silent partners in the business. The way it was going there'd be precious little of the business left, and their investment would be up the swannee. It wouldn't matter at all if she and Dan were still together, but now they were apart and going to be apart permanently, Pippa just couldn't see how she was going to be able to buy Dan out, which was her preferred option, and what to do about the farm was hanging over her like a dark black cloud.

There was a ring on the doorbell. Pippa frowned. She wasn't expecting anyone – the kids were at school, Richard was working in Birmingham at the marketing firm where he was financial director, and Dan was in the fields. She put her papers away and got up to answer the door. A smartly dressed young man in a pinstripe suit was standing on the doorstep

– Jehovah's Witness she thought immediately. He flashed a white toothed grin at her, held up a business card and said, 'Laurence Fairburne, LK Holdings Ltd. We're acquiring property in the area and wondered if you'd be interested in selling up?'

# Chapter Three

'I hope you sent him away with a flea in his ear,' said Dan, when he came to pick the children up at the weekend. He stood, framed in the doorway, so tall, strong and dependable. It was still hard to believe that things had changed so catastrophically.

It had taken a while for Pippa to pluck up the courage to tell him about her unwanted visitor. The truth was that, even with all of the ongoing counselling, Dan could still be somewhat unpredictable since his accident, and she never knew what was going to spark off a rage in him, which some idiot from a posh company wanting to buy them out was likely to. Dan's black moods were the main – the only – reason they'd split up; Pippa had been prepared to live with them but Dan hadn't.

'It's the look in your eyes, that does it,' he'd said to her once, after the heartbreaking occasion when he'd frightened the boys so much, they'd run away from him. Pippa had tried not to show her horror at his behaviour, but it was nigh on impossible. So she'd tried to preserve passive neutrality ever since. But it wasn't easy.

'Of course I did, but I thought you should know,' Pippa said, returning to the matter in hand. 'It's not just that either. Remember those people we saw at Blackstock Farm before Christmas? I'm wondering if they've got anything to do with this.'

Dan whistled.

'You think LK Holdings is looking at buying up all the land round here?'

'I don't know,' said Pippa, 'but I wouldn't be surprised. I don't think that guy is going to take no for an answer.'

Her gut instinct at Christmas hadn't reassured her, and it wasn't reassuring her now. She had the uneasy feeling they were under siege, and she wasn't sure she had the strength to withstand the onslaught alone.

'They can't do anything unless we sell,' Dan pointed out, 'which we're not obliged to do.'

'I don't think it's quite as straightforward as that,' said Pippa. 'We may not have a choice.'

'Oh?' Dan looked at her quizzically.

Pippa paused, her heart was racing and she felt slightly sick. It was now or never; time to face up to the inevitable. 'The thing is, if we're going to go through with the divorce, it's time we started to talk about the future of the farm.'

'I'll buy you out,' said Dan. 'You keep the farmhouse, and I'll buy the business.'

'I'm not sure you can,' said Pippa, the anxious gnawing feeling in her stomach returning. 'I've been looking through the accounts, and to put it bluntly, the business is a mess. We hardly made any money last year, and . . .'

Her voice trailed off. She so longed for him to turn that dazzling smile of his on her, and say, 'No worries, Mrs Micawber, something will turn up,' as he would have done in the past. But that wasn't going to happen now, or ever again. That was in the past, and the past was gone, however much she wished it hadn't. This was their reality now.

'And maybe selling up would be a good idea?' Dan looked

at her incredulously. 'Pippa, I can't believe you of all people would say that. This farm is a family farm, *our* family farm. What about the boys?'

What about the boys? she felt like saying, maybe they don't need this millstone around their necks? But she kept quiet. Dan was right. This farm was where she'd grown up; it was her heritage and she loved it with every fibre of her being. Pippa had always regarded herself and Dan as stewards, tending the land to pass it onto the next generation. She'd never imagined doing anything else, and she knew how much the children loved it too. Particularly Nathan who was already talking about studying agriculture. How had it come to this? She shouldn't even be contemplating taking his or George's future away as a possibility.

'What does Richard think?' Dan said, taking her by surprise.

'I haven't talked to him about it,' said Pippa. The thought hadn't even occurred to her. 'Not till I'd discussed it with you. It's none of his business.'

'Isn't it?' Dan's voice sounded bitter, which was confusing. He'd seemed all for Richard and Pippa as a couple at Christmas. Pippa's heart leapt a little as she allowed herself to entertain a ridiculous smidgeon of hope. Maybe Dan would finally break through his barriers and tell her he'd made a mistake. She looked at him expectantly, but suddenly he changed tack. 'Look, Pippa, I don't want to sell, and you don't want to sell, do you?'

'No, of course not.'

'Then, we won't,' said Dan. 'Come on, we can work things out. Chin up. Anything is possible, if you put your mind to it.'

And there, for a moment, was the old Dan, *her* Dan. It was all Pippa could do not to weep.

\* \* \*

57

*They say you should never put your daughter on the stage . . . but the same could apply to getting your baby in front of a camera. As a way to earn money for childcare, it seemed like a no brainer to take my daughter to the Tot's Modelling Agency and see if she could start paying her way. After all, every baby is photogenic, and cute and adorable, aren't they? . . .*

*Wrong!*

*For starters do you know how hard it is to get a baby to smile when she doesn't want to? Despite the best efforts of the photographer who was waving cuddly toys and pulling faces like they were going out of fashion, my bouncing baby just wouldn't perform . . . even with me crouched behind her stuffing treats in her mouth in between takes. Turns out not every baby is loved by the camera after all . . .*

Cat smiled as she read Mel's latest piece for a mother and baby mag. Mel had captured perfectly the absurdity of trying to take photos of a small baby. She was proud of her daughter for managing to get a regular gig to earn her some money, while she carried on with her studies. They were going to need all the help they could get now she'd lost the TV show, particularly when Mel went to university next year. Cat and Noel both wanted to support their daughter, but Cat wanted her to take responsibility for Lou Lou too. It was a delicate balancing act.

'That's brilliant, Mel,' she said. 'You're a natural. And it was a great idea to get Lou Lou some modelling work.'

Despite her wry take on it, the modelling day had actually gone well, and Lou Lou had already had several further sessions, which meant Mel could save something for her future.

Mel blushed. 'It does help having a famous journalist mum,' she said.

'Not that famous,' sighed Cat, 'I feel like I'm being put out on the scrap heap.'

Cat had pitched a few more cooking ideas to Anna, including a cookbook for young urbanites, but had been met with a stone wall so far. Anna had been far more candid than Cat would have liked, 'At the moment your face doesn't fit, darling,' she'd said, 'but I'm sure we'll find something for you before too long.'

She hadn't sounded very sure, and Cat was beginning to think she needed a radical rethink of her entire career.

'Don't be daft, Mum,' said Mel, giving her a hug. 'I think you're an inspiration.'

Cat blinked back unexpected tears. It never ceased to amaze her how surprising her children could be sometimes. While she missed them being little, she loved the fact that they were growing into their own people.

'You have to say that, you're my daughter,' she laughed. 'Anyway, I'm proud of you too. This is great. You never know, you may even get another book out of it.'

'That would be great,' said Mel. 'There's so much good material here. I haven't even got started on the Pushy Mums yet.'

Cat had witnessed the Pushy Mums herself, when she'd taken Lou Lou to a photoshoot for Mel. They were usually done up to the nines, plastered in fake tan and tottering in high heels, determined that their little darlings were going to succeed in the modelling world, where clearly many of them had not.

'Brilliant,' said Cat. 'So long as it doesn't interfere with your exams, though. Earning money is important, but your studies come first.'

Mel pulled a face. 'I know.'

Cat sighed. 'I wish I could do more to help. The timing of this bloody TV thing couldn't be worse. If that was still going ahead, we'd have a bit more leeway, and could take some pressure off you.'

'Oh Mum,' said Mel, looking a bit teary herself, 'you do so much for me already. If you didn't help out as much, I couldn't even think about going to university. And when you look after Lou Lou it stops you from working.'

'Well just because life's thrown you an unexpected curveball, Dad and I don't want you to not have the best future possible. Besides, you know I love looking after Lou Lou.' It was true – Cat did. It reminded her of having her own babies again, and she hadn't realised how much she missed them being small. 'The important thing is that your education doesn't suffer. I'm happy to sacrifice anything for that.'

'I don't believe it!' Gabe came haring in in a blistering mood, while Marianne was standing by the cooker dishing out the twins' tea.

The twins, both sitting eagerly at the cosy kitchen table waiting for their food, were startled by their dad's unexpectedly belligerent tone, burst into tears and stopped Gabriel in his tracks.

'Oh damn,' he said, looking stricken. 'Don't fret, Harry, Daddy was just being grumpy.'

He picked his son up and started to tickle him, while Marianne did the same to Daisy, and they were soon giggling away as if nothing had happened. Would that grown-ups could cheer up so quickly, Marianne thought. By the time they'd finished tea, the twins had long forgotten Gabriel's bad mood, and they were happily dispatched to the lounge to watch *In the Night Garden* before bed. Time to turn her attention to her husband.

Marianne put the kettle on and said, 'So go on, what's the problem?'

'You know the other day we saw those guys in Old Joe's field?' said Gabriel.

'Yes?' said Marianne, she'd been so busy since then, she'd half forgotten about it, 'what of them?'

'I've found out what they are doing,' said Gabriel. 'There are planning applications on every tree down the lane. They want to build a new hotel, leisure centre and golf course on the site. They want to go all the way to the bottom of Old Joe's property and take in parts of Hope Christmas woods too. It's insane.'

'But they can't!' said Marianne. The woods was a favourite haunt of hers with the children as they were too little still to manage long walks to the top of the hill, particularly one lovely little area where a local artisan had carved statues out of fallen logs. 'That will destroy the views from the hill, let alone the wildlife and the space for the sheep to roam. Hope Christmas will never be the same again.'

Hope Christmas was such a special place, Marianne had always felt. It had the most perfect High Street, complete with lovely little trinket shops, a great bookshop, black and white buildings and even a quaint old antiques market. There was a thriving market during the week, and it had a lovely friendly community. Too small for major hotels, there were plenty of b&bs in town, catering for walkers and families of all ages, the usual kind of visitor to the town. A massive complex like this would have huge repercussions for the area, not least in the fact that it would change the landscape which brought the walkers in the first place.

'They can, and they will, apparently,' said Gabriel. 'I ran into Archie Speers, and he said that Joe's farm has passed to a great-nephew who isn't interested and is going to sell up and doesn't care what happens to the land.'

'But what about Archie's land, doesn't some of it intersect with Joe's?'

'Yup,' said Gabriel, 'and they want to buy that bit off Archie.'

'I hope Archie said no,' said Marianne, looking appalled. This was looking serious. If they wanted to stop this development the whole town was going to have to get on board.

'I think Archie's in a difficult position, to be honest,' said Gabriel. 'You know he's managing that farm all on his own. He's been talking about downsizing for some time. It's going to affect him either way. He may as well make some money out of it, I guess.'

He stared gloomily out of the kitchen window. Marianne only had to look at him to know what he was thinking. Gabriel was a country boy through and through: Hope Christmas was bound up in the fabric of his soul. A development on this scale could destroy the place they loved forever.

'And Dan said they've had people sniffing round there asking about buying their farm,' Gabe continued. 'I hadn't twigged there might be a connection with the developers till today. If everyone sells up, we won't stand a chance.'

'Pippa and Dan won't sell,' said Marianne quickly. The thought of Pippa's farm going was unthinkable.

'They wouldn't have in the past,' said Gabriel, looking sad, 'and according to Dan, they're still not planning to, but he hinted that things are a bit tight financially. I have a terrible feeling everything will be different once the divorce goes through.'

Marianne felt a cold clutch of fear on her heart. She had always assumed they'd stay here forever. The farms down the lane seemed immutable and unchanging, along with the valley, woods and hills which she loved so much. She couldn't bear the thought of all that beauty being destroyed and a massive hotel complex being erected instead.

'I wouldn't mind so much,' said Gabriel, 'if they were actually building something that would benefit the whole town – starter homes that local kids could afford would be good. Or even a hotel for the walkers and usual visitors. But this isn't what anyone needs. Not only will this development encroach too much on the hillside and destroy the views and the wildlife, but it sounds like it's at the luxury end of the market. I'm guessing it will attract people who are more interested in making use of the facilities on site, than spending any time or money in Hope Christmas. I don't think it's going to do the local economy any good at all.'

'It might not be as bad as that,' said Marianne.

Gabriel gave her a withering look, so she added, 'Ok, then, let's not just sit fretting, we need a plan of action.'

'Like what?'

'Doing what we did with the eco town,' said Marianne firmly. When she'd first come to Hope Christmas, she and Gabe had been part of a successful campaign to prevent an eco town being built not too far away which, before work was halted, had caused a flood that nearly destroyed the town. 'We need to act and fast. I'll ring Pippa straight away.'

Gabriel looked sceptical.

'I don't know if that would work this time, this company, LK Holdings I think they're called, actually owns the land.

And with the eco town we had the fact it was a potential environmental disaster on our side.'

'We've done it before, we can do it again,' said Marianne. 'And if *we* don't fight to save Hope Christmas, no one else will.'

# My Broken Brain

### Day Twenty Eight. 5am

I really don't know if this is helping. Seems like a lot of psychological bollocks to me. It's early in the morning and I can't sleep, so here I am staring at a blank screen. For what? I don't know what to say, and when I do write stuff down it makes me feel worse. I start thinking about what I've lost – particularly the kids. I miss them so much, even though I see them every day. Thinking about it makes everything seem much blacker. I'm not sure it's worth the aggro, and quite frankly I'd rather be milking cows.

Or spending time with Pippa. But that's not even an option anymore. I can't afford to go there. When I think about her, it feels like I'm being punched in the guts. I know I've done the right thing letting her go. I was holding her back, stopping her from having the future she deserves. She needs a whole man, not a damaged one.

But Jo keeps telling me to persevere . . . So here I am again . . .

The thing is, I feel such a failure. My marriage was the one thing I thought I could always count on in my life. I thought it would pull me through anything. I knew Pippa was always going to be there for me, that we would grow old and contented together.

I don't remember much about the accident. Just bits from the hospital: Pippa crying and not knowing why; the kids looking scared; my mum being sad. And then this fog in my brain. A fog which never quite seems to have lifted since. I know Pippa says she can cope with my mood swings, and the blackness that sometimes swamps me, and the way I get vague from time to time, but I just can't ask her to do it. I love her too much to take her down with me.

But now she's talking about selling the farm. Seems we can't afford to run it if we're not married anymore. I thought leaving Pippa was for the best, but now things seem worse than ever and it's killing me. But Pippa deserves her chance at happiness. I have to hang on to that. It's the only thing I've got.

I didn't talk to anyone about getting divorced. Maybe I should have, but what was the point? I walked out on my marriage a year ago, for the sake of my family; I wasn't doing any of them any good. And though every day away from them is painful and difficult, I know I'm doing the right thing. For all of us . . .

*February*

# Chapter Four

'Lucy, sweetheart, be reasonable,' Pippa was saying as she tried to get her daughter into bed, 'you know it's way past your bedtime.'

Lucy just glared at her and stuck her feet out from beneath the covers, the feet that Pippa had just firmly tucked in. She had gone rigid all over, and Pippa was finding it impossible to move her. Lucy was getting so big, the time was going to come when she couldn't manage this at all. As it was, with Lucy in recalcitrant mood, Pippa felt like she could be there all night.

She knew why Lucy wasn't playing ball of course. It was because Richard was here. Lucy made no bones about her dislike of Richard, despite his best efforts to appease her. They'd had days out, just the three of them, Richard had bought her presents. 'He can't just buy me, you know,' Lucy had typed angrily on her keyboard, when Pippa had told her off for not being grateful.

She couldn't blame her beautiful special daughter. From the terrible moment when they'd had the diagnosis that Lucy had cerebral palsy and would always be wheelchair bound, Dan had been there to support, help and care for Lucy. She was closer to him than even the boys were. What had Pippa been thinking? She'd walk in with a new man and everything would be ok? Of course Lucy was going to resent anyone who she thought was taking her beloved dad's place. It was entirely natural for her to feel that way. Nathan and George moaned about it too, to a lesser degree, but they were better at hiding it, and with more independence than Lucy could ever hope to have, could arrange to be out when Richard was round. Lucy didn't have that option, Pippa thought ruefully – no wonder she was kicking up.

But what was Pippa supposed to do? Not see him at all? Not bring him into the house? Or should she be a nun for the rest of her life, because Lucy couldn't cope with another man in her dad's place? The eternal dilemma of the newly single mum made that bit more tricky because of the complications of Lucy's life.

That was an unworthy thought, and Pippa scotched it from her brain. It was always difficult for children whose parents split up, with Lucy the problems were compounded that's all.

'Please, Luce, I did let you stay up later.'

A sop to her daughter to try and soften her a bit. It hadn't worked. Lucy was still looking at her mulishly from under the covers. It didn't help that Lucy was also hitting puberty and very definitely hormonal. Normally a sunny child, her mood swings had become much more marked in recent months. Pippa had a feeling that the next few years were going to be *very* challenging. If Dan hadn't left, she'd feel up to coping – Dan had always made dealing with Lucy's issues seem a shared burden – but now she felt bleak facing it alone. How was she going to manage?

'Stop being naughty,' said Pippa as Lucy resolutely stuck her legs out of the bed, again, for the third, or fourth time. Jeez. How long was she planning to keep this up?

'Not being naughty,' Lucy typed on her computer sulkily.

'Yes you are,' said Pippa firmly. 'You know you won't get up in the morning if you don't go to bed now.'

Lucy stuck her tongue out in response, but did eventually allow herself to be tucked in. She even gave Pippa a kiss good night – she was an affectionate child, and for all her posturing, she still wanted a hug at bedtime.

Pippa sighed, as she turned out the light. She hoped Lucy could come to terms with what was going on. How could she ever contemplate seriously having a future with Richard if Lucy hated him?

Pippa knew this happened to other people, yet the circumstances of her split with Dan had left her uncertain about what to do or where to go next. Richard would turn up unannounced and cook her dinner, 'Just because,' he'd say with a ready smile, or organise football tickets for the boys. And he never took Lucy's strops to heart, 'She'll get over it, Pippa,' he'd say, 'don't worry so much, it will be fine.'

Richard was good for her. He made her feel safe and comfortable and *looked after*. Pippa, who had spent so many years looking after other people, was enjoying that. And despite a sneaking suspicion that Lucy might after all know her better than she knew herself and be right, she wasn't going to stop seeing Richard. At least not yet. There was no need to make it serious. A light-hearted love affair after all the serious doom and gloom of the last two years would do her good. Or so she told herself.

'She's settled then?' Richard said. He was sitting in front of the TV looking at home. Pippa tried (and failed) to picture him there all the time. Too soon for that, Pippa, too soon.

Richard held out a glass of wine and she sat down next

to him and snuggled up. This felt cosy and nice. She should stop analysing and just go with the flow.

'Just about,' said Pippa. 'I'm sorry she's so naughty when you're here.'

Even before the bedtime fuss, Lucy had been in an incredibly bad mood. Deliberately tipping her plate on the floor when Richard had mildly suggested she should finish the dinner she was making a point of not eating because he was there.

'Don't worry about it,' said Richard equably. 'She's had a lot to deal with in a short time and she's asserting herself.'

'Thanks, for being so understanding,' said Pippa. 'I know she doesn't make it easy on you.'

Richard put his arm around her and pulled her tight.

'Or on you, Pip,' he said, kissing her. 'You're amazing you know that?'

It gave Pippa a warm, fuzzy feeling to be told that. Too often she felt like a catastrophic failure. It was nice to think someone thought she was amazing. Particularly someone as good looking and caring as Richard. She was doing the right thing. Lucy would come round eventually.

They settled back to watch some dross on TV, and Pippa felt herself destress. After half an hour, she was feeling much better.

That was until Richard put a spanner in the works.

'So has there been any more news about the development opposite?'

Pippa groaned. She didn't want to think about that right now. Marianne had already been on at her about starting up a campaign, but at the moment she wasn't sure she had the energy. She would have preferred not to discuss it with Richard either, but he'd seen the planning notices pinned up down the lane, and his take on things was very different from hers.

'Not really,' said Pippa. 'I know it's going to be too big and out of keeping with the area and not what any of us want.'

'Maybe you're looking at this the wrong way round,' said Richard. 'Perhaps you should take advantage of it.'

'Advantage how?' said Pippa.

'Why not be part of it?' said Richard. 'When you and Dan divorce, you'll have to think of the farm. Why not sell some of your land? Make things easier for you both?'

'But we don't want to sell,' said Pippa. 'This farm has been in my family for three generations.'

'Things change,' said Richard. 'And you've said yourself the farm is losing money.'

'I know,' said Pippa, suddenly angry that he was suggesting things that had already gone through her mind. 'But sell it? I don't think I could.'

Marianne took the phone call. It was Eve's mum, Joan.

'Hello, is Gabriel there?' she asked. She sounded jittery and nervous.

'Sorry, he's not in yet,' said Marianne.

She looked out of the window into the gloom of a February evening. Gabriel was still out – the lambing season was getting going in earnest now, and he was very busy, working all hours helping deliver the new lambs. Marianne helped out when she could, but she couldn't help Gabe in the evenings, so Dan or Gabriel's dad often came out to lend a hand.

The twins were tucked up in bed, Steven was away at school, even their new pet lamb, Dolly, was asleep in her basket in the corner of the kitchen. It was likely to be several hours before Gabriel came in. Marianne felt lost and lonely and not in the mood to deal with Eve's mum who could be very difficult and demanding.

'Ah,' said Joan, 'have you any idea when he's likely to be back?'

'I'm afraid not,' said Marianne, wondering why Joan was ringing them, it wasn't as if they were often in touch. 'Can I help at all?'

'It's about Eve . . .'

It would be. Eve had been part of the fabric of her relationship with Gabriel since day one. Marianne had met Gabriel just after Eve had left him, and she'd seen for herself the pain she'd caused him, particularly when she'd come back to Hope Christmas and tried to win custody of Steven. And more recently, when she'd come back to live in the area, and suggested Steven go to the choir school in Middleminster. It was what Steven wanted, but it had caused Gabriel considerable heartache.

And over the last couple of months since Eve had been ill again, Marianne knew he was worrying about her. He couldn't help himself. Gabriel had spent so many years worrying about Eve, he still felt guilty when he thought she needed him. When was it ever *not* about Eve? Chiding herself for being uncharitable – Eve couldn't help being ill, despite the problems it gave them – Marianne forced herself to say, 'How is she? Gabriel said she's doing really well.'

Gabriel had been taking Steven to see his mother at regular intervals, and even popped in to the hospital once or twice on his own. One of the many wonderful things about Gabriel was his kindness and consideration. Marianne knew that he still cared about his ex wife and worried about her when she was ill, but his kindness and consideration could also be bloody frustrating at times. Eve had left *him*, and it wasn't Gabe's fault that she was ill now. Marianne tried not to let it get to her, but sometimes, it grated that her husband was still so involved in his ex wife's life.

'Yes, she is,' said Joan. 'And they're thinking of letting her come home.'

'That's wonderful,' said Marianne, still curious as to what it had to do with them. Despite her frustrations about the way Eve's problems impacted on them, Marianne *was* pleased Eve was better (as Joan must be too, the last few weeks must have been a nightmare), but it wasn't really her problem. 'So she'll be coming back to stay with you, I presume?'

'Ah, she would . . .' the unspoken 'but' hovered between them.

Here it came, the real reason Joan was ringing.

'Unfortunately, I've booked a cruise,' said Joan, 'and it's not possible to cancel at this late stage . . .'

You selfish cow, thought Marianne, her sympathy for Joan dissipating instantly. Eve was Joan's only child. No wonder she had rejection issues.

'. . . so I was wondering . . . the thing is, Eve has nowhere to go. So could she . . .'

'. . . come to us?' said Marianne. The cheek of the woman! Not prepared to take responsibility for her sick daughter (whose illness she was probably to blame for – she'd given Eve a rackety dysfunctional childhood) and yet expecting her ex son-in-law to pick up the pieces.

'It will only be temporary till she sorts herself out,' said Joan persuasively. 'She'll hardly be in your way.'

Wanting to throttle the woman, Marianne gritted her teeth. 'I can't promise anything, Joan,' she said, 'I need to talk it through with Gabriel first.'

'If you could let me know as soon as possible?' Joan clearly didn't have a clue that her call was unwelcome.

'I'll let you know when Gabe and I have had a discussion,' said Marianne firmly, putting the phone down with a satisfying bang. Bloody woman. How dare she? But then, Eve couldn't be left on her own. It wasn't her fault she had a lousy mum.

And in her heart, she knew there wasn't really any talking to Gabriel about it. Eve would be coming to stay and that was that.

Gabriel walked in at that moment, complaining about the cold. He stopped dead when he saw the look on Marianne's face.

'What?' Gabriel asked.

'That was Joan,' said Marianne. 'Eve's coming out of hospital and she has nowhere to stay.'

Gabriel sat down with a thud.

'Bugger,' said Gabriel. 'Can't she stay with her mum?'

'Joan's going on a cruise apparently,' said Marianne. 'No doubt it would cramp her style.'

'No doubt,' said Gabriel drily. 'Well we can't have her. We've got enough on our plate. I'll ring Joan back and say no.'

Marianne let out the breath she didn't know she was holding. She'd been so sure Gabe would say yes straight away. She felt unkind, but Gabe was right, they did have enough to deal with.

But when Gabe spoke to Joan his resolve lasted all of five minutes. Marianne could hear from Gabe's responses how insistent she was being.

'And there really is no one else?' he said eventually, pulling a face at Marianne.

'. . . No of course I don't want her to relapse,' he added, which made Marianne's blood boil, as if Gabe were responsible for Eve's illness.

In the end, she saw him give a helpless little shrug and say, 'Of course she can stay here.'

He put the phone down and turned to Marianne, who was looking at him in horror. 'I'm sorry,' he said, 'but what else could I do?'

Cat was online researching recipes. She wondered what she was going to do now that *A Shropshire Christmas* wasn't going to be filling the screens of the nation. After her latest long chat with Anna about it, they'd concluded she'd go ahead with the book any way as her publishers were still happy to be on board. In the meantime, Cat would pursue other avenues.

'You could always try a reality TV show,' suggested Anna.

It had been a joke when Marianne mentioned it, but to Cat's horror, Anna was serious.

'I'm sure Paige would love me to, but I don't think so,' said Cat with a snort. 'Besides, I couldn't leave the kids that long.'

It seemed to Cat sometimes, her kids needed her more the older they got. As well as Mel's AS levels, which of course were a huge priority, James had GCSEs to contend with. Not that you'd know, he was so laid back about them Cat felt she had to be on top of him all the time, making sure he was getting some work done.

'You worry too much, Mum,' he said. 'It will be fine.'

And it probably would be, James had such a happy-go-lucky nature, things probably would turn out well for him whatever happened. And though he had given up on his own career as a teenage TV chef, which had sprung up on the back of Cat's TV work, he always had that to fall back on if all else failed.

Paige was another matter entirely. Her life was one long drama – even making GCSE choices was turning into a daily argument, with Noel's mild suggestions that Textiles and Tourism weren't perhaps the most academic subjects she could take, causing an explosion of 'You don't understand anything!'. True Mel had been quite explosive at that age, but Paige was taking it to a whole new level. Most of her tantrums related to her phone, to which she was addicted. She was always on snapchat and ask.fm, neither of which Cat remotely understood. Every time she got to grips with a new technology it seemed to change, and she and Noel waged a constant and wearying war of attrition against it.

Ruby, who at ten, was still reasonably straightforward, was even more techie than Paige. It exhausted Cat to be constantly telling both of them to get off their phones, only to find Ruby ten minutes later hooked up with the iPad. Honestly, technology, it was the bane of a modern parent's life.

Who was it who'd told her when she'd moaned about dealing with the difficulties of toddlers and babies, 'It will get worse'? They'd been right. Despite the turmoil Lou Lou had wrought upon their lives, Cat found looking after her relatively uncomplicated. She went to bed when she was put there, was asleep by seven, and didn't answer back.

Cat found a file for a Christmas cake that she'd come across a while ago, and printed it off, before starting to type, *'Thinking about making a Christmas cake takes a lot of forward planning. In an ideal world, you should make it in October, but those of us with lives to live have been known to squeeze it in in November . . .'* without much enthusiasm. She felt so much less interested in the book now it wasn't going to be a TV series. How very shallow of her. But she enjoyed the buzz of being in front of the cameras and was going to miss it.

Don't be daft, Cat, she scolded herself. It's only one show.

But what if it wasn't? What if all her TV work dried up? After all, she was in her mid forties and a woman. Time and TV weren't on her side. She felt it herself in her daily life. Whenever she was out with Lou Lou, inevitably all the talk was about the baby, and no one noticed her, but it was more than that. She knew her teenage self would be furious by her middle aged disappointment, but she never even got wolf whistled anymore. And last time she'd been in London, a man in his thirties had politely given her his seat in a manner which had made her feel both old, ugly and decrepit.

Useless to tell herself that looks didn't matter; she had age and wisdom on her side. Useless to know that Noel still found her sexy. A TV director no longer thought she could cut it. She was getting wrinkles, going grey, wore glasses, and had an unsightly ring of tummy fat that resolutely refused to go. She felt fat, old and frumpy. And worse than that, she felt *invisible*.

# Chapter Five

Marianne heard the key in the lock and Gabriel's voice saying with false cheer, 'Here we are, home at last!'

She got up from the sofa, where she'd been reading to the twins, to greet Gabriel, Eve and Steven, who had insisted on going to the hospital to pick his mum up. The twins followed Marianne curiously, and clung to her legs, looking at this strange woman whom they'd last seen some months ago.

'Eve, how lovely to see you,' Marianne said with forced enthusiasm, giving Eve what she hoped felt like a welcoming hug. The hallway seemed narrow and constricted. Suddenly there were too many people in it, and Marianne had a pang of trepidation about what they were doing. Was this really the right environment for Eve? But then again what was the alternative? She clearly had nowhere to go, and it wasn't her fault she was ill. Giving Eve somewhere safe to come was the right thing to do, however hard it was going to be. Marianne and Gabriel had discussed it at length, and agreed they'd have to make the best of it. But it was a little odd having your husband's ex to stay in the house they'd once shared.

Eve clearly felt the same.

'This is weird,' she said, looking quite nervy. Weight had

never been an issue for Eve, but Marianne was shocked at how thin she had got.

'I hope it's not too weird,' said Marianne, giving her as welcoming smile as possible and trying not to feel too concerned about the size of the enormous suitcase Eve had brought with her. Marianne's heart sank. Just how long was Eve planning to stay? Gabriel shot a grimaced look at her, and she felt slightly reassured. 'Come on, why don't you come and sit in the kitchen and have a cup of tea.'

But as they walked into the kitchen, Dolly, who was one of the nosiest lambs they'd ever fostered, chose that moment to come out of her basket and investigate who was there. She came straight up to Eve and nibbled at her leg. Eve promptly screamed and threw her arms in the air, hitting Gabe so hard on the nose it started to bleed. While Marianne went to grab a tissue, Dolly took advantage of the confusion to bolt out of the door.

'Dolly, no!' shouted Marianne, but it was too late, the lamb was pelting round the hall causing chaos. In the space of seconds she had knocked over a couple of vases, and chewed some carpet. She took a quizzical look around her, and decided upstairs looked like a fun place to be.

'Steven stop her!' shouted Marianne, as she shoved some tissue at Gabe who was standing with his head back pinching his nose, while Eve continued to scream like a banshee.

'Dolly, stop!' yelled Steven as he went tearing after her, followed by the twins in hot pursuit, deciding it would be really fun to join in the chase. It took ten minutes, a lot of thumping and shouting from upstairs, but eventually Steven came back into the kitchen triumphantly holding a wriggling Dolly in his arms.

'Got her!' he announced with a victorious grin.

'Well done,' said Marianne, sitting a rather shaken Eve down. 'Eve I'm so sorry about that. I forgot Dolly was in here.'

'Why have you got a sheep in the house?' Eve looked dumbstruck by such an idea.

'We always have baby lambs in the kitchen,' said Steven. 'Don't you remember?'

'I must have forgotten,' said Eve.

'The mother died,' said Gabriel, 'so I brought her in. The twins love her. Sorry, I forgot you weren't too keen on animals. She won't be here much longer, once she's weaned I'll let her out with the flock again.'

'It doesn't matter,' said Eve, with the ghost of a smile, 'I'm sure I'll cope.'

'Why doesn't Steven show you your room?' said Marianne tactfully.

'That would be lovely, thank you,' Eve said, giving Steven such a radiant smile, Marianne could suddenly see why he was so devoted to the mother who had let him down pretty much his whole life.

'Follow me, Mum,' Steven got up with alacrity. He looked so pleased to see his mum, Marianne felt churlish for being so negative. It had been tough on him having Eve in hospital all this time, it would be good for him to have her here.

'I'll take your bags,' offered Gabriel, who seemed to have succumbed to the smile too. Eve radiated a sort of helpless waiflike air. It was probably impossible for any man to resist.

'Must practise that,' muttered Marianne as they all disappeared upstairs to one of two spare bedrooms she and Gabriel had created when they'd had their extension done the previous year. It was left to Marianne to sort out some lunch and clear up after the twins. She tried not to feel like a skivvy, but it was hard.

And got progressively harder as the day progressed. Eve took to her room to lie down, as she was tired, and she'd apparently been told to rest. Marianne soon found herself in constant demand to make tea, bring up lunch and generally run around after her.

'She's ill, remember,' Marianne kept telling herself between gritted teeth, but it was difficult not to feel grumpy, particularly as Gabriel disappeared off to the fields, once he'd seen Eve settled, before Marianne had had a chance to ask him to take the twins with him, something he often did on a Saturday. They were hyped up and overexcited by the new arrival (and Dolly's rampage), and Marianne didn't want to take them out and leave Steven alone with his mum. Though he'd coped with things very well, he'd been very shaken up at Christmas, confiding in her that it was the scariest thing that had ever happened to him, 'I really thought she was going to be stuck in the bathroom forever,' he'd told her. 'I hope she never does that again.' When she asked him about it now, Steven kept telling her he was fine, but Marianne didn't think it was fair to put him in a position where he might have to be responsible for his mum again.

So she stayed in, chucking the children out in the garden for half an hour so they could run off their energy, getting on with the jobs that needed doing, trying to put on a cheerful, welcoming face for Eve, and feeling deeply resentful of Gabriel.

'So what do Ralph and Michael think about this new hotel business?' Cat asked Noel. She'd heard from Pippa and Marianne that developers were looking at the fields next to them, and like them was concerned about the effects on her adopted home town. In the years since she'd been here, she'd grown to love Hope Christmas, as the unspoilt haven that it was. She'd hate to see that change.

'They're as appalled as the rest of us,' said Noel. Noel's employer, Ralph, and his nephew Michael, were passionate about sustainable development and Ralph had been hugely instrumental in preventing the building of the eco town a few years earlier, even though his other nephew Luke, had been all for it. If anyone knew about what was being planned it would be Ralph and Michael. They always seemed to have their fingers on very unlikely pulses. But not this time, apparently. 'It's all been very secretive. We didn't even know planning permission had been applied for till the notices went up,' continued Noel. 'The trouble is the land belongs to someone who's willing to sell, and quite entitled to do so.'

'I suppose so. Pippa and Marianne are getting a campaign going,' said Cat, feeling gloomy. 'It's not as if we even need a spa hotel here. There are plenty dotted about the countryside in old stately homes. This is the wrong place for it. The tourists who come here aren't remotely interested in spa breaks.'

'You sound like Pippa,' said Noel, who like the rest of them had been strong armed into helping Pippa's last campaign to save the respite care centre Lucy went to. 'I take it you're getting involved?'

'Certainly am,' said Cat. 'Although I'm not sure I'm going to be able to help on the TV front like last time. I feel like I've disappeared off the face of the earth. Every single idea I've suggested to Anna recently, she's thrown back. And no TV producer seems to want to talk to me. I'm beginning to think my TV career is over.'

'There's more to life than TV,' said Noel, giving her a hug. 'And at least you still have the books. There's life in the old dog yet.'

'Oi, less of the old,' said Cat, hitting him playfully.

'And on the bright side, last year you were moaning about being away from home too much, at least you'll be here more.'

'True,' said Cat, thinking of the times when she'd complained about shoots taking her out of the house. 'But I'm not quite sure I'm ready for retirement yet. Besides, we can't afford it.'

'Oh I don't know,' said Noel, looking at her in a deliciously flirtatious way. 'You're still young and seductive enough for me. If I could push for early retirement we could both be at home some more.'

He gave her a lascivious grin, and she hit him again. But she was secretly pleased. All these years together and they still fancied each other. That was something. The rest of the world might think she was invisible, but her gorgeous husband didn't, and that was what really mattered.

'Yeah, right,' Cat said, laughing, 'and who'd look after Lou Lou and pay for the kids' uni fees?'

As if on cue, Lou Lou woke from her nap and started crying. Cat sighed. Sometimes it felt as if her life were going backwards.

'This feels familiar,' said Pippa as she, Cat and Marianne squeezed round a window table in the corner of Vera's café, and Lou Lou slept in her buggy, clutching hold of her toy rabbit.

As usual the place was packed, and there was a lot of buzz about the proposed new development. Typically, the group of old age pensioners, who met in Vera's regularly for a chat, were up in arms, led by the indomitable Miss Woods, who was a well-known character in the town. But to Pippa's dismay, she'd heard one or two of the younger

85

Yummy Mummy types – Keeley Jacobs and Angie Townley who Pippa always got muddled up as they were both dyed blond with high top ponytails, fake tans, long eyelashes and caked in make up – offer their support for the plans. They were newcomers from Birmingham, clearly missing city life and saying how great it would be to get their spray tans done in the new hotel. Pippa had assumed everyone would be against the development, and it was a bit of a shock to discover that wasn't the case. It would make things harder for their campaign if there was support for it in the town.

'It does, doesn't it?' said Cat, with a grin. 'It doesn't seem so long ago since we were organising how to save Lucy's respite care. We won that campaign, we can win this one.'

'I hope you're right,' said Marianne, 'but this does feel horribly close to home. And I'm worried that a big firm like LK Holdings won't really care what we think. Plus I've been talking to Vera, and she seems to think a lot of people are really for the hotel. It will bring work into the town. You know it's hard for youngsters to get jobs round here, that's why they mostly leave.'

'Except that it probably won't,' argued Pippa. 'It will be cheaper to bring in a load of Eastern Europeans than pay the locals. So it will destroy the landscape and not bring in any jobs. Double whammy.'

'Faint heart never won against big builders, or something,' said Cat. 'Come on, we need to stay positive.'

'Perhaps we should look at the impact on the environment first,' said Pippa, 'how it will affect the wildlife, that kind of thing.'

'It just seems the wrong place for such a big hotel,' said Marianne. 'And probably too expensive for most people to go. I don't see how it's going to benefit the local community.'

'According to Noel, who's managed to bend the ear of

someone on the council, it's going to be aimed at the luxury end of the market – an exclusive leisure complex, with spa facilities, a top of the range golf course, and luxury villas to rent, plus the hotel,' said Cat.

'Why do I get the feeling you lot are plotting again?' a familiar voice joined them, with a twinkle, a smile and a doffed cap.

'Ralph, how lovely to see you,' said Cat, giving him a warm smile. Ralph was the sort of person who always made you feel better about life, and he had the knack of turning up unannounced, with a plan in mind.

'And you,' said Ralph Nicholas, with a grave smile. 'So, have you got very far? I assume you are talking about the luxury leisure complex?'

'Yes we are. And not really,' said Marianne, ruefully. 'We're not quite sure where to start.'

'Perhaps you should approach the company direct, appeal to their better nature?' suggested Ralph. 'I *do* believe there might be an opportunity to meet some of the LK Holdings people at some meet and greets in the near future.'

'And do what?' asked Pippa.

'I don't know,' said Ralph with a smile. 'Three lovely ladies, a few easily flattered businessmen. I'm sure you'll think of *something*.'

# Chapter Six

'It's all right, I'm happy to babysit,' said Eve with a bewitching smile. 'Look on it as a thank you from me, for letting me stay.'

'Well if you're sure,' said Marianne cautiously. She knew from the past that Eve could not always be relied on to look after Steven, could she really entrust the twins to her? She felt bad for thinking it, because Eve seemed so much better. She was taking her medication, going to regular counselling and had even put on weight. Being with the twins also seemed to be doing her good, she seemed to brighten up around them and was really trying hard. But still, Marianne couldn't help fretting, and to her embarrassment, Eve picked up on her angst.

'Please don't worry,' she said. 'If I was feeling too ill to cope I would tell you. I wouldn't want to be in a position where I couldn't look after the children properly. Come on, it's Valentine's night and you two could do with a break. The twins are in bed. I'm just sitting downstairs. What could possibly go wrong?'

A lot, Marianne felt, but it seemed churlish to say anything. She looked anxiously at Gabriel, hoping he'd back her up.

'Do you think it will be ok?' she whispered, while Eve was distracted looking at the tv guide.

'I think so,' Gabriel whispered back, 'she might not have been the best mum, but she'd never hurt anyone.'

Out loud he said, 'Eve's right, Marianne, we haven't had a night out in ages. It's really kind of her to offer.'

'Yes, it is,' said Marianne. 'I suppose we don't have to be out for long, and we're not going to be far away . . .'

'So we're agreed,' said Eve, 'that's brilliant. You two have made me feel so at home, I want to give something back.'

Which was such a sweet sentiment, Marianne felt even worse, and though she muttered something to Gabriel about her worries as they were getting ready, his response of, 'I know she's not been well, but Eve's not stupid, she'll let us know if she can't cope,' only served to make her feel unkind. God, was she turning into someone who was prejudiced against mental illness? She hoped not, but she couldn't help worrying. If something went wrong it would never be *meant*. It's just that Eve was by nature a self-absorbed person, and she wasn't used to thinking about anyone else.

But Gabe was probably right, Marianne was worrying unnecessarily. If Steven hadn't been away at school he could have helped out, but he was, and Eve was on hand. And she *was* really good with the twins, who enjoyed her company. They had taken to running up to her, calling 'Evie! Evie!' whenever she came in the room. Eve had a knack of getting on the floor with them and playing inventive games; in fact, annoyingly, sometimes she seemed better at it than Marianne. But then again, Marianne thought, Eve didn't have anything to do apart from swan about all day, and was immediately taken aback by the bitchiness of the thought. Deciding she was being far too negative, she resolved that as they had the chance of a night off, she and Gabe should make the most of it.

But that still didn't stop her fretting when it came to them leaving.

'You have got our mobile numbers, haven't you?' said Marianne for the dozenth time, as they were heading out the door. 'Call us if there's a problem or you need us to come back.' Gabe gave her a coaxing nudge and Marianne finally relented.

It was a brisk clear night and their breath fogged in front of them.

'So where shall we go?' said Gabriel, as they set off hand in hand down the lane.

'Gabe! You mean you haven't booked anything?' said Marianne in dismay. 'We'll never get a table, you idiot.'

'You don't think the Grove will have something?' said Gabriel.

The Grove was a new trendy restaurant which had opened recently.

'We could try,' said Marianne, 'it's still quite early, but I doubt it somehow.'

As Marianne predicted, they arrived at the Grove to be told there were no tables till 9pm. It was the same at the curry house and the Chinese. At Whispers, Hope Christmas' poshest restaurant, they didn't even bother to ask.

'I told you,' said Marianne crossly So much for having a relaxing evening, this wasn't going at all according to plan.

'If you hadn't been making such a fuss about leaving, I would have sorted something out,' snapped Gabriel, who was clearly angry with himself for not having done so.

By the time they found themselves squashed up at the Hopesay Arms, they were both thoroughly grumpy with one another. Even more so, when Roger the new landlord apologetically informed them a table wouldn't be free till 8.30pm.

'I think we'll be lucky to get a table by then,' Marianne carped as she looked around the crowded pub. 'At this rate it's going to be nine o'clock before we eat.'

'There's nothing we can do about it, now,' said Gabriel. 'We may as well enjoy ourselves.'

'I didn't want to be out too late,' said Marianne snappily.

'It can't be helped,' was Gabriel's terse reply.

This was no good, they were heading for an argument. To deflect it, as soon as they'd settled down at a small table by the fire with their drinks, Marianne rang Eve to let her know they were going to be a bit later.

'Everything's fine,' said Eve. 'The twins are fast asleep. Now go and enjoy yourselves.'

And to her surprise, after the tetchy start, enjoy herself she did. Gabe seemed more relaxed away from the house, and so, she realised, was she. Soon they were chatting and laughing away, and she found herself staring into those lovely brown eyes of his, and wondering why she ever got cross with him.

'I believe we may have a table for you a bit sooner,' said Roger, pointing them to the restaurant area, where they saw Ralph Nicholas leaving.

'I forgot it was Valentine's night,' he said. 'An old codger like me doesn't want to be taking up space when other people need it. Stupid of me, really. Do have my table.'

'Ralph, you're a guardian angel!' said Marianne. 'Are you sure?'

'Of course I'm sure,' said Ralph with a broad grin, 'I don't like to see two lovely young people at odds with one another.'

How did he always know everything? Marianne wondered as Roger showed her to their table. She turned back to wave her thanks at him, but Ralph had already vanished.

And after that, the evening was thoroughly magical. Gabriel ordered champagne, they both had steak and chips, and for the first time they actually talked about having Eve in the house.

'I know it's tough on you, Marianne,' said Gabriel, lacing his hands through hers. 'But honestly, it's not easy for me either. She drives me mad, the length of time she spends in the bathroom.'

'And the fact she never picks up a towel,' said Marianne. 'I feel like her servant half the time.'

'It won't be forever,' said Gabriel. 'And she doesn't have anywhere else.'

'I know,' said Marianne. 'You're such a softie. It's why I love you so much.'

She leaned forward to kiss him.

'And I love you,' said Gabe, his kiss sending a delicious promise of pleasures to come. 'I know it's hard at the moment with Eve staying, but you and the kids are everything I need. Don't forget that.'

'I won't,' said Marianne, and her heart skipped a beat. She'd been being silly, feeling pushed out because Eve was in the house. There was nothing to worry about. Gabriel was still hers. All was well with the world.


'Hey, what's going on?' Cat came in the house after a long and fruitless day meeting various TV executives to promote ideas for future programmes that no one wanted – Cat could have screamed for the number of times she'd been told today, 'It's a great idea, but not quite what we're looking for'– to find the kitchen bathed in soft candlelight, and the table set for two.

Mel was overseeing proceedings, holding a damp haired, babygroed, very sleepy Lou Lou in her arms.

'Paige, will you stop texting!—' Cat smiled in amusement, that was normally her line '—I said fold the napkins properly, not dump them down. Rubes, be careful with the glasses.'

To her amazement, Paige and Ruby, who would get out of any domestic duties if they could, were scurrying around like the busiest of bees helping sort the table out.

In the corner, by the oven, James was slaving away. Though he had recently professed to not wanting to continue the TV cookery career which had started when he was twelve, finding it too much 'hassle', he still enjoyed cooking in his own time.

'Sit down, and have a glass of this.' Noel appeared by her side, taking her coat and thrusting a glass of champers in her hand, and forcing her to sit down at the kitchen table. 'Happy Valentine's, darling.'

'Aw guys,' said Cat, 'that's lovely. You didn't have to.'

'Well I thought, realistically, the chances of us getting out tonight were about a million to one against,' said Noel, 'so an evening in seemed like the next best thing.'

This was true, as the children got older it seemed to get harder and harder for her and Noel to have a night alone, not easier. 'The kids have done the rest.'

'Go on,' urged Paige, who was incredibly nosy, 'what have you got each other?'

'None of your business, young lady,' said Noel, which made Cat suspect he'd bought her underwear.

'And I haven't even bought Dad a card,' admitted Cat, blushing with mortification. 'I'd completely forgotten.'

It turned out to be dinner not quite for two, as Lou Lou got a second wind and ended up on her lap through most of it. In the meantime Ruby kept coming in to tell very bad jokes and James fretted at the stainless steel oven, showing an unusual anxiety about the state of his lobster thermidor. Mel and Paige spent so much time anxiously hovering around them, to make sure things went smoothly, in the end, Cat pulled them all in and made them sit down.

It was years since they'd had this much fun with each other on Valentine's Day – it was, as Noel always said, only a day, which was hyped up by the card industry. But the way Cat had been feeling about herself recently, it was nice to feel appreciated and loved for who she was. Cat looked around at her children, bustling about the kitchen for her and Noel, and she felt her heart burst with love and pride.

'Thanks, guys, that was wonderful,' she said, 'but do you know what? Valentine's isn't just about me and Dad, it's about you lot too. We love you very very much. Thank you.'

'Ugh, soppy alert,' said Ruby, until Noel tickled her.

The kids cleaned up, Mel put Lou Lou to bed, and then at Cat's insistence, they all sat down to play the Game of Life, a family favourite. As usual James won outright, through a combination of blagging, persistence and downright cheating in places. There was much laughter and good cheer, and Cat felt her spirits lift.

She looked round at her family with satisfaction. It was rare that they spent much time together these days, and as her family grew up, would soon be rarer still. Best she make the most of it.

'You ready?' Richard appeared at the door, as Pippa came down the stairs and her heart skipped a beat. Normally when they met, Richard was dressed casually, but tonight, he'd made an effort with a smart shirt and tie, casual dark blue jacket, and chinos, which accentuated his rangy good looks. She had a sudden longing to run her hands through his greying hair, and the surge of desire that shot through her took her by surprise.

'Almost,' said Pippa, feeling her mouth go dry. She usually saw Richard at home, or occasionally at his house if her mum could babysit. But going out, on a proper date, was making her feel absurdly nervous. It felt like a new phase in their relationship, as if they were taking things up a gear, and her stomach twisted in knots as she wondered if she was ready for that.

But as his face lit up with a smile and his green eyes dazzled her, Pippa blushed, hoping he couldn't read her thoughts. Maybe she was finally moving on. It was a long long time since she'd felt this combination of nerves, sickness and excitement.

'You look lovely,' Lucy typed, and stuck her thumbs up in approval, for once behaving herself while Richard was there. That was encouraging. Perhaps Lucy was getting used to the new situation at last.

'So you do,' said Margaret, Pippa's mum, and hugged her.

'Be good,' typed Lucy, and gave her mum a radiant smile. Pippa bent down to give her daughter an extra special kiss goodnight, relieved she was being good. Life would be so much easier if Lucy really were beginning to accept Richard.

'Now you two have a lovely time,' said Mum, in a way that Pippa couldn't quite understand.

Richard didn't say much, as he escorted her to his car.

'You don't mind driving?' said Pippa, looking puzzled.

'No it's fine,' said Richard.

'So where are we going?' Pippa said. 'Surely you can tell me now.'

But Richard refused to be drawn, merely saying she'd see soon enough.

After half an hour driving down the dark country lanes

of Shropshire, Richard finally pulled off the road down a barely lit country drive.

Pippa gasped in awe as they pulled up in front of the Westcott Country Manor – a hotel that had recently made it into the top twenty luxury hotels in the country. It was rumoured all manner of celebrities used it as a country hideaway.

'Oh Richard!' said Pippa, 'we're not having dinner here?'

'More than that,' said Richard. 'I took the liberty of getting your mum to pack a bag. I thought you – we – deserved a night off.'

It was true that the nights that Richard stayed over were infrequent and could be fraught if Lucy were there. Pippa preferred to coincide them with nights when Lucy was at respite care, to avoid the inevitable sulks which greeted Richard in the morning.

'What about the children?' said Pippa. 'And the farm?'

'Your dad's coming later, and your parents are both staying over,' said Richard. 'And the boys said they'd help with the milking. It's all sorted.'

Pippa was staggered, he'd done all this for her? She was touched by his thought and consideration.

'Richard, I don't know what to say,' said Pippa, fleetingly wondering how Dan would take the news that she'd spent a night away from home with Richard, then telling herself it wasn't anything to do with him.

She had never seen such luxury, or spent time anywhere like this. On the rare occasions she and Dan had managed to get away together, it had always been to cheap budget hotels.

'Don't say anything,' said Richard. 'Just enjoy. You deserve it.'

In a daze, Pippa followed him into the hotel, where

Richard checked in, while Pippa gazed around at her surroundings, hoping her jaw wasn't dropping to the floor. She followed him up the stairs, to their room, with its massive bed, and plush carpets. She felt dazzled by the luxury.

'I know it's still early days for us,' Richard said, pouring her a glass of champagne, 'and I get that it's complicated with Dan, but I'm so glad I found you, Pippa. Happy Valentine's Day, here's to us.'

Pippa swallowed hard. This was all wonderful, and she felt she was in a romantic bubble, as if she had suddenly been transported to a Richard Curtis movie, but even now, it was hard to just relax into this. Then she thought, bugger it, I deserve a treat.

'Thanks, Richard,' she said, 'and for taking things slowly. I really appreciate it.'

'To us,' said Richard, 'and to the future.'

'Whatever it holds,' said Pippa, raising her glass. At the moment, she didn't have a clue.

# My Broken Brain

## Day Thirty Six 10pm

Jo asked me in counselling today, how I feel.

Ha. That's a good one.

I'm a middle aged man, living at his parents', away from my kids, trying to make sense of how I lost my life. I'm writing this on my laptop, in the bedroom I slept in as a boy. And my wife – sorry, ex-wife – has just spent a night away with her new partner.

How the hell am I supposed to feel? *Angry.* Angry is how I bloody feel. And I know I have no right to.

I cannot imagine where I go from here. Pippa's finally signed the divorce papers. So now we can proceed. She's making a go of things with Richard. Which is what I wanted for her. I can't bear the fact that I've made her so unhappy. I wanted her to have a future to look forward to. But I wasn't expecting this. The way it would make me feel. Because even though I've engineered it, and I thought it was what I wanted for her. It *hurts*. So badly.

Go figure, Holliday, you inconsistent git.

Time to work out what comes next. And where we go from here.

Never mind my brain being broken. My family's broken too.

I feel like Humpty Dumpty. Who's going to put me back together again?

*March*

# Chapter Seven

'So you've finally signed the divorce papers?' said Cat.

She was sitting in Pippa's kitchen with Lou Lou wriggling on her lap. Cat planned to take her out to look at the animals in a while. She seemed to enjoy that. Pointing out the cows and mooing, and laughing at the chickens which wandered about the yard.

'Yes,' said Pippa, a slight flicker of almost indiscernible sadness crossing her face. 'I'd been putting off the inevitable. I should have done it ages ago. It wasn't fair on either Dan or Richard. But it just seems so – final – you know?'

'I think I do,' said Cat, remembering the bleak time when they were still living in London and she thought she'd lost Noel. She could imagine all too well how hard it would be to let go.

'So what changed?'

Pippa blushed.

'Oh,' said Cat, 'the dirty mid-week bonk worked then.'

'You *knew* about that?' said Pippa, mortified.

'Marianne and I both did,' laughed Cat. 'Richard asked our advice about where to take you. We suggested a lovely country hotel.'

Richard had pestered both her and Marianne for weeks as to whether or not he should take Pippa away. Knowing that Pippa needed a push in the right direction, they'd both said yes.

Cat looked at her friend slyly. 'I take it that did the trick?'

'Shut up,' said Pippa, blushing again. 'It was lovely if you must know, but it made me see I had to make a proper choice, or lose Richard too. He's been very patient with me, but I feel like I may have been stringing him along a bit without meaning to.'

'Don't be so hard on yourself,' said Cat, 'with what you've been through, you needed to take your time. Still, onwards and upwards, eh?'

'Absolutely,' said Pippa. 'No more harking back to Dan. Richard is gorgeous and lovely and very very sexy. Time to look forward, not back.'

'And the kids are ok with things?' asked Cat, knowing that Pippa had been having trouble getting them to accept Richard.

'The boys don't say much, but they seem to be ok,' said Pippa. 'I've explained to them, that if Dan had wanted it, I'd have gone back to him like a shot. However, as he doesn't, I've got to find a life of my own again, and I think they understand that. Lucy on the other hand . . .' She sighed heavily. 'It's been harder to explain to her – you know how close she is to Dan. She's really difficult whenever Richard's about, in fact she's quite difficult a lot of the time now. Hormones kicking in, I expect. That doesn't help.'

'I know that feeling,' said Cat. 'We've got two hormonal teenagers, one pre teen, and me on the cusp of the meno-pause. Our house can be hellish at times. It's a wonder Noel and James don't move out.'

Pippa laughed.

'You're making me glad I've only got one girl,' she said. 'Anyway, I'm sure Lucy will get used to things in time. And to be honest, however our relationship pans out, I'm glad Richard took me away. I did have a really lovely time.'

'So the hotel was nice then?' said Cat.

'Nice? It was fabulous,' said Pippa. 'I've never been anywhere so luxurious. We should go there with Marianne and have a spa day. They were advertising some introductory special offers. Here, let me get the leaflet.'

Pippa got up and went out of the room, and Lou Lou wriggled out of Cat's lap. She had recently started walking and toddled over to the farm cat, pointing at it, saying 'cat' proudly, a new word she had recently learnt. The cat gave such a look of disdain, Cat laughed out loud, but she did consent to let Lou Lou stroke her rather energetically, till Pippa returned.

'Just look at this,' said Pippa, as Cat scooped Lou Lou up in her arms, before she started to pull the cat's tail too vigorously.

'That looks amazing,' said Cat, poring over the pictures of steam baths, hot stone massages and Ayurvedic treatments, and an invitational offer to become favoured clients for the day. 'I feel a girlie day out coming on. Hang on . . .' she paused and looked at the leaflet more closely, 'LK Holdings – isn't that the company who are behind the new development?'

'Is it?' said Pippa. 'Do you know, I hadn't even noticed. How shallow am I? In that case we should definitely go and check it out. Know your enemy and all that.'

'That sounds like a great idea,' said Cat. 'I've always fancied myself as a spy. Particularly if there's a Jacuzzi thrown in.'

Pippa was feeling much better about everything. With the divorce papers signed, and the decree nisi granted she felt like a big burden had been lifted from her shoulders. They still had to wait for the decree absolute, but the deed was done. Spring was round the corner, and it was time to get on with the rest of her life. If she did still sometimes feel sad at what she'd lost, she had to park those feelings and hide them away. They weren't doing her any good, best bury them deep.

Since the trip to the hotel, she and Richard had grown much closer. He had taken to staying over a couple of times a week, although he always checked if it was ok with Lucy first. Every other weekend, when Dan had the kids, they also tried to have a date night. Either Pippa would go to Richard's and he would cook for her, or they'd take a trip into Hope Christmas and go out to dinner at Whispers.

If when he was over, Richard sensed Lucy was being uncooperative, he would back off and go home. Pippa appreciated his tact and sensitivity. While it wasn't winning Lucy round quickly, the boys seemed to understand the efforts Richard was making, and appreciated the fact that he didn't try too hard to be their friend. He was also incredibly understanding about the slightly strange situation she found herself in with Dan, regarding the practical aspects of running the farm, and would make himself scarce if Dan came in to discuss something of importance.

'I don't want to get in your way,' he'd say, and take himself off into the lounge to watch tv with the kids, or go upstairs with his laptop and do some work.

Pippa felt tremendously grateful to him for making it so easy, particularly as she and Dan seemed to be getting on much better now all that was between them was organising the farm. All the tension that had built up over the last couple of years seemed to be slowly dissipating, and she felt much more relaxed in Dan's presence than she had done for a long time.

The only potential blot on the landscape was that Pippa was getting worried about what was going to happen to the farm. Now the divorce was nearly official, Pippa felt she should take on more of the practical jobs on the farm than she'd done in the past, and not expect Dan to do everything. Since money was tight, they couldn't afford too much labour. And while Gabriel was often on hand to help out, she knew they couldn't always rely on him. He had enough to do on his own farm.

The boys were a great help too, often getting up early in the morning to help milk the cows before school if she or Dan couldn't do it. But next year Nathan would have GCSEs, and Pippa wanted him to concentrate on his schoolwork. More likely than not he was going to become a farmer – he was looking into doing a BTech in Farm Management later on – it was in his blood, and he loved it, but Pippa was determined he would have proper choices to make, not end up in farming by default. Though if that was what he really wanted to do, she'd be happy for him to take over the farm in the future, *if* they survived that long.

Despite the divorce, Pippa and Dan still hadn't discussed the business properly yet. She hadn't asked him for maintenance, because the farm gave them everything they needed, and he could barely sustain himself alone. At some point they would have to deal with the practicalities, but it was giving Pippa a headache just thinking about it. It was easier to keep things the way they were.

The one difficulty she was having with Richard was that he couldn't understand why she was 'letting things slide', as he put it. Once or twice he'd brought the subject up, saying 'Come on, Pippa, you've got to face up to this sometime,' but she'd resisted the conversation. Because the practical thing, the sensible thing was to sell the farm and split their assets. And with LK Holdings hovering about, they could probably get a really good offer on the farm, as Richard had tried to hint to her on a number of occasions.

'You don't understand,' she'd tried to explain to him, 'my heart is here and always will be.'

She'd grown up on the farm, in this house, with Gabriel next door. They'd both taken on the heritage of their fore-fathers; Pippa didn't want to be the one who threw in the towel.

Richard couldn't begin to understand. He was a townie through and through. And although he liked living in the country, he just couldn't see that farming was in her blood. And somehow she had to save her heritage. Whatever it cost.

'So I was thinking, now the twins are doing a couple of long days at nursery, I might sign up for some agency teaching,' said Marianne over a rare supper alone with Gabriel. Eve had had a bad day, and was upstairs 'resting'. The twins had already had their tea, given Dolly her bedtime bottle of milk, and were sitting in pyjamas watching *Peppa Pig*, waiting for Gabriel to chase them up to bed – a nightly ritual when he came in early enough.

'Oh?' said Gabriel, 'what's brought this on? I thought you didn't want to go back to teaching just yet.'

'I didn't think I did,' admitted Marianne, 'but I do miss it, and I'm getting a bit frustrated at home, particularly on the days when the twins are out all day.'

She didn't like to say that living on top of Eve, as she had been for over a month now, was getting to them both.

They were such different people. Marianne liked to get up and get things done, whereas Eve liked to take her time and sit around drinking tea and chewing the fat. She was always offering to help, but in reality she'd lose interest pretty quickly, stopping to watch something on TV, or picking up a magazine. It drove Marianne nuts, but what could she do? They were living in the same house, and despite Joan having returned from her cruise, there had been no mention of Eve going to stay there, so there was nothing Marianne could do. She had to get on with Eve.

'You could always come out and help me,' said Gabriel.

'Yes, but it wouldn't bring in any extra cash,' she argued.

'We'll survive,' said Gabriel.

'The money would come in handy, you know it would,' said Marianne.

'True,' agreed Gabriel, not saying what she knew he was thinking – having an extra person in the house who was contributing nothing to the household was an added expense. Perhaps as a result of having lived with Darren, her last partner, who was a rich businessman, Eve seemed to have no idea of basic economies, leaving lights on, turning up heating, running baths she forgot about and eating vast amounts for someone who was annoyingly skinny. She'd offer to get the shopping, but always came back with expensive items they didn't need, and never brought back any change from the money Marianne gave her.

Marianne dearly wanted to ask how much longer Eve was staying, but Gabriel seemed to have developed a blind spot as far as his ex-wife was concerned, saying 'I can't upset her, Marianne, you know that. I'm sure she'll move on when she's ready.'

So Marianne didn't feel she could push it. She knew

Gabriel still felt absurdly responsible for Eve, 'I always felt I could have done more to help her,' he'd confided in Marianne more than once – which was daft from where Marianne was sitting – and this was his chance to put things right.

Marianne couldn't fault Gabe's motivation. She knew he was being kind to Eve, but he was putting his head in the sand about it so the subject was becoming very difficult for Marianne to broach. She couldn't tell him that one of the reasons she was desperate to get out of the house was that she no longer felt it was her own.

Whenever she came in, Eve seemed to have changed some knick knacks around, and put expensive vases and glassware all over the place. Funny how she couldn't afford rent, but she could afford *that* – despite Marianne saying with the twins around it was dangerous (and she'd been proved right – at least two glasses had gone for a burton for which Marianne had felt obliged to pay). Nor could Eve be persuaded that lighting candles in the house was a bad idea with small children, a dog, and a pet lamb (who though big enough to go back to the fold, still hadn't quite made it out of the kitchen, the twins were too enamoured of her).

She wanted to tell Gabriel all this but didn't know how. It seemed so petty. Besides, Eve was always there, and tonight was a very rare occasion when she wasn't. Which gave Marianne the confidence to venture—

'You don't think we could – perhaps—'

'Perhaps what?'

'Ask Eve for some rent,' she said, 'then maybe I wouldn't have to work.'

'Oh Lord. I've been so selfish – of course I should be paying you rent. Why didn't you say?' To Marianne's horror, Eve had chosen that moment to come downstairs and heard every word. 'Here let me go to the bank right now and draw some money out.'

'That won't be necessary,' said Gabe. 'We asked you to stay here, remember? We wouldn't dream of asking you for any money. It's fine, isn't it, Marianne?'

He looked at her with such pleading, Marianne didn't know what else to do.

'Absolutely,' said Marianne between gritted teeth. But she was furious. How could Gabriel do this to her? When did *her* feelings get taken into account?

'Oh you're so kind, the pair of you,' said Eve, her eyes welling up (that was another thing about Eve, she was so good at producing tears), 'I don't know what I'd do without you. I'll be out of your hair soon, I promise.'

Hurrah, thought Marianne silently, but Gabe just leant forward and said, 'You can stay as long as you need, Eve, you know that. We'll manage won't we, Marianne?'

'Of course,' said Marianne with a sinking heart. 'It's our pleasure.'

At this rate, Eve would be there forever.

'And, Marianne,' added Gabe casually, 'I think you're right. It would really help if you got a job. Do you good to get out of the house.'

'Great,' said Marianne, with false cheer, and looked over to see Eve smiling at her sweetly. She'd got what she wanted, so why did she feel she'd been outmanoeuvred?

# Chapter Eight

'So do you think it's time we talked about the farm?'

Pippa nearly dropped the pot of tea she was pouring for Dan. She'd thought the farm was a subject they'd agreed on for the time being, but maybe not.

Once a day, usually mid morning, Dan would silently appear for a cup of tea and slice of cake. Sometimes it felt like a parody of her former life. But Dan was so formal with her now; although she was glad they could at least be civilized about things. And the children liked it – Lucy in particular – when he popped back at teatime. The special bond they shared hadn't been lost, despite what had happened. If anything, it had grown stronger. Lucy seemed to empathically know when her dad was feeling low; he on the other hand could josh her out of her strops in a way that Pippa never could. The last time Dan had been round, Lucy had gone into a complete meltdown because Pippa had made something she didn't like for tea. It was only Dan playing aeroplanes with her, as if she was two, and threatening to eat it for her, that had got her out of it. Perhaps the physical trauma Dan had been through gave him a greater insight into their daughter's condition. Whatever the reason, Pippa saw it and was glad.

Pippa carefully wiped up the tea she'd spilt.

'Um, what's brought this on?' she said. 'I thought we'd agreed we weren't going to do anything about the farm at the moment.' They were still waiting for the divorce to be finalised, but Dan had been adamant nothing was going to change in the short term.

'We had,' said Dan, 'but I was in the field that backs onto Blackstock Farm, this morning, and there were people up there again. Lots more people. They had maps, and were taking photographs. They've already applied for planning permission, seems to me that LK Holdings are really serious about the site. Which started me thinking . . .'

'Don't want to do that,' joked Pippa, feeling a little anxious about what might be coming next, 'never know what kind of trouble thinking can get you into.'

'I'm being serious,' said Dan. 'I'm just wondering if we had a bit of a knee-jerk reaction to that guy knocking on the door and making us an offer. Maybe we should sell up after all. Then you and Richard could find somewhere together, and I'd be free to start up again elsewhere, or who knows, do something different.'

'But the farm . . .' said Pippa.

'I know,' said Dan.

And that was the point, he *did* know. The farm had been their commitment to the future. A future that was no longer possible. She knew what it was costing him to ask her this.

His eyes held her and looked so sad she was tempted to hug him, but she knew from past experience that he would flinch and move away, and she'd long ago inured herself against that. It was still too painful.

'Wait a minute,' she said. 'Richard and I – well I don't even know what Richard and I have. It's too soon. We're certainly not planning to live together at the moment.'

'But you might in the future,' said Dan. 'And I really

don't want to stand in your way, when the time comes. I'm holding you back, Pippa. You know I am.'

'Oh Dan,' Pippa's eyes filled with tears, 'you aren't. You don't. I just thought . . .'

'That things would be different?' said Dan gently. 'But they're not, and they can't be. We're nearly divorced now, Pippa. Hell, you've got a new partner, and yet we're still carrying on as if nothing has changed. We can't do that forever.'

'What about the boys?' said Pippa. 'You know how keen Nathan is to go to agricultural college. He's born to be a farmer. Can't we hold on at least until he's old enough to get more involved?'

'Pippa, I don't think we have that luxury,' said Dan. 'I know how hard you work to keep control of the finances, but I'm not stupid. I can see the bills piling up. I just think this would be a solution to our problems.'

Pippa looked out of the kitchen window, at the hills at the end of their lane, where Gabriel's sheep were grazing happily, as those belonging to her family had for over a hundred years. She felt her stomach contract with a feeling of anxiety that was becoming all too familiar of late. Her heart, her soul was here. She couldn't, wouldn't give it up without a fight.

'What if I find another way?' said Pippa. 'If I could get the finances together and buy you out? Would you agree to that?'

'But Pippa—'

'But Pippa, nothing,' she said, 'would you, or wouldn't you? I don't think you really want to lose the farm for Nathan either, do you?'

She was bargaining on him hating the thought of it.

'No,' admitted Dan, 'I really don't. I just can't see another way out.'

114

'Well then,' said Pippa, a sense of determination growing in her, fortified by Dan's acquiescence, 'I shall have to see what I can do.'

Marianne went downstairs at 6am to put the kettle on. Gabe was already up and about, ready to go and see to the ewes and their newborn lambs. Marianne had given Dolly, still resident in the kitchen, a bottle of milk; she was rapidly outgrowing her basket. Really they should send her out with the other lambs now, but the twins were so attached to her and Marianne who always felt a total townie when it came to sending the lambs to market felt she couldn't quite stomach sending Dolly out in the fields, knowing she was going to the slaughterhouse later in the season.

Gabe, with the typical pragmatism of a farmer had said, 'At least we've given her a good life.' But he could no more resist the wide-eyed wonder of the twins (who hadn't yet made the connection between their beloved pet and the roast lamb they enjoyed so much for Sunday dinner) than she could. Very soon they were going to have a fully grown sheep careering round their kitchen, thanks to their soft-heartedness. Only Eve, who'd never quite recovered from the shock of their meeting, didn't like Dolly. In fact Eve was so completely anti-animal, it seemed miraculous to Marianne that she had ever entertained the life of a farmer's wife. She was so eminently unsuited to it.

Marianne mechanically made the children sandwiches. She had Gabe's mum, Jean, on call to do the nursery run if she got a phone call from the agency saying she had work. Twice last week, she had been asked to step in and had had to drive halfway round the county. Eve had offered to help out, but not only did Marianne doubt she'd get up in time, she also worried that Eve mightn't remember to go (from what Gabriel had told her, she very often forgot to pick Steven up when he was little), so she asked Gabriel to pick them up instead.

Gabriel hadn't exactly been enthusiastic about it, 'You know I can't be sure of getting there,' he'd pointed out reasonably, but she felt frustrated. When she'd first met him all those years ago, he'd often picked Steven up from school, though Pippa had also helped out a lot. Now it was as though Marianne was being taken for granted, always there, and if she wanted to work, it was her job to sort out childcare. If she ever got a job again permanently, she'd have to do something about that.

'When are they likely to phone?' Gabe came out of the kitchen, taking a cup of tea with alacrity, but eating nothing. He usually liked to come back around nine for his breakfast.

'It was about seven last week,' said Marianne.

She didn't like to say she wasn't really sure yet about the supply teaching. It seemed bitty and inconsistent and she hated not teaching the same children every day, but they were in the middle of the school year, and jobs were hard to come by. Particularly part time ones, which is what she really wanted. It was unfair to keep relying on Gabe's mum on the off chance that she was going to get a job for the day. She'd have to sort something out, but then paying for a childminder when she might not get any work seemed like a waste of money.

As if mirroring her thoughts, Gabe said, 'I hope you get something more permanent soon. This is so frustrating for you.'

'I know,' said Marianne, 'but what can I do. I feel bad for your mum too, that I can't give her more notice.'

'No, don't worry,' said Gabriel. 'She's always happy to help.'

'I know,' said Marianne, 'but if I get anything more permanent I'll try and get a new childminder.'

'But that defeats the purpose of you working,' said Gabriel, 'especially if it's not every day.'

'So what do you suggest?' asked Marianne, feeling grumpy. It was too early in the morning for this conversation.

'We could ask Eve,' said Gabe, 'it would be good for her, give her something to do. I'm worried that she's not got any sense of purpose. I think helping us could really help her. It's the obvious solution.'

Marianne wanted to say over my dead body, but Gabe was right, it was an obvious solution, even if she didn't like it. She was saved from replying by the phone ringing. A year five class in Whitchurch required her services.

'We'll talk about this later,' she said, getting her mobile out to text Jean. She looked at her watch, the journey was nearly an hour, and she needed to be there at eight. 'I'm going to have to dash, can you sort the kids out for your mum?'

'Will do,' said Gabriel a bit grumpily, 'but I can't do it every time.'

'I know,' said Marianne. She went to get ready with a sinking heart. This had seemed like such a good idea. But what if she'd bitten off more than she could chew?

Cat was at the park with Lou Lou, gently pushing her in a swing. Since she'd started looking after her granddaughter, Cat had got much fitter. She was walking miles pushing the buggy, just as she had when Mel was small. Back then, pounding the streets of North London, always on a timetable, worried about being late, pumped with adrenaline, rushing around and a diet of coffee had ensured she stayed thin. Now she could feel a midlife tummy crisis occurring. No wonder she didn't fit on TV anymore. She'd seen a really cruel piece in one of the many TV based rags about how 'the TV Kitchen Totty' had turned into 'a tub of lard'. It was grossly unfair and very hurtful. She'd put on a bit of weight certainly, but she was hardly obese. She was so frustrated by what was happening to her, she'd started a new blog, *Invisible Woman*, which judging by the hits she was getting had really struck a chord.

'Time to go home.' Cat prised her reluctant grand-daughter out of the swing and into her buggy. It was all very well Lou Lou having fun, but Cat had forgotten how much you froze to death pushing swings.

She walked back up the path to town and was delighted to see Miss Woods and Ralph Nicholas deep in conversation. Her favourite old people in Hope Christmas.

'What are you two plotting?' she asked with a grin.

'Just chatting about this wretched plan for the new hotel,' said Miss Woods. 'Honestly, these property people. They think they can waltz in here and take over.'

'Unless we find a way of stopping them,' said Cat.

'That is exactly what I was saying to Ralph,' agreed Miss Woods. 'I gather there are some plans afoot in that direction?'

'We haven't got very far,' said Cat, 'but there's a meeting in the village hall in a couple of weeks.'

'Glad to hear it,' said Miss Woods. 'I'd like to give that London lot a run for their money, and show them that the people of Hope Christmas aren't pushovers and can't be taken over on a whim. I've been asking around, and there are plenty of people up in arms about this: Diana Carew,

Batty Jack from the turkey farm, Vera and Albert from the café, to name but a few.'

'I couldn't agree with you more,' said Cat, 'we should be more than a match for those in favour.'

'We certainly will be,' said Miss Woods with relish. 'We'll show them we're not going to take this lying down. Bring it on, I say!'

# *Chapter Nine*

Pippa was online looking at ideas – anything to see if there were ways to make money from the farm that they hadn't thought of. She felt sick to the pit of her stomach with the worry of it all. The baking that Pippa had been doing for several years for Vera's in town was great, but it wasn't enough.

She looked at ice cream manufacturing – supermarkets paid so little for their milk it felt barely worth their while selling it sometimes. She'd read somewhere about a farm who'd made a mint on home-made ice cream, but now of course she couldn't find the article. It sounded like a good solution, but she couldn't do it alone. She wondered idly, now that Cat had more time on her hands, whether she could co-opt her into help.

She started a list.

1. Ice cream?

2. More baking – but how??? There was only so much time in the day and she was up at five as it was.

3. Festivals? They had a lot of land. The Hope Christmas Summer Fest was a regular feature on the calendar, maybe she could rent out land to campers? Or perhaps she should start her own mini Glastonbury. Then she thought about seeing Miss Woods' reaction at a Parish Council Meeting if she suggested it. Maybe not.

4. Camping? She and Dan had talked about letting out some of their fallow fields in the past, but it had never come to anything. Plenty of people did do it locally. Mind you . . . health and safety, and insurance was an issue with all these things. And did they really want loads of strangers traipsing past the house and driving up the lane? They got enough walkers up here as it was.

5. B&B? Ditto.

Bugger, this was getting her nowhere. It was late, she'd organised the first campaign meeting for the next day, and she needed to get to bed. Richard was on a work trip to town for a few days, so she'd decided to make the most of his absence to get her ideas together.

'I'm not sure if you're realistically going to be able to turn things round,' he'd said in an infuriatingly reasonable manner, when she'd broached the subject of diversification, and to avoid an argument, she'd kept quiet. But maybe if she presented Richard with a fait accompli, he'd change his mind. She hoped so. She felt instinctively Richard would prefer it if she weren't so keen to save the farm. If they were to have a future together, she ought to take note of that. *If* . . . That was the million dollar question. She was enjoying spending time with him, and appreciated everything he did for her, but sometimes she wondered if they were too different to make a proper go of things.

She should try not to worry about Richard too much and concentrate on the farm. If they ended up having to sell, she wanted to be sure she'd explored every option.

Sighing, she was just about to shut down the computer, when she saw an advert pop up on a website she'd been looking at.

*Easter Eggstravaganza*, it said. *Come to Farmer Bill's for some Eggcellent fun*. It was just a little farm, doing some Easter fun days, but it got her thinking.

6, Pippa wrote down, Theme based Farm Days. Now *that* might be an idea.

'This is a bit of a disappointing turnout,' said Cat to Noel, as she walked through the door of the village hall, rebuilt after the floods seven years previously. She'd expected the place to be heaving, but it was only half full. The usual suspects were there: Vera and Albert from the café, 'It makes me so mad to think of what they are planning to do to our woods,' said Vera, her face flushing pink with frustration. 'Why can't they build their hotel somewhere else?'

'I couldn't agree more,' boomed Diana Carew, the bossiest and most overbearing woman in Hope Christmas. She steamed up to them, with a determined look that Cat knew meant she felt entitled to take over proceedings. Diana was good-hearted, but she needed containing. Luckily, Pippa had already set up a table at the front of the room, from where she was planning to talk.

Cat nodded her agreement and then she and Noel found their way to seats next to Marianne and Gabriel, who'd obviously been there for some time.

'Not as many as I thought,' said Cat, 'which is a shame.'

'Maybe people haven't worked out yet how serious this is,' said Marianne. 'After all, none of us have seen the plans.'

There was a steady hum of conversation as people settled down into their seats and Pippa called the meeting to order.

'Thanks so much for coming to this preliminary meeting to discuss the proposals for Blackstock Farm,' said Pippa. 'As you're all probably aware, LK Holdings are planning to build a huge hotel complex and leisure centre in the area of Blackstock Farm, and the woods near it, and I'm sure you're all as worried as I am about what that development will entail.'

'I'm not!' shouted a voice from behind Cat, 'they're buying my land.'

She turned round to look at a small, lean, red faced farmer, with greying hair, who was looking quite pleased with himself.

'Who's he?' asked Cat.

'Archie Speers,' said Marianne, 'part of his land backs onto Blackstock Farm. He's dead keen to sell.'

'Yes, we know, Archie,' Pippa swiftly riposted, 'but it's not all about *you*.'

The hall erupted in laughter, and Pippa moved on and did what she was so good at, describing in clear and precise detail why this development was a bad thing for the town and the area in general.

'We all know what a special place Hope Christmas is,' said Pippa. 'It has its own unique charm, which risks being lost if this development goes ahead. And I'm sure none of us want that.'

'But it could bring much needed jobs into the area,' someone shouted from the back.

'And the leisure facilities could be really good,' said a youngish, ginger-haired woman near the front, who Marianne whispered was Jenny Ingles, who worked in the local estate agents.

Jenny turned round to a younger contingent of women, whom Cat recognised from the café as the very orange Yummy Mummys, 'I mean, I'm sure you guys would love to go to a gym locally and not schlep into Shrewsbury.'

'Too right,' said Keeley Jacobs, her hair drawn so tightly into a ponytail on top of her head, it made her look like some strange kind of alien. 'I think it's a great idea.'

Cat and Marianne looked at one another in dismay. This wasn't going at all well. They had been aware that there was some support for the scheme but were not prepared for quite this much.

'Well I don't,' Miss Woods boomed, standing up and tapping her stick on the floor decisively. 'It will change the very character of this place and not for the better.'

'Silly old bat,' muttered one of the Yummy Mummies, and the meeting threatened to break down into chaos until Pippa called a halt.

'Clearly feelings on this issue are running high,' she said. 'And at the moment, we don't have a complete picture of what LK Holdings are planning. It may be they are thinking of a development more in keeping with the area – they have been known to invest in wildlife sanctuaries in the past. So who knows, that may be what they are planning here. In the meantime, if we all keep our eyes and ears open for any new developments, we can start to think about what action we can take.'

'I hope they don't build a wildlife sanctuary, what a waste of space that would be,' muttered Angie Townley, Keeley's great crony, who was sitting behind Cat, 'I fancy having a local spa and beauty centre, that would be cool.'

Cat turned to Marianne in despair, they didn't have to say anything, it was clear they were thinking the same thing. This might turn out to be a whole lot more difficult than any of them had thought.

Marianne stood in a class of Year 4s with a pounding head. She'd not slept well the night before after the unsatisfactory meeting. It seemed like there was a lot of public support for the hotel plans, and it made her feel anxious. Were she and Gabriel going to end up living opposite a massive hotel complex? It would mean more traffic on their little lane, destruction of some of the wonderful views, visitors who might not be sympathetic to the area, and all in all be a huge headache. She really hoped it wasn't going to happen.

She tried to concentrate on the task in hand: numeracy with a bunch of eight-year-olds who were even less interested in it than she was. Dutifully, she tried to take them through fractions, and multiplication, but they were very badly behaved and she ended up sending two of them to the headmaster before first break. It was going to be a very long day.

And so it proved. By lunchtime, the children's behaviour was wilder than ever, and Marianne had received several sympathetic nods from other teachers in the staff room. 'Their actual teacher is off with stress,' explained one of them at lunchtime, and Marianne wasn't at all surprised. They were the most nightmarish class she'd ever had to deal with.

By the time she'd got to the end of the day and separated three fights, told four children off for using language she had only learnt when she left home, and stopped three very unpleasant girls picking on the smallest boy in the class, Marianne had a pounding headache. She made a mental note that she was never ever going to agree to work in this school again. And to add insult to injury it was on the far side of the county, so it had cost her a fortune in petrol too.

Marianne was beginning to wonder if doing supply teaching was worth it. If she was going to have to pay for childcare on top of this, then she'd be in massive trouble. But to find a job closer to home seemed to be proving impossible. She got in the car and switched the engine on. It sputtered and died. Resolutely, she turned the key in the ignition again, and nothing. She checked the fuel gauge, wondering if she'd been stupid enough to forget to fill up. Having been dashing in and out so much lately, it was quite likely. To her relief it was still half full, so why wouldn't the car start? It was as though there was no power in it. Then she realised there *was* no power in it. She'd been a complete idiot after all, and left the lights on. It had been a damp foggy morning, and the traffic had been terrible. She'd had the lights on all the way, and arrived late. In her hurry to get through the door, she hadn't turned them off. The battery was flat. Damn, damn and triple damn.

She looked around her for any signs of life, and then spotted a man she'd vaguely seen round the building that morning.

'I'm so sorry to trouble you,' she said, 'in fact, I feel a bit embarrassed to tell you this, but my battery has gone flat. I've got some jump leads in the car. You couldn't possibly give me a jump start could you?'

'My pleasure,' said the man. 'Wait a minute, I'll bring the car round.'

He was as good as his word, driving round to get as close as he could to Marianne's car, showing her the correct way to connect the leads together.

Within seconds the car had started.

'Thank you so much,' said Marianne with relief.

It turned out her helpful stranger was the deputy head of the school she'd been working at. He was so young, Marianne had thought he must be a junior member of staff. Which was a bit embarrassing. She drove off at speed, worried she was going to be late back.

The journey home was quicker than she'd anticipated, so she was glad to pull into the driveway in time to sort the twins' tea out. But to her surprise the house was in darkness. She came into the kitchen to find a scribbled note from Gabriel.

*Sorry. Kids with Mum. Had to go out on fields and Mum couldn't come over here. Eve out somewhere.*
*Love Gx*

Great. Now she was going to have to pick up two hungry hyper kids. What an end to her day. She was about to go out again, when she suddenly became aware of an insistent beeping sound and realised the answerphone had been flashing since she came in.

'Marianne, this is Mum, can you ring me?'

Marianne frowned. Her mum didn't sound quite right, and besides it was Tuesday, she never rang her on a Tuesday. She always rang on a Sunday. Something must be wrong. Heart pounding, Marianne checked her mobile. Two missed calls. Mum *never* rang her mobile.

Marianne picked up the phone with shaking fingers and dialled home.

'Mum? Is everything ok?'

Her mum's voice sounded tinny and far away.

'Oh Marianne,' she said. 'It's your dad. He's had a heart attack. You need to come right away.'

# My Broken Brain

## Day Sixty Six. 4am

So I seem to be doing really well in the cocking things up department. Sometimes I think this brain injury has robbed me of any sense at all. Which is why I'm sitting here, wide awake with a blinding headache, when I should be sleeping.

We have to sort out a sensible future, but my head gets fogged up thinking about it all. Pippa's always been much better about that sort of thing than me. Even before my accident accounts have always made my brain hurt. It's even worse now. Maybe we should let the developers in. God knows we could do with the money, and from what I heard at the meeting Pippa organised, there are a lot of people in town who think it's a good idea.

If we had the money, it would give us the freedom to start again, *properly* . . .

But I know Pippa. She will never give up without a fight. And I don't want her to either. It's our legacy to the kids and I don't want to see that farm go. But when the divorce is finally through we're going to have to make some decisions about the farm once and for all.

This is a half life, and it's killing me. I'm close to Pippa, and yet know that's all gone. I need a clean break, she needs a fresh start.

I want to save the farm. I hope we can save it. But what if we can't? What then?

## Part Two

## *It's going to take some time*

# 15 years ago

## Married Christmas

'I still can't believe we're actually in,' said Pippa, looking thrilled to bits. The farmhouse was still full of boxes, though they'd decided to defer unpacking the rest of them till after Christmas. There was a lot of work to do to bring it up to the twenty first century – during their tenure here, Pippa's parents hadn't done much modernisation – but finally, the farm was theirs. Pippa's parents had decided to retire and were moving to an old farmhouse belonging to Pippa's grandfather, while Dan and Pippa bought the farm off them. They couldn't afford it outright, but Pippa's dad had generously agreed to come in as a silent partner till such time as it was viable for them to buy him out altogether.

'This farm has been in our family for over three generations,' he had said gruffly, 'I want my new grandson to be brought up here.'

Dan still felt touched by the gesture, and by the faith his new father-in-law had shown him. He hoped he could live up to that expectation. At the moment it felt like an awesome responsibility. But equally it was a responsibility and adventure he got to share with Pippa. Pippa who lit up every day of his life. He could never go wrong with her by his side.

'Come on, Dan, we've got to get a move on. We still have to get the Christmas tree decorated,' said Pippa, giving him a dazzling smile. 'I'm not missing carols in the square for anything.'

She waddled towards the tree, and started decorating it with tinsel and baubles, and then turned round, aware that Dan was silently laughing at her.

'What?' she said crossly.

'Nothing. You,' he said, his heart swellling with love as he went over to kiss her on the head. 'I was just thinking, even though you look like an uncomfortable duck, I still think you're the most gorgeous thing I have ever seen in my life.'

'Oh Daniel,' she said, throwing her arms around him, 'you do say the nicest things.'

She leant against him, and he felt her mould into shape with him, as if she fitted there quite naturally. She stretched up to kiss him on the lips.

'I do love you, Dan Holliday,' she said happily. 'I just can't believe we're here together in our very own home. It's so perfect.'

She kissed him again.

'Happy Christmas, Dan,' she said.

'Happy Christmas,' Dan echoed, pulling her close to him, and listening to the bells ringing out for Christmas Eve. He didn't think he'd ever felt more content in his life.

'Never mind, Fairy Tale in New York,' he said, 'I'll settle with Fairy Tale in Hope Christmas.'

*April*

# *Chapter Ten*

Marianne sat in a small cubicle, close to the nurse's station, sitting by her father's bedside listening to his slow rhythmic breathing, and wondered, as she had every day for the last week, whether today would be his last. A *week*. A whole week of him being like this: comatose, apparently oblivious to the world. And it felt no easier than it had on that first day, when seeing her dad covered in wires and tubes had been a massive shock. Stupid really, but she'd never imagined a world without her father's reassuring presence. He was so solid and *there*, it was impossible to think of life without him, and now she was staring the prospect starkly in the face. He lay there, a pale still figure, surrounded by monitors and with tubes attached to him, who bore little resemblance to the man she knew and loved. How could he possibly die?

It would have been hard enough to deal with this anyway, but Mum had fallen completely apart. She appeared incapable of making decisions, and spent most of her time sitting beside Dad sobbing, which wasn't, Marianne felt, the most helpful reaction. Initially she'd refused to leave Dad's side, but as the situation stabilised and it looked as though he was going to pull through, Marianne had persuaded her to go home from time to time, to rest and occasionally eat, while she stayed with Dad alone. Guiltily, she preferred it without Mum. It allowed her to grieve for the father she was losing in her own private way.

She kept trying to picture Dad as he normally was, bright, funny, full of life, but the image kept eluding her. The days of sitting here, looking at his pale face, listening to his stertorous breathing, day in and day out, were taking their toll. Try as hard as she might, Marianne couldn't visualise her dad in any other way than this. It was as if the figure on the bed had obliterated a whole lifetime of memories, and it made her want to weep.

To make matters worse, she felt terribly alone. Gabriel had to stay at the farm, and look after the twins – she hadn't wanted them to see Grandpa like this – and her beloved brother Matt was travelling with his husband, Marcus, and they were trying to get a flight back. So it had been her and Mum, and occasionally, Mum's sister, Auntie Vi, together all week. And Marianne had never felt so lonely.

Marianne sighed, and held her dad's hand. Willing him to wake up. She kept up a steady patter about what the twins were up to, filling him in on how Dolly the sheep was getting so big and was causing so much chaos that Marianne had had to fit a stair gate in the kitchen to keep her in.

'You should see her, Dad,' she said. 'It's quite ridiculous, we've got a semi grown sheep living in the kitchen. And she's bonded so well with Patch, I swear she thinks he's her mum.'

Marianne knew that would amuse him. Dad had found the whole notion of a sheep in the house hilarious. She hoped he could hear what she was saying, and it was making him feel better, somewhere deep inside.

The more she talked, the more she missed her family,

but it was better they weren't here, and thanks to Pippa and Jean, who were generously sharing childcare duties to help Gabe out, she didn't have to worry about what was happening at home.

'You just concentrate on your dad, love,' said Jean, in a way that made Marianne love her mother-in-law even more than she already did, 'that's the important thing. You don't worry about what's happening here.'

Even Eve had chipped in to help, and according to Gabriel, had been amazing. Marianne wasn't sure if that made her feel better or worse. Every night as she clambered into her childhood bed, in the room in the bland suburban house she'd grown up in, which Mum had scarcely changed since her teenage years, it felt all wrong. More than anything, she wanted to be at home with Gabe and the twins and Steven, and for none of this to have happened.

But happen it had. She sighed again and squeezed Dad's hand, desperate for some response.

'I do wish you'd wake up, Dad, even if only for a minute.'

But there was no reply. Just the laboured sound of his breathing. Marianne felt like weeping, but found she couldn't. Besides, Mum was doing enough crying for the pair of them. She let go of his hand and got up and stared out of the window at the drab London streets, wondering how long this was going to go on for, wishing everything would be all right.

The sound of her dad moving in the bed made her turn round to check he was all right.

'Hello, love,' a familiar and very welcome voice said, and Dad, her lovely dad, opened his eyes a fraction and was smiling at her. 'What are you doing here?' were his first words, and his second were, 'I could murder a cup of tea.'

\* \* \*

139

'So what do you think we should do next?' said Pippa. 'I don't know about you, but I'm still really disappointed with the way that public meeting went. I thought more people would show up. And I'm worried how many of those that did seemed in favour of the hotel. Maybe we're the only ones who are really bothered about it.'

Pippa was hosting a creche today. Lucy was happily sitting playing with the twins, who were fascinated by the computer she used to communicate with everyone, and Lou Lou was tottering happily between them. Gabe had dropped the twins earlier. He looked exhausted, having taken a fleeting trip down south to see Marianne's dad, who was slowly improving, but still not out of the woods. Marianne had been away for nearly a fortnight. Gabe was managing, but Pippa could see it was all getting a bit much. At her suggestion, the twins had cut their usual swimming class and were spending the day with Pippa instead. Steven was home for the weekend, and helping Gabriel on the farm, which was also a blessing.

Cat had come round too, to give Pippa a hand, and also to prevent Lou Lou breaking into Mel's all important revision time. Mel was apparently inclined to use playing with Lou Lou as an excuse not to study, so Cat felt the best thing was to take Lou Lou out. It was just like the old days having little ones around. Though Pippa had forgotten quite how exhausting it was, trying to have a conversation and entertain the under-fives.

'I think,' said Cat, picking Lou Lou up as she banged her head for the umpteenth time, 'we should take the fight to them. I noticed on some of the brochures Noel brought back from work, that they're looking for local investors. Could we pose as some interested parties?'

'Isn't that a bit fraudulent?' said Pippa.

'That's a point,' said Cat. 'Or we could go along and look, as interested locals. We don't have to say we're against the development. I believe they're having a swanky gathering at one of their hotels which is just outside Shrewsbury. We can go and see what we can find out.'

'It's an idea,' said Pippa, rescuing Daisy from where she'd got stuck behind the welsh dresser, in a three-year-old version of hide-and-seek, which seemed to consist of Daisy, Harry and Lou Lou all shutting their eyes and counting to ten (or in Lou Lou's case saying 'Two' very often and very loudly), while Lucy watched them, laughing. 'So long as we don't do anything illegal.'

'I wasn't intending us to,' laughed Cat. 'Right time to go I think,' she added, grabbing Lou Lou before she started investigating the dog's food bowl.

'I'll find out more about this open house thing, and let you know,' said Cat.

'That would be great,' said Pippa. 'Thanks for being so positive. I was beginning to lose heart a bit.'

'Don't,' said Cat. 'It was just one meeting, and we do have lots of people on our side: Vera, Albert, Miss Woods, I even saw Batty Jack the other day and he's very keen to get involved. We can do this, I know we can.'

Cat was pushing Lou Lou's buggy down the lane, when she heard a motorbike pull up beside her. It was Michael Nicholas, clad in his customary leathers, and distinctive flaming orange helmet. It was a while since she'd seen him around, Noel had told her he'd been working abroad for his uncle. It was good to see him back in town. As with Ralph, everything always seemed to turn out better when Michael was about.

'I didn't know you were back,' she said.

'Uncle Ralph decided to call in reinforcements,' said Michael. 'I gather the planning meeting didn't go well.'

'It was disappointing,' admitted Cat. 'Not very many people turned up. And a lot of those that did seemed to think it's a great idea.'

'Or maybe they were just thinking someone else would sort the problem out,' said Michael. 'People can be very apathetic, till they actually realise how things can affect them.'

'Good point,' said Cat, 'we'll have to show them what's going on, won't we?'

'I think once people get wind of how big this complex is, they'll think again. LK Holdings are holding an open house soon. Go and take a look.'

'I had heard,' said Cat. 'Pippa and I are both going to try and be there. Just to see what we're up against. I'm not sure how confident I feel though. I've looked into their previous developments, and ninety nine times out of a hundred, they seem to get planning permission.'

'Let's make this the one in a hundred, then,' said Michael.

'That sounds easier said than done,' said Cat.

'Nothing's impossible, Cat,' said Michael. 'Don't give up the fight too soon.'

He turned the throttle of his engine, and was about to drive off, when he turned round and said, 'Oh and by the way, Cat, rumour has it that the CEO of LK Holdings is going to be there. Name of Felix Macintyre. Big in to birds apparently, particularly birds of prey. I don't know if that's any help to you.'

He roared off leaving Cat puzzled. She had no idea what Michael might have meant.

It was only when she turned into her road and she saw

142

a bird whistle overhead and land in the hedgerow that she got an idea. So Felix Macintyre was into birds. There were plenty of birds nesting in the woods near Blackstock Farm. Slowly a plan started to form in her head . . .

# Chapter Eleven

*As a well-known artist once put it, I feel like I'm not really here . . . Since I've hit my mid-forties I may as well be an invisible woman. No one tells you this will happen when you're young. Back then you're too busy fending off unwelcome attention from men to imagine what it will be like when no one NOTICES YOU AT ALL . . .*

Cat was in the middle of a rant on her blog, when the phone rang. It was Anna, trilling, 'Good news, darling, good news. The TV bods have changed their minds.'

'What, they do want to go ahead with *A Shropshire Christmas*?' Cat was stunned. She'd spent weeks working on the book, maybe it hadn't been a waste of time after all.

'Don't get too excited,' said Anna. 'They don't want you to do another cookery show, they've decided on a different kind of programme. Less cooking, and more country.'

'Meaning?' said Cat cautiously.

'They want it to be more of a celebration of all things rural, protecting wildlife, that kind of thing.'

Cat wasn't sure whether to laugh or cry. Though she'd lived in Hope Christmas for over seven years, she was hardly an expert in the countryside. There must be loads more qualified presenters than her.

'But I don't know anything about wildlife,' said Cat with a wail.

'Well best you mug up, my dear,' said Anna grandly. 'If you say no, you do realise they'll just give it to someone else.'

'Yes, yes, I get it,' sighed Cat. There wasn't any choice. It was either take it, or see her career backslide further, and it was better than nothing.

Noel was at least pleased to hear about it when he came home, ostensibly for lunch, but mainly to play with Lou Lou, on whom he completely doted. Cat loved seeing them together, and it made her laugh that he always kept up the fiction that he was just popping in, when she knew he wanted to spend as much time with their granddaughter as possible.

'It is good news, Cat,' he said, 'and even though Lou Lou's modelling is helping cover the nursery fees, it's not like we couldn't do with the money.'

'I guess,' said Cat. 'I know I live in the country, but I'm singularly unqualified to *talk* about it.'

'A mere bagatelle,' said Noel. 'We know plenty of people who are. Where's your get-up-and-go?'

Got up and gone, she felt like saying. She'd lost a lot of confidence when the cookery programme was dropped, could she do this instead? They'd need more nursery days for Lou Lou if she did, but Noel was right, they could do with the money.

'Have you heard when this meet and greet thing that LK Holdings are having is yet?' she asked, changing the subject.

'In a few weeks,' said Noel. 'I haven't got a date yet, but I think it's going to be some time in May.'

'Let me know as soon as you find out,' said Cat. 'Pippa and I have a plan. Starting with a girlie spa day.'

Noel raised his eyebrows. 'And this is going to help, how?'

'We thought we'd make perfect spies, go in as guests and see what we can find out.'

'Hmm, and who's paying for *that*?' said Noel.

'My last book,' said Cat. 'I'm not *entirely* on the scrap heap yet.'

Pippa was out walking, as she often did when life got too much. She found it therapeutic tramping over the hills of her childhood, particularly up to the waterfall which was a favourite spot. A good walk never failed to lift her spirits. Which today had been blighted by yet another letter from LK Holdings, actually inviting her and Dan to one of several meet and greets in May, to see things from the LK Holdings perspective, and get a feel for the plans in place for Hope Christmas. The subtext being, *And your land, should you choose to sell.* At least it gave her a legitimate reason to be there, she supposed.

Richard had caught sight of the letter and hadn't understood her reluctance to make the most of the opportunity being presented to her.

'You work so hard,' he said, 'for so little. And how are you really going to keep this place running without Dan? You have so much to do already. You can't do it alone.' He was still struggling to see things from her point of view. It was incredibly frustrating.

'The boys can help,' said Pippa stubbornly, 'and I can diversify.' She really didn't want this conversation now, or ever.

'Diversify, how?' said Richard, and in that minute, Pippa knew she couldn't tell him her dreams for the farm, because he wouldn't share them. How could she go forward with someone who she couldn't share her dreams with?

They'd argued, which made Pippa feel miserable and then Richard had left to go to work, and she'd come up here, to try and work out if there was a way she could sort things so that both she and Richard could be happy.

Reaching the top of the waterfall, she sat down in the heather and stared across at the valley, hills and woods. They couldn't build a hotel complex here, they couldn't. It would change everything she loved and held dear. Their quiet lane would be busier, the fields would be destroyed and the hillsides marked with buildings which had no place being there.

'If we all work together, I'm sure we can stop them.'

Pippa was startled and scrambled up to see Ralph Nicholas, with his dog, standing on the brow of the hill staring in the same direction. 'I hope we can,' said Pippa. 'But it worries me, I feel there's so much against us this time.'

'I know we can,' said Ralph, doffing his cap as he made to leave. 'Oh by the way, I believe there may be merlins nesting in the valley. Isn't that lovely?'

And he walked away whistling.

'Aren't they birds of prey?' asked Pippa, but Ralph had vanished down the path.

Marianne was packing to go home. Finally. The crisis had passed. Dad was much better and had finally been allowed out of hospital, where Mum was treating him like a piece of precious china, and driving him completely demented. Matt and Marcus had at long last managed to get a flight between continents and had arrived the night before to take over.

'Are you sure?' Marianne had asked for the umpteenth time, feeling guilty they were having to break off the trip of a lifetime. But then, she felt guilty that Mum was starting to irritate her and she wasn't at home with Gabriel and the children. Guilt was beginning to feel like her default setting. In this situation, there was always someone she was letting down.

'Of course I'm sure, sis,' said Matt cheerfully. 'You've done your bit. Time for me to do mine. Besides, you need to get back to that gorgeous husband and those fabulous kids of yours.'

It was true, she did. She missed them all with an ache that was almost physical. And unworthy though she knew it was of her, Marianne felt increasingly uneasy about how long Gabe had been left with Eve. Suppose she? Suppose he? Then told herself off for imagining things. It was ridiculous to even contemplate such a thing. She'd spent too long away from home and was being paranoid. Even if Eve made a pass at Gabriel, she knew he'd never respond. He was far too honourable.

But something didn't feel right. Gabriel seemed so distant on the phone. Didn't really seem in the same place as she was. Asking perfunctorily after her dad, snapping occasionally when she'd said she couldn't get home sooner, then apologising for being so tired. And then Marianne felt guilty all over again. He must be finding things tough too. It couldn't be easy juggling the farm and nursery runs, even with the help he was getting. Jean and Pippa had been fantastic, and even Eve had picked up from nursery once or twice. Although that had stopped when Pippa let slip that Eve had forgotten one day, and the twins had been waiting till gone 1pm, just as Steven had so many times in his childhood. Fury with Gabriel for being stupid enough (desperate enough, Pippa had assured her) to let Eve have any responsibility with their children had led to incomprehension that he hadn't told her. She felt very far away from home, and Gabe, and wished he didn't seem so distant on the phone.

Shaking her head with irritation at herself for being so silly, Marianne carried her bags downstairs.

'Now you will be ok, won't you, Mum?' said Marianne. 'The boys will look after you. And I've left a lasagne in the fridge for tonight.'

'Don't fuss so,' said Mum, familiar tears spring to her eyes. 'We'll be fine.'

Tears sprang to Marianne's eyes too. And she hugged her mum.

'Thanks for everything, Marianne,' said Mum, 'I couldn't have done it without you.'

Which made Marianne howl, and hug her even harder. It wasn't often that she bonded with her mother. And this was such a rotten reason for them to become close.

She went into the lounge to say goodbye to Dad, who was sitting in his favourite chair, watching a DIY programme.

'Now you get better soon,' she said, giving him a hug. 'You gave us all a fright.'

'I'm fine,' said Dad. 'Fighting fit, me.'

Marianne gave him a big grin, and said 'That's the spirit,' but she couldn't help fretting that he looked small and frail sitting there, nothing like the strong, physical man she'd always known. Would he ever be the same again?

'Right, I'm off,' she said as brightly as she could. She hugged Matt and Marcus, gave Mum another kiss, and got in the car, hoping that the traffic wouldn't be too bad.

Several hold ups on the M40 later, meant she hit Birmingham at rush hour, which she'd been trying to avoid, so she sat in a traffic jam for an hour, tantalisingly counting each slow mile home. She was so desperate to see the twins, she hoped Gabe wouldn't have put them to bed before she got back.

In the event, she arrived home at seven, the twins' bedtime. Letting herself in quietly, she went into the lounge unannounced to surprise them.

And there on the floor she found Gabriel and Eve, sitting playing snap with the twins, in their pyjamas, looking for all the world like a cosy happy family.

# Chapter Twelve

'Marianne.' Gabriel scrambled to his feet, looking – guilty? Surely not—? She was being paranoid again. 'We weren't expecting you so soon, from your last text it sounded like you'd be hours.'

Clearly not, the words were on the tip of her tongue, but Marianne kept her mouth shut. She didn't want to start an argument the minute she walked through the door.

'The traffic cleared quickly once I got to the M54,' said Marianne lightly. 'I thought I'd surprise you.'

'Mummy!' The twins came flying over to her, nearly knocking her down in their enthusiasm. She smothered them with kisses and hugs, blinking back the tears. She'd missed them so much.

'And it's a wonderful surprise,' at last Gabriel enveloped her in a great big hug, and Marianne felt herself succumb to it. But a part of her felt awkward. Eve was still there, a witness to her homecoming. Awkward that she suddenly felt tongue-tied in Gabriel's presence. And worst of all, awkward that both of them had shared this man, and this house, and aware that at the moment, *she* felt like the outsider.

'Have you brought us a present, Mummy?' Daisy wanted to know, as she snuggled up to Marianne. 'Eve said you would.'

'Oh.' Marianne felt an immediate pang. She should have thought to bring them something. Why hadn't she thought of that? But how idiotic of Eve to tell the twins something, when she had no idea if it were true or not.

'Present, present,' said Harry excitedly.

'Sorry, sweeties, Mummy's been too busy looking after Grandpa to get to the shops,' said Marianne. 'But never mind. I'm home now. That's a present, isn't it?'

'That's not a present,' said Harry sulkily.

'Want a present,' said Daisy, looking doe-eyed and moody.

Marianne felt like strangling Eve, who clearly picked up on the vibe as she swiftly disappeared to the kitchen to make tea.

'Now now,' said Gabriel, 'you know you can't always have presents,' which caused Daisy to have a minor meltdown.

'But I want a present!' she screamed, bright red in the face. 'Eve said you'd bring one!'

'Eve made a mistake,' said Marianne, trying to remain calm, and thinking this was not at all the homecoming she'd been planning. 'Now it's time for bed.'

At which point Harry joined in the screaming, 'Don't want bed!' he shouted, throwing himself at Marianne, and kicking her wildly.

'I hate you, Mummy!' shouted Daisy, and threw herself on the sofa screaming even louder.

What on earth was happening? The twins never behaved like this.

'Bed, now!' roared Gabriel, which had the effect of shutting them up temporarily, silently and sulkily they made their way up the stairs.

When they got there, they refused to let Marianne put them to bed.

'Want Eve!' wailed Daisy.

'Well you can want,' Marianne was tempted to say, but bit her lip. She was exhausted and wrung out. She didn't have the energy for this at the moment.

'Sorry,' said Eve who'd come upstairs with the tea. 'They've got a bit out of routine since you were away. They seem to like me reading them stories.'

*They like me reading stories*, Marianne wanted to say, but didn't, instead leaving Eve to it, she went downstairs with a heavy heart. She felt like a stranger in her own house.

'Wine?' said Gabriel. 'Dinner's in the oven.'

'Please,' she said gratefully. 'Have they been like that the whole time?'

'Not the whole time,' said Gabriel, 'but they have been unsettled, particularly at bedtime. Eve's been a great help.'

'I bet,' said Marianne bitterly.

'What's that supposed to mean?' Gabriel looked puzzled.

'You looked very cosy when I came in,' Marianne blurted out the words, and instantly regretted them.

'Marianne! Don't be so ridiculous,' said Gabe. 'You've not been here for a whole fortnight, and I needed all the help I could get. As it happens, Eve was bloody useless at picking them up, but it does turn out she's really good at stories. They wouldn't settle for me, but they seemed to for her.'

'And I've been having such a great time on my fortnight away,' said Marianne.

Gabe stopped mid-sentence, looking stricken. He ran his hands through his wavy brown hair, and stared at her with those lovely deep brown eyes.

'Oh god,' he said. 'I'm so sorry. It's been so rough here without you. I know it's not been any fun for you either. How is your dad?'

'Better,' said Marianne. 'But it's been horrible. And I missed you all so much.'

'And I missed you too,' said Gabe. 'Come here, you idiot.'

He pulled her close to him, and she sank into his arms. 'Sorry this wasn't the homecoming you were quite expecting.'

'Sorry for being so paranoid,' said Marianne. 'Look at me, I'm such a mess. I can't stop crying.'

'I know something that will cheer you up,' said Gabriel, 'the kids have been making Easter cards for you.'

He produced a picture of something which could resemble a bunny, with the words To Mummy, Love Daisy xx scrawled on it, and another featuring an exploding Easter Egg, which just had Harry and lots of kisses on it.

'Oh that's wonderful,' said Marianne, feeling instantly better. 'Shit, I'd completely forgotten about Easter. That's this weekend, isn't it?'

'It's ok, Eve went out and got eggs,' said Gabriel, and Marianne tried not to flinch. 'And we're invited to Pippa's for breakfast on Monday morning.'

'Monday? What's happening on Monday?' asked Marianne.

'The Monday Muddle,' said Gabriel.

'I'd forgotten all about the bloody Monday Muddle,' said Marianne. How could she have forgotten about one of the major highlights in the Hope Christmas year? The Monday Muddle was a mad race through town, chasing a leather ball. Whoever brought the ball home was declared King of the Muddle. Gabriel had even won it one year. 'I've only been away for a fortnight but it feels longer.'

'Too long,' said Gabriel, taking her into his arms and kissing her. 'You're never allowed to go away for that long again, you hear, Mrs North?'

'Perfectly, Mr North,' said Marianne and kissed him back. For the first time in days, she felt ok.

'Are you really going to take part in the Monday Muddle?' Cat asked Noel as she served out the Easter Sunday roast. 'At your age? Isn't it dangerous?'

The Monday Muddle was such a scrum, there were always injuries. She wasn't quite sure she wanted Noel to take part.

'Oh probably,' said Noel cheerfully. 'But Michael Nicholas and a couple of the younger guys from work are going, so I thought I'd give it a bash.'

'I can't wait till I'm eighteen and I can take part,' said James, who had been wanting to do the Monday Muddle since their first year in Hope Christmas.

'Well don't say I didn't warn you,' said Cat, 'I'm not planning to take you to A&E when you hurt yourself.'

Angela, who had come for Easter and was sitting playing peekaboo with Lou Lou, at the dinner table, looked up and said, 'What a lot of nonsense. Sounds like a ridiculous idea to me.'

'It's just a local tradition,' said Cat. 'If you come and live here, you can watch if you like.'

'Ah about that,' said Angela. Cat knew or thought she knew what was coming. Since Christmas, they'd been trying to persuade Angela to move nearer to them, even promising to convert their garage into a granny flat. But Angela was determined she wanted to stay put, and didn't yet want to give up her independence.

The trouble was, she'd had a couple more falls recently, and though Angela made light of them, Cat and Noel were getting quite worried. Noel had had to go down to Bedford to sort her out the last time. Sooner or later, something had to change.

'Your sister wants me to move in with her,' announced Angela to Noel.

'Really?' said Cat in surprise. Angela had always favoured Kay over Noel, so she shouldn't be surprised by her mother-in-law's choice, but Kay was incredibly selfish. Cat found it hard to fathom that she'd actually *offered* to have Angela to stay.

'Really,' said Angela firmly. 'She has more space than you, and she's nearer. She's adamant that she wants me to come, and she and David are converting their downstairs. I can move in in May.'

'But what about your house?'

'On the market,' said Angela. 'Now don't worry, it's all settled. I'm going to be quite all right. Kay and I will have a lovely time together. More potato anyone?'

Noel glanced at Cat, and she shrugged her shoulders. She'd always assumed they would take responsibility for Angela. Noel's brother Joe was lovely, but feckless, and Kay had always seemed too selfish to her to get involved. Angela was a grown woman, and knew her own mind. But Cat knew she'd always idolised Kay, and could see no fault in her only daughter. Cat hoped that that wasn't about to change . . .

'Monday Muddle!' There was a roar from the crowd as the competitors took off in a surge, down the field, racing after the elusive ball, among them Noel Tinsall, much to Cat's chagrin.

'I can barely look,' she confessed to Pippa, as they stood together at the cake stall. The Monday Muddle was a community event, the whole town coming out to watch, and buy produce from the stalls which sprang up in the field near the start line. Lucy was ostensibly helping them man the stall, but she was eating nearly as many cakes as she was selling. She was doing it in such a cheeky fashion that Pippa didn't have the heart to tell her off. It was so lovely seeing her cheerful.

'Look who's coming,' Lucy tapped out on her computer, her grin growing even broader.

Pippa felt herself grow absurdly nervous as Dan came wandering over to see them. Which was ridiculous. They were now officially divorced, the decree absolute when it finally came, feeling like something of a damp squib. She felt her marriage should have ended on more of a fanfare than that. But ended it finally had, and there was nothing more between her and Dan; she was with Richard now, she could be polite. But she rarely saw him away from the farm, and dressed in smartish jeans, shirt and denim jacket, his dark hair looking ruffled, he looked gorgeous. She shouldn't think like that, she scolded herself, she no longer had the right.

Time was when Dan had led the Monday Muddle. Time was when he ran (and won) it year after year. But on medical advice, he hadn't run it since his accident, though a foolish bit of Pippa thought that maybe with another bang on the head, they'd get the old Dan back. A forlorn hope she knew. Though Dan had made a brilliant recovery, the injury had changed him permanently. And nothing could ever change that.

Putting on a smile, she said, 'Hi, how are you?' He'd spent the Easter weekend with his parents, and been busy with the newborn calves on the farm. It seemed ages since she'd seen him properly.

Dan hugged Lucy, and tickled her chin, before stealing a cake from her.

'Oi, that will be 50p,' she typed.

'Even for me?' he teased.

'Even for you,' typed Lucy.

'I'm fine,' said Dan, eventually turning his attention to Pippa. 'You?'

'Great,' said Pippa brightly. She had a feeling he wanted to say something, but she couldn't work out what.

'I've been thinking, Pippa,' he began.

'About?'

'The farm. The future,' said Dan.

'Oh that,' said Pippa, her heart sinking. 'I thought we'd agreed . . .'

'I know what I said last time we spoke about it, but the more I think about it, the more I think we're just not going to get a better offer than LK Holdings.'

'But, Dan,' argued Pippa, 'I haven't had time to work everything out yet.'

'Pippa, I know you've got lots of ideas,' said Dan, 'but how many of them are really feasible? Even if they do work, we're staring bankruptcy in the face. I don't think we've got the luxury of time on our side.'

Pippa felt she'd been punched in the stomach. Dan had always believed in her in the past. He'd always given her the benefit of the doubt, when her ideas were fledglings just hatching out. He'd never just dismissed them out of hand. Things really were different.

'Oh Dan,' she said, the familiar sickness returning to the pit of her stomach. 'Come on give it chance. If I could at least try out some of my ideas. I'm sure I could get a loan from the bank to tide us over . . .' She told him about the themed events and school visits.

'But it's a big if, isn't it, Pippa?' he said sadly. 'We're running out of time, and I can't see the bank lending you enough money.'

'We have to try,' said Pippa stubbornly.

'We?' said Dan. 'It's got to be down to you now. You and Richard. What does he think of all these ideas of yours?'

Richard? Richard wanted her to sell. She hadn't said she would or she wouldn't, and he seemed to have assumed that in time she'd come round to his way of thinking. Somehow she hadn't found time to disabuse him of the notion. She felt dismayed that both Richard and Dan were so dead set against her keeping the farm.

'I haven't told him about them,' admitted Pippa. Richard was down south visiting his mum for Easter and spending time with his daughter.

'Naughty Mummy,' typed Lucy slyly.

'Shh,' said Pippa. 'Look, Dan, I'm not trying to be difficult, I'm really not. But I just can't bear the thought of giving up without trying everything.'

'No you wouldn't would you?' Dan gave her a wry look. 'You wouldn't be Pippa, if you did.' He sighed. 'Maybe something will turn up.'

'Maybe it will,' said Pippa, but she felt more doubtful than she had for a long time. Dan wasn't backing her, Richard would never understand. Did she really have the guts to go for this alone?

There was a shout from the far end of the field. The Muddlers had made it through the first hurdle, and were heading back through the field, to go over the hill and through the woods, leading back to the finish line.

'Muddle!' came the roar. A crowd of muddy men had jumped on top of one another, in a desperate attempt to get the ball. Suddenly one was kicking and pulling his way out. With superhuman strength, he pushed his way from the scrum, got up and streaked across the field.

'Good god,' said Pippa, suddenly recognising him. 'It isn't. It can't be— Oh my god, I'd better warn Marianne.'

'Why?' asked Cat.

'It's someone I haven't seen in Hope Christmas for a very long time,' said Pippa, as the crowd cheered the new leader on.

'Who is it?'

'It's Luke Nicholas, Marianne's ex-fiancé,' said Pippa. 'He's back in town. And that can only be very bad news.'

# My Broken Brain

## Day Seventy Five 9pm

I think we need to bow to the inevitable. The farm is barely making any money at the moment. Certainly not enough that either of us could buy the other out.

And there is a way out, if we sell to LK Holdings. We can't go on like this. I don't know about Pippa, but it's crucifying me . . .

I feel like I am trapped in my old life yoked to the farm I've loved and worked for all these years. And it's confusing for the children. Nathan and George have both asked me separately when we've been working together on the farm, if everything's going to be ok. And the answer is, I just don't know.

I wanted to give Pippa a chance to sort things out. I know she's got some great ideas. But I think we have to face facts. The farm is making a loss, and I don't think we can turn it round. Not this time.

Pippa doesn't agree of course. I might have known she wouldn't; always fighting to the very last – one of the many reasons I love her

But this time, I don't think it's a fight she can win . . .

*May*

# Chapter Thirteen

'This is the life,' said Cat, sipping Prosecco on a sun lounger, wearing a soft dressing gown and feeling very relaxed. She'd already had a head massage and was looking forward to a body wrap in another hour or so. Cat was still pinching herself that the three of them had managed their night away, and only feeling marginally guilty about abandoning her offspring, which was good going for her. 'One lovely family-free day in a posh hotel with spa treatments and Prosecco. What's not to like?'

'Don't forget we're here as spies,' warned Pippa. 'And we're in enemy territory, don't forget.'

'I'm not quite sure what we're going to accomplish,' said Marianne, doubtfully.

'Oh ye of little faith,' said Pippa. 'I've already befriended one of the waitresses, and she's been telling me some very interesting stuff about the employment practices here.'

'Oh?' said Cat. 'Like what?'

'Well they tend to hire very young staff for a start, and pay them a pittance, so if they do the same in Hope Christmas, it's hardly going to help local people get jobs.'

Hope Christmas was the sort of place where people came with young families, and when those families were grown, they left and went away, only returning when they had families of their own. Paige was already moaning about how little there was to do in Hope Christmas, Cat had no doubt she'd be off at the first opportunity. So if LK Holdings thought they'd find their staff from the local population, they'd be sadly mistaken. There was a dearth of young people crying out for jobs in the hotel industry; those looking for work tended to be older, so this new hotel wouldn't help them.

'They also tend to work on zero hour contracts,' continued Pippa, 'so the turnover of staff is massive. Again something we don't want. We need businesses that bring stability to the area.'

'So who do they get working for them?' said Cat.

'Foreigners, mostly,' said Pippa, 'and people who don't have much choice.'

'That doesn't tie in with their so called ethical stance,' snorted Cat, who'd been doing some research into LK Holdings. 'According to their mission statement, they want to provide twenty-first century leisure solutions in an ethical, sustainable way.'

'Yeah, right,' said Marianne. She looked around her. 'Still, it is rather lovely here. And I can't tell you what a relief it is to have some downtime.'

'How's your dad?' enquired Pippa.

'Oh he's much better, thanks,' said Marianne. 'Matt and Marcus are still there, but I shall go and see him in a couple of weeks when Mum's on her own again. At the moment, it's not really Dad I'm worrying about.'

'Things no better with Eve, then?' asked Cat sympathetically.

'Nope,' said Marianne. 'She keeps making noises about going back to work, but then I find her staring into space, or lying on her bed, saying she's too ill to get up. And of course, that's where she gets me every time. She isn't well enough to work yet.'

'Oh Marianne,' said Pippa. 'I'm sure it's only temporary.'

'I just wish . . .' Marianne looked wistful.

'What?'

'I just wish Gabe wasn't quite so protective of Eve,' she said. 'I'm probably being silly to mind, it's not like he wants her back . . .'

'I don't think that's silly at all,' said Cat. 'He should take more care of you.'

'Only say the word and I'll bash my stupid cousin over the head,' said Pippa.

'It's fine, really,' Marianne attempted to sound unconcerned. 'I'm probably fretting about nothing. Anyway. What are we planning to do while we're here?'

'One of us could break into their filing cabinets while they're hosting their meet and greet thing,' suggested Cat. Having found out that LK Holdings were planning the first of several open evenings for interested parties in the Hope Christmas project for this weekend, they had coincided their spa treat.

'I doubt we'll need to do that,' laughed Pippa. 'But if we can sneak into the evening thing, I believe the plans are going to be up there, so we can take a look at them. Besides, Felix Macintyre, the CEO of LK Holdings is definitely here on a special visit, I overheard the reception staff talking about it. He wants to see how things are going. I intend to accidentally bump into him and sound him out – see how wedded he is to the project.'

'Is he likely to change his mind?' asked Marianne. 'I mean, look at this place? I can see why they want to build more like it. But it doesn't exactly fit in with concerns about the environment.'

'Ah, that's where you're wrong,' said Cat. 'Felix Macintyre, from what I've read about him, is quite keen on being seen as one of the good guys. He's invested in a lot of educational projects, and he's passionate about wildlife.'

'So maybe we can persuade him that instead of a hotel, what the area needs is a wildlife sanctuary, with an educational slant. It's a much more suitable tourist attraction for the area than what he's proposing,' said Marianne

'It's worth a try,' said Cat, sipping her Prosecco. 'Though I doubt he'd think that was commercial enough, to be honest. In the meantime, I have to say this was a splendid idea. A whole weekend away from being granny and overseeing fraught teens as they prepare for exams. Bliss!'

She sank back into her sun lounger and shut her eyes. She was so tired. Lou Lou had been up half the night, and as Mel was revising like a demon at the moment, Cat had her granddaughter in bed with them. Small children in a bed did not a good night's sleep make. She'd forgotten how exhausting it was.

Dimly aware she should be following Pippa's conversation, Cat drifted off into a pleasant reverie instead. She was awoken by a strangled gasp from Marianne.

'Oh my god,' she said, 'it's *him*.'

Marianne took a deep quaff of her Prosecco. Apart from three weeks ago, when she'd spotted him from afar holding the Muddle Trophy high, covered in mud, being triumphantly carried through the crowds to the pub, she'd last seen Luke Nicholas over seven years ago. He'd broken her heart. And now here he was. Back in Hope Christmas. Back in her life. She was shocked by how much it rattled her.

He was still fit and lithe, even after all this time. She watched, mesmerised as he dived into the plunge pool, and swam back and forth with swift clean strokes. Boy, he could still cut it. There was something compelling about the way he swam, ploughing effortlessly through the water, as if he were born to it.

*Stop it!* Marianne said to herself. It must be the Prosecco talking, and her latent insecurities about Gabriel. Luke Nicholas might still be good looking, with a body to die for, but he was an uncaring, heartless bastard who hadn't loved her enough to marry her. Whereas Gabriel . . . isn't paying you much attention at the moment, the thought popped into her head, unbidden.

She brought up Gabriel's reassuring face in front of her. Gabriel with his lovely dark curly hair, beautiful eyes and kind face. Gabriel who would never treat her badly.

*Are you sure?* A sneaky little voice in her head said. *What about Eve? Should you have left them alone again? And Gabe did want you to go . . .* in fact he'd seemed so keen for her to leave the house they'd actually had an argument about it. Which was ridiculous. Gabe's last words had been 'I only want you to have a nice time, I can't think what the problem is,' which made her feel stupid and irrational.

Which was pretty much how Marianne felt most of the time these days. She hated the little paranoid voice in her head which had showed up repeatedly since she'd got back from London. There was nothing going on with Eve and Gabriel, she was just stressed and tired and imagining things.

Marianne gripped her glass fiercely and took another deep sip. Thinking like this was the way madness lay . . . Gabriel loved her. He felt he should look after Eve that was all. And he'd only wanted her to go away because he said she deserved the break. She was being silly.

'Who?' said Pippa, responding to Marianne's shriek.

'Luke Nicholas,' Marianne gulped. 'What on earth is he doing here?'

'Heaven knows,' said Pippa. 'Try and ignore him.'

'I'll do my best,' Marianne said and tried to concentrate on what Pippa was saying instead. She was talking about trying to make contact with Felix Macintyre, who apparently had a soft side.

'You know he's got this thing about birds, particularly birds of prey?' Cat was saying. 'I was wondering if we could use that, somehow. Are there any special birds in the woods which need protecting? I've been trying to work out a way of making that an issue.'

'Oh yes!' said Pippa. 'Ralph Nicholas tells me there are merlins living in the woods. I looked them up and they're quite rare. Maybe if Felix Macintyre were to find out about them, he'd think again about building on the woods at least.'

'Bit of a long shot,' said Marianne sceptically, 'but I suppose it's worth a try.'

Out of the corner of her eye, Marianne saw that Luke was getting out of the pool. He shook the water off his magnificent body, flung on a towelling robe, and strode confidently and arrogantly around the pool. She swallowed hard, her palms felt sweaty and her heart was racing.

Oh god, had he spotted her? No, please, no.

'Marianne?' The smile was as wide and welcoming as she remembered. The eyes as bright and warm. 'I can't believe it's you. You look fabulous.'

Marianne felt herself squirm. She wanted the ground to swallow her up. Even after all this time, he could have an effect on her. It was infuriating. Most of her was thinking, don't be daft, I'm wearing a dressing gown, am without make up, and my hair is straggling down my neck, but a small disloyal part of her felt thrilled, particularly when he said, 'I can't believe you've got two kids. You don't look a day older than when we last met—' (remind yourself of that Marianne, he was a bastard, remember?) '—Gabriel's a very lucky man. I was a fool to let you go.'

Despite herself, Marianne melted a little. There was something satisfying in thinking that Luke Nicholas still found her attractive, and might actually realise he'd made a mistake.

'What are you doing here?' she asked.

'Oh a boring work thing,' Luke mentioned casually. 'We're planning a new hotel complex in Hope Christmas, had you heard?'

'It might have been mentioned,' squeaked Marianne. She might have known Luke Nicholas was involved.

'Drink? In the bar? Later? For old time's sake?' he said, and before she knew it, she found herself agreeing. And he'd disappeared in a wave of manliness.

'What?' she asked as Pippa and Cat dissolved into hysterics.

'Nothing,' they replied in unison.

'It's only a drink in the bar,' she said, feeling defensive. 'And I can try and see if I can get him to spill the beans about the development.'

'Good idea,' said Pippa. 'You can be our very own Mata Hari.'

It was only a drink. She was married. Luke knew that. But her pulse was racing, and a part of her felt ridiculously excited.

'Right, girls, so we all know what to do?' asked Pippa as the three of them snuck past reception in their glad rags and made their way to the ballroom where the meet and greet was taking place.

'I have my dictaphone switched on, and my smartphone at the ready to take snaps,' said Cat.

'I'm going to make a beeline for Luke and see if I can sweet talk any information out of him,' said Marianne.

'Excellent,' said Pippa. 'And I am going to nobble Felix Macintyre and entice him with the rare birds angle. Maybe it will help stall things a little if we can persuade him they need protecting.'

Their first hurdle came in the form of the supercilious waiter, handing out champagne.

'Your invitation, madam?' he said.

Pippa had been expecting this. Taking a deep breath and confidently grabbing a glass of champagne, she waved her invite in front of him.

'Is this invitation valid for today?'

Oh dear, Mr Supercilious wasn't going to be put off easily.

'I think there's been some kind of mistake,' said Cat smoothly, waving a press pass in front of him. 'We all got sent the wrong invites. But it's ok because I've set up an interview with Felix Macintyre for the *Sunday Times*, and I know he's very excited about it.'

'Oh look, is that Luke Nicholas? Haven't seen him in ages,' said Marianne, smiling sweetly, grabbing a drink and slipping past the waiter.

'Must dash, got to mingle,' said Pippa, brightly. She slugged her drink and strode through the doors as if she belonged here, while Cat darted off in a different direction, leaving Mr Supercilious open-mouthed but unsure which of the three to follow.

Luckily it was easy to get lost in the crowd, so Pippa

made her way to the far end of the room, where a huge display was proudly taking up space.

*Hope Christmas Developments. A Leisure Plan for the Future.*

Pippa gasped with shock.

'Jeez, it's enormous,' said Cat who'd just joined her. They both stared at the plans in disbelief.

There was Pippa's farm, and Gabriel's, and all the land between theirs and Old Joe's, and the woods beyond. And it was transformed on the map into golf courses and driving ranges, with a massive set of buildings, comprising of a huge hotel, and several holiday houses.

Cat swiftly took some photos, and excused herself, 'I'm going to send these to Noel, so he and Ralph can see what we're up against.'

Pippa stood for some moments in front of the display, feeling a sense of overwhelming despair. How could they even begin to fight against this?

'Magnificent, isn't it? It will bring Hope Christmas into the twenty first century,' declared a plump middle aged man with an American accent. 'I gather it's a cute little place in the middle of nowhere in need of a shake up.'

Gritting her teeth, and trying to play the part, Pippa smiled sweetly, and said, 'Yes, it is. So you think your development is really going to help the town? It looks rather large.'

'Sure it is,' said her new friend, putting an avuncular arm on her shoulder. 'See, they get leisure, we bring jobs to the town, there're new holiday lets. It's a win win.'

'Not for the people of Hope Christmas,' muttered Pippa, but out loud she said, 'My name's Pippa Holliday. I'm a local resident, I'd love to hear more about your plans.'

'Felix Macintyre, CEO of LK Holdings,' the man said,

confirming Pippa's suspicions. 'I'd be delighted to tell you more about what we're proposing.'

'And you have no opposition to the development?'

'No serious stuff,' said the man confidently. 'You always get a few looney tunes, wanting to save the planet, but when they see the benefits, they'll soon come round.'

'What about the wildlife?' asked Pippa. 'You do realise there are badgers and all sorts in those woods.'

'Which is why we've promised to create a wildlife sanctuary further up the valley,' he said. 'We'll just move them.'

'Move them?' Pippa was gobsmacked.

'Sure it's easy,' said Felix. 'There's plenty of space.'

Pippa was so nonplussed for a moment, she couldn't think of anything to say.

'Ok,' she said eventually, 'but what if I were to tell you there were birds of prey breeding in the woods? You might find it not so easy to move them, particularly in nesting season.'

'Birds?' Felix's interest immediately piqued. 'What birds? No one said anything about any birds.'

'I have heard,' said Pippa, 'that this year we even have merlins nesting in the woods. Our local bird twitchers are getting very excited about it.'

'Merlins?' said Felix. 'That would be great. I've always wanted to see merlins in the wild. Do you really think they're there?'

'Absolutely,' said Pippa, crossing her fingers behind her back and hoping Ralph was right. 'And their habitat is right in the area you're planning to build on.'

'You're kidding me?' said Felix. 'I'll make a date with Hope Christmas next time I'm over. This I have to see.'

# Chapter Fourteen

'So you've promised Felix Macintyre merlins in the woods?'
Cat burst out laughing, as they gathered together back at
the bar. 'What possessed you?'

'No idea,' said Pippa, pulling a face. 'Desperation, I think.
And it could be true. Ralph seemed to think there are some
birds of prey nesting there. I was just so gobsmacked by
those bloody plans. They're bigger than I thought. I don't
think we're going to be able to stop this as easily as I'd
hoped.'

She sighed. It wasn't like Pippa to feel overwhelmed, but
for once she did. LK Holdings was a massive multinational
company, used to getting its own way. There was enough
local support for planning to be waived through relatively
easily. Pippa hated the thought of the fields and woods she
loved being destroyed like this, but she had a terrible feeling
that whatever they tried to do to stop it, the development
was going to go ahead anyway.

'Nonsense,' said Cat, stoutly. 'We just have to find a way
round it. I managed to have one or two conversations with
executives who'd had a bit too much champagne, and I
don't think it's a done deal. The Hope Christmas site is
only one of several options. And the guy I was talking to
said they'd had such a lot of opposition in one place they

tried to build, they eventually withdrew. Noel and Ralph are going through the pictures I sent. I know they've been looking at alternative ideas to present to LK Holdings. They think something like a back-to-nature type of place, with cabins in the woods, is probably more in keeping with the area, but we shall see.'

'I suppose we could work on the wildlife angle with Felix Macintyre some more,' said Pippa. 'He didn't seem averse to the idea of a sanctuary. Mind you, he hasn't a clue really. He seemed to think we could just pick the wildlife up and transplant it elsewhere. And I'm guessing he's not that altruistic. Whatever happens it's business and he wants to turn a profit.'

'But at least you've touched base with him,' said Marianne, 'that's something.'

'Maybe,' said Pippa, 'but I've still got to find some wretched birds for him to look at. As far as I know, it's only a rumour that the damned things exist.'

'I'll get onto Miss Woods,' said Cat. 'I bet it's the kind of thing she'd know. I've got to research the local wildlife anyway, for these programmes I'm presenting, so I can kill two birds with one stone. Well, metaphorically of course'

'I hope we can persuade Felix Macintyre,' said Marianne. 'There's no way Gabriel or I want to give up the farm, but if the complex LK Holdings is suggesting is that huge, we may be forced to. I don't know how we'd be able to carry on if something like that was on our doorstep. Particularly if you sell, Pippa.'

'I am *not* going to sell,' said Pippa stubbornly. 'Farming is part of who I am. And it's for the kids' future too.'

'Does Richard understand the way you feel?' said Cat.

Pippa grimaced. 'Not in the slightest. He thinks I should

sell, I don't. It's an impasse. I've given up talking to him about it.'

'Ouch,' said Cat.

'I know,' said Pippa. 'Which is why we've got to stop the development, whatever it takes.'

Despite the slight air of gloom that had descended on them now they could see the scale of what they were up against, Cat was enjoying herself. It was rare these days that she got to spend time with her girlfriends, and despite the real reason for being here, she had had a lovely, self-indulgent day. Noel had kept her updated during the day about various domestic mishaps: Lou Lou had been up early, Mel had had another exam-related meltdown, James had not. Paige had been in trouble for being out too long, Ruby had argued with James, Lou Lou had tipped her lunch over her head. The list was endless, and made Cat even more grateful of the break. It was wonderful for once not to have to deal with all this stuff.

When she checked in to talk to him about his reaction to the development plans, she found him fuming.

'You'll never guess what Kay's done?' he said.

'What now?' The last Cat had heard, Angela would be moving in within the month.

'Mum's moved in already, accepted an offer on the flat for a fraction of what it's worth, without consulting Joe or me, and now Kay's persuaded Mum to give her Power of Attorney. She's not gaga. It's hardly necessary.'

'Maybe she was just being practical?' suggested Cat, although she doubted it somehow.

'Knowing Kay, she's being mercenary,' said Noel. 'I bet she's after Mum's money.'

Cat thought privately that the money wasn't likely to go

that far between three anyway – Angela having had a Sking mentality since she'd been widowed, spend now and think about tomorrow later. And who could blame her when her children could all be mercenary? Dearly as she loved him, even Noel could get sucked in – the three of them had argued about money at his dad's funeral.

'Well if it's what your mum wants . . .' Cat said.

'But is it?' said Noel. 'Kay's always been able to wind Mum round her little finger. I think she's persuaded Mum it's for the best, but I'm not convinced.'

'There's nothing we can do,' said Cat, 'except pick up the pieces if it all goes wrong. Besides, look on the bright side. At least she won't be coming to live with us.'

'Problem?' asked Pippa, when Cat switched off her mobile.

'Nothing another glass of Prosecco won't cure,' said Cat. 'Aye, aye, Marianne, I think your admirer's here.'

Luke Nicholas had exited the ballroom and was looking round with very definite purpose. Spotting them, he made a beeline for their table.

'Shut up,' said Marianne giggling. She'd clearly had a lot to drink. 'I've already spent ages chatting to him.'

'And did you get anything out of him?' asked Cat.

'Not a lot to be honest,' said Marianne. 'Unsurprisingly, he thinks it is the best thing to happen to Hope Christmas for a very long time. But then he thought that about the eco town, and look how that turned out.'

'Well maybe this is your chance to find out some more,' said Cat, pinching Marianne as Luke approached the table.

'Can I get you another drink?' he asked.

'We're fine, thanks,' said Marianne firmly, but she was blushing and looking a little coy.

'Oh go on,' said Luke, 'I don't believe that for a minute.

Waiter! Champagne over here. I take it you're all making the most of our special weekend Spa offer?'

'Yes it's great,' said Cat. 'Lovely hotel.'

'We're hoping to build something of the kind in Hope Christmas.'

'So we've heard,' said Pippa. Cat put a calming hand on her. No point giving the game away.

'And with that in mind, Marianne, can I borrow you for a moment?'

Marianne looked at them in panic, but Pippa mouthed, 'Go on, see what you can find out, we're only over here.'

'Do you think that's a good idea?' said Cat a little worried. 'Marianne has had a lot to drink.'

'It'll be fine,' said Pippa. 'We're here to rescue her if she needs it, and she might find out something useful.'

Marianne felt a little light-headed as Luke led her to the bar. Until tonight, it was ages since she'd been so physically close to him and she had to admit the intervening years had been kind to him. He still had the fair hair swept back from his face, and the bright blue eyes, and charming manner. It was hard not to be drawn to him, despite everything she knew.

When they'd spoken earlier they'd been in a crowd, but now they were on their own. Despite herself, she couldn't help her heart from thumping like a steam train. She hoped he couldn't hear it too. She felt stupid for being so excited. She was married, and Luke hadn't wanted her before, so why would he be remotely interested now, unless he had a motive? But she couldn't help enjoying the way he was looking her up and down with appreciation. It felt like a long time since Gabriel had looked at her like that.

It was so rare for Marianne to have the opportunity to

dress up these days, she'd enjoyed shimmying into a burgundy velvet number, slipping into high heels, putting on red lipstick and doing her hair up. It was nice to feel grown up and sexy for once and not a boring mum and housewife. She felt a little flutter of appreciation that Luke clearly found her attractive.

'Motherhood suits you,' Luke said, appraising her.

'Thank you,' said Marianne, blushing. Remember he's a bastard, she told herself. 'Now what did you want to talk about?' she added, trying to get herself back on more even footing.

'It's a bit delicate actually,' he said. 'But I couldn't believe my luck when I saw you were here. Seemed like the perfect opportunity to chat.'

'Chat about what?' said Marianne, though she had a good idea.

'I gather our people have been in touch already about your farm?'

'It's not for sale, Luke,' said Marianne. 'Even if I wanted to, which I don't, Gabriel would never sell.'

'We don't really need that much more land,' said Luke, 'just a little of yours and some of Pippa's. Without it, we can't do all the things we planned. Here let me show you.'

So that's what this was all about. She might have known he had an ulterior motive.

He brought out an iPad, and launched a small film about the development, showing a light, spacious building, with luxurious bedrooms, and a spa attached, much like the one she'd visited today. On the outside was a sweeping landscape of golf greens, and gardens, with peacocks prancing in front of the hotel. It looked amazing, even Marianne had to admit. If it had been anywhere else . . .

'So without our land you really couldn't do all this?' said

Marianne, surprised to find that she and Gabriel might have a bargaining tool. This was interesting. Perhaps they could do something with that.

'We really can't,' said Luke. 'And we understand about the balance with nature, so we're going to keep as much of the wood as we can, even plant more trees, and have a little wildlife sanctuary.'

'You make it sound idyllic,' said Marianne.

'It will be,' said Luke suavely, 'I can guarantee that.'

She almost laughed at his eagerness. Still the same old Luke, flirtatious, charming, full of crap. He didn't give a damn about the wildlife. It was bound to be another disaster, like the eco town he'd rashly tried to create a few years earlier.

'I know what you're thinking,' said Luke, 'but it won't be like the eco town. I've learnt my lesson.'

'You have?' Marianne laughed, finished her drink and turned to go.

'In more ways than one,' he said and lightly touched her fingers. 'Like I said earlier, Gabriel's a very lucky man.'

'And I'm a lucky woman,' said Marianne firmly, though she was blushing. She fled to her table in confusion. Nothing had happened, so why did she feel so guilty?

# Chapter Fifteen

'Will you turn that music down, I'm trying to revise!' Mel was standing at the top of the stairs yelling to James, who was in his room listening to some rap at a hundred decibels. It *was* too noisy. Cat could see Mel's point.

'I'm revising too,' protested James. 'It helps me concentrate.'

'Really?' said Cat. 'Well if you *have* to listen to music that loud, can you at least put your headphones in? And Mel, try not to get quite so stressed. Everything is going to be fine.'

'How can it be fine?' shrieked Mel. 'I don't know *anything*. I'm going to fail them all and have to resit another year. I'm never going to get to uni at this rate.'

'I'm sure you know more than you think,' said Cat, trying to pacify her. 'Getting hysterical won't help.'

'Oh you just don't understand!' Mel disappeared into her room, where she would probably now stay for the next couple of hours, presumably revising. Cat felt for her. A lot was riding on these exams for Mel. She looked pale and thin, and Cat wasn't surprised that she was so stressed. She'd had to take a step back and watch her friends go on to sixth form without her and listen while they'd all applied for uni, which had been one of the reasons why she'd chosen to go to a sixth form college where no one knew her. The thought of slipping back still further was clearly troubling her. Not only that, if she passed the first hurdle this year with AS levels and then went onto get her A levels and a place at university in Birmingham next year, she wouldn't be going away from home like her peers but commuting. It was the best that could be done in the circumstances, but sometimes Cat's heart ached for her daughter. It was tough on her that she wouldn't have the lighthearted experience her friends were going to have. Neither of them would be without Lou Lou, but it was a difficult plough for her to furrow.

A wail came from downstairs, and Cat went to rescue Paige who'd been sitting with Lou Lou for five minutes, in between snapchats. Cat suspected there had been a lot of selfies of Paige and Lou Lou doing the rounds in the last few minutes. Lou Lou was wailing loudly to see Mel, but was easily distracted by making pastry shapes with Cat, which was messy and fun, and occupied her till bath time, when Mel came, full of apologies, to take over. Cat left them to it, Mel singing nursery rhymes and Lou Lou splashing happily away. She loved the nutty rhythm of her household, however frustrating it might sometimes be.

Cat came into the lounge to find Noel on the phone, his face like thunder, and she guessed he was having another row with Kay.

'So you're determined to accept that offer still?' he said. 'What's the rush? Why not give Mum some more time to make up her mind.'

Angry shouting from the other end.

'Really? Well I find that hard to believe.'

'Wine?' mouthed Cat.

'Please,' Noel mouthed back, before returning to his

183

conversation, which got curter by the minute. 'Hmm, yes, if you say so . . .' another pause but with less shouting, 'Well I still think we could get more for it. And it would have been nice to have been consulted . . .' which led to more frantic shouting, 'I know you're there and we're not, but Cat and I would have been more than happy to have her – Oh.' He held the phone and looked at it in disbelief. 'She's just put the phone down on me,' he said.

'What's the problem now?' said Cat.

'The house sale seems to be going full steam ahead,' said Noel. 'Kay's practically exchanged contracts. And wants me to go down next weekend to help pack up. It's the least I can do, apparently.'

'Can't Dave help?' said Cat. 'If they're so keen to go ahead, I'm not sure why you're needed.'

'Dave's working apparently, and Joe's busy, and Kay can't spare the time.'

'Ok. I'll come too,' said Cat.

'What about the kids and revision?' said Noel.

'Paige and Ruby can come with us to help out and look after Lou Lou. James and Mel will just have to cope for the day,' said Cat. 'You can't go and do all that alone. Besides, it's not going to take one trip is it?'

'Cat, are you sure?'

'Noel, you were there for me with my mum,' said Cat. 'It's the least I can do to be there for yours.'


'Richard, just hear me out, will you,' said Pippa, standing in the kitchen looking at Richard in dismay. She was trying to share her plans with him, but he just didn't seem to be getting it. 'If we can persuade LK Holdings to change their ideas about the development, the farm won't be under threat.'

'But what about your finances?' said Richard. 'Pippa, you've got to start being realistic. I know you don't want to talk about them, but I'm not stupid. Even I can see it's a struggle.'

'And that's why I'm making plans to diversify,' argued Pippa. She was furious with him. Why couldn't he give her the benefit of the doubt? 'I've got lots of ideas, some of them will work, I know they will.'

'Pippa, I really think you're taking on too much,' said Richard, trying to pacify her which made her more angry. He was treating her like a silly little girl, and it was infuriating. *Dan would never patronise you*, the thought snuck in despite her attempts to stop it. 'I can't see how you'll be able to manage all this and everything you already do. And it seems a huge risk.'

'Have some faith in me,' said Pippa in dismay. 'I can do this, I know I can.'

'I know you think you can,' said Richard with a mollifying grin that failed to dissipate her irritation.

'I know I can,' she said, glaring at him.

'Ok, say you do approach LK Holdings about taking a different line, do you really think you can persuade their CEO to change his mind about the hotel complex?' said Richard. 'He's hardly likely to be swayed by environmental concerns.'

'But that's just the thing,' said Pippa, she had to try and make him see. 'Felix Macintyre *does* have a history of getting involved with wildlife sanctuaries and the like. And he's obsessed with rare birds. There might be a way of using that.'

'There might,' said Richard with scepticism. 'But that aside, there's still the problem of the farm.'

'Which I am addressing,' said Pippa. 'We've weathered other storms, we can weather this one.'

'But maybe you won't have to,' argued Richard. 'Things change.'

'Of course, they do. They have to, if we're to survive,' said Pippa, deliberately misreading him. Richard had begun hinting about the future already, seeming to think that their relationship was moving forward more than Pippa did. Pippa was content to live in the present for now. She didn't want to look too far ahead, and this argument was proving to her that she shouldn't anyway. She and Richard were too far apart on what was a vital issue for Pippa. They couldn't even consider planning a life together till they resolved it. 'The farm is for the kids. I've always felt I've held it in trust for them.'

'None of us want to leave,' typed Lucy, who'd been sitting glowering in the corner.

Although Lucy had been trying more of late, she still wasn't happy having Richard around. She made her feelings so abundantly clear – wheeling her chair sulkily out of the room as soon as he walked into it, being sullen when Richard was around – it would have been funny in any other circumstances.

Pippa desperately wanted Lucy to approve of Richard, but she wasn't being won over, despite his best efforts. And although he had experience with his own daughter who also had cerebral palsy, she could tell it was hard for him, especially when Lucy had typed once in his presence, 'He's not my dad, he doesn't tell me what to do.' Pippa saw the hurt in his eyes and felt caught between a rock and a hard place. Whatever she did, she risked upsetting one or other of them.

'With all due respect, Lucy, it's not your decision,' said Richard.

'Neither is it yours!' She typed back furiously, giving him

a look of malevolence, Pippa hadn't known she was capable of. She swung her wheelchair away from the table and stormed out of the room – well as far as she could storm in a wheelchair. In the process, she caught one of the wheels on Richard's leg.

'Lucy!' Pippa said in dismay.

'She did that on purpose,' said Richard, nursing his leg.

'I'm sure she didn't,' said Pippa, not sure in the slightest. 'We probably shouldn't have been discussing it in front of her. This is the only home she's known, she's bound to be unsettled by talk of selling up.'

'It doesn't have to be,' said Richard. 'You could all move in with me.'

'You are joking?' said Pippa, thinking hell, no, this is far too soon. 'It's a lovely idea, but I'm sorry, I'm not ready for that yet.'

'It was just a thought,' said Richard, backtracking, 'it would mean you could sell to Dan, and you wouldn't have to worry about this stuff.'

'But I want to worry about this stuff,' said Pippa, wishing he would understand. He didn't get her at all, if he thought it would be that easy for her.

'At least think about it?'

Pippa sighed and laced her fingers through his. It would be such an easy way out of her problems, and Dan would get to keep the farm. She was half tempted, but was that what she really wanted?

'Ok,' she found herself agreeing, more to keep the peace than for any other reason. 'I'll think about it.'

But as she stared out as the sun set over the hills, and she listened to the crows cawing into the summer's night, she wondered why on earth she had.

\* \* \*

187

Marianne had had a long, hot, hard day teaching a reception class, who had been lovely, but were exhausting. It was so difficult to get them to sit still on the carpet and listen to even the simplest of instructions. Another school to try and avoid. No more reception classes. There had been a reason why she trained to teach Year 4 and above. To add to the general stress, her mum had rung at 6am to say her dad's breathing was bad and asking what she should do.

'Call an ambulance,' Marianne suggested, feeling panicky. She hated being so far away. If only she lived nearer.

'I'm not sure,' Mum said. 'Perhaps I should wait a bit.'

'Look, Mum if you're that worried, I think you should at least call 999.'

'All right,' said Mum. 'I just don't like making a fuss.'

'It's not making a fuss,' said Marianne. 'If Dad's ill, he's ill.'

Agreeing to call back and let her know what happened, Mum rang off, then rang back ten minutes later to say Dad had settled again and was breathing more easily.

When Marianne managed to check in later in the middle of a day mainly administering crowd control to her enthusiastic class of four and five year olds, Mum had spoken to the GP who told her to ring 999 if Dad got any worse.

'But it's all right, really, Marianne,' she said, when Marianne suggested coming down, 'I was just being silly. He's sleeping now. I'm sure he'll be fine.'

Unable to ignore the nagging feeling of anxiety, Marianne drove home at the end of the day, stressed and worried, to find the house in total chaos. Jean had picked the twins up from nursery, but Eve had sent her home, saying she could cope. Her idea of coping was to fill the children full of chocolate, so they were sky high when Marianne walked in. The lounge was a tip, and the TV on so loud it gave Marianne an instant headache, and Dolly was baaing loudly in the kitchen as no one had fed her.

Marianne's attempts to get the children to eat tea – chicken nuggets and chips seeming to be all that Eve could rustle up – were met with blank refusals and tears, as was her suggestion that (tea uneaten) they went to bed.

'No!' declared Harry defiantly.

'No!' said Daisy, planting herself heavily next to him.

'Oh let them play a little longer,' said Eve. 'It's so difficult for them to sleep on these light summer evenings.'

'Don't want to go to bed!' the twins yelled.

'Well you have to,' yelled Marianne back, cursing Eve to the high heavens, hating herself for shouting and dragging her recalcitrant offspring up the stairs, ignoring Eve's comments of, 'Well it never did Stevie any harm,' having apparently forgotten that she'd spent much of Steven's childhood absent.

The twins were eventually got into pyjamas and into bed, but were keeping up a steady wail of 'We don't want to go to bed!' when Gabriel walked in.

'Do you really think Eve's not well enough to work still?' said Marianne in exasperation. 'She's well enough to cause complete chaos here.'

'I'll have a word with her in the morning,' said Gabriel. 'I'm sure we can sort something out.'

'Well you'd better do it soon,' snapped Marianne, 'because I have had enough.'

'Ok, ok,' said Gabriel. 'Look I am really sorry. I didn't know that you were feeling quite like this. I'll deal with it, I promise.' But she knew him of old. Gabe couldn't help worrying about Eve, and if she got upset about the thought of going back to work, he'd give in. Gabriel was nothing if not empathetic, she just wished his empathy came her way a bit more.

The twins were just calming down a bit when the phone rang, and Marianne nearly shot out of her skin. The feelings of dread from earlier on, returned.

'Yes, I see,' Gabriel was saying, 'I'll just get her. It's your mum,' he said with a peculiar look on his face. Without asking she knew the news was very bad.

'Oh Marianne,' her mum sobbed down the phone. 'I'm at the hospital. I don't know what to do. It's your dad. Marianne. I'm so sorry, love, but he's dead.'

# My Broken Brain

I've been sitting thinking all night. Thoughts whirling through my head. I want to do the right thing, the best thing for all of us.

It seems the development plans are even worse than we thought. I don't know how we could survive if a complex that size was on our doorstep. We're barely managing as we are. Pippa's got some mad scheme for trying to stop it, but even Pippa, god bless her mad enthusiasm, is going to have trouble holding back this juggernaut. Gabriel tells me we might have some negotiating clout, as they are very keen to buy bits of our land. Pippa won't want to hear that of course.

But I look at the boys and worry for their future. And for Lucy's. What will happen to her, when we're not around? I think it's time we faced facts and cut loose.

Pippa's going to kill me, but I'm going to tell her we should sell.

*June*

# Chapter Sixteen

'So how can I help with this campaign?' Miss Woods was sitting ramrod straight on her mobility scooter, ready to take on the world. She was a local legend of indeterminate age – Pippa would have hazarded anywhere between 80 and 100 – whose indomitable spirit made her a valuable ally. 'I know that first meeting wasn't well attended, but since the meet and greets LK Holdings have been running, there's been a definite shift in opinion. I think more people are waking up on what this hotel complex might do to the area and are feeling alarmed about it. You should tap into that energy.'

'There are still a lot of people in favour, though,' said Pippa. 'The Yummy Mummies from the café can't wait to have somewhere to go to get their fake tans done.'

Pippa had just come from the café, where a crowd of Yummy Mummies (and some not quite so yummy), led as ever by Keeley Jacobs and Angie Townley, had all been talking in screeching, excited tones about the new development. There seemed to be a general consensus that having a spa and luxury leisure centre on their doorstep was a good thing. And depressingly no one seemed to care about the effect on the local environment. Even Jenny Ingles, from the local estate agents, who'd been Pippa's babysitter years ago, was enthusiastic.

'I just think it will bring more people into the town,' said Jenny, 'and a better class of tourist.'

Pippa quite liked the class of tourists they did have. They loved the quaint nature of the town with its teashops, quirky bookshop, antiques market and butcher's and greengrocer's selling fresh local produce. They also appreciated the beauty of the hills they invariably walked in. Pippa doubted any visitors to the new hotel would even get out of the complex to notice their surroundings.

'But there are still plenty of people who disagree,' said Miss Woods stoutly. 'Batty Jack is already formulating ideas as to how we can sabotage their plans: leaving gates open for sheep to wander into the land was one idea, or releasing his turkeys into the yard when the surveyors are there.'

Pippa laughed. Batty Jack, the local turkey farmer who had gained his moniker from the bats living in one of his barns, was another local celebrity. He could always be guaranteed to bring his own unique methods to any situation. And he'd certainly get them noticed.

'So, don't give up just yet, young Pippa,' Miss Woods declared staunchly, waving her walking stick alarmingly in Pippa's face. 'What's your plan of action?'

'We have had one idea,' said Pippa. 'Felix Macintyre has a big thing about birds of prey. Merlins are his thing apparently. Ralph Nicholas seemed to think there might be some nesting in the woods. If that's true, we could try and use it as a means to persuade Felix that Hope Christmas is the wrong place for this development.'

'Ah yes, Cat Tinsall already approached me about this,' Miss Woods boomed. 'If he wants merlins, we'll give them to him. Or if not, something similar. I know there are kestrels about, and they often get confused with merlins. We don't have to get close enough for him to check, especially if there are a lot of us making noise, they won't stay anywhere too long.'

'That sounds a bit like cheating,' said Pippa, grinning. She loved Miss Woods' can-do approach to life.

'All's fair in love and war,' said Miss Woods. 'Besides, I hear that young scoundrel Luke Nicholas is involved. Since when has he ever played fair?'

'Very true,' said Pippa, laughing. 'So all I need to do is organise a sighting, and bob's your uncle.'

'That's the spirit,' said Miss Woods.

'You make it sound so easy.'

'Easy? Easy? If things had been easy, we'd never have won the war,' said Miss Woods.

Pippa laughed again. 'Thanks, Miss Woods, you've cheered me up. I shall go home straight away and organise some leaflets which we can distribute in the town so people can start to see what we're up against.'

'Good idea,' said Miss Woods, and set off on her mobility scooter, wobbling down the road in her usual erratic fashion.

Pippa walked home where she found Richard, ensconced in the kitchen working on his laptop. She had a perfectly good office he could use, and yet here he was. Pippa tried not to feel irritated. Richard meant well, and she *had* told him to feel at home. She just hadn't meant him to take it so literally. The kitchen was *her* domain. Dan had always understood that.

Be fair, she scolded herself. Richard's not Dan. You can't expect him to know you inside out yet. That was the trouble with new relationships, she was finding, all the handy shorthanded understandings you had in a long term

197

relationship were missing. Which meant it felt much more of a minefield.

Plastering a smile on her face, she said cheerfully, 'How's it going?'

'Fine,' said Richard. 'How's your morning been?'

'Just been planning some skulduggery with Miss Woods,' said Pippa.

'Miss who?'

'Miss Woods. You must have seen her. Old bird who bombs around town on her mobility scooter.'

'Oh her,' said Richard, as if he were barely interested. 'So what skulduggery are you planning?'

Feeling a little foolish, Pippa told him about the bird spotting idea. It sounded lame. It *was* lame.

'It'll never work,' said Richard, not holding back. 'Even if Felix wotsit likes birds, he's more interested in business. LK Holdings won't be put off that easily. They can smell the money. You must realise that.'

'I do,' said Pippa, a bit cross with his lack of support 'but I want to show them there might be another way. A better way. And at least we can delay them a bit if they think they have to take rare birds into consideration.'

'Oh wake up and smell the coffee, Pippa,' said Richard, startling her with his outburst. 'No one is going to stop a development like that for the sake of a few birds. I really think you should sell up.'

'Well I don't!' Pippa snapped. She was furious. How dare he lecture her? 'And it's my farm, not yours.'

'But *our* future,' said Richard.

Pippa didn't answer. What was there to say? She hadn't liked to think too far ahead, but it was only reasonable of him to. She'd been hoping he wasn't serious about her

198

moving in with him, but she was clearly wrong. He'd been giving it far more thought than she had.

'Let's not have this discussion now,' said Pippa. 'Nothing's happening immediately. And I don't want to have a row.'

'Me neither,' said Richard, and he kissed her on the cheek. She could feel he wanted her to say something. But she couldn't. Our future, he'd said. Was that what she really wanted?

*You ok? Am around for coffee when you're back if needed. Cat xxx*

Marianne read the text, and her spirits lifted a little. Cat had already spoken to her on the phone. She'd been really understanding, having lost her mum not too long ago. Everyone had been kind, and they'd had so many offers of help with the farm so Gabriel could come to London with her, it had been overwhelming.

'Of course, I'm not letting you go alone,' had been his first words when she came off the phone to Mum. She'd wanted to get straight in the car, but Matt had said firmly, 'You've got stuff to sort out your end, Marianne. I can hold the fort here. Auntie Vi's staying too. You come when you're ready.'

So they had taken a day to organise themselves, and now finally they were powering down the M40.

It was a beautiful sunny day. Completely at odds with her mood. Marianne felt she had fallen down a deep dark hole, one she couldn't climb out of. The sun was shining, but it felt like it didn't touch her. Dad had gone. Even after the last few months, when she'd started to envisage it happening, it didn't seem possible. How could Dad just *not* be there anymore? However kind and understanding people were, nothing could take away her pain and loss.

199

'You ok?' said Gabe, looking across at her anxiously. He squeezed her hand.

'No,' said Marianne, squeezing back a tear. 'But I'll survive.' She wondered if she could. How long did grief last? How did anyone ever get over something like this? Marianne felt as if her life had been ripped in half. She couldn't shake the image of Dad in his hospital bed, when he was first ill. She tried to conjure up other, earlier images, but failed dismally. Was she only going to remember him from these last few grim months, a small frail creature, not like the dad she had loved her whole life? She couldn't even recall their last conversation properly. Something banal, about the children. If she'd known—

If she'd known, what more could she have said? Whenever it happened, it was always going to be too soon. She was always going to wish for another day, another chance to hug him and tell him she loved him. Always.

'I need a wee!' Daisy announced suddenly.

'I do too,' added Harry.

'Bugger,' said Gabriel, 'we've just passed a service station, I don't know when the next one is.'

'But I need to go now,' wailed Daisy.

'Why didn't you say so before, darling?' said Marianne.

'Because I didn't need one *then*,' said Daisy, with infuriating three-year-old logic.

For the first time since she'd heard the news about Dad, Marianne managed a smile.

'That would have made Dad laugh so much,' she said to Gabriel. 'He always said Matt and I needed the loo at the most inconvenient times when we were little.'

She laughed at the memory, and then turned back to the twins, 'You'll just have to hold for a bit. Not long now.'

Luckily a sign announced the next service station as less

than thirty miles away. The twins kept up a steady stream of moaning till they got there, but much to Marianne's relief they arrived without mishap.

As she got out of the car and took them into the service station, Marianne was hit by another memory of holding her dad's hand on a similar occasion. She must have been four or five, and Dad had taken her on his own to see her grandparents. It had been so exciting that it was just the two of them. They'd stopped at a service station for chips and hot chocolate, and he'd teased her about getting a chocolate moustache. Suddenly the tears that wouldn't come before spilt over. Her dad. Her lovely dad was gone. And for the first time since Marianne had heard the news, she really understood what it meant. Dad had gone and she was never going to see him again.

Cat was busy sorting out the boxes that Kay had deemed worthy of bringing home. In fact, left to Kay, most of the contents of Angela's house would have gone to the tip. Although Kay had said she was busy, she clearly couldn't stop interfering and had come over to put a spanner in the works, as Noel put it. She wanted to get rid of everything without looking at it, and Cat had had a job to persuade her not to chuck the baby out with the bathwater. Then there'd been the unedifying sight of Noel and Kay arguing over bits of furniture they both coveted. It had given her a headache and made her feel grateful that she was an only child. She hoped her own children wouldn't be fighting over her and Noel's belongings in thirty years' time.

In the meantime, Angela seemed well – less Angelaish – a shadow of her former self. Much meeker and more inclined to do Kay's bidding. It was as if she couldn't be bothered to fight. It had been a long time since Angela's former moniker of Granny Nightmare had been accurate, but Cat found herself wishing that Angela would revert to her normal feisty self. Or at least stand up to Kay more, who seemed to be on a roll, dictating events and demanding everything went her way.

'Are you sure you know what you're letting yourself in for?' Cat asked Kay, privately thinking her sister-in-law didn't have a clue. 'It's not easy living with your mum.'

'It'll be fine,' Kay said airily. 'My mum's not like yours was, away with the fairies. She'll be perfectly happy in the granny annexe.'

Cat bit her tongue for the sake of family harmony, but she could have crowned her. Like her mother, tact was not Kay's strong point. For once she thought maybe Noel had been right, Kay had been dropped on the head as a baby.

'I'm just saying it's not easy,' said Cat, 'and you'll all have to make adjustments. Are you sure your mum wouldn't be happier living independently nearby instead?'

'No, we've discussed it,' said Kay breezily. 'Mum still doesn't feel confident since her last fall' – because you keep nannying her, thought Cat – 'this way she can keep some independence and I can keep my eye on her.' (And have babysitting on tap, thought Cat uncharitably.)

Cat had her doubts about how long Angela's confidence would stay rocked, given her strength of personality, but certainly her mother-in-law seemed frailer than she had. Maybe her moving in with Kay was for the best. At least it meant she and Noel didn't have to have Angela with them. Cat felt guilty for the thought, but the idea of having great granny, as well as a grandchild, in the house, while battling teens was a bit more than she could contemplate right now.

She checked her watch. Time to pick up Lou Lou from nursery. Mel, who was on study leave, offered to do it, but Cat had wanted her to revise instead. Which of course meant *she* wasn't working so hard. One day she'd get this work-life balance thing sorted out once and for all. But not today. Today she'd carry on sandwich caring. After all, she'd had enough practice.

# Chapter Seventeen

Marianne sighed as she climbed into bed with Gabriel. The twins were asleep and her mum had gone to bed with a valium.

'That was a long day,' said Gabriel, cuddling up to her. 'How are you doing?'

'The longest,' said Marianne. 'And I feel crap, but I'm glad it's over.'

Gabriel held her tightly and she let soft tears fall on his shoulder. He'd been a rock since they'd got here, helping her and Mum sort out the funeral arrangements, registering the death, and the thousand and one things that apparently needed doing when someone died. At the weekend, he'd popped back to fetch Steven, who'd been very fond of Marianne's dad and asked to come.

To her immense surprise, Mum had asked Steven to sing a solo at the funeral.

'I'd love to,' Steven had agreed shyly, when Marianne suggested it. 'I liked your dad. He was fun.'

That made Marianne weep more than she thought it would be possible to. Dad had always made a point of taking time with Steven. She was touched that his efforts had not gone unappreciated.

Marianne was grateful for the twins who didn't

understand what was happening and kept asking where Heaven was and when would Grandpa come back from there, they were so sweet it made her smile. As if he'd gone on holiday, and would come back to them soon. Marianne envied them their innocence. A dull lead weight had settled in her stomach. She still couldn't believe she would never see Dad again. She felt as if the whole balance of her world had shifted and gone out of kilter. Nothing would ever be the same again.

But the one good thing had been Gabe. Suddenly she'd got him back. She wondered that she'd ever felt she'd lost him. He seemed nearly as upset by Dad's death as she was – 'I just can't take it in,' he kept saying – and as they lay there together, comforting one another, he said, 'I'm sorry, Marianne. I feel like I've let you down these last few months. I know it's been tough on you to have Eve around. You've been wonderful to have her, it can't have been easy.'

'No it hasn't,' said Marianne. 'But I'm not *that* wonderful, I know I've not been as accepting of her as I could have been.'

They lay staring into the darkness and then Gabriel started talking.

'It's just I've always felt so responsible for Eve, you know. I realise it's ridiculous, but ever since I met her, I've had to take care of her. And it's a hard habit to break. I'm sorry, I should never have put her above you. It won't happen again.'

Marianne squeezed him tight.

'I know,' she said. 'And it has driven me mad at times, but I do understand.'

'I don't deserve you,' said Gabe, kissing her, and Marianne felt a huge sense of relief.

'No you don't,' she said, 'but luckily for you, you have a wonderful wife, and I forgive you.'

'When we get back, I'll gently start talking to Eve about getting a job and moving on,' said Gabriel. 'She *is* a lot better, it's time she stood on her own two feet again.'

'Are you sure?' said Marianne. 'I know it's hard for her and for you not to worry about her.'

'I'm sure,' said Gabriel. 'Having Eve in the house hasn't been good for us, and one thing the last week has shown me is how lucky I am to have you.'

'How lucky *we* are,' said Marianne, leaning against his chest, and listening to the rise and fall of his breathing. She let out a deep sigh. The road ahead was tough, without a doubt. But with Gabriel at her side, she knew she could get through it. Together, they could get through anything.

'So you really think there might be merlins in the woods, after all?' said Cat over a well-earned cappuccino in the café. She and Pippa had spent the morning delivering leaflets throughout the town calling for action and another public meeting. 'And Felix Macintyre has agreed to come and see them?'

'No and yes,' said Pippa. 'There are definitely kestrels, according to Miss Woods, and they're similar to merlins. And with any luck they won't come close enough for him to get a clear look.'

'And you're going to bend Felix Macintyre's ear about the importance of preserving the area as a wildlife site?' said Cat.

'That's the plan,' said Pippa. 'If he really is keen on rare birds, and everything I've read about him suggests it's an obsession of his, I think we can persuade him that Hope Christmas is the wrong site for his hotel.'

'Me too,' said Cat. 'It's definitely worth a try.'

'You know me,' said Pippa. 'I'll always give it a go. Even if no one else is on board.'

'You've still not persuaded Richard to back your plans then?'

Pippa pulled a face.

'It's so frustrating. I've got such great ideas, and neither Richard nor Dan are prepared to hear me out.'

'Oh I am sorry,' said Cat. 'What kind of things did you have in mind?

'I was thinking of trying to come up with some seasonally themed attractions, to get people in. You know, like a Summer Sizzler and Halloween Spooktacular – we could put on some tractor rides, and have seasonal activities that kids would enjoy,' said Pippa. 'We've got the space to do it. I was even thinking about having something special at Christmas, and getting Santa in. Ralph Nicholas has reindeer, I was going to ask if I could hire some from him.'

'That's a brilliant idea,' said Cat. 'When Richard sees something concrete, I'm sure he'll come round.'

'I think that's highly unlikely,' said Pippa with a sigh. 'Richard wants me to sell up and move in with him.'

'Wow!' Cat searched her friend's face for clues. 'That's great isn't it? The moving in bit, I mean not the selling. Shows he's serious.'

'I don't know,' Pippa said, fiddling with her cup. 'I think I'm being unfair to Richard. I do like him. He's kind and funny and he's made me feel better about Dan. But we're so different, and he really doesn't get where I'm coming from about the farm. It's so fundamental to me, and if he can't see that, I don't really know where we go from there.'

'I can see that is a big problem,' said Cat. 'Maybe you just need time.'

'Maybe,' said Pippa, 'but I'm beginning to think I might be better off being single. I know Dan's not coming back, I've accepted that now, but I don't have to be in a relationship. And I'm starting to think I shouldn't be. Besides, Lucy hates Richard.'

'Isn't Lucy just being a typical stroppy preteen?' said Cat. 'God knows Paige and Ruby would give me hell if Noel and I split up and I found someone else.'

'But Lucy's not an ordinary girl is she?' said Pippa. 'And she's struggled the most of the kids since Dan left. I don't want her to suffer because of my decisions.'

'Yes, but you still have the right to a life,' said Cat. 'You don't have to be a nun.'

'I know,' said Pippa, 'I just think I may have rushed it. Richard was there, being kind when I needed him. Oh shit, am I only going out with him from gratitude? That's terrible.'

'I'm sure you're not,' said Cat. 'It's not like you don't fancy Richard or anything. It's still early days.'

'I guess,' said Pippa but she didn't look convinced. 'Anyway, enough of that. Are you going to join us in the woods?'

'Sounds like a hoot,' said Cat. 'You can count me in.'

Dan was having a coffee mid Saturday morning with Pippa. It was still something he did occasionally at weekends when it wasn't his turn to have the kids. They all loved seeing him, and the boys had even deigned to spend ten minutes away from the Playstation to spend time with their dad. The sight of her normally laidback teenagers still being prepared to cuddle up to their dad warmed Pippa's heart. Whatever else had happened, Pippa was glad that Dan still had good relationships with them all. Though she had noticed with a pang, as Richard had been around more, Dan had been around less.

Lucy was giggling so happily in her dad's presence, Pippa felt worse than ever. It didn't seem fair that Lucy had to live apart from Dan, even though it wasn't Pippa's decision. Logically, she knew she hadn't chosen this situation, but it didn't make her hate it any less. She really enjoyed Richard's company, and he had helped her get over Dan, But how could she ever be with Richard, when Dan made their daughter this happy? How could she ever be with anyone? Pippa felt torn. And if she was really keen on Richard, she'd find a way . . . Which suggested to her that she wasn't as keen on him as she ought to be.

Pippa got on with cooking while Dan and Lucy chatted together, so naturally and cosily for a moment she could almost pretend that nothing had changed and Dan was still living here. Then Richard came in. He'd stayed over, been tired from work and was only emerging now. He wasn't used to farmer's hours – a fact Pippa was trying hard not to hold against him – and had only just got out of bed. She reminded herself he worked very long hours in Birmingham during the week, as the financial director of a marketing firm, but it wasn't easy for her to imagine him living here at the farm. Nor was it easy to picture herself selling up and moving the family into his. She should tell him, she really should . . .

'Morning, love,' said Richard, kissing her on the cheek and putting a proprietorial hand on her shoulder. She tried not to bristle, but she felt uncomfortable with this overt display of affection in front of Dan. 'Any chance of a coffee?'

'Yes, sure,' said Pippa, getting up to pour him one, inwardly seething. She didn't dare look at Lucy, or Dan for that matter.

Lucy quickly made her excuses and rolled her way into the lounge. Dan was about to follow her, but Richard stopped him.

'Sorry, Dan, I wondered if you'd mind having a word, as we're all here, it's about the farm.'

'What about it?' Dan's voice was wary.

'Well, as you know Pippa and I have been together a while now, and we've been discussing taking things further—'

'I haven't—' Pippa started to protest, but Richard was on a roll.

'So we were wondering about you buying out the farm instead, to allow the boys the option of still having it in the future. I know how concerned Pippa is about that.'

'Richard, I never said yes to any of this,' said Pippa angrily.

'You said you'd think about it,' said Richard.

'Not the same thing,' said Pippa, 'besides what about my plans?'

She'd shown Dan a few of her ideas, and thought he'd been interested.

'I'm not convinced they're going to work,' said Dan, to her dismay. 'I know last time we spoke I said we should sell, but Dad had suggested this as a possibility too. Maybe if between us we can raise a bank loan, it might be doable. I don't want the boys to lose out, and the last thing I want to do is to hold you two back.'

I haven't said yes, yet, Pippa wanted to say, but she was so upset by Dan's reaction to her ideas, she found herself unable to say anything. *Her* Dan would have listened to her. Her Dan would have fought for her. It was time to face reality. Her Dan was gone for good. She was tilting at windmills and always had been.

# Chapter Eighteen

Marianne breathed a sigh of relief, as they drove down the lane to the farm. The sun was shining, the birds were singing, the sheep baaing on the hills, and she felt a lightening of her spirits, for the first time since her dad had died. It felt so lovely to be home. Time to get back to normal, even if she still felt odd and spaced out by what had happened. It would be good to get back into routine. The twins had slept most of the way back, which had made the journey a lot easier, and Gabe had done the driving so she'd been able to have a kip too. Marianne hadn't slept much in the last week.

To her surprise, Mum had insisted not only that Matt and Marcus fly back off to India to resume their world tour, but that she and Gabriel went back home.

'The twins need their routine, Steven needs to get back to school, and Gabriel has work to do,' she said, and when Marianne had protested, 'But what about you?' she'd smiled a sad smile and said, 'I'll manage. Besides, I have to get used to being on my own now.'

Marianne felt simultaneously guilty and grateful to have been let off the hook. It was true, the twins were all over the place, and it had been too crowded for all of them at Mum's house. They all needed to get back to their lives, but she still felt guilty about leaving Mum, and made her promise she would come up and visit soon.

If she was honest, Marianne was amazed at how well her mum was coping so far. She was demonstrating a stoicism and pragmatism that Marianne hadn't been aware her mother was capable of. She'd always relied so much on Dad, Marianne had been sure she'd fall apart. Instead, she'd been stronger than either Marianne or Matt at the funeral, and kept up a cheerful determination in front of them, which had made Marianne love her mother more than she'd done in her entire life. Dad was the one she'd always been close to. Maybe now she and Mum could get on better. Marianne hoped so. At least then something positive would have come out of Dad dying.

'Glad to be home?' Gabe said as Steven helped them carry their bags to the front door, making the most of the twins still being asleep.

'You bet,' said Marianne. She kissed him. 'Thanks for everything, Gabe. I couldn't have got through it without you.'

'I didn't do anything,' said Gabriel, 'but glad if I helped.'

He squeezed her hand and she felt a thrill of joy that he was hers and everything between them was restored and back the way it should be.

'Ugh, you two,' said Steven, 'do you have to?'

'Yes, young man, we do,' said Gabriel, giving his son a friendly shove. 'One day when you're grown up you'll understand.'

'I don't think I'll ever understand *that*,' said Steven, the look of disgust on his face sending both Gabriel and Marianne into paroxysms of laughter.

'Right, I'll dump the bags and get straight out to the sheep,' said Gabriel as he went to open the door. It was a bit stiff, so he gave it a good shove, and then, 'What the—?'

'What's the matter?' said Marianne as she followed him in.

The hallway was in chaos. The wallpaper was half stripped, the banister sanded down and there was a dust-sheet half on and half off the floor (the cause of the sticking door), and the sound of piteous baaing was coming from the kitchen.

'Dolly sounds fed up,' said Gabriel. 'What on earth is going on?' He made his way carefully through the hallway to the kitchen, and opened the door. Dolly had clearly been waiting on the other side, because she charged out, almost knocking Gabriel over, and causing a tin of paint to go flying.

'Shit!' said Gabriel as it tipped all over the bit of carpet which was exposed, and Dolly shot past him and out of the front door.

'What the hell is going on?' said Marianne furiously.

'Oh.' Eve appeared at the top of the stairs looking stricken. 'It was meant to be a surprise. I thought I'd decorate while you were away. I hope you don't mind?'

'Mum! You just don't understand! All my exams were shit. I'm going to fail everything, and have to resit the year. I've cocked everything up again!'

Mel slammed the kitchen door and fled up the stairs in floods of tears, causing Lou Lou to pucker up and form tears of her own.

Mel had finished her last exam, and had just had her first day back at college. She'd been quite happy about her performance before she caught up with her mates and made the mistake of dissecting every last detail. The result was a massive panic attack which had left Mel in the depths of despair, and nothing Cat could say or do seemed to help.

Sighing, she cuddled Lou Lou to calm her down, and soon had her sitting playing with her bricks. James too had finished his exams, with much less fuss, it had to be said, than Mel. 'I can't see what you're getting so wound up about,' he said, 'it's only exams,' but then not quite so much was riding on it for him.

Now James had broken up for the summer, he seemed to spend most of his time playing Grand Theft Auto and drinking endless cups of coffee, despite Cat's hints that he might like to get himself a job. Mind you, that seemed to have been pretty much what he was doing during his revision period. If he'd spent as much time looking at his books as he had waiting for the kettle to boil, she was sure he'd have got As and A*s all round. She marvelled at the differences between her two eldest children. Mel could do with a dose of James' laidback attitude, and James needed a rocket up his arse. Such was the way of family life.

'Can you keep an eye on Lou Lou?' she asked him. 'I need to go and calm your sister down.'

'I bet she hasn't done that badly,' said James. 'Girls always exaggerate.'

'You're probably right, but try to be kind,' said Cat. 'I won't be long, and in the meantime, get off that wretched computer while you look after your niece, and make sure you stay off it.'

'Yeah, yeah,' James waved her away and sat down on the floor to help construct things out of bricks with Lou Lou. Cat grinned. She loved seeing them together. Who knew her gangly, tall teenage son, who was normally far too cool to display emotion, would have been so soppy about a toddler?

She left them to it and went to find Mel who was lying on her bed staring into space, her eyes red with sobbing.

'Oh Mel,' said Cat, 'were they really that bad?'

'Worse,' said Mel. 'Oh god, I've stuffed up again.'

'No you haven't,' said Cat. 'A) it might not be as bad as you think and b) exams aren't everything. With your blog and book, you've got the start of a career. You don't even have to go to uni if you don't want to. Nothing's set in stone.'

'But I do want to go to uni,' said Mel, 'I really do. And I can't see myself ever getting in at this rate.'

'Well, love,' said Cat, sitting down and holding her hand, 'if you don't, you don't. It's not the end of the world. And whatever you do, remember, Dad and I are so proud of you.'

'You are?' said Mel, looking pleased, and Cat smiled as she saw the similarity with Lou Lou, when someone praised her.

'Of course I am. Now come downstairs, have a cup of tea and some cake, and play with your gorgeous daughter. Whatever happens we'll get through it. You'll see.'

It was a sunny day and the birds were tweeting across the valley as Pippa went to the yard to start herding the cows in for milking. Despite Richard's continued reservations about her ideas, she felt she was at least doing something to save the farm. She looked around her, at this place which had been her whole life. She wasn't going to give it up. Not for Richard, or anyone.

'Penny for 'em.' Dan appeared in muddy overalls, big wellies, looking totally scruffy, and still able to make her heart stop unexpectedly. This was stupid, she was over him. She was. Over. Him.

'Just thinking what a lovely day it is,' said Pippa, 'and how much I love this place.'

'Me too,' said Dan. He paused and looked at her a little sadly. 'Pippa, I know neither of us want to sell up, but Dad and I have been over the figures a dozen times, and we just can't get them to work. I'm really sorry, but I can't afford to buy you out, however much I want to.'

'Well let's work together to save the farm then,' said Pippa. 'I know *we're* divorced, but we still want the same things for our children. We only need to keep things going for a few more years till the boys are old enough to take it on.'

'Pippa you are unstoppable,' Dan roared with laughter. 'You never give up do you? It's what I've always loved about you.'

There was a pause, and Pippa's heart beat more, a little faster. Stop it, Pippa, stop it, she scolded herself, but couldn't help her reactions. Dan hadn't said anything that emotional to her for months.

'Oh you know me?' she said lightly. 'Never one to roll over lightly and take it.'

'Yes, I do know you,' said Dan, and his eyes were sad.

Pippa wanted to hug him, anything to take away that melancholy look on his face but instead, she said, 'Shall we get on?' The cows were lowing in their stalls, clearly fed up. 'Time and milking wait for no man.'

All the time she was herding the cows into the milking stalls and attaching them to the machines, her thoughts were whirling. She couldn't get his words out of her head. Dan had been so cold and distant to her for so long and made it plain he didn't have feelings for her anymore, but what if he still did? She'd been so sure he didn't want her, but if he did, where did that leave her and Richard?

This is ridiculous, she told herself. Dan divorced you,

remember? It's in the past. Maybe he does regret it, but it's too late now. Too late. The words made her feel infinitely sad.

But afterwards, when Dan followed her back to the kitchen, she felt a little flutter of hope. Although it was soon overcome with guilt. Was she leading Richard on, by still having feelings for Dan?

As she pondered this, Richard came in. He was working from home again.

'Hi Dan,' he said, extending a hand, before putting a possessive arm around Pippa again. 'Has Pippa told you our good news?'

'No,' said Dan, looking at them quizzically.

'We're not going to wait till the farm's settled, we're moving in together,' said Richard, 'I thought you should be the first to know.'

'But—' Pippa was stuck in shock – what had happened there? She hadn't agreed to anything. Richard had just assumed.

'Well that's fantastic,' said Dan, extending a hand, and Pippa felt herself collapse. She'd been imagining things. Dan seemed genuinely pleased for them. They were divorced. Time to move on.

# My Broken Brain

*Oh sod what day it is. I only know it's 4am, again.*

Another completely sleepless night. I'm sitting here, looking out of the window as a pink sun slowly breaks through the clouds of grey, just trying to work out how I can have got things so spectacularly wrong.

All this time, I thought I wanted what was best for Pippa. And I know I'm not it. Since my accident, I've only brought her down.

So, I pushed her away from me, not letting her get close once, even though it hurt like hell. I've shored up my feelings and hidden them from her so she can have a happier life without me.

And I've succeeded beyond my expectations. Pippa *is* happy. Just as I wanted her to be. She's with Richard and they're going to move in together. It's right for her; it's what I wanted for her. And I *should* be glad.

Except, I'm not. What do you make of that, counsellor, Jo? Weren't expecting that, were you? Me neither.

Turns out I'm an idiot. By pushing Pippa away, I've lost her forever, and made the biggest mistake of my life.

# Part Three

## A thousand memories

# Nine Years Ago

## Christmas with Lucy

'Time for bed, munchkins, otherwise Santa will never come!' Pippa came into the lounge where the boys, Dan and Lucy were watching *The Snowman*, entranced. Lucy was sitting in her chair gurgling in delight and for the first time all day, the boys were sitting still, and not tearing round the house hyped up by overexcitement. The room was strung with paper chains Pippa had made with Nathan and George, and lit with fairy lights. The Christmas tree, top heavy with tinsel applied again by the boys, was sparkling in the corner, with a few presents Santa wasn't bringing already piled up underneath.

Lucy was fascinated by the Christmas tree, staring for hours enthralled by the lights and baubles. As ever, it was her enjoyment of little things which lifted your spirits, Dan thought. This year had been so difficult, finally having the diagnosis of cerebral palsy, they'd so long suspected, when their beautiful daughter had failed to develop in the ways that her brothers had done. It was only Pippa's tenacity and determination to push the professionals to commit to a diagnosis that had got them this far. Being Pippa, she would never be put off by a 'What does the mother know?'

223

dismissive response. Though by and large, once they'd got into the system, the support they'd had from both doctors and care workers had been phenomenal; it was the journey to get there which had been so hard.

And then the shock of the diagnosis. Even when they'd expected it, somehow to be told that your precious child is less than perfect in the conventional sense, was a devastating blow. Coupled with the realisation that their family life was never going to be the same, that for the rest of their lives Lucy's needs would forever take them in a different direction to the one they'd imagined. They loved their daughter dearly, but they also mourned the possible life they had planned for her, and worried about how they would all cope in the future.

It had been tough coming to terms with that. And yet, somehow, they *had* come to terms with it. Partly because Lucy, with her sparkly smile and mischievous personality seemed to have the character to rise above the problems inherent in her condition, and partly because, she was still their precious daughter and always would be.

And here they were at Christmas, all together, a family bonded by a special kind of love, and a very special child.

Lucy clapped her hands when Pippa mentioned Santa, and the boys were clamouring to put out mince pies and a sherry for the reindeer, and a carrot for Rudolf. Lucy had been too little to take part in the tradition last year, and was wreathed with smiles at the thought of it all. Dan lifted her up – she was so small and frail, he felt like she would break in his arms sometimes – and carried her into the kitchen, so she could feel part of everything. Nathan gave her the carrot to hold, and George walked back to the lounge carefully holding onto the sherry, and making sure it didn't spill.

'Can we write Santa a note?' said Nathan.

'Of course,' said Pippa, grabbing pens and paper.

Nathan carefully took a pen, and started writing his letter, while George just drew a picture of their family and wrote George, and five kisses. Lucy indicated she wanted to write something too, so Dan helped her hold a pen, and watched her draw unintelligible squiggles on the paper.

'Is this Santa?' he asked, looking at a blob in the middle of the page, and Lucy nodded happily. 'Well, I'm sure he'll be really pleased,' said Dan.

'It really is bedtime now,' said Pippa to groans from the boys about not being tired, but they didn't grumble long, when she added, 'the sooner you go to sleep, the sooner Santa gets here.'

She chased them up the stairs, and Dan carried Lucy into her room. The boys came in to kiss their sister in a nightly ritual – in the way of children the world over, they accepted that their sister was different, and loved her just the same – and then Pippa came and together they tucked Lucy in.

'Just think, Luce,' said Pippa, placing Lucy's stocking on the bed, 'when you wake up Santa will have been, won't that be lovely?'

Lucy's grin melted his heart. She was as happy as any other three-year-old going to bed on Christmas Eve. Perhaps not so different after all . . .

*July*

# Chapter Nineteen

'Save our birds!'

'No building in the woods!'

'No Hotels Here!'

The sun was beating down on the town square which was full of people waving placards and holding posters. There were so many people, they were spilling out onto the road, stopping traffic. Pippa looked around her with quiet satisfaction. True she'd had one or two aggressive types shouting at her for being a Nimby: one lady going so far as to wave her fist in Pippa's face, and say, 'You're depriving people of valuable jobs, you know!' but for the most part everyone was good humoured.

When Felix Macintyre arrived later, and she drove him up to the woods, where one or two stalwarts, including Batty Jack had taken to camping – 'Somebody needs to keep an eye out on them bastards,' he said. 'Don't want them sneaking up behind our backs' – he'd be able to see how strongly people felt. And if he thought there was a chance of spying his precious merlins, then maybe he'd think again.

'You all set?' Miss Woods came sailing up on her scooter.

'I think so,' said Pippa. 'The plan is I take Mr Macintyre round the woods, and point out the likely places you might spot merlins. We should at least see the kestrels and hopefully that should make him think again about destroying their habitat. Then we can try and persuade him that a more educational slant here might be a better idea, although I appreciate that's not very likely.'

'Seeing the force of local opposition against the idea should give him pause for thought,' said Miss Woods.

Just then a big black limo swept up and out climbed the great man himself. He turned to his companion – Pippa's heart sank to see Luke Nicholas – and said sotto voce, 'I thought you told me the whole town *wanted* this development.'

'There are plenty who do want it, Felix, I can assure you of that,' said Luke smoothly. Felix Macintyre, however, was clearly perturbed by the reception. Pippa decided to strike while the iron was hot.

'Hello, Mr Macintyre,' Pippa beamed, stepping towards him in greeting.

'Please call me Felix. How lovely to see you again,' Felix replied with genuine warmth.

'Felix, we wondered whether you would like to come and visit the woods? We might see some merlins if we're lucky,' she said with her fingers crossed behind her back. 'We think a pair may have been nesting there this spring; there could be babies.'

'That sounds, swell,' he answered, and she grinned as she saw Luke grimace. In his shiny suit and gleaming shoes, he couldn't have looked more unprepared for a tramp in the woods. Felix on the other hand looked as though he'd come ready for a hike in the Rockies. Though Pippa noticed his boots were brand new and ridiculously shiny. Honestly, city dwellers. They had no idea about the country.

'After you,' said Felix and Pippa and her band of followers marched up the valley to the woods.

'This is a cute little place,' he said to Pippa, as they made their way to the path through a field full of daisies, butter-cups, and dandelions that led to the woods, 'I had no idea.'

'Isn't it? Which is why we're concerned about your plans,' said Pippa. 'I'm not sure that a huge hotel complex is what Hope Christmas needs. And I think when you see the birds in their natural habitat . . .'

'If we see any,' sneered Luke.

'Luke seems to think you're bullshitting me,' Felix explained.

Oh bugger! Pippa thought rapidly.

'We're not bullshitting about the beauty of the place, and the need to preserve the landscape for future generations. Just look around you.'

'It sure is beautiful,' admitted Felix, 'we'll see.'

He marched ahead, every now and then peering through his binoculars as if he was expecting to be caught out.

'Do you think we'll convince him?' whispered Marianne, as she and Pippa trailed after him.

'If I've got anything to do with it, we will,' said Pippa.

The motley crew wound its way up the valley. You had to hand it to Pippa, Marianne thought, she could always be relied on to get a crowd going. People were chanting and cheering all the way, until Pippa shushed them as they reached the woods. In the distance, Marianne could make out a few hammocks, where Batty Jack and his cronies had been sleeping. They had made themselves scarce for now, as they didn't want to disturb any birds that might be there.

'Mr Macintyre is very keen to see our merlins. So if you all wait here, I'll show him where they've been spotted.'

To her dismay, Luke who'd been shadowing Felix Macintyre, elected not to follow him, and came sidling up to her.

'Birds or no birds,' he said, 'the old man is going to go ahead with his plans, so you may as well accept it now and give up on all of this.'

'It's not what people round here want,' argued Marianne. 'You should think again.'

'In my experience, people never know what they want till it's right in front of them,' said Luke, firmly holding her gaze. 'The hotel and spa will bring people into town and give it new life.'

'I doubt that very much,' said Marianne, reeling off a list of her concerns. 'You're going to destroy a local beauty spot, which is one of the many reasons people come here; most of the locals won't be able to afford the facilities; and the sort of people who go there are hardly going to be shopping in Hope Christmas or interested in the countryside. It will be a disaster.'

'You never did have a head for business, did you?' said Luke in a patronising manner, which Marianne found infuriating. To think she had begun to find him attractive again. It must have been the Prosecco.

'But I do know what people round here want,' said Marianne, 'which is something you've never grasped.'

'It's not too late for you to be part of this,' Luke said. 'Your land would come in useful, and I'm sure you could do with an injection of cash.'

Infuriatingly, he was right about that, but Marianne wasn't about to say so.

'Well keep talking,' she smiled sweetly. 'But it would have to be a pretty big offer to make us change our minds.'

There was no harm in keeping him dangling a little . . .

Just then, Pippa and Felix emerged from the woods, the latter full of excitement. 'I can't believe it,' he was saying. 'Fancy seeing merlins in the wild. It's a shame we couldn't get a closer look.'

'We didn't want to disturb them,' said Pippa, 'and they don't settle for long.'

'True, true,' said Felix. 'And it was a damned nuisance that dog came out of nowhere and frightened the birds away.'

Dog? What dog? Marianne wondered.

Two minutes later Ralph Nicholas hove into view with his cocker spaniel trotting beside him.

'So sorry about that, old boy, Charlie here gets a bit carried away when he thinks he's smelt rabbit.'

'No matter,' said Felix. 'At least I caught a glimpse of the birds. Remarkable. Quite remarkable. You should have seen them, Luke, son.'

Luke, son, looked as if he would rather swallow his own bile.

'Hello, Luke old boy. Fancy meeting you here,' said Ralph with a dazzling smile. 'On the side of the angels as ever.'

'Uncle Ralph,' said Luke with open distaste.

'Now, now, Charlie, behave.'

Marianne stifled a smile as Charlie decided to cock his leg against Luke Nicholas' shiny shoes.

It couldn't have happened to a nicer bloke.

'I can't believe Ralph Nicholas' dog peed all over Luke's leg,' giggled Cat.

'I know,' said Pippa, 'and he also arrived at the fortuitous moment before Felix realised he wasn't looking at a pair of merlins but kestrels. I was glad I didn't have to face any awkward questions, I can tell you. I have a feeling Mr Macintyre knows his onions and would have found me out if we'd got any closer.'

'So what next?' said Cat.

'There's another public meeting next Monday, prior to the county council meeting where they pass planning permission,' said Pippa. 'I think we can expect more interest than last time. Although it might get messy. There are still more people in favour of the hotel complex than I'd like. Do you think you can make it?'

'Sure thing,' said Cat. 'And you'll be pleased to know I've co-opted the director of my country series into featuring this story as part of a country life under threat episode.'

Cat had already started filming the new series, and despite feeling a bit of a duck out of water, she was having fun. The first day of shooting had gone well, if a bit scary. She'd spent the day at a bird sanctuary and had spoken to camera while holding a very pissed off falcon. Despite the stress it had caused her, Cat had enjoyed herself. She'd missed being in front of the camera.

'We've already shot some footage elsewhere in the county where they've brought in unsuitable developments and the difference it's made to the locals. This will be a good counterbalance. I'll see if we can get some cameras along to film the action and get people's thoughts.'

'Oh Cat, that's great. I've already contacted the local press,' said Pippa. 'They were a great support last time.'

'That's brilliant,' said Cat. 'You'll see, we'll have them running for the hills in next to no time.'

'I'm glad you're confident,' said Pippa, 'because I'm feeling a bit wobbly . . .'

She paused. She didn't like to think what would happen

if they didn't succeed. Then her plans for the farm would probably be next to useless, and she and Dan might as well sell up.

'You don't really think you'd have to let the farm go?' said Cat.

'I don't want to,' said Pippa, 'but we're struggling at the moment, and Richard thinks we're mad not to take LK Holding's offer. Maybe we are.'

'What about your plans for the farm?' said Cat. 'Won't they help?'

'I hope so,' said Pippa, 'I genuinely think I can turn it round. If we capitalise on the visitors in the summer, aiming for the family market with tractor rides and the like, and a small petting zoo, I'm sure we can get people in. We should have some calves, and Gabe will have some youngish lambs still, who can be fed. I've earmarked the lower field for some changes, and the bank manager has agreed a loan. So that's something, but . . .'

'But what?'

'Richard thinks I'm wasting my time.'

'Does that matter?' said Cat. 'It's not Richard's farm.'

'And it's not mine either, is it?' said Pippa. 'Dan has to have a say in all of this.'

'So what does he think?'

'Dan has barely spoken to me,' said Pippa. 'Not since Richard announced we were moving in together.'

'You are?' said Cat, surprised. 'Isn't that a bit sudden?'

'Yeah, well it is for me,' said Pippa, 'but not for Richard apparently. He rather forced the issue.'

Cat looked at her friend.

'If you don't mind me saying,' she said, 'you don't look that happy about it.'

'I am,' said Pippa quickly – too quickly – 'it's just, I wasn't expecting it so soon, that's all. I'm not long divorced. I think I need some space.'

'Well tell him,' said Cat. 'I'm sure he'll understand.'

'Yeah, you're right,' said Pippa, but she didn't sound convinced.

# *Chapter Twenty*

'Gabe? Are you in?' shouted Marianne, as she stumbled in with the twins over the bags of rubbish and paint pots still lining the hall where Eve, having persuaded them that it would cause more chaos if she stopped what she was doing, was continuing with her decorating efforts. The little she had done so far was stunning, but most of the time she seemed to be sitting in the kitchen drinking tea and perusing decorating mags. Marianne would have preferred less perfection and a little more action. The walls were filled with different shades of blue, while Eve chose the perfect one. Marianne had tried saying in vain, she didn't care, she just wanted it finished, but was always met with a, 'But Marianne, please let me. It's my way of saying thank you', which made Marianne feel once more like a stranger in her own home.

It was hard to argue with that, and Gabriel agreed, 'Just accept it in the spirit it's offered,' he counselled, 'she's got precious all else to focus on.'

Which was true. After six months on sick pay and a round of job cuts, Eve had recently taken voluntary redundancy. She had taken the news badly and it had knocked her back a bit. She was quite often anxious, and her moods could be volatile. One minute she would be passive and docile, another bright-eyed and manic. Eve was still fragile and Marianne could see she needed a focus. It would just be nice if she found a different kind of focus. Like looking for somewhere else to live, maybe. But without a job, that would be impossible. So Gabe's talk had been put on hold.

'In here,' Marianne could hear laughter coming from the kitchen, where she found Gabriel sharing a cup of tea with Eve.

The kitchen looked like a bomb had hit it, and Dolly was snuffling up against Gabriel's legs in search of food. Really, it was time they moved her out to the fields, she was nearly fully grown. But the twins wouldn't hear of it.

'I thought you might like some muffins,' said Eve, producing them triumphantly from the oven. 'Sorry I made a mess.'

'Ooh, muffins,' the twins eyed them with delight. 'Can we, Mummy?'

'Of course,' said Marianne, feeling defeated.

'They are delicious,' said Gabriel. He looked apologetically at her, as if to say, What can I do? And Marianne felt churlish. Eve didn't mean any harm, in fact she was very kind. But she was thoughtless, and had been in their space too long. The trouble was, how could they ask her to leave, when she had nowhere to go?


'Yay, college is over till September!' Mel came into the kitchen looking both exhausted and triumphant. Her sixth form college was finishing a few days before Ruby and Paige's school, much to their disgust.

'It's not fair,' Ruby said, 'why can't our school finish today?'

'Because life isn't fair, sweetie,' said Cat, giving her youngest daughter a hug and sending her to school. It might not be fair, but Cat was pleased Mel was getting a break. She had worked so hard and deserved it.

'Yay for the holidays!' said Cat, giving her daughter a hug. 'Look, Lou Lou, Mummy's home for the summer, isn't that lovely?'

'Luvvy!' said Lou Lou, tottering up to her mother, who whisked her up in the air and gave her an enormous hug.

'Let's celebrate,' said Mel. 'Why don't we go up to the woods, and have a picnic by the stream.'

'Excellent idea,' said Cat, 'because tomorrow I have to do some filming, and you, madam, need to look after your daughter. Unless you had other plans.'

A look passed over Mel's face, but was gone instantly.

'Some of the girls wanted to go to Alton Towers for the day,' she said.

'Oh Mel, you should have said,' said Cat. 'I can't get out of it now. Bugger.'

'It doesn't matter,' said Mel, 'it was only a spur of the moment thing. We're all going to the pub on Friday anyway.' But she looked so sad, Cat felt like hugging her. Damn Andy Pisldon, the love rat who had literally left Mel holding the baby, he had a lot to answer for.

'Let's see what we can sort out,' said Cat. 'I don't have to go out till ten, and James never goes out. I'm sure he wouldn't mind babysitting.'

They got a picnic ready, put Lou Lou in her buggy, and managed even to prevail on James to join them, before tramping up to the woods. The path was luckily not too steep, and as the weather had been dry, they didn't get stuck in the mud as was often the case. Reaching a clearing by a shallow bit of stream, they stopped and let Lou Lou out to scramble by the banks and do what she liked to do best, throw stones into the water, with James helping her.

'Isn't this perfect?' said Cat, as she watched her granddaughter carefully, while Mel lay back on the picnic blanket, soaking up the sun.

'Isn't it? I can't believe I have no more college till September,' said Mel. 'Bliss.'

'Make the most of it,' smiled Cat, 'September will be here all too soon.'

'I think I ought to get a job,' said Mel, 'to help out a bit.'

'One thing at a time,' said Cat. 'You've spent all year having to be out and not be at home with Lou Lou, I think you should enjoy her while you can. There'll be time enough for jobs later. Besides, you are still working on that cookery book, aren't you? That's enough for now.'

'Unfair,' said James, 'you keep on at me to get a job.'

'That's because you're a lazy tyke who needs to get off his backside,' said Cat, looking at her son fondly. He was so tall now, in that half state between man and boy, but still the same old James, laidback and lazy. 'Mel has a lot more on her plate than you.'

James continued to grumble, but his heart clearly wasn't in it, as he had moved on to trying to catch fish to impress Lou Lou, who was clapping her hands and laughing.

'I wish I could be like other people!' burst out Mel, suddenly, 'is that bad of me? I wouldn't be without Lou Lou, you know I wouldn't, but . . .'

'It's hard I know,' said Cat, 'but it's the way it is. You can't change it, love.'

'And next year, it's going to get harder,' said Mel. 'I don't know how I'm going to cope with uni, and leaving her, even if I am living at home.'

Just then a bird flew past with a worm in its mouth. It disappeared into the hedgerow from where a chorus of cheeping sounds was coming.

'See that bird,' said Cat. 'She has to leave her chicks to make sure they're fed. It's part of her job, just like it's part of yours.'

'You're comparing me to a bird?' said Mel. 'Gee thanks, Mum.'

'Mum, you are so weird,' said James.

'You know what I mean,' said Cat, 'besides, look at your gorgeous daughter. She's worth it, isn't she?'

'Yes,' said Mel, smiling, 'she is.'

Pippa was out in the yard sluicing it down and feeling morose. She shooed away stray chickens who kept getting in her way. Lucy was in a very stroppy mood and had refused dinner. She wouldn't say why, but Pippa knew it was about Richard, who kept making enthusiastic plans for their future. Pippa kept trying to restrain him – there never seemed to be a good time to say slow down, please – but he was like a puppy with a bone, and was so excited by the idea, she found it difficult to curtail him. It was making her frantic with worry. While Nathan and George both claimed to be 'cool' with the idea, Lucy was furious with her and making no bones about it.

'Does Dad know about this?' she'd typed angrily.

'Yes,' said Pippa.

'Bet he's happy!' Pippa could almost feel the venom coming off the keyboard.

'Lucy, sweetheart, we've been over this. Your dad split up with *me*. It's not what I wanted, but what he wanted. I'm sorry, but it's true.'

'But you don't have to move in with Richard!' came the swift response, and Lucy glared at her with a fury Pippa hadn't known her sweet daughter capable of.

There it was again, that guilt-inducing angst. Pippa wasn't

even sure she wanted to live with Richard, she certainly couldn't live with him while Lucy was feeling like this. She had many late nights worrying about it. Why was everything so complicated?

'Lucy, let's talk about this—' began Pippa, but Lucy ignored her and wheeled herself into the lounge where she and George were watching *The Big Bang Theory* back to back with *How I Met Your Mother*. Pippa had felt the need to get out of the house, so had come out to the yard to take her mind off things.

'You look fed up,' said Dan, looking dusty and tanned from a day in the fields mending fences with Gabriel. 'What's up?'

'You wouldn't want to know,' said Pippa, putting down her broom and wiping her brow. It was a hot evening and thirsty work. 'Fancy a beer? I was just about to call it a day, and the kids would be pleased to see you.'

'Is Richard in?'

'No,' said Pippa, 'would it matter if he were?'

'Well, things are a bit different now, aren't they?' Dan looked embarrassed and was staring at his feet as if he found them suddenly fascinating.

Pippa felt stiff and awkward. Oh god, was this how it was going to be if she moved in with Richard? Lucy not speaking to her? Dan making her feel uncomfortable? Her not 100 per cent committed? Richard was a nice, kind man. He deserved better.

'You don't look very happy,' said Dan. 'Is everything ok?'

Nothing's really been ok since you left, was what Pippa wanted to say. Being with Richard had been papering over the cracks, she could see that now. She'd wanted to believe she could move on, and leave the past behind, but it wasn't as easy as that. And Pippa certainly couldn't tell Dan what was in her head, so she said instead, 'Lucy just being arsey.'

'Oh?' said Dan.

'She's not told you then?' said Pippa. 'How pissed off she is about me and Richard? I've tried to explain it to her, it doesn't change things, she can't see it.'

'Would it help if I talked to her?' said Dan.

'I can't seem to get through to her anymore.' said Pippa blinking back tears.

'Oh Pippa,' said Dan softly. 'I'm sorry. This is all my fault. I put you here. I'll make sure Lucy sees that. I'll go home and freshen up and come round tonight at bedtime so I can chat with Lucy, and you and Richard can go out for a bite to eat. You'll see, it will be ok.'

He kissed her on the top of her head, and strode out of the farmyard.

Pippa watched him go. Dan. The man she'd married. The man she thought she'd never lose. Generously giving her up to someone else.

This wasn't how it was meant to be.

# Chapter Twenty-One

The village hall was packed, Cat noticed with satisfaction. Marianne and Gabriel were gathering signatures for a petition to be presented to their new Green MP Sarah Carnforth, who'd replaced the previous incumbent, Tom Brooker, after a by-election called following his fall from grace caused by one expenses scandal too many.

Miss Woods was talking long and loudly to whoever would listen about the evils of corporate life, while Diana Carew, her preposterously large bosoms bouncing in front of her, was declaring vociferously that no one was going to get her into a spa tub, not even if they paid her.

'As if that fat old bat would even fit in a spa tub,' Keeley Jacobs said cattily.

'God these people,' said Angie Townley, 'what century are they living in?'

Ouch, thought Cat as she and her cameraman Tony, wandered about among the crowd, getting some atmospheric shots, there were plenty of dissenters here today. She hoped the mood wouldn't turn ugly.

'So feelings here in Hope Christmas are running high against the new hotel development being proposed. Vera Edwards, you run the local post office, what is it that you object to?'

'It's not the idea of another hotel, that's a problem,' said Vera blushing pink, as she always did when anyone paid her any attention. 'We welcome tourists here; they're the lifeblood of the town. But this hotel complex won't cater for our normal tourists, it's far too luxurious and it's in the wrong place. They're in danger of destroying the very reason people come here. The woods they're planning to build on are a haven of wildlife. It would be criminal if that were lost for the sake of big money. We none of us want to see that happen.'

'And I understand there is some very special wildlife in the woods at the moment, isn't that right, Miss Woods?' continued Cat.

'Yes indeed,' declared Miss Woods. 'We've got some merlins living there – small birds of prey, a little like a kestrel. They're quite shy, but we've had several sightings.'

'And yet another reason for not having the hotel here, I'm guessing,' finished Cat before she went on her way.

Making her way through the crowds, Cat tried to include as many differing points of view as she could, in the interests of fairness. Jenny Ingles, from the local estate agents, was totally pro the development, naturally.

'It's going to be good for the town,' she argued, 'and it will help people like my Tom who was made redundant after Christmas and needs a new job.'

And it turned out that the Yummy Mummies weren't the only ones keen on the use of the spa facilities and gym.

'Let's face it,' declared Ann Young, a relative newcomer to the area who'd just retired to Hope Christmas from London, 'the gym facilities here are extremely limited. Hope Christmas needs something like this.'

If you wanted Fitness First, why did you leave London? Cat felt like saying, but she bit her lip and turned to Batty

Jack who started extolling the virtues of sleeping out in the open every night, which wasn't quite what she was after. Eventually about to declare it a wrap, Cat became aware that Diana Carew was holding court.

'We need this development like a hole in the head. What good is it going to do us, I ask you? Everyone talks about globalisation these days, globalisation, my eye!' she concluded, 'my eye!' Cat was able to escape, thankfully, to the back, just as Pippa called the meeting to order.

Marianne and Gabriel squeezed in next to Vera and Albert.

'This is just like old times,' said Vera with a smile.

'Isn't it?' grinned Marianne. 'To think we all got together thanks, in part, to the campaign to save the Post Office. And here we all are again.'

She and Gabriel had been thrown together by the campaign Pippa had started to save Vera's post office, while it had also been the catalyst for Vera and Albert to finally reveal their true feelings. The worst kept secret in Hope Christmas at the time had been their undeclared love for one another. Everyone could see it, but they'd both been too shy to say it.

'Only I don't feel so confident about saving our fields,' said Gabe gloomily. 'LK Holdings have a lot of money to throw around and Old Joe's great-nephew won't be the only one to take notice, I'm sure.'

'We've done it before, we can do it again,' said Marianne. 'Besides, we do at least have something they want. I told you Luke Nicholas is prepared to negotiate for our land.'

'Like I'm going to let that happen,' snorted Gabriel.

'It's so frustrating,' said Vera, looking fretful. 'I hate the thought of us all being swamped by these big companies.'

'Me too,' said Marianne.

'By the way,' continued Vera, 'do you know of anyone looking for work? Only Albert and I have decided we want a bit more time to ourselves and we could do with some help in the Post Office.'

Gabriel and Marianne looked at one another. Marianne didn't want to push, but squeezing her hand, Gabe said, 'As it happens, we do. Eve used to help out in the village shop ages ago. It might do her good to get out of the house to come and help you.'

That would be a result. Getting Eve a job would be one step further on the road to giving her the means to be independent again.

They were shushed as Pippa began to speak. She started by making an impassioned speech, as only Pippa could, about the need to save their land and community, raising laughter, when she spoke about her attempts to persuade Felix Macintyre that having merlins in the woods were a good enough reason for him not to build there.

'But, sadly, the birds alone won't do it,' she said. 'We may have given Mr Macintyre and LK Holdings pause for thought, but that's it. We have to make them see that this development is simply in the wrong place, and not what this community needs. So if everyone here could write to them, and not just to them, to the planning committee, the county council, to our new MP, Sarah Carnforth, that will show how strong the feeling here is. I've written a draft letter which has the key points, which you're welcome to crib – please it's vital that every voice is heard. The more of us who complain, the more they have to listen.'

Pippa sat down to a wave of applause, followed by some bad-tempered shouting from a couple of the Yummy Mummies who thought their point of view wasn't being heard. Then a strange little man, called Otis Hooper, who was dressed in clothes which would have looked shabby on Wurzel Gummidge and who lived at the back of the woods, leapt up and started pontificating. He seemed to be saying (when he finally got to the point) that any merlins in the woods were a bad thing, as they were birds of prey so would attack the other wildlife, and therefore the development should go ahead, which was quite a piece of skew-eyed logic. Ralph eventually managed to leap in to shut him up and wrapped the evening with a speech urging everyone to attend the planning meeting to be held in September.

'They're hoping by sneaking it in at the end of summer, very few people will be around to complain,' said Ralph. 'Let's play them at their own game and prove them wrong.'

'Brilliant, Pippa,' said Cat at the end of the meeting. 'I think we've got some great footage.'

'Thanks,' said Pippa. 'It's a great start, but there's a long way to go.'

'Fancy a drink?' asked Cat.

'Not tonight,' said Pippa. 'Mum's babysitting and Richard said he'd take me out for dinner.'

'Well done, Pippa.' Dan was standing at the back when she left. 'If anyone can save our woods it will be you.'

'That's the plan,' said Pippa. 'And thanks for speaking to Lucy.'

Lucy, though not reconciled to her and Richard, at least was less grumpy about it. She had even apologised for being rude. When Pippa had thanked her, Lucy had typed crossly, 'Dad made me,' which made them both laugh.

'It's the least I can do,' said Dan lightly. 'By the way, your lift is here.'

He nodded to where Richard was sitting in the car, waiting for her.

Pippa felt a stab of irritation. She'd asked him to come in. He knew how important this was to her. But no, it didn't matter to him. As far as Richard was concerned, the campaign was a waste of time, and the sooner she was shot of the farm the better.

'How did it go?' he said, as she got in the car, and strapped on her belt.

'Fine, I think,' said Pippa, 'but this is only the beginning. There's a long way to go and a lot to do. After the planning meeting in September we'll see what we're up against.'

'You know they'll ignore you, don't you?' said Richard, as he steered the car down the driveway of Whispers, their favourite restaurant. Or actually not their. *His*. What had got into her tonight? She was feeling very grumpy.

'Oh let's be positive,' said Pippa. 'Try and have some faith, why don't you?'

'Just being realistic,' said Richard as they sat down at the table.

'Well, don't,' said Pippa. 'This is important to me. It could be vital to us as a family.'

'But it doesn't have to be,' said Richard. 'When you sell the farm and move in with me, it won't be so important. We can use some of the money to adapt the house to Lucy, and you wouldn't have to work so hard.'

'But I like working,' said Pippa, 'I couldn't sit around being a decorative housewife. I'd go nuts.'

'You wouldn't have to,' said Richard. 'I've seen you in action. You could do charity fundraising, run your own business. The world's your oyster.'

'No,' said Pippa, with sudden clarity. 'My world is farming and my family. I want to leave a legacy for my children, and that's that.'

Richard reached into his pocket and suddenly she felt

sick. He couldn't be, could he? They'd hardly been together any time at all. But Richard was an all or nothing kind of guy. She might have known he'd rush things.

'Would you say that even if I gave you this?' He opened his palm and in it lay a box which he opened to reveal a huge diamond ring.

Oh god. She'd got this all wrong and it had to stop now. She'd been half asleep for the last few months, thinking moving on from Dan meant being with Richard. But this was so wrong. They weren't right together.

'I'm sorry, Richard, but the answer is no,' she said, feeling terrible, but knowing she had to do it. 'You're lovely and I'm really fond of you, but my future is with the farm, even if I have to go it alone. You won't ever want to be part of that, and we both know it. I'm really sorry, but we can never be together, not in the way that you want.'

# My Broken Brain

### *Day 100 and something . . . 7pm*

The law of unintended consequences. Or how to bugger things up more than you can imagine.

Lucy's happiness means more to me than my own. After my accident, I knew I'd changed. Didn't think I could be a good husband. Or a good father. And after frightening my sons half to death – and me too, the look in their eyes when I shouted at them, haunts me still – I thought it was better if I left.

I wanted Pippa to find happiness again. I thought it would help, give a purpose to all this.

I didn't think about what Lucy wanted.

And what Lucy wants is for me to come home. Despite everything that's happened, she still has faith in me. A faith I'm not sure I deserve.

But instead, she's having to deal with her mum moving in

with another man. Thanks to my actions, my poor little girl is heartbroken.

What have I done?

*August*

# Chapter Twenty-Two

'Have we forgotten anything, do you think?'

Marianne was fretting as they drove out of the farmyard with the Land Rover laden down. Gabriel's parents stood at the doorway, waving them off.

'Only the kitchen sink,' laughed Gabriel, as he expertly manoeuvred the Land Rover up the lane.

'Shut up,' said Marianne.

But with three children, her mum (meeting them off the train at Barmouth) and Eve, who looked as if she wouldn't get a holiday otherwise, all slumming it in a caravan park for a week, she'd not taken any chances, and had come, she hoped, prepared for anything. Thankfully, they'd been able to leave Patch behind, otherwise Marianne wasn't sure she'd have been able to cope. The twins had really wanted to take Dolly, who had finally graduated from kitchen to fields, and the children missed her. Marianne had had to be very firm.

'Dolly lives in the fields, now,' she said, 'she'll be too uncomfortable in the car.'

As it was, Marianne wasn't sure if she were going on holiday, or going to need a holiday to recover. Guiltily, she wished it were just her and Gabe off for a week to the lovely LK Holdings hotel she and the girls had stayed in. Now *that* would have been relaxing.

'We're all going on a summer holiday!' started up Gabriel, before a, 'Lame, Dad, really lame,' from Steven shut him up.

Marianne glanced at him, squeezed in next to Eve and lots of luggage, with Harry and Daisy squashed in at the back with even more. He was engrossed with his iPod, either playing some game, or pinging his mates about this being the most boring trip ever. He'd already made no bones about the fact that it wasn't his idea of fun.

Marianne felt a pang. When Eve had been with Darren and had had money, at least Steven had had exciting holidays. But what was there for a fourteen-year-old boy on a Welsh caravan site? The twins would be happy as larry, playing on the beach, enjoying the rubbish entertainment at the bar, eating fish and chips; Mum would be happy to be with her grandchildren; she and Gabe would manage because it was a family holiday and at least it was a break from the farm, and Eve would be getting a freebie, so if she wasn't happy, Marianne didn't really care. But poor old Steven was going to get fed up really quickly.

'I hope this week won't be too boring for you, Steven,' she said.

Steven shrugged his shoulders. 'It'll be ok, I expect.'

'Maybe you and Dad can go off and do something fun together,' suggested Marianne, hoping that would help.

'Maybe,' said Steven, looking non-committal.

Oh dear. This wasn't at all promising. At least it was only a week.

Half an hour into the journey, there was a wail from Daisy.

'I feel sick,' she cried, and promptly was.

'Oh, gross!' said Steven, while Daisy screamed the place down, and then Harry decided to join in.

'Didn't you give her travel sick pills?' said Gabriel, accusingly. He always got tense when he was driving on a family holiday.

'Yes,' said Marianne. 'It must be these windy roads.' That Daisy was a champion vomiter, they'd discovered early on in their family car experiences, but this was a first even for her. 'She must be overexcited.'

Gabriel found the nearest safe place to park, and Marianne got out of the car, extricated a snivelling Daisy from her seat, and went through the joyous experience of cleaning up.

'It stinks,' moaned Steven as they set off again. Marianne had come equipped with antibacterial spray, but it wasn't enough to keep the smell away.

'Open the window,' said Marianne unfeelingly, but changed her mind as they hit a torrential downpour. It seemed as if they were heading into a storm.

'I need a wee!' It was Harry's turn to yell.

There hadn't been a sign for a service station for ages, so they hadn't been able to stop, and judging by the road signs, there wasn't going to be one for miles.

'I'll pull over as soon as I can,' said Gabriel, which wasn't very soon, and the yells from the back became even more urgent.

'Can't wait!' Harry was crying, his face bright red with effort.

'Too late,' said Marianne with a sigh, when Gabriel was finally able to pull over.

Sitting with the tailgate up, she changed the second of her children in the pouring rain. They hadn't even arrived yet and she'd nearly used up all the spare clothes she had for the journey.

It was going to be a very long week.

\* \* \*

257

'This is great,' said Cat, as she, Lou Lou and Ruby hopped off the tractor ride, which took them on a small circuit of Pippa's farm. It was a sunny day, and the farm was buzzing.

To Pippa's delight, a steady stream of summer visitors had availed themselves of the opportunity to visit the farm, and it was great to see small children everywhere, excitedly oohing and aahing at the animals. There were parents with babies in backpacks, and toddlers in buggies, older children clamouring to go on tractor rides. The numbers had exceeded her wildest expectations.

She'd roped in the boys and their friends to help out with the small animals, and though there wasn't a lot of variety, she'd got chickens, lambs, a couple of goats, and a few rabbits and guinea pigs, which were going down a storm with the younger ones. So much so that she'd even been asked if any were for sale. Now there *was* an idea . . .

The greatest success of all was the hay barn, where George and Nathan, veterans since their youth, had hooked up a variety of slides and jumps. Who needed a ball pit, when you had hay to jump in? Admittedly the cost of liability insurance was diabolically high, and the working days were even longer than normal, but if this many people kept coming through the doors all summer, it would be worth it.

Lucy was enjoying herself too, sitting in the entrance taking money, selling home-made jams and chutney by the dozen. It turned out she was a talented saleswoman, she only had to smile at people, and they immediately fell in love and parted with their money. She had been so much happier since Richard left, even if Pippa had had any doubts, they would have been quashed by the sight of her daughter.

Her teenage strops seemed to have vanished overnight and Lucy had reverted once more to being the happy-go-lucky, easy-going child she'd always been. Pippa was staggered at how much impact Richard had had on Lucy's behaviour. How she could have ever considered putting her own happiness above Lucy's, Pippa couldn't now imagine. She felt she'd been caught up in a weird bubble for several months, where her sensible head had gone walkabout and she'd been oblivious to what really mattered. Maybe that's what rebound relationships did to you.

And *she* was happier too, Pippa realised. She was sleeping better and felt as if a great weight had lifted from her shoulders, as she had finally taken control of her own life. Ever since Dan had left, it felt as if she had let events dictate to her what to do, and now finally she was taking charge of her own destiny. It was up to her to save the farm. But if only it were that simple.

Uneasily, she looked across the road. The surveyors had been back and forth over the last few weeks, and there had been a couple of rotivators in one of the fields. Batty Jack was running a war of attrition, letting sheep and turkeys into the fields on a regular basis, as promised, and deflating the tyres on the surveyors' cars (illegal or not) just to annoy them. He seemed to have the knack of invisibility though, and avoided detection, despite the installation of CCTV on gates at Blackstock Farm. He and his fellow campers seemed well ensconced in the woods now, and were daily joined by newcomers. There was real momentum growing for the campaign, but still Pippa felt anxious.

Despite Jack's efforts, with a month to go before the planning meeting, there seemed to be an awful lot of activity on the land, with old fences being knocked down and security fencing and lighting going up in the yard. And the voices in Hope Christmas who were pro the hotel seemed to be growing in number daily. There had been several bad-tempered clashes in the letters pages of the local paper. Pippa was growing genuinely concerned that they might not, after all, be able to stop the hotel being built. But at least by the look of things she could save the farm. And that was something.

'Don't like the plane! Don't like the plane!' Lou Lou was sitting next to Mel wailing her head off as the engines started and the plane took off.

Cat didn't entirely blame her granddaughter. She wasn't all that sold on flying either. But to celebrate Mel's eighteenth birthday, and as a reward for all the hard work she (and some of the effort James) had put into their exams, Noel and Cat had decided they'd stretch to a villa this year for the family holiday, instead of two cramped apartments.

She hadn't factored in Lou Lou's reaction to flying. They'd never taken their own children on a plane so young – life had always been fraught enough without holidays abroad – and Cat hadn't quite twigged how much noise a pissed off toddler could make on a plane.

A lot as it turned out.

'It's all right, sweetheart,' Mel was holding her daughter close and soothing her with a lollipop, 'this will help if your ears are hurting.'

Which apparently, as the whole plane could hear, they were.

James started pulling funny faces at her, which thankfully managed to calm her down. That was a relief. Cat had visions of them being the most unpopular family on the plane. No one liked crying children on planes, not even ones you were related to.

Once they were safely airborne, Lou Lou settled down

with pens and paper, Paige and Ruby hooked themselves into their iPods, and James and Mel sat quietly chatting. Cat leant back and relaxed her head on Noel's shoulder.

'This may well be our last family holiday,' she said. 'Who knows what Mel will want to do next year. We must make the most of it.'

'I think they'll be coming for a while longer yet,' said Noel. 'The kids keep telling me they'll come as long as they don't have to pay.'

Cat laughed. 'But you know what I mean. They're growing up, and it's all changing.'

'I know,' said Noel, 'but just think, then we can go on holidays together, just the two of us.'

'Now that *is* something worth looking forward to,' said Cat, taking his hand. It seemed like a lifetime ago since they'd gone away on holidays, just the two of them. It would be nice to revive that lovely intimacy they'd had on trips to Greece, Portugal, Italy, when they'd been young and carefree and the thought of children was a distant fantasy. 'Though I can't begin to imagine it.'

'Me neither,' said Noel. 'But I shall look forward to it.'

He raised a glass. 'To Happy Holidays, Cat.'

'Happy Holidays, Noel,' echoed Cat.

# Chapter Twenty-Three

'This is definitely the life,' said Cat as the family sat themselves down at a restaurant by the sea, in the pretty town of Puerto de Pollensa in Majorca. All except Paige, who had been so thrilled to find a wifi link for the first time today, she was standing by the restaurant entrance happily snapchatting her friends. The sun was setting, casting golden shadows on the purple bougainvillea that covered the walled area where they were sitting, and the sea was lapping gently at the shore. Two small kittens played happily in the corner, much to Lou Lou's delight, as she sat contentedly scribbling on some paper that Mel had brought with her, and sucking the lollipop given her by the waiter. Ruby was happy as she'd spotted pizza on the menu. She'd tried calamari this holiday, but that was the extent of her daring, pizza and chicken had remained her diet for the rest of the time. James had dashed straight into the kitchen to make friends with the chef and swap recipes, as he had in every restaurant they'd been in all holiday. He'd come back with so many tips, Cat felt a new Mediterranean cookbook coming on. Perhaps they could do it together, if James could be bothered.

Paige, meanwhile, stunning at fourteen, was turning heads wherever they went, and enjoying the adulation much more than her parents, who were on alert to make sure she didn't fall for some unsuitable thirty-something waiter – after Mel, Cat felt they couldn't be too careful.

Mel seemed to be having a nice time too, relaxing for the first time in months, and really enjoying playing with Lou Lou. It was doing them both good.

Cat looked at her family. She was so proud of them, and so lucky to have them. It didn't seem possible that all those years of hard work had disappeared, nor that in the next year her eldest would be beginning her own journey into the world, while her youngest was making the transition to secondary school. But it was true. And it was making Cat feel old, and besides her gorgeous daughters, ugly.

'For the beautiful Mama,' the waiter had brought her a rose. Cat thought he meant it for Mel, as had happened frequently on this holiday, but he proffered it to her.

'So young for all these children,' the waiter said gallantly.

It was cheesy and it was a lie to butter up tourists, but who was Cat to complain? Perhaps not so old and ugly after all.

Marianne was sitting on a freezing cold beach, having an altogether different holiday experience. Watching two miserable and cold children attempting to build sandcastles was no fun at all. She and Gabe had tried their best, but the weather was lousy, it was cold and damp, and rain was threatening from the sea.

'Bugger this,' she said. 'Let's go and find fish and chips.'

Eve and Steven had elected to spend the day together, as Eve didn't 'do' beaches, or at least not cold wet ones in Wales, and Marianne's mum had looked at the weather and opted to stay in the caravan. To Marianne's amusement, she'd muttered something about morning bingo in the bar area.

'You don't want to go back to the caravan park do you?' said Gabriel with a grin.

'No, I bloody don't.'

The caravan park had been a great disappointment. The play area promised in the brochure had consisted of a couple of swings, a rickety slide and a roundabout even the twins thought was boring; the indoor swimming pool was out of action, and it had been too cold to use the outdoor one. The heating in the caravan was non-existent, and they were spending a fortune on electricity cards to keep vaguely warm. They'd barely bathed the children all week, who were so hyped up from being cooped up indoors, Marianne had a feeling they were turning feral.

'Hardly the Costa del Sol, is it?' said Gabriel. 'I know how to show you the good life.'

'You certainly do. Remind me next year to say no if you mention a caravan holiday again,' said Marianne, as they packed up and carried their junk back to the car. They got the twins' raincoats on and brollies up just in time, as a torrential burst of rain came sweeping across the bay. It was bleakly beautiful here, with wonderful empty sandy beaches, and mountains in the background that seemed to go back as far as the eye could see. Today, they were shrouded in mist yet again. In different circumstances, Marianne might have enjoyed it, but it was hard to stay positive when you were perpetually damp and spending a fortune on staying warm and dry.

'What the hell are we going to do this afternoon?' said Gabriel as they squeezed their way into a packed fish and chip shop.

'Um, let's see' – Marianne consulted her iPhone – 'there's an aquarium—'

'Quariam,' clapped Daisy.

'Fishes please,' said Harry.

'Thirty miles away,' said Marianne. Oh god, a long drive in the rain to an aquarium which probably had three fish in it. Was it worth the aggro?

'It beats sitting in the caravan listening to the rain come down,' said Gabriel, which was true. They'd spent a lot of the previous day doing that and the twins had been wild by the end of it.

'True,' said Marianne, 'and whatever the weather, at least we're all together.'

And at the end of the day on a family holiday, that's what it was all about.


'So this is working out you think?' said Dan, as he came into see the children after feeding the cows.

'Yes, I think so. Come and look at the books,' said Pippa. 'If I can get the Halloween thing and the Winter Wonderland off the ground, we should be in a much better place than we were at the start of the year. Enough to keep the bank manager happy for a bit, at any rate. And if we carry on like it . . .'

'Yes?'

'We might not have to sell. It's worth the risk, don't you think?'

'What about Richard?'

'Ah, Richard.' Pippa hadn't quite got round to telling Dan about Richard, and she'd asked the children to wait for her to find a good moment. Which this seemed to be.

'What do you mean, ah Richard?' said Dan.

'He asked me to marry him,' said Pippa.

'Congratulations,' said Dan. She searched his face to see if he was upset by the news, but he didn't appear to be, particularly.

'And I said no,' finished Pippa.

'You – what?' Dan looked stunned. 'But I thought you and he . . .'

'I wasn't ready,' said Pippa, silently thinking I may never be ready to marry anyone else ever again.

'Oh,' said Dan. 'I'm sorry.'

'Don't be,' said Pippa, 'it was for the best. But it means – well if you want things to stay the same, they can. At least for now. You and I can be curators for the kids until they're older, and they can buy us out if and when they're ready to.'

'And what about what happens across the lane?' said Dan, nodding in the direction of Old Joe's farm. 'It's a lot of money they're offering us.'

'I know,' said Pippa, 'but I really do want to make a go of this. And I'll do it alone if I have to.'

She meant it to. Somehow, even if she had to work every hour of every day for the rest of her life, she would succeed in keeping the farm. She was disappointed by Dan's silence. She'd hoped for more.

'If that's not what you want, I'll try and raise the capital somehow,' Pippa was gabbling, she was so desperate for Dan to agree.

'I'll think about it,' he said. 'Let's wait and see what the planning committee decide. If the hotel goes ahead, it might make it difficult for your plans to go ahead.'

'Thanks for the vote of confidence.'

'That's not what I meant,' said Dan. 'I'm trying to be practical. We might not be able to change the tide.'

'I'm going to have a damned good go,' said Pippa. 'I'll change my name to Cnut, if you want me to.'

'And if anyone succeeds, it will be you,' said Dan, 'but this . . . we're living a kind of half life. I think it would be better for us both to start afresh.'

Pippa looked at him in dismay. She'd hoped without Richard being around, Dan would have been more likely to see things her way, but he seemed less interested than ever.

The only way she was going to do this, it seemed, was completely on her own.

# Chapter Twenty-Four

'Thank god we're home,' Marianne said as they piled through the door. Though there had been moments of fun, the holiday had been mainly high farce. Culminating in Eve having a dramatic hissy fit with Steven (Steven refused to say about what) one day and storming off in the wind and the rain. Steven and Gabriel had tracked her down to a late night café – thankfully not a pub – where she'd sat sobbing for half an hour about how lonely she was. It transpired Eve hadn't been taking her medication while they were away. The first thing Gabriel organised when they got back was a trip to the emergency doctor, who warned her that she might have to go back to hospital if she continued in this vein, which seemed to be enough to make her very meek and regretful. Particularly when Steven told her off.

'You can't keep doing this, Mum,' he said, angrier than Marianne had ever seen him before. 'Dad and Marianne don't deserve it. And neither do I.'

Eve had been totally stricken and remorseful after that, and when she recovered from her bout of crying, even apologised to Marianne, 'I'm sorry if my being here has made it difficult for you and Gabriel,' she said. 'When I started work, Vera mentioned possibly moving into the flat above the café. I might take her up on it. I've been in your hair too long.'

Marianne was so taken aback by this, she mumbled something about there being no hurry, but then she wished she'd been firmer.

'It will work out,' said Gabriel. 'Don't worry.'

Which was easy for him to say.

So yes, Marianne was glad to be home, even though it meant all hands to the deck to bring the harvest in, from theirs and Pippa's fields. Marianne alternated between staying with the twins and providing provisions as necessary, and going out on the fields with Gabe and Steven. The hours were long, but there was something immensely satisfying about driving back down country lanes in the tractor as the sun set, exhausted from the physical labour, but knowing a job had been well done.

Pippa informed her that in their absence the surveyors from Blackstock Farm had been looking over at their fields, measuring up and taking photos, which was a bit disconcerting, but Marianne had seen no evidence of anyone till one day, she'd taken the twins and Patch down to the stream for a picnic. She was surprised and dismayed to see Luke Nicholas with two other men in fluorescent jackets, who seemed to be checking out the landscape.

'Hi,' said Marianne, though she didn't feel in the slightest like talking to him. 'Isn't this common land?'

'It is,' said Luke, with that devastating smile, which would have once turned her insides to mush, 'but the boundary is disputed, and we're checking out if we can spread as far as here.'

'And I shall go home and check too,' said Marianne. 'Because if I have anything to do with it you won't be able to build here.'

'Marianne, Marianne, what can I do to persuade you differently?' said Luke.

'Nothing,' said Marianne.

She was vaguely aware of a pair of birds, hovering in the sky above them. Kestrels? She wondered. Or were they the merlins Pippa was so desperate to prove were there?

'But we'll be bringing jobs into the area,' said Luke smoothly.

'Like your eco town?' Marianne asked slyly.

'That was in the wrong place,' said Luke.

'So is this,' argued Marianne.

'You're wrong, it's going to be beneficial for Hope Christmas,' said Luke.

'I don't see how,' said Marianne.

She wished he'd go away. He'd ruined the peace of the afternoon, and unsettled her. This was not how she wanted to spend her days, encountering Luke Nicholas when she least expected it. It made her more determined than ever to oppose the hotel. If Luke were working opposite, life wouldn't be pleasant at all.

Pippa was also thinking about the hotel. Felix Macintyre seemed to have disappeared off the face of the earth, and not bitten on the wildlife idea, which was a pity. As far as Pippa knew there hadn't even been any merlin sightings lately, but from what Jack was telling her, there had been attempts to steal wild bird's eggs, which was a bit worrying. Jack had gathered more people in his makeshift camp, and was reporting aggro from some of the locals keen on the hotel. It made Pippa feel uneasy to think that the development was causing so much upset, she hoped Hope Christmas wasn't going to tear itself in half over the issue.

The wildlife angle had been a long shot, but they needed

to do more. With the planning meeting coming up, Pippa was throwing herself into action. She had been tweeting regularly using the hashtag #savethewoods, plastering the town with leaflets, bombarding the council with letters, and badgering Sarah Carnforth as much as possible, so it didn't slip off her agenda. Luckily, Sarah seemed to totally get what they were after.

'You do realise, though don't you, Pippa,' she said, 'if they lose, they'll just come back with another planning application, or they can take it to the Secretary of State, and if the planning is then approved, you can only appeal through the High Court.'

'That seems grossly unfair,' said Pippa.

Sarah shrugged. 'Who said planning laws were fair. It's the way it is.'

'Well they're not going to have it easy,' said Pippa, 'none of us are going to take this lying down. We'll install ourselves in the woods and pelt them with eggs if necessary.'

'I can't be party to anything illegal,' Sarah insisted hurriedly.

'I wouldn't expect you to be,' said Pippa 'and I was joking. Though the thought of chucking something smelly all over Luke Nicholas and his smarmy crew is rather appealing.'

Miss Woods, on the other hand, was all up for some urban guerrilla action.

'I was quite the campaigner back in the day,' she said. 'I marched against Nam in the 60s, banned the bomb in the 70s and spent a fair proportion of time in the 80s at Greenham Common. I still know a lot of people who can help us, and I'm perfectly happy to join the camp in the woods.'

'I look forward to seeing that,' laughed Pippa.

'A bit of mud doesn't faze me,' said Miss Woods stoutly,

'and I'll make sure we have enough troops to keep the place guarded while we argue things out in the courts.'

Pippa laughed and felt better. Somehow, Miss Woods always made her feel *anything* was possible. Which was just as well, because if she thought too hard about the impossibility of the task ahead it was overwhelming. But then again, she was used to that.

Cat was on edge all morning, as Mel had gone to college on the bus to get her results. She'd promised to ring as soon as she knew, so Cat was busy distracting herself by sitting in her back garden, enjoying the sunshine, and looking up Mediterranean recipes to adapt for her new cookbook, while Ruby played with Lou Lou. She was thinking of calling it *The Mediterranean Diet: A Healthy Way to Live*, and so far Anna was being cautiously encouraging. Maybe she could still have a career doing what she loved. Though she had to admit the country programmes she was getting involved in were fascinating, and it was nice to have another string to her bow, cookery was her first love. She had learnt a lot on these new programmes, but it wasn't the same.

James was upstairs on his Xbox, resolutely pretending he didn't have results next week, while Paige was still in bed, probably texting all her friends. In two years' time it would be her turn, which didn't seem possible somehow. Cat couldn't believe how quickly her children had grown up. The speed at which life seemed to fly past these days, Lou Lou would be at secondary school before they knew it.

'Ruby, run!' Lou Lou was staggering up and down the garden in her pretty little sundress and sunhat, while Ruby played chasing games.

It was a lovely tranquil scene, with the sun bright in an

aquamarine sky. In the distance birds called to one another from the trees, and sheep baaed in the bracken. The hills were awash with bright pink heather, and her own garden was abundant with geraniums, fuchsia and nasturtiums.

*It's no coincidence that people living a Mediterranean diet live longer*, Cat wrote. *As a healthy way of life, it's been long proven, and with the recipes in this book, I can help you recreate some of that healthy living in your daily routine.*

She looked up and sighed, she had been stuck on the same line for the last half an hour. She just couldn't concentrate on what she was doing today.

If Mel hadn't done well, she'd be disappointed and after all that hard work, it seemed unfair. She'd been so stressed over the exam period, juggling her revision with Lou Lou, her blog and her writing, it would be really devastating if she didn't succeed. Cat knew how much these exams meant to her daughter; she deserved to do well.

The phone rang, and Cat nearly jumped out of her skin.

At first she couldn't hear anything, just the sound of incoherent sobs. Oh god, it had gone badly. Cat frantically started to go into organising mode.

'Mel,' she said, 'sweetheart, it doesn't matter, if you didn't get the grades. We can sort something out. You can resit them next year.'

'Mum, I did it,' said Mel. 'I got 4 As.'

And then Cat too, burst into tears.

273

# My Broken Brain

*Day 140 or something. I'm beyond caring. 5am*

Turns out Pippa isn't planning to move in with Richard. I'm glad for the kids' sake, particularly Lucy's. She seems so much happier. Which is great news. Like getting my old daughter back.

Lucy asked me the other day if that meant I was going to move back in. The twenty million dollar question. She really thinks it's still possible. But she's only a child, she can't see how things really are.

How can I go back now?

We're divorced. Pippa's carving a life as a single woman. And now her focus is saving the farm. And she's doing a great job of it.

I've spent nearly three years pushing Pippa away. And it's the one thing I've succeeded in doing well.

I'd say Pippa doesn't need me anymore.

Nice one, Holliday.

I just wish I could make Lucy see, that however we both feel, it's for the best.

One day, it might stop hurting so much.

*September*

# Chapter Twenty-Five

A warm September sun shone out of an azure blue sky. In the woods the magpies were keeping up a consistent chatter. While the swallows swooped through the sky in huge clusters, getting ready no doubt for their trip down south. Pippa wished they could find some evidence of the merlins, but it seemed if they had been there, they were long gone now. Not only that but Jack had reported bits of nest having been destroyed along with some fragments of egg shells. It seemed like their enemies might have chased the birds away.

'So if you can move along, and yes, there's room for more tents up here, and we're stringing some hammocks in the trees, for those who like that kind of thing . . .' Miss Woods was imperiously giving orders as the expansion of the Hope Christmas camp began in earnest. Miss Woods, it turned out seemed to have a myriad of connections with the anarchic underworld, and all sorts of professional protestors had turned up to lend a hand.

Pippa stood watching in awe as so many strangers arrived to give up their time and efforts for her protest. There were banners and posters, and tents, and people making tea and coffee. A warm camaraderie had sprung up between the locals and the incomers, and lots of friendly banter. It was really rather wonderful. She was glad she'd managed to persuade both the local newspaper, and the TV to come down. It should make the evening bulletin.

'From little acorns, great trees grow,' said Ralph who'd appeared as if by magic, with Charlie. 'Any sign of your merlins yet?'

'Sadly no,' said Pippa, 'we think someone might have chased them away.'

'You never know,' said Ralph, 'they might not have gone far.'

'Maybe,' said Pippa. 'There is so much other wildlife as well though. We need to persuade LK Holdings that what's here needs protecting, and that they're developing in the wrong place.'

'Agreed,' said Ralph, 'and I'm sure you're just the person to do it.'

It was nice that someone could be certain of the outcome.

'Miss Woods is doing a great job,' said Pippa, looking over at the makeshift camp, 'if it was down to her efforts alone, I wouldn't be at all worried.'

'The more noise we make . . .' said Ralph.

Pippa smiled. She did feel a bit more hopeful. Ralph had a knack of making everything seem better.

They had had such a huge outpouring of support, including her Twitter campaign, which was taking on a life of its own, with #savethewoods trending. Although there'd also been the inevitable trolling from disaffected parties – Pippa had traced the particularly vehement *Die you bitch* comments to one of Keeley's cronies, who'd been warned off coming anywhere near the woods and threatened with the police – in the main, people had been on their side. Maybe the council would listen to public opinion. After all, they'd succeeded in saving Vera's post office, and Lucy's respite care home. Anything was possible if you put your mind to it. They could do this.

Just then a familiar face came up to her, looking rather sheepish, and holding a placard.

'Richard?' Pippa was gobsmacked. She hadn't heard from him in several weeks. What on earth was he doing here?

'Look, I know you don't want to be with me, anymore,' he said in a rush, 'and that's fine. But I've been thinking about everything you've been doing, and I may have been wrong about your woods. If nothing else, I underestimated you. So I'd really like to help. What would you like me to do?'

Cat was on the phone. Angela was haranguing her about Kay's latest misdemeanours. The honeymoon period was clearly over.

'She doesn't allow me any freedom!' complained Angela. 'She treats me like a child.'

'Would you like to come to us for the weekend?' suggested Cat. 'Give you both a break from each other.'

Her heart sank at the thought. It was coming up to the end of the holidays, and she'd earmarked the weekend for Ruby's new school uniform, and other back to school kind of activities. Plus, she'd promised to look in on Pippa's camp at some point. Oh well, Angela would just have to go with the flow.

'Could I?' said Angela. 'That would be wonderful. Noel can come and pick me up on Saturday morning.'

Saturday morning was always manic in their house and all the activities were starting again. Ruby had ballet, James football, and Paige piano.

'How about Lou Lou, Ruby and I come down on Friday and get you,' said Cat tactfully. 'That might be easier.'

'Well, if you're sure,' said Angela.

'Of course I am,' Cat lied, 'but is it really as bad as all that?'

'Worse,' said Angela. 'She doles out my own money to me. Can you believe it? As if I were a child. I feel in prison. You have to come and rescue me.'

Cat had questioned the wisdom of letting Kay have access to her mother's bank account – apparently it was 'easier' if she had Angela's cash card, as now she was more immobile she couldn't get out as much – but had been shouted down. Seemed that she'd been right.

Resolving to get Noel to have a word with his sister, who like her mother, could be a control freak, Cat put the phone down. Honestly, it would have been easier to have had Angela living with them, with all the upheaval that entailed, than being on the end of the phone listening to the latest dramas. She needed to drive down to Bedford on Friday like a hole in the head.

'Look, Nana, look. I done painting,' Lou Lou came up to her smiling. She was covered from head to toe in paint. And somehow, during the course of the conversation, so was the kitchen table.

Cat sighed as she went to clear up. It didn't seem five minutes ago that she was clearing up after Ruby when she'd done similar. Sometimes, she felt she was living in groundhog day.

Marianne had asked Jean to come and babysit, and she and Steven were headed for the woods to join the protest. Steven was going back to school the following week, and Marianne had been enjoying a few days with him exclusively. Her stepson had a lot of his father in him, and was good company. He had also been really helpful when Eve had finally moved out into the flat above Vera's café, and

Marianne had enjoyed packing up Eve's stuff with him, and helping her get settled in. Since Eve had left, they had a bit more time with each other, and Marianne was relishing it guiltily. She still couldn't believe the little boy she'd known when she first came to Hope Christmas was growing up into such a handsome young teenager. And a fine one at that. Kind, considerate, and immensely good fun to be around.

'So tell me,' she said, taking advantage of this opportunity to have a chat with her stepson for the first time in a while, 'how are things with your mum? Have you managed to sort out what was bothering her on holiday?'

Steven shook his head.

'Not exactly,' he said, looking sad. 'I want to help her, but she doesn't always want my help. She thinks I'm a kid still and I'm not.'

'She probably doesn't want to worry you,' said Marianne. 'And maybe she feels guilty.'

'Oh I know she feels guilty,' said Steven, 'she's always apologising for how crap she was when I was little. But it's ok, I get it. It's her illness. She can't help it.'

'That's very mature of you, Steven,' said Marianne. 'I think she's lucky you feel that way.'

'Well I do,' said Steven, 'and I've been thinking – well this is what we were rowing about actually . . .'

He looked awkward and unsure of his ground, so Marianne prompted him, 'And?'

'I know Dad will go mad,' he said, 'but I worry about Mum all on her own. She's much worse when she's lonely. She was better all the time she was with Darren. I think I want to go and live with her for a bit, keep her company.'

'Oh,' said Marianne, quite taken aback. She knew Gabriel would be furious.

'But Mum said no, on account of Dad, and I know Dad will never agree, so . . .'

'If that's what you really want, I'll talk to him about it,' said Marianne, as they approached the campsite. 'You never know, maybe he'll be up for it. We'll talk about it later, I promise.'

Steven looked doubtful, but they couldn't discuss it further, because as soon as they arrived, Miss Woods whisked Steven off to help put up tents, and sort out banners, while Marianne went to find Pippa, who was mid TV interview.

'How's it going?' asked Marianne, as Pippa finished.

'Good, I think,' said Pippa. 'It's hard to tell though. While we have a lot of support, there are still plenty of people who are against us.'

Marianne smiled. 'Have faith. Pippa the Campaign Queen never fails.'

'We'll see,' said Pippa. 'Can you do me a favour and help me hand out tea and biscuits to all these amazing people who've turned up. Honestly, I'm overwhelmed.'

'I see someone has come out of the woodwork to help,' said Marianne, with a sly look, pointing Richard's way. She and Cat had hoped after all Pippa's problems, she might get a happy ending, but it clearly wasn't to be.

Pippa blushed. 'Well I wasn't expecting him.'

'And?' asked Marianne archly.

'And, nothing,' confessed Pippa. 'I'm quite enjoying being on my own at the moment. I don't think I need the complication of Richard again. I'm not sure it's worth all the hassle. I'd rather keep the farm alone, than give it up, settle with Richard, and then regret it.'

Marianne smiled. 'Yeah, I get that,' she said. 'I just want you to be happy.'

'And I am, or as happy as I'm going to be,' said Pippa, 'so don't worry about me. I'm fine.'

At the end of a long, positive and enjoyable day, Marianne and Steven walked home, leaving the campers to settle down in their hammocks and tents. As they left, someone was sorting out a barbecue, and the sound of guitars had started, Marianne reflected on what Pippa had said. Happiness didn't always come from being with a partner. She thought about what Steven had discussed with her earlier. It sounded as though Eve was really lonely. Now she wasn't actually living under their roof, Marianne found it easier to feel sorry for her. Eve had had a hard life, and in the last couple of years, things had gone badly wrong for her. So to her surprise, Marianne found herself saying, 'You know what you mentioned earlier, about your mum. I think you might be right, perhaps living with her is something you should think about.'

# Chapter Twenty-Six

'Here we are,' said Cat as she opened the front door and let Angela in.

She'd been shocked by the state of her mother-in-law, when she arrived at Kay's. Angela looked thin and tired, and smaller than when Cat had last seen her, as if she'd diminished somehow. She'd leant on Cat's arm coming to and from the car – Angela had never leant on anyone in her entire life – and to Cat's dismay, had seemed a little bewildered at first, as if forgetting for a moment why Cat was there. Cat felt a sinking in her stomach. Please, no. Don't let Angela go the same way as Mum, that seemed so unfair. Angela might not be her own mum, but she'd been a damned good stand in since Cat's mother, Louise, had first become ill.

Before they left, Kay had bossily told Cat what Angela needed, and Angela what Angela needed, until Cat wanted to scream. Kay had taken to talking to her mum as if she were a slow and very stupid child, and it infuriated Cat. It was just as well Noel hadn't been with her, he'd have been furious, and there'd have only been another argument.

But it was worrying. Where had her lively – if sometimes demanding and difficult – mother-in-law gone? Angela just seemed to take it meekly, though there had been a flash of fire, when Kay had tried to put her coat on for her. 'I'm not a complete imbecile you know,' she'd snapped, causing Kay to sigh a martyred sigh, and whisper to Cat, 'Good luck with her. You've no idea what it's been like. Had I known . . .'

Cat, who had a very good idea what it could be like, had bit back the retort that it was all Kay's idea to have Angela with her, but instead smiled sweetly, and said, 'I'm sure we'll cope,' and steered her mother-in-law out of the house. The atmosphere had felt unwelcoming, stuffy and down-right hostile. No wonder Angela couldn't wait to get out.

'Come on, Angela,' she'd said cheerfully. 'We'll get you home, and tomorrow we can go on a lovely long walk in the hills.'

One thing Angela always loved about coming to Hope Christmas was walking in the hills.

'Oh no!' said Kay in horror. 'You can't be serious. Mum isn't fit enough for that. She needs rest and silence. She won't be up for it.'

'Oh,' said Cat, her mother-in-law wasn't that old, and had been perfectly capable of walking five miles last time she came to stay. 'I'm sure we'll manage.'

It wasn't her place to have a family row – Noel managed them quite well without her help – so she was delighted when they got back home and settled Angela in.

Angela seemed happy enough, too, enjoying playing with Lou Lou, and drinking a cup of tea. Her earlier vagueness seemed to have disappeared, and Cat breathed a sigh of relief. Perhaps it would be ok after all.

'What's all this about Steven going to live with Eve?' Gabriel came in from the fields with Steven, looking like thunder. Oh dear. Steven had obviously taken it upon himself to tell his dad their idea. Marianne had been waiting for the right moment. This evidently wasn't it. 'What on earth were you thinking? What if she's ill again? Steven's only fourteen for god's sake. It's not on.'

'But it would be different if I was living with Mum,' protested Steven, 'then she might not get ill.'

'And you think I didn't spend several years thinking that?' Gabriel said angrily. 'It's not going to happen, Steven. You being there won't make your mum better. When you're old enough, you'll understand.'

'I am not a kid anymore! Why don't you ever listen?' shouted Steven, and ran up the stairs in fury, slamming his bedroom door shut.

'Why didn't you discuss this with me, first?' Gabriel demanded, he was still very angry, and Marianne couldn't blame him. This wasn't the way she'd anticipated him finding out.

'It came up in conversation yesterday,' said Marianne. 'I wasn't trying to cause a problem. It was Steven's idea, and I think he might have a point. It seems to me Eve is very lonely and maybe Steven living there would help her.'

'You've changed your tune,' said Gabriel, 'I thought you couldn't wait to get shot of her. Now it transpires, it's my son you can't want to get shot of.'

'That's not fair,' said Marianne. 'I love having Steven here, of course I do. I want what's best for him. Look, I'm sorry, it was just an idea. I wish I hadn't brought it up.'

'After everything that's happened, and all that we went through to keep Steven with us last time,' said Gabriel. 'You know what Eve's like. This will be a fad. I can't believe you'd even think I'd let that happen.'

'But it's different now,' argued Marianne. 'This isn't Eve's idea, it's Steven's He's old enough to know his own mind – and we've got the twins.'

'So that's ok, then,' said Gabriel, 'we can lose Steven, because he's not *ours*, but we've still got the twins.'

'That's not what I meant,' said Marianne, 'you're being difficult.'

'I'm not the one suggesting breaking our family up,' said Gabriel belligerently.

'And neither am I,' said Marianne, 'I just feel sorry for Eve—'

'So do I,' said Gabriel. 'And I'm happy she still sees Steven, but his home is here, and always will be.'

'But she's so lonely, Gabe,' said Marianne, 'don't you think—'

'No I don't,' said Gabriel. 'Eve's living in the village now and can meet plenty of people there. We've done enough to help her. It's not our problem, Marianne, not anymore.'

Pippa was on the phone sorting out the hiring of equipment for the Halloween Spooktacular she was planning. It was turning out to be quite a headache, but a fun headache. She'd roped in a number of students from the Drama College in Shrewsbury to play scary parts, hired a couple of smoke machines, worked out a maze in one of the barns with Nathan and George's help, and despite all the usual bureaucratic nonsense, it actually felt like it was coming together. She'd looked into how other farms did similar things, and spoken to several farmers who reckoned it was their most profitable activity of the year, so she was hoping for great things.

Although, she was hoping for even better from Christmas. She'd planned to create Santa's Snow Palace in the biggest barn, and even wangled some reindeer from Ralph's estate.

Ralph had also kindly agreed to be Father Christmas, and with the help of the drama students as elves, she was hoping she could create a really magical feel. If both ventures were successful, Pippa felt they had a good chance of starting the New Year with a nice healthy profit, which meant she should be able to run more events next year. She was still feeling incredibly nervous about the future of the farm, but *if* things worked out the way she hoped, in a couple of years she might finally be in a position to buy Dan out.

Since Richard had reappeared to help with the campaign, Dan seemed once again to have melted into the background. He never came into the kitchen for a cup of tea anymore, and when he brought the children home, refused to spend any more time with Pippa than he had to. She'd made it clear to the children that Richard wasn't about to come back on the scene, but whether the message had got through to Dan or not, she didn't know.

It was true she had seen Richard a couple of times, but having quickly established their relative positions on the farm remained the same, she'd made sure he knew that their relationship was not going anywhere, and he appeared to have accepted it. To his credit, it hadn't stopped Richard from being involved in the campaign, frequently turning up to 'man the barricades' as he put it, which made her smile. Richard was hardly the radical type.

Dan, on the other hand, seemed to be resolutely ignoring the campaign, which made her sad. She knew he loved those woods as much as she did. Time was, he'd have been there fighting with her. Every inch of the way.

When she came off the phone, she realised Dan was silently standing in the kitchen, patiently waiting for her to finish. She was surprised, as it had been several weeks since he'd voluntarily come in the house.

'Is everything ok?' she asked.

'Fine,' said Dan, 'but I thought you ought to know. I've just run into Ralph Nicholas. And they've brought the planning meeting forward.'

'Oh?' said Pippa, the meeting was planned for next week.

'Yes,' said Dan. 'It's tonight, the planning meeting is tonight.'

# Chapter Twenty-Seven

Marianne drove down the lane, late as usual. Pippa had rung her to let her know what was happening, and she'd filled Gabriel in, before leaving him to put the kids to bed, while she hotfooted to Shrewsbury where the planning meeting was taking place. Pippa had already gone, otherwise they'd have shared a lift. Marianne felt bad dumping Gabriel in it, particularly as they had barely spoken since the row about Eve, but she wanted to be there to hear the verdict.

When Marianne arrived, she discovered a noisy demonstration outside the council office by some of the campsite followers, who were holding up placards and shouting 'Save our woods!', while on the other side of the entrance a rival group were shouting, 'What do we want? A hotel for Hope Christmas! When do we want it? Now!'

Inside it was even more chaotic. So many people had turned up for the vote, the council chambers were full and people were milling around outside listening to the action from speakers which were wired into the meeting room. Despite the two opposing groups, the atmosphere was mild and festive. Some people had brought sandwiches and Miss Woods was dispensing tea from a large flask. Batty Jack appeared to have a flask of his own, which Marianne suspected didn't contain tea.

'Have I missed anything?' asked Marianne, as she found Pippa in the crowd.

'They haven't got to us yet,' said Pippa. 'We're the fourth item I think, and they're on the second.'

She glanced around, looking at the hotel supporters' group who were piled in one corner talking amongst themselves animatedly.

'There are a lot of people here who want the hotel,' she said. 'That might have an impact on the council's decision.'

'And more who don't,' said Marianne, pointing out the crowd round Miss Woods, and the people still pouring in the door, who judging by their unkempt clothing had come from the camp.

'I suppose,' said Pippa, but she still looked jittery.

Marianne could make out an interminable mumble from the speakers over the sounds of the crowds, as one of the councillors was spouting forth about an ongoing problem with drains.

'How come the meeting got moved?' said Marianne. 'I thought it was at the end of the month.'

'So did we,' said Pippa. 'Sneaky bastards thought they'd get it in before anyone noticed. Luckily Ralph found out, and they hadn't bargained for the Hope Christmas grapevine. Once Miss Woods had let Diana Carew know, the whole town knew.'

'What's your gut feeling saying?' asked Marianne.

'My gut feeling seems to have gone awol tonight,' said Pippa, ruefully. 'Word on the street is that the councillors are pretty divided on the issue, and with so many people in the town supporting the development it's not going to be clear cut. The balance could still be in our favour though.'

An hour or so passed, during which Marianne regretted

rushing off so quickly, as the meeting and chat seemed to go on forever. She was feeling literally sick with nerves by nine o'clock, when they finally moved onto the Hope Christmas Woods. What if they didn't succeed? What then? Their whole lives would be turned upside down.

The arguments flowed. Some councillors feeling there had been enough building in the area, one declaring, to so many cheers from the public gallery the chairman threatened expulsions, that she'd had enough of the 'ravishing of our precious countryside'. But depressingly the tone of the argument seemed more in favour of the proposals than against, with several councillors, none of whom lived anywhere near Hope Christmas, seeming to think it would be fantastic for Shropshire to have more luxury hotels. Marianne was surprised they weren't demanding one in every town, they seemed so enthusiastic. They were met with huge cheers from the Yummy Mummies and their friends.

Marianne looked at Pippa anxiously. They'd been hoping that the planning wouldn't be granted. What if they were wrong?

Cat and Noel snuck into the County Council building hopelessly late, just as a councillor from the other side of the county closed his argument.

'He's given a very strong case for the hotel bringing in much needed jobs not just for Hope Christmas, but the outlying villages,' whispered Pippa, filling them in as they took their seats.

Tony Morrow, their local councillor, got up to speak, pointing out that Hope Christmas already had a thriving tourist economy, and asking for whose benefit the hotel complex was – hardworking locals who couldn't afford the prices of spa treatments? Or rich people who would spend the whole weekend being pampered there without stepping foot in Hope Christmas? 'Yes, the hotel complex will bring people to the area but they won't spend money here,' he said, reeling off an impressive list of statistics about hotels that LK Holdings had brought into previous areas, which had caused more problems than they'd solved. 'If anything, it is likely to have a detrimental effect on the local economy, which is not what we need, not for this special place, which we know and love,' he concluded triumphantly to thunderous applause and more whoops and cheers from the gallery.

'Go, Tony Morrow!' said Cat. 'I never knew he had it in him.' Tony Morrow had always struck her as a rather ineffectual councillor. Cat had once had dealings with him concerning traffic calming measures near the primary school, and he'd been about as much use as a wet weekend in November.

The speaker after Tony proved to be not quite so compelling. 'It's so important that we don't let business decisions destroy our environment,' she droned so drearily Cat felt like screaming. She found herself drifting off, thinking back to the chaos she and Noel had left at home. Paige had come home with a detention slip for having cheeked her teacher, Mel was in the dumps about how difficult A level year was going to be, and Angela had declared firmly she wanted to stay on for another week, resulting in a long and tedious phone call with Kay, trying to subtly explain that her mother was in fact a grown up, of sound mind and could stay as long as she liked.

Noel had started the conversation, but it had got so heated, Cat had had to finish it, promising to take the greatest care of her mother-in-law (as if she wouldn't) and that they'd review the situation in a week. It had been quite a relief to leave the house . . .

She turned back as Ms Boring sat down to muted applause, and Simon Clancy, the councillor for Hope Christmas South (otherwise known as Smooth Simon), locally rumoured to be in the pockets of any number of entrepreneurial builders, got up to speak.

Cat looked at Pippa anxiously. Smooth Simon was known to be one hell of an operator. God alone knew what *he* was going to have to say.

Pippa's heart sank as Simon Clancy talked. Producing facts and figures that demonstrated the benefits that LK Holdings' plans would bring to the area. 'This can only be a good thing for our town and community,' he said with such conviction, he clearly had the council eating out of his hand. Indeed, his voice was so mesmerising and enticing, for a minute there, he even had Pippa thinking he had a point. Oh hell, it was going to be incredibly hard standing up against this.

'One of the contentious issues of this project, is how we balance the legitimate needs of nature with the forward-looking plans for a modern outlook for Hope Christmas,' Simon was saying. 'People are no longer prepared to stay in b&bs and poky little hotels for a weekend away. They want luxury, and spas and the things this hotel can offer. For too long we've been saying the two things are incompatible, but LK Holdings have assured me they will protect the wildlife on the site – they are even suggesting turning part of it into a small sanctuary, which I think would address many of the concerns that my constituents have, and which I also share. Felix Macintyre, the CEO, is certainly keen for this to happen, and Luke Nicholas, his second in command, who is himself a local, also wants to retain the character of the area.'

'Luke Nicholas!' snorted Noel, with whom he'd had dealings when the eco town was being proposed. 'Since when has he cared about the local area?'

'Ssh,' said Pippa, as Simon continued.

'To vote against the proposal, is to leave Hope Christmas far behind. So I urge you tonight, to vote for it, and give the village what it needs to bring itself thoroughly into the twenty first century.'

He sat down to wild applause from the council chambers and boos from the public gallery. Again the chair shushed them, and called everyone to order, but Simon's speech had left everyone restive. There were shouts from the pro crowd of 'Give us our hotel now!' which were met with 'Don't destroy the woods!' from their side. The debate continued for a further fifteen minutes, but it seemed to be going nowhere, so the chair finally said, 'We are now going to have the vote. So I declare half an hour's pause before we resume.'

'That's it,' said Noel gloomily. 'Bloody Simon Clancy's swung it the wrong way. If only Tony Morrow had spoken last.'

'We haven't lost yet,' said Pippa stubbornly, but her heart was sinking. They always knew it was going to be tight, but now? It was too close to call.

The half an hour turned into an hour, and a sombre silence fell over the crowd, the cheery rebellious spirits of earlier dying down as both sides realised the count could go either way.

Finally at midnight, when Pippa felt she might scream with the tension, the chair called everyone to order.

'Concerning planning permission for Hope Christmas

Woods, and Blackstock Farm, planning is hereby granted to LK Holdings,' he said to utter pandemonium.

There were huge cheers from the Yummy Mummies, who were hugging each other with glee, and groans of despair from the campers, who looked stunned by the announcement.

'That's not right!' shouted someone from the upper gallery.

'Whose side are you on?' shouted another, while the chair's cries for calm were completely drowned out.

Pippa felt sick to the stomach as the chair struggled to make his voice heard. 'And just to reiterate,' he said, 'there is no right to appeal.'

It was over. They'd lost.

# My Broken Brain

*Worst day in a long while. 1am*

Pippa's just rung to say it's all over. The campaign failed and the fields opposite ours are going to be turned into a hotel.

Despite all Pippa's hard work.

I know she's devastated; so am I. Neither of us wanted this. It's the beginning of the end. The farm won't be able to survive with that opposite us.

Now I really don't think we have any choice. We have to sell up. And I am utterly heartbroken. For Pippa. For the kids. For me. At least if Pippa and I were still together, we could support one another through this. But we're not.

So here I am, alone, in the dark, feeling more fractured than ever.

# Part Four

## *Got my feet on holy ground*

# Last Year

## Christmas Alone

Dan got into the Land Rover and started it up while his mum and dad fiddled about, as ever. Mum was flapping that she'd forgotten something (not presents, Dan had brought them over the previous day, nor booze, because Dan had done that too) ah, apparently it was the cake, which she'd insisted on making to 'save poor Pippa time'. The implications of 'poor Pippa' were not lost on him. It was his fault he was living back at his parents and it was his fault that Pippa had a new boyfriend, Richard, who apparently was going to come for Christmas. Pippa had rung Dan apologetically the day before to ask if it would be all right for Richard to join them, as his own family Christmas wasn't happening. It was Dan's fault too that instead of spending Christmas where he belonged, with his wife and children, he was visiting with his parents, a stranger in his own home. He didn't need Mum to rub it in. He was already feeling lousy enough as it was.

Last year it had been too painful to have Christmas together, so Pippa had gone to Marianne's, and Dan had spent the day working on the farm, before having a late lunch with his parents and retiring to bed. It had been too dismal for words, so when Pippa told him the children were desperate to have Christmas Day together, Dan couldn't say no. The boys had asked him outright in front of his parents if he was coming for Christmas, and Lucy only had to look at him with those begging eyes of hers, and it was a done deal. He could never refuse his daughter anything, however awkward things might be round the Christmas table.

And he did think things were getting better. More civilised. He saw Pippa most days, popping in for tea at some point, trying to make sure he was around for the kids at the end of the day, if he could be, and of course, they still had the farm to run together. At some point they were going to have to come to some decision about the farm. Dan was uncomfortably aware that since his accident, productivity wasn't quite what it had been, and though Pippa was playing the state of the accounts down, he knew in his heart that they were in big trouble. In the past, he wouldn't have cared, somehow they could have worked things out, but now, he just didn't know. They couldn't keep working like this for ever, particularly not with Richard on the scene.

Dan yawned as Mum and Dad finally got in the car, and he drove off to the farm. After a quick Christmas Eve visit to see the kids, when he'd had to swallow his pride and accept that Richard was sitting in *their* lounge watching Christmas TV with *his* family, he'd come home and sat up brooding all night. A year earlier he told Pippa it was all over. He was different since his accident, for him things could never be the same again, and he didn't want Pippa's pity. He loved Pippa, he would always love Pippa, and that was why he had to leave her. He couldn't bear the thought of her becoming resentful with him, because he wasn't the man she married. She said it didn't matter; he knew it did.

And so he'd hardened his heart, and let her go, and now she was starting afresh with someone new. Which was good. It was great in fact. It meant that she was over him, and he couldn't hurt her anymore. And if he kept building the barriers up between them, soon not being with her wouldn't hurt him anymore, either.

By the time they drove into the courtyard of the farm, and were getting out greeting everyone and exchanging Christmas gifts, Dan knew what he had to do. Today, he would give Pippa the best gift of all. He would set her free, so she could have a new life, however much it hurt to do so.

That's what you did for the person you loved.

*October*

## Chapter Twenty-Eight

'It's not over till the fat lady sings,' said Pippa, stubbornly refusing to accept they'd lost, as she and Miss Woods pored over minutes of council meeting notes, trying to work out their next plan of action. Their options appeared to be limited. Planning permission having been granted, it was going to be difficult, if not impossible, to appeal against it. Though Pippa didn't want to admit it, particularly as the Yummy Mummies were being so triumphant every time she went into the café, it did look as though they might be at the end of the road.

In the meantime, they were losing support fast; the camp was slowly disbanding. Winter was coming and the woods weren't exactly a comfortable place to live, particularly not on misty, damp mornings like today. There was a hard core of the visitors who'd promised to stay whatever it took, but the majority had evaporated, back to their normal lives, or the next campaign, or whatever it was they did. Pippa couldn't blame them. The fight looked lost, they might as well go to pastures new, to more winnable campaigns. It hadn't been their fight in the first place.

'What about Ralph's right of way?' she said. 'Surely they can't build on that without his permission?'

'I'd have thought they couldn't,' said Miss Woods, 'but

it does leave us in stalemate. And it won't stop them building everything else.'

'Oh god,' said Pippa gloomily. 'It's going to happen, isn't it? Whatever we do, this time, I don't think it's going to be enough.'

'Don't give up just yet,' said Miss Woods doughtily. 'We'll have to think of something else. Perhaps if they saw what a success you're making of the farm, they could come up with a more imaginative use of the land . . .'

'Maybe,' said Pippa, admiring Miss Woods' resilience, but somehow doubtful that she could be right. That was one bright spot: bookings were healthy for the Spooktacular weekends, the first of which was taking place this weekend. The boys were beside themselves with excitement, looking forward to donning chains and jumping out at people. And Lucy had bossily insisted she was going on the gate, to take people's entrance fees. Only Dan had remained aloof. She'd hoped he'd be persuaded to help out, for the children's sake if not hers, but he seemed to have retreated somewhere very far away and she couldn't reach him. Pippa was more hurt than she would let on to anyone. Her party line if she was asked, was that she was happier on her own, but she wasn't – not really. She missed Dan with a fierce ache, and she was sad that he felt he had no place at her side anymore. All the things they'd fought for together over the years, and now they were barely speaking.

Marianne was also feeling down. Since the planning meeting, there had been more and more activity on the fields opposite theirs, with cars and vans in and out every day. And despite Batty Jack's continued raids on the site, it wasn't making any difference. She wasn't as hopeful as Pippa and felt it was only a matter of time before the bulldozers moved in.

The situation at home was also making her miserable. Though Gabriel had refused to discuss Steven moving in with Eve any further, Marianne knew he was still angry with her, and was brooding about it. An uneasy truce had built up between the three of them on the subject. They skirted around the issue, and Steven hadn't raised it again. He came back to Hope Christmas from school at the weekend as normal, played with the twins, helped on the farm, saw his mum, but said nothing about his future.

But Marianne couldn't stop thinking about it. All these years she'd felt tremendously sorry for Eve, and at times, furious with her too, but now she could see how lonely Eve was. She'd lost her rich boyfriend, her lovely house, her job, and she'd long ago lost her son. And all because of the cruel misfortune of her illness. It didn't make her the easiest of people to deal with, but it was a hard affliction to cope with in your life. Thinking about it made Marianne feel immensely lucky. She had their house, the children, Gabriel. Everything Eve didn't have. Would it be so very hard to let her son live with her, especially if he wanted to?

She didn't like to broach the subject anymore with Gabe, she knew what his reaction would be, but instead, for the first time, she found herself seeking Eve out, going for coffee with her on days when she wasn't working, suggesting a brisk walk on days when she could see Eve was struggling. Because although Eve was continuing to improve all the time, now she was getting to know her better, Marianne could see the effort of staying well was a huge burden on Eve's shoulders.

'It's like it never goes away,' she explained to Marianne on a sunny day when they wandered up to the local reservoir. 'Even when I'm well, it's still lurking there in the background. I know I'll never be properly better, but I can live with that now, I think. And as long as I keep taking my medication, I can keep it at bay.'

When Marianne heard that, she resolved that somehow she had to break the impasse. Somehow she had to make Gabe see that it would be good for Steven to be living with Eve. It was the right thing to do, she felt sure.

'How was your day?' Cat said as Mel came through the door, and watched with joy as Lou Lou launched herself on her mother, 'Mummee!!'

'Ok,' said Mel. 'I missed this little monkey.'

Two seconds later when Lou Lou had a strop about bath time, Mel sighed, 'What was I saying?'

'You used to do that when I came home from work,' reassured Cat. 'It's her punishment to you for being away. Don't fret.'

'God, what's she going to be like next year, when I'm at uni?' said Mel, with a sigh.

'Worse?' said Cat. 'But that's parenthood for you.'

'Gee thanks, Mum, you've made me feel so much better,' said Mel, before disappearing upstairs with a screaming child, while Cat got on with preparing the tea.

Paige wandered in, as usual with her head attached to an electronic device, snapchatting away or whatever it was she was doing, deigning momentarily to engage with anything other than her iPhone to say, 'When's tea?'

'Half an hour,' said Cat. 'And don't you have homework?'

Paige waved her hand airily.

'Homework, what's that, Mum?' said Noel laughing. '"There are more important things to think about like texting and tweeting.'

'Of course, how silly of me,' said Cat, mimicking banging her head against a brick wall, 'why would I imagine something as minor as homework would get in the way of social networking?'

'Sorry, what?' said Paige vaguely, looking up from whatever she'd snapchatted to her friends.

Noel and Cat exchanged glances and burst out laughing.

'Nothing, darling,' said Cat. 'Just keep taking the selfies and you'll be fine.'

Ruby rang five minutes later needing to be picked up from drama, so Cat set off in the car, as she seemed to do constantly these days. Always picking someone up or dropping them off. Mel was the only one yet able to drive, and she had so much on, Cat never liked to ask her. Noel was often not around at the right time. Cat felt like she was a permanent taxi service.

She'd just got in when the phone rang. It was Kay. Now what? Cat wasn't sure she was ready for any more of Kay's dramatics. Angela had finally returned to Kay's a couple of weeks earlier, and as far as Cat was aware, things had settled back in. She'd certainly seemed happy enough, whenever Cat spoke to her on the phone, and Kay and Noel hadn't had any more screaming matches, which was a blessing.

'Cat, have you heard from Mum?' asked Kay, sounding anxious.

'No, not today,' said Cat. 'Why, should I have?'

'She's gone missing. I swear she does this to me on purpose. She knows I have high blood pressure and the doctor says I shouldn't get stressed.' Kay's voice grew high and reedy, 'I can't believe she'd do this to me. So selfish.'

And she's not the only one, thought Cat.

'What happened?' she asked, sensing there was more to this than met the eye, which it transpired, there was.

'All I said to her yesterday was I wondered if living alone was getting too much for her,' said Kay, 'and she went off the deep end.'

'She doesn't live alone, she lives with you,' said Cat automatically, registering concern.

'Living independently, I mean,' said Kay. 'Cat you have no idea what it's like, She is so confused all the time, and it's awful to admit about your own mother, but I really don't think she's quite right in the head.'

'She seemed fine when she was with us,' said Cat, 'maybe she's not very well.'

'There's nothing wrong with her physically,' snapped Kay. 'It's her mind that's going. You don't see her every day.'

This was true, but Angela *had* stayed with them for over a week, and had seemed reasonably with it. Thinking it was wiser to change the subject, Cat said, 'So when did she go missing?'

'Well that's it,' said Kay, 'I don't know. I went to work and she was fine, and came back and the house was all locked up and she wasn't there. And she's not answering her mobile. I mean what's the point of a mobile if it's always switched off? It's a damned nuisance.'

'Have you called the police?' asked Cat, remembering her mother's escapades when the Alzheimer's had started, and beginning to feel anxious.

'Whatever for?' said Kay. 'She's punishing me, I know she is. I do everything for her, and look how she behaves. It's outrageous. So bloody ungrateful.'

And so hard for her to feel grateful *all* the time, thought Cat, but kept her thoughts to herself.

'Well, I think maybe you should,' said Cat. 'Something might have happened to her.'

'Nothing will have happened to her,' snorted Kay. 'She's indestructible.'

314

'Well give it another half an hour,' said Cat, 'but I'd be inclined to ring them anyway, particularly if you say she's confused.'

She thought about all the times Mum had gone missing. Was this the beginning of the end for Angela? She really hoped not. She couldn't bear the thought of Angela going through what Mum had been through, and Noel suffering the way she had. Kay hung up, promising to ring back later and Cat tried to ring Angela – not that she expected her mother-in-law to answer or indeed for it even to be switched on.

'Oh bloody hell,' said Noel, 'where on earth do you think she can be?'

'No idea,' said Cat, who was trying to stop her imagination running riot. Anything could have happened to her. 'Look, I'll just have another trawl of your mum's friends and see if any of them know anything.'

She flicked through her address book, trying the few numbers of Angela's friends and relatives she'd got, but nothing. It was no good, she was just going to have to ring Kay back and persuade her to call the police. Cat was on the verge of doing so, when there was a knock on the door. On the step stood a fraught and rather bedraggled looking Angela, with several bags and an enormous suitcase.

'I know it's ridiculous at my age,' she said, 'but I can't stand living there a moment longer. I'm running away from home.'

# Chapter Twenty-Nine

'So what are you going to do with your runaway?' said Pippa in amusement, when Cat called in for a much needed cup of coffee. Angela had now been with them for over a week, and was showing no signs of wanting to go home, despite Kay's frantic phone calls and suggestions that Angela wasn't in her right mind and needed sectioning. As a precaution, Cat had taken Angela to the doctor, who'd pronounced her slight confusion was the result of a long term urine infection. Within seconds of being on antibiotics, or so it seemed to Cat, Angela had been as right as rain, as sharp as she'd ever been, and not in the slightest bit in danger of losing her marbles.

'I don't know,' said Cat. 'She's refusing point blank to speak to Kay, and I can't really blame her. Noel's also refusing to speak to Kay – though I'm not quite sure why he's taking the moral high ground, it's not like he was all that keen for Angela to live with us. So I keep having to field Kay's phone calls and calm her down, she's quite hysterical. She keeps shouting down the phone that it's a plot and we're after Angela's money. Which is ridiculous, and anyway we can't keep her permanently unless we convert the garage. The house is bursting at the seams. Paige and Ruby are currently sharing, so Angela can have a room, and they're fighting like cat and dog, and Lou Lou's routine seems to have been upset since Angela's been there, which is making Mel fret. The only calm one in the house is James. But even with a bomb under him, I don't expect he'd lose his cool.'

Pippa laughed. 'Boys are certainly different,' she said. 'My two are similar, they're so laid-back sometimes I think they'll never get off their backsides and do anything, but with Lucy I get fireworks.'

'How are things your end?' asked Cat, pleased for a moment not to have to think any more about her domestic chaos. 'Has Richard given up the idea of you getting back together?'

Last she'd heard, Richard was back on the scene and Pippa had been trying to tactfully persuade him that she wasn't interested in pursuing their relationship further.

'Thankfully, yes,' said Pippa, 'and he has been surprisingly helpful about the campaign. Not that it's doing us any good. Miss Woods and I have been looking at it from every angle we can, but I think I might have to admit defeat this time. I think we've got to face the fact we've lost.'

'No,' said Cat. 'After everything you've done. I honestly didn't think the planning application was going to be the end of the road. And I thought our TV segments might make a difference.'

Cat's TV series hadn't aired yet, but had had a lot of interest in the press, and she'd done several radio interviews on the subject.

'I really hoped all the PR I got might help,' she said. 'I've got another article coming out in one of the Sunday mags soon, but it was probably a long shot.'

'It did,' said Pippa, 'everything helped, but it wasn't enough. It's so much harder for us to appeal now the plans have been approved.'

'Isn't there anything else we can do?' said Cat. 'Noel and Michael are still looking at the possibility of some alternative ideas.'

'Short of persuading Felix Macintyre to come here again, and see that there's an alternative I don't know that there is. And he's showing no signs of doing that, unfortunately. I'm really disappointed. He seemed so excited about the merlins, I thought he might really change his mind. But apparently he's been away on business a lot. Maybe he doesn't realise how far things have advanced.'

'That's such a shame,' said Cat. 'What does Ralph say?'

'Ralph's been called away to London,' said Pippa, 'he's been trying to find some deeds to a right of way that have gone missing. He seems to think it might be useful. I thought Noel would have told you.'

'He may have mentioned it,' said Cat, 'but to be honest, I've been so caught up in what's going on at home, I've really not been paying much attention.'

'You're going to need a bigger house if Angela stays much longer,' said Pippa.

'Don't,' said Cat, 'just don't.'

Pippa stood on the freezing cold and dark October night at a stand selling hot dogs and burgers, feeling sick with nerves, as people poured through the gate of her farm. Well not people – her clientele seemed to be mainly giggling teens and young couples. She'd had no idea so many of them would come. It was a great relief that they'd actually not only sold tickets, but that people had turned up. But that wasn't the end of it. For this to work, they all had to have a great evening, otherwise there was no point. Lucy sat imperiously in her wheelchair taking tickets off people, with Pippa's mum, Margaret, beside her to help.

The boys, together with the actors Pippa had hired, were taking the first victims round the farm, and it was all in all proving a very successful evening, judging by the screams. Pippa just hoped the takings would make it worth their while. On paper she should just turn a profit, but it was touch and go, and the evening had been more expensive than she'd thought. It just needed one bad night of rain or fog, for people not to turn up, and she'd be back to square one again. Best not think about that.

'This is great, Pippa,' Marianne and the twins had just been to the play barn, which had been set up for littlies. Although Pippa had mainly planned an evening for older kids, she'd laid on some entertainment for the younger ones. And she was organising fireworks for the last weekend in October, and hoping families would come. 'I think we might be ready for a hot dog and hot chocolate each.'

'Coming right up,' said Pippa. 'Where have Gabriel and Steven got to?'

'They're trying out the Haunted House,' said Marianne. 'I thought it might be too much for the twins.'

'Wise idea,' said Pippa. 'Thanks so much for coming, I'm really grateful for the support.'

'We wouldn't have missed it for the world,' said Marianne. 'And the twins are really getting excited by the idea of seeing Santa and his reindeer.'

'One thing at a time,' said Pippa. 'Santa's a very busy man.' She was hoping Ralph Nicholas wasn't going to stay in London too long, or she'd be in *big* trouble.

Marianne smiled and led the twins away to sit on two bales of hay and have their food and drink, while Pippa served other customers.

The evening went by with a swing, business was brisk,

and judging by the excited screams coming from the rides, people seemed to be enjoying themselves. Halfway through, Margaret ushered a very tired Lucy to bed, while Pippa's dad took over at the entrance until it got too late for newcomers to come in, and he came to help Pippa instead. By midnight the last of the revellers were off the premises. It had been a brilliant night and, when they checked the takings, one that had wildly exceeded Pippa's expectations. She high-fived everyone in delight.

'Excellent work, team,' she said. 'Now we just have to do it all again tomorrow.'

It was 1am before she went to bed, but she was too excited by the success of the evening to sleep. As she stood at her bedroom window staring out at the farm, she felt a quiet sense of satisfaction. She might not have saved the wood, but she could still save the farm. She could give the boys that at least.

*And you?* a voice said in her head, *What did you get?*

She brushed it aside. What did it matter what she got? She was doing this for her family, wasn't that enough? But she couldn't stop the thought creeping in that, once upon a time, she'd have celebrated the night with Dan – once upon a time. Now, she was doing this alone. And it was hard not to feel sad about that.

Marianne was on her way home from the nursery run, on a cold and dank day, when she saw the diggers slowly coming up the road, which led to their lane, Blackstock Farm and the woods.

'Oh no,' she said. 'Oh no.' After everyone's hard work the inevitable was happening. A white heat overcame Marianne suddenly. Filled with fury – how dare they do this to the place she called home, how dare they? – she

320

flew home without even thinking about what she was doing, grabbed some chain and padlocks, and raced towards the gate. She promptly chained herself to the gate post and then rang Pippa.

'Pippa?' she asked. 'Are you free? Only I'm doing a one woman protest here, and it's rather lonely.'

The diggers were travelling in slow convoy up the lane, which was narrow and today quite muddy. They halted suddenly as they came to the gate and saw Marianne chained to it.

The guy in the lead digger hopped out.

'Look, we don't need any trouble,' he said.

'And I don't want to cause any,' said Marianne sweetly, 'but here we are.'

'Hands off our woods!' She suddenly heard shouting from behind her and turned to see Batty Jack leading a group of the protesters who were still camped out in the woods, making their way to the gate, from the far end of the fields waving placards and shouting loudly.

Marianne had never been so pleased to see anyone, because standing here all alone, now the first wave of adrenaline had worn off and the results of her impetuous actions were being taken so seriously, she felt a bit daft. Not a natural campaigner, she wasn't entirely sure what to do next. She needn't have worried. Imperiously and unsteadily up the lane, came Miss Woods on her mobility scooter, along with Vera and Albert, and even Diana Carew. Good grief. She'd never seen Diana Carew as an anarchist.

The two groups met, one crowding round the tractors, waving placards, the other setting up a noisy and raucous chorus of, 'We shall not be moved'.

The first digger guy looked unsurprisingly out of his depth. He immediately got on to his mobile phone.

'Looks like we've got trouble, boss,' he said. 'With a capital T.'

There was obviously not a very happy response from the other end, when he'd finished explaining what was happening.

'You said there'd be no protesters,' the digger man was saying unhappily, 'but there are loads of them, waving their banners, and everything.'

The boss was clearly angry and making it apparent it was up to Digger Man to sort things out, as the phone call ended abruptly and he started to try and demonstrate his authority.

'Ok, you've had your fun, people,' he said. 'Time to move on now, this is private property, we have a legal right to be here.'

'Ah, but do you have a moral right?' said Marianne, fired up by the sight of Miss Woods berating Digger Man's companion.

'I'm just trying to do my job,' pleaded Digger Man.

'That's what the Nazis said, and look how that turned out,' said Marianne, 'but I'm afraid we're not going anywhere. So put that in your pipe and smoke it.'

# Chapter Thirty

Two hours later, Marianne was really not quite so sure of her ground. They seemed to have reached an impasse, with Digger Man and his mates standing off to one side, having called the police, who weren't in any hurry to show up, and Marianne and the protesters on the other. The people on the ground were sitting quietly not causing any trouble, so even when the police did show up, they were reluctant to remove a bunch of old ladies, particularly one on a mobility scooter, and were equally reluctant to deal with Marianne. But time it seemed would not wait for the great cogs of business to stop turning, and Digger Man was getting a series of phone calls which were getting increasingly irate.

'Right . . . yes I know . . . well, nothing,' Digger Man was saying, 'I mean the police say they can do nothing. Oh. So you're coming here? Right. Thank you.'

Digger Man looked like he might be sick.

'Problem?' asked Marianne, flashing him a brilliant smile.

'No,' said Digger Man, but he looked rattled. 'My boss is on his way,' he said, clearly trying to look assertive. '*Then* we'll see how far you lot can stop things from happening.'

'Hmmph,' said Miss Woods, who'd parked her scooter next to the fence, and was standing looking fierce leaning on her stick. 'You do realise this is only a temporary measure, don't you? They'll get rid of us today, and be back again tomorrow.'

'I know,' said Marianne, 'but every day we cause disruption, means another day when they can't start work. Maybe if we keep it up long enough they'll get fed up.'

'Maybe,' said Miss Woods. 'Oh, look Pippa's bringing us refreshments. Marvellous.'

In fact, Pippa was doing more than that. She'd clearly been busy in the time since Marianne had phoned her. She was being followed not only by another gang of protesters, but also Cat's film crew, several journalists and the local MP.

'Thought you might need some back up,' she said with a grin.

Cat got to work immediately. She thought she'd got enough footage, but this was too good an opportunity to miss for the campaign, and would be a nice extra to put in the programme, to show how much people cared about the development.

'Things are coming to a head here in Hope Christmas,' she said to camera. 'With planning permission on Blackstock Farm granted, the local residents are getting desperate. We're here with Marianne North who has chained herself to a gate to prevent the developers coming in. This seems a bit drastic, Marianne, what do you hope to gain from it?'

'Time,' said Marianne firmly. 'More time to talk to the developers, and make them see this isn't the way forward.'

Marianne talked for several minutes more, till Cat called a halt.

'That's great,' she said.

She turned to Miss Woods, who gave her typical succinct and clear cut version of events, followed by Diana Carew who as usual wanted to get into the action and declared that it was 'jolly exciting'. For the sake of fairness, she turned her attention to some of the Yummy Mummies, who'd got wind of the situation and driven up in their people carriers, and were tottering down the lane in unsuitable heels. They were very loud and angry about the fact that Marianne might ruin the plans for their precious spa. 'Some people are so selfish,' Keeley Jacobs declared with such a flounce it was all Cat could do not to burst out laughing.

Managing to just about contain her composure, Cat turned to the man leading the first digger, and asked, 'So how do you feel about destroying the natural habitat of so much wildlife, particularly the rare birds of prey which nest here?'

'Piffle,' a voice came from behind her. 'We all know there are no birds of prey here. They'd have been spotted months ago. You lot are doing what people like you always do, stopping ordinary decent business folk going about their legitimate business. Now Marianne,' the voice continued, 'you've made your point. Do be a good girl and unchain yourself from that fence.'

Cat turned round and couldn't disguise her surprise any more than Marianne who'd just said, 'Oh fuck,' to the camera.

There, in top to toe Armani, stood Luke Nicholas.

Pippa turned to Luke and said, 'She doesn't have to listen to you. None of us do.'

'I think you'll find she does,' said Luke, brandishing a bit of paper. 'The police have informed me they'll arrest anyone who stands on the land of LK Holdings, which includes your little friends on the other side of the fence,

325

and Marianne if she doesn't unchain herself. Now be sensible and give it up.'

'Yes give up!' shouted the Yummy Mummies en masse.

'Get this on camera,' shouted Cat to her cameraman, and he moved in to get a close up of Marianne looking desperate and determined, saying 'Never!'

'Never,' shouted Miss Woods, waving her walking stick and looking as if she was having the time of her life.

'Never,' declared Vera and Albert.

'Never!' boomed Diana Carew, who looked so out of place it was all Pippa could do not to laugh out loud.

'Never!' shouted Batty Jack, before yelling to his friends, 'let 'em out, folks, let those babes run.'

As if by magic, all the people from the camp released turkeys, hidden in baskets they'd brought with them. Gobbling away like mad, the turkeys veered in every direction, causing at least two of the Yummy Mummies to go arse over tit, and Luke to momentarily lose his cool and shout, 'Where the fuck have they come from? Get rid of the bloody things!' as Cat obligingly held the microphone to his face. For several glorious moments, pandemonium ensued, but gradually the turkeys were caught and order was restored.

Then it was all over brutally quickly. The police simply cut the chains Marianne had used to tether herself to the fence.

'I'm not going to go quietly,' said Marianne, 'this is harrassment.'

'Quiet or not,' said the copper who had freed her, 'you're coming with us.'

'You, what?' asked Marianne.

'You heard, I'm arresting you for disturbing the peace.'

'You're kidding me?' said Marianne.

''Fraid not,' the officer said.

'Can you pick the kids up for me?' she shouted at Pippa as she was escorted to the waiting police car. She was soon joined by Miss Woods, who had been most vociferous in her objections, and hilariously by Diana Carew, who not to be outdone by Miss Woods, called one of the policemen a little gobshite. Then Vera and Albert placed themselves on the ground in front of the diggers and also had to be dragged away. As the patrol cars drove off one by one, Cat ran after the police with a microphone shouting, 'How does it feel to arrest old ladies and mums?'

But it was to no avail, the protesters were cleared and the diggers finally made their way into the farm, to the sound of many boos from both sides of the fence, though the protesters on the farm side had the sense to scatter in the fields, to escape arrest.

By this time it was nearly 2pm. At least there wasn't a lot more the diggers could do today.

'Face it, Pippa, this is over,' Luke said with a smug grin. 'You've given it your best shot, but it's time that we got on with our work.'

Just then a bird flew out of the wood and past Luke's shoulder, leaving a messy deposit on his coat as it did so.

It was small and swift, with a sharp beak and a blue head, and it soared through the sky and then hovered above them. Pippa was so busy laughing at Luke's irritation as he tried to clean off his coat, that at first she didn't quite realise the import of what she'd seen.

A small bird – a small *hovering* bird.

'Hang on a minute,' she said, as the bird swept down and picked up a stray mouse with its claws. Quickly she took a photo with her phone.

'Your boss still keen on merlins?' she said.

'He has a bit of a bird obsession,' said Luke, 'but you know as well as I do, Pippa, there are no merlins here. That's why he greenlighted the project.'

'Really?' said Pippa with a smile. 'I wouldn't be too sure of that if I were you.'

# My Broken Brain

*I have no idea how long I've been doing this . . . 8pm*

It's taken me nearly two years to see it. But every day as I look across at Blackstock Farm, and think about what they're planning, then I look at the farm and think about what we had together, it's slowly hitting me that I've got it completely wrong.

I thought I was helping Pippa, and maybe I am, because she seems to be managing fine without me. Whenever I see her she's bright and breezy and full of plans and ideas for the future. A future which can never include me.

Well, as my nan would have said, wagging her finger at me, when I'd got into trouble, You've only yourself to blame.

And I do blame myself. What seemed like the best idea at the time has turned out to be the worst. I pushed Pippa away when she wanted to help me. It's too late to eat humble pie and ask her back.

Why would she want me anyway? After what I did to her.

She *is* better off without me.

The trouble is: I'm worse off without her. And there's nothing I can do about it.

Only yourself to blame, Holliday. Only yourself.

# Chapter Thirty-One

'I still can't believe you got yourself arrested,' laughed Pippa. 'All the campaigning I've done, and I've never seen the inside of a cell. I'm impressed.'

She had popped in to see if Marianne was all right after her ordeal, as she felt quite guilty, particularly as Gabriel had been a bit snotty with her when she'd brought the twins home.

'I'm really sorry, I didn't think even Luke Nicholas would be such a dickhead as to get people arrested. Honestly you and three old ladies, and Albert, what a good day's work for the boys in blue.'

'Don't be,' said Marianne. 'It was quite funny really. Especially seeing the look on Luke's face. Besides, all that happened was I sat in a police car for twenty minutes, and in a cell for half an hour. As soon as they had word that the diggers were in the farm, they let me go. All very polite and British.'

'Was Gabe ok about it in the end? He seemed a bit cross when I took the children home.'

'He wasn't best pleased, mainly because of me leaving them,' said Marianne. 'He was quite happy for me to make my protest, less happy that I got arrested.'

'I am sorry,' said Pippa. 'Auntie Jean was there too, and she seemed to think it was quite funny.'

'Bless her,' said Marianne, 'she *did* think it was funny.'

'Have you and Gabe sorted out your differences about Steven?' asked Pippa.

'We're just not talking about it,' said Marianne, 'which is mature. And now for reasons I can't fathom, he's got a bee in his bonnet that I only did this protest thing to get nearer to Luke. Quite why I don't know. Ever since we met him at the spa, he's been a bit funny about Luke. I've told him he has nothing to be jealous of, but there you go.'

'Men!' said Pippa. 'They can be so stupid. Do you want me to have a word?'

'No, I don't think it will help, to be honest,' said Marianne, with a sigh. 'He's cross with me at the moment, but he'll get over it.'

'Well, I'm really sorry if your efforts to stop the diggers caused more problems for you,' said Pippa, 'but thanks for trying.'

'Don't be,' said Marianne. 'Gabe would still be angry even if I hadn't got arrested. It's a shame that it hasn't done any good, though. They've been out in force all week ploughing up fields.'

'Maybe not,' said Pippa, 'but I'm sure we can find other delaying tactics. In the night some of the campers broke in and put wheel clamps on all the diggers. It won't stop them, but it's another spanner in the works.'

'But they'll get over that, and the next hurdle,' said Marianne gloomily. 'Whatever we do, this hotel is going to get built.'

'Oh I don't know,' said Pippa. 'I wouldn't give up, *just* yet.'

'Why?' asked Marianne.

'Because after you left that day, a bird flew over and crapped on Luke's head.'

'So?' said Marianne looking puzzled.

'Not any old bird,' said Pippa. 'A merlin. Ralph was right, there are merlins in the woods. So I sent a photo to Felix Macintyre, and a message asking him to hold off digging until we can investigate further.'

'And have you heard back?' asked Marianne.

'The bugger's abroad doing some deal,' said Pippa. 'But until he gets back, I've got the guys on diversionary detail. At the very least it will come to his attention fairly soon that work isn't progressing as it should. Time is money and all that. It might bring him back and this time we really can show him some merlins.'

'It's a bit of a long shot,' said Marianne.

'I know,' sighed Pippa, 'but it's all I've got. If we can delay them till the weather turns, it will be Christmas before you know it. You never know. Miracles have happened in Hope Christmas before.'

Miracles have happened at Christmas. Marianne wondered if Pippa were right about that, as the twins ran ahead of her, shrieking with delight. They were on their favourite walk through the muddy woods where the wood carvings lived. The twins squealed with pleasure when they came across statues of owls and otters, and even a crocodile.

'Mummy, Mummy, there's a new one!' Daisy came running back, and dragged her towards a gap in the path, where a new clean carving stood. It was of a pair of nesting birds. They looked like, yes they were, merlins, and someone had carved Save The Woods in the tree next to them. Marianne laughed out loud – that cheered her up enormously.

Maybe Pippa was right about Christmas. It was true that she and Gabe had first got together at Christmas, the year she'd put on her first Nativity in Hope Christmas. It had always felt doubly special to her since. And only two years ago, when Eve and her then partner Darren had been threatening to take Steven away from them, it was at Christmas that they discovered Eve had changed her mind. But surely that was coincidence.

'Don't believe in miracles myself.' Michael Nicholas was parked in the lane, as they emerged from the wood, the children chattering nineteen to the dozen about their favourite statues. It was uncanny how he and Ralph always seemed to appear out of the blue. Uncannier still how they always seemed to know exactly what you were thinking too . . .

'I hear you had an encounter with the boys in blue,' continued Michael. 'Bit radical for you?'

'Maybe a bit,' said Marianne, 'and I'm not sure it was worth it. Your cousin is determined this hotel is going to get built.'

'Hmm,' said Michael, 'he doesn't always get his own way you know, so long as there are people to stand against him.'

'There are plenty of them here,' said Marianne with a smile. 'You make it sound so easy.'

'Oh nothing worth fighting for is easy,' said Michael, 'but I think you already know that, Marianne,' and he roared off up the lane on his motorbike, leaving Marianne with the feeling that they weren't just talking about the campaign.

She walked back into town, holding the twins' hands tight, feeling very blessed that she had such beautiful, healthy children. Sometimes, it was too easy to get bogged down in the minutiae of life and forget about what was really important.

'Hot chocolate, kids?' she said, feeling they deserved a treat.

'Yes please!' was the eager response, so she took them to the café, to find Eve working as, after their brief brush with the law, Vera and Albert were back campaigning in the woods again.

'They weren't put off by being arrested, then?' said Marianne.

'Nope,' grinned Eve, 'they seemed to find it entertaining.'

Marianne settled the twins down with a drink, and ordered herself a coffee. As it was quiet, Eve came over and joined them.

'I've got some news,' she said.

'What's that?' said Marianne.

'Well, I know I've made it hard on you and Gabe this year—'

Marianne protested, but Eve waved her off, 'You're just being polite. Steven told me it's causing problems between you, and I'd hate to do that to you, you've both been so kind. Now that I'm feeling so much better, I can see what a nightmare I was when I was living with you, and I'm sorry.'

'You were ill,' said Marianne, who felt it wouldn't be helpful to admit quite how stressful it had been having Eve to stay. 'And we were glad to help.'

'Anyway, it's been great being here, and I'm grateful to Vera for the flat and the job, but I don't want to serve coffee for the rest of my life. So, I've decided come the new year I'm going to look for another job. I'm not much cop to Steven when I'm around, I only drag him down. So I'm going back to London, permanently.'

\* \* \*

335

Cat was at home playing with Lou Lou and chatting to Angela, when the phone rang.

'If that's Kay I'm not talking to her except through my solicitor,' said Angela.

Before Cat had got to the phone, Lou Lou had already picked it up and said, 'Hallo' and was about to put it down and say it again as she did with her favourite toy.

'Hallo?' The voice on the other end sounded cross. 'Who's that?'

'I'm very sorry,' said Cat, taking the phone from Lou Lou before she managed to end the call. 'My granddaughter picked up the phone. Can I help you?'

'I am speaking to Cat Tinsall?'

'You are,' said Cat, unsure as to who it was.

'Brilliant,' said the voice. 'I was just wondering if you were available at short notice.'

'Erm, I might be,' said Cat, looking into the lounge and wondering *quite* how short the notice might be, and what she needed to be available for.

'Excellent, I've been let down. My name's Josh Anderson, of Backtrack Productions, and I'm directing a Christmas Cookery Short Cuts programme, which is going to be shown live nightly during December. How about it?'

'Sounds great,' said Cat, slightly stunned, contemplating what had happened to being too old. 'Why me though?'

'All the youngsters are off partying,' said Josh, 'A mature woman won't be. You fit the bill.'

So a backhanded compliment then.

'I'll have to think about it,' said Cat, 'and sort some stuff out, but provisionally, yes.'

'Marvellous, look forward to working with you,' said Josh, and put the phone down.

Fan – bloody – tastic. Cat sat back in total shock. This

was amazing. She hadn't asked about money or any other sensible details. But she had another job, doing what she loved.

'Yes!' Cat jumped up and punched the air. She was back, albeit in a very small way. She didn't care. It was a job. And someone wanted her to do it.

'What was all that about?' said Angela.

Yikes. There was the small problem of what to do about Angela and Lou Lou, but she'd have to cross that bridge when she came to it.

So Cat told her.

'Brilliant news,' said Angela. 'You're wasted doing programmes about cows.'

'It's called diversification,' grinned Cat, 'or putting up with what you can get.'

'Still,' sniffed Angela, 'this is much more up your street.'

'It is,' said Cat, 'but . . .' in the last few months with less work on, she'd been shouldering the domestic burden more. How was she going to manage both again?

'But nothing,' said Angela. 'Don't stop to think about it. Just take it. You don't have to say anything. I can see me being here isn't helping you at all, and I don't want you fretting about me on top of all the other things you have to deal with. It's time I took matters into my own hands. I'm going to find myself somewhere else to live.'

# Chapter Thirty-Two

Cat was frantically making Christmas lists – not just for herself, but for the programmes she was due to start filming, which were aimed at people wanting to have a smooth run up to Christmas. She was busy making script notes wondering just how organised could anyone be on December 1. Should the tree be up? Cake made? Turkey ordered? Presumably all three. Turkeys for her were easy – she always got hers from Batty Jack, who reared his birds with such tender loving care he named each one of them, and while he had no compunction about killing them, couldn't ever eat creatures he referred to as friends – but not everyone lived in the country.

This is *insane*, Cat found herself scoring it all out. *What are we talking about here, people. It's one day of the year. One day, and yet we stress ourselves so much about it . . .*

She broke off. It was true, bloody true. Every year she went into panic mode around the middle of October, and stayed in it until Boxing Day when she relaxed. Cat suddenly felt after all these years of planning, it would be nice if someone else could take charge for a change.

'Maybe you should, Lou Lou,' she said, looking at her granddaughter who was colouring in reindeer pictures, she'd been given at nursery, where all the talk was of the day out to Winter Wonderland, at Pippa's farm, where they could see real live reindeer and meet Santa.

'Although I'm getting a bit worried about the reindeer,' Pippa had confided in Cat, 'as Ralph hasn't come back to me about them. I've got visions of shoving fake horns on the cows instead.'

'Lou Lou wouldn't notice,' Cat roared with laughter at this vision, but she had a feeling Pippa didn't find it *quite* so funny.

Angela had gone home to give them a break – well not home, she had refused point blank to go back to Kay's house and moved into a hotel down the road and was still insisting she wanted to buy herself a flat in Hope Christmas instead. Noel and Cat thought it seemed like the ideal solution, but Kay was not at all convinced. Last time she'd rung, she'd accused Cat of poisoning her mother's mind and being after her inheritance, which seemed a bit rich from someone who seemed to be controlling the purse strings. Families.

Her phone rang and she saw it was Mel. Mel had been a bit distant lately, keeping her head down at home, working immensely hard and turning down it seemed most social invitations, though Cat was always happy to babysit. Instead, she came in from college, played with Lou Lou, put her to bed, then locked herself away studying, except for the occasional weekend nights, when she worked in the local pub. It must be hard for her to feel so responsible, when her friends were more carefree, but she never complained.

Of late there had also been a couple of mysterious phone calls at the dinner table, which Mel had dashed off to take privately. Cat suspected there might be a boy on the scene, but didn't ask. She missed her daughter's confidences, but she guessed Mel would tell her in her own good time. Cat didn't think Mel would make the same mistake twice, she hoped not anyway.

'Hi, love, you ok?' said Cat.

'Fine,' said Mel. 'Only, would you mind if—'

'If what?'

'It's really short notice' – the words came out in a rush – 'but there's a party tonight, and—' there was a pause as if Mel was trying to find the words, '—I've been invited.'

'That's great,' said Cat, who worried that Mel didn't have much of a social life.

'Really?' the relief in Mel's voice was comical. 'So you wouldn't mind having Lou Lou, so I could stay over?'

'Mel, sweetheart, you're eighteen years old, of course you can stay over.'

'Mum, you're a star,' said Mel. 'I'll see you later.' The relief in her voice was hilarious.

*Definitely* a boy.

'Good, you're home,' said Marianne, one Friday night, as Gabriel walked through the door. 'Right, go and have a shower and get changed. The twins are in bed. Your mum's babysitting. We're going out.'

'We are?' said Gabriel.

'We are,' said Marianne firmly. Since her chat with Michael, she'd been working out a way she and Gabe could get back onto a more regular footing. They'd been so busy recently they barely spoke to each other apart from about things relating to the children, and Marianne was aware they couldn't carry on like this. And now Eve had told Marianne her plans to move to London, the problem of whether Steven should go and live with her had become irrelevant, as he would have to move schools in order to do so, and he loved Middleminster too much to do that.

340

So Marianne decided to take the bull by the horns and get Gabriel out for a night to thrash out the things that were bothering them both. It seemed like the ideal opportunity to get over this invisible barrier that had sprung up between them.

Marianne felt tense as they set off down the lane, as Gabriel had barely said two words since coming home. But as soon as they hit the High Street, he turned to her and said, 'You're right. We need a night out, thanks for organising it.' Then he gave her a kiss and took her hand, and she thought with relief, this is going to be easy.

And it was. Over an Indian they found themselves slowly unwinding, talking first about the twins, then about Steven's Christmas carol concert which was coming up, and then finally, about Eve.

'So Eve's planning to move back to London,' said Gabriel, the relief in his voice palpable.

'Apparently,' said Marianne carefully. 'So that's good, isn't it?'

They both paused, then at the same time:

'I'm sorry—' began Marianne.

'I shouldn't have bitten your head off—' said Gabriel.

Followed simultaneously by, 'It's ok!' at which point they both burst out laughing and Marianne felt the tight knot which had been in her stomach for weeks now, slowly unwind.

'I didn't mean to upset you, Gabe,' Marianne said. 'I was just trying to think what was best for both Steven and Eve.'

'I know,' said Gabriel, taking her hand. 'It's just Eve and I have battled over Steven for so many years, and I can't stand it. I shouldn't have taken it out on you.'

Then everything felt ok, and they sank a bottle of wine

to celebrate. It was nearly ten when they left the restaurant.

'One for luck in the Hopesay?' said Gabriel, holding her hand tightly as they tottered up the road.

'Why not?' said Marianne who was feeling decidedly tipsy.

They entered the pub, which was packed, so Gabriel went to the bar while Marianne squeezed into a seat in the corner. While she was waiting for Gabe to come back with the drinks, to her very unwelcome surprise, Luke Nicholas was bearing down on her.

'Marianne, my lovely,' he carolled, he too seemed more than a bit tipsy, 'how wonderful to see you.'

He insisted on sitting down at a table and leant over to give her a kiss that lasted that little bit too long. Marianne squirmed uncomfortably at his touch.

'Have you given any more thought to selling up?' he said. 'You know you can't fight us anymore, why not join us?'

He leaned forward and put his hand on her leg.

Marianne laughed nervously and tried to wriggle away.

'Sorry, Luke we could never do that.'

'Pity,' he said, 'I think you're making a big mistake.'

Then with one last kiss, he got up and left her, just as Gabriel came towards the table with their drinks, looking like thunder.


'Pippa, are you busy?'

Busy, when wasn't she busy? She looked up from the accounts to see Dan framed in the doorway. But Pippa was pleased to see him. It had been several weeks since they'd done anything more than nod at each other.

Though she knew she had no right to, Pippa wished he'd get more involved with the plans for the farm and with the woods campaign. It was crazy of her to still feel like this, but divorced or not, she still wanted things to be the way they were, would there ever be a day when she didn't?

'Not too busy. Do you want tea?'

'That would be lovely,' said Dan, and sat down. 'Don't suppose there's any . . .'

'. . . Cake?' finished Pippa. 'You know there's always cake in this house. Unless the boys have eaten it all.'

They sat down and for a fleeting moment it was like old times. The times Pippa missed, even though she knew she shouldn't.

But then it changed.

'I know we keep skirting round this,' Dan said, 'but I do think we need to get our finances straight. I can see what a brilliant go you're making of the farm, and I don't want to hold you back. So in the New Year, I'm going to go and manage Jim Davenport's farm – since his stroke he's been struggling, and he's prepared to pay well. When you're ready to, I'd like you to buy me out. You've been right about the farm all along, it should be held in trust for the children. I want the boys to have it, when they're old enough. What do you think?'

I think this is mad, she wanted to say, I think we've lost everything that was ever good in our lives, apart from the children, but she said nothing. Dan was right, they couldn't go on the way they were, and he had the right to a fresh start. She should let him go.

'Of course,' said Pippa, 'I'll look around for someone to come and manage the farm, and we'll start the New Year with a clean slate. Thanks for being so generous.'

'It's not generous, Pippa,' he said, 'you deserve the best. And I can't give you that anymore.'

Suddenly a weird instinct kicked in.

'Does she have a name?'

'Who?' said Dan, looking guilty.

'Your fresh start,' said Pippa. 'I'm pleased for you, Dan, if that's what you want?'

'Andrea,' mumbled Dan. 'I met her online.'

Online dating. She felt as if she'd been kicked in the stomach. *He'd been online dating.* But then why shouldn't he have been?

'Great. Good for you,' said Pippa much more brightly than she felt.

She went to shake his hand, feeling faintly foolish, and then he pulled her into a warm tight hug, from which she never wanted to be let go.

'This really is it then,' she said, hoping he wouldn't hear the muffled tears in her voice.

'Guess so,' he said, the tears in his all too apparent.

Then he was gone, and she was alone in the kitchen, which no longer felt warm and bright, but cold and very very lonely.

# *Chapter Thirty-Three*

'So there we were, having a really lovely evening, and just at the point when I thought I'd finally got through to Gabe, bloody Luke Nicholas had to screw it all up,' said Marianne. 'Now he's got it into his head that there's something going on between us, which there's *not*, obviously, but Gabe just won't listen.'

'Give him time,' said Pippa, 'stubborn as a mule, my cousin.'

'And don't I know it,' said Marianne. 'What about you? Have you got any further with buying Dan out?'

'Working on it,' said Pippa. 'I think if we can get a good crowd in for the Winter Wonderland and I take my parents up on the offer of a loan, I might be able to persuade the bank manager in six months that I can do it.'

'Well that's something,' said Marianne. 'Progress for the year – Pippa to be self-sufficient.'

'Yes,' said Pippa, and looked sad. Marianne felt for her friend. She wished things could be different for her. Mind you, at the moment, she wished things could be different for her too. Gabriel had retreated into a sullen silence again, and this time she really didn't know how she was going to get him out of it.

'What's the latest on the woods?' said Marianne, who'd

slightly lost track of things thanks to a week in which first Daisy and then Harry had succumbed to a stomach bug.

'It's all gone a bit quiet on that front,' said Pippa. 'Thankfully the weather has held things up a lot' (it had been raining fairly constantly for the last couple of weeks) 'and Miss Woods has been organising raids on the worksite – they keep finding tools missing and the like. They tried to put in a better perimeter fence but Batty Jack and his crew have cut a hole through it from a ditch near the woods, and they keep going on guerrilla missions at night, moving equipment about and spraying Save the Woods messages on the yard.'

'Won't they get into trouble for defacing property?' said Marianne.

'I hope not, I do keep impressing on Jack the need to stay legal, though luckily with so many protesters, it's difficult for the police to pin the blame on one individual. And at least the paint they use is water soluble, so it comes off really easily. It's about being a nuisance really.'

'What about Felix Macintyre?' Marianne wanted to know. 'Did he respond to your pictures?'

'No,' said Pippa. 'It's such a bugger, as the merlins have been spotted several times now. It was a bit of a wild hope really.'

'Never say die,' said Marianne. 'We've just got to keep plugging on.'

But on the way back home, she was dismayed to see a couple of diggers coming down the lane. Work was still going ahead, despite the weather, and despite the protests it was looking increasingly unlikely that Luke Nicholas could be stopped. Feeling infuriated, Marianne burst onto the site, where she found Luke instructing his foreman.

'You really don't get it, do you?' she said angrily. 'You

don't live here, Luke, you don't even really like it here, you just want to exploit it. I wish you'd bugger off.'

'Oh Marianne, you say the nicest things,' said Luke. 'But you're wrong, I'm here to help Hope Christmas. We're going to make things better, not worse. And if you don't get off this property, I'll have you arrested again.'

'I don't see how,' said Marianne. But all the drive soon left her when she saw Gabriel standing in the corner of the field opposite, looking furious.

Oh no, he'd probably read that completely wrong. Bugger, bugger, and bugger again.

'So today, we're making and icing the Christmas cake,' said Cat smiling to the camera.

'Kissmass Cake,' agreed Lou Lou, standing on a stool next to her, waving a wooden spoon rather wildly.

'Now I know amazingly organised people will have done this weeks ago,' continued Cat, 'but if you're like me and have left it far too late, this recipe will get you out of a hole. And if you really don't have time, buy one in Marks and I'll show you how you can jazz it up.'

'That's great,' said Giles, the director. 'Now if we can just pan out over the ingredients, we'll get started on how it works.'

Several gruelling hours later, with plenty of stops to accommodate Lou Lou (who'd been roped in when Cat had been unable to find a babysitter, and Giles had decided she added cute factor: her starring role amounted to stirring the cake and making a wish), Giles pronounced himself satisfied. 'That will be up next week,' he said, 'for December 1. This afternoon we'll do decorating the cake.'

'Right,' she said, 'but madam here needs a proper break and so do I. Fancy some lunch?' To make the programme feel more homely, Giles had insisted on filming at Cat's house, which suited her as it meant less for her to organise.

'That's kind,' said Giles, 'but Finn' (the cameraman) 'and I will pop out to the pub, if that's ok.'

'No problem,' said Cat, thinking it gave her time to tidy up.

It was going to be a long week, filming these short segments every day, but she hoped it was going to be worth it.

Just as she was settling Lou Lou down to lunch, her phone rang. Angela. Cat's heart sank. Now what?

'Cat,' said Angela. 'You have to help me. I came over to have a sensible discussion with Kay, and she's locked me in the house and won't let me out. You have to come and rescue me, *now*.'

Pippa was in the woods, surveying the earthworks which had been dug so far. The diggers still hadn't got very far thanks to the bad weather. On top of that, Miss Woods was still organising those campers left to employ delaying tactics. Sooner or later, someone was going to break the law. There had already been a discussion about putting sugar in petrol tanks, and Pippa was worried they'd get themselves arrested, and in serious trouble. So far things had been fairly amicable, and she didn't want things to turn nasty. From what Marianne told her of their last encounter, Luke Nicholas was losing the plot fast. They might not have much time left. They could possibly stall things up to Christmas, but after then, who knew what would happen? All Pippa knew was that they were on borrowed time.

'So nothing doing today then?' Pippa asked Miss Woods, who was standing surveying the scene when she arrived.

'They've come out, sniffed about a bit and gone back

348

into their huts,' said Miss Woods, with a satisfied grin. 'I believe the weather forecast is for more rain, with snow and sleet to follow.'

'But we can't stop them forever,' said Pippa gloomily. 'I just wish I'd had a response from Felix Macintyre, and that we could have the chance to make him change his mind.'

'You never know,' said Miss Woods, 'I gather from the troops that Luke Nicholas is getting an ear bashing from Mr Macintyre about the lateness of the project, and maybe planning to inspect it himself.'

'That would be brilliant,' said Pippa, 'because I think I've found where the birds are nesting and it's bang near where he wants to pull down some trees and put up his spa. If nothing else will persuade him to change his mind maybe that will.'

'. . . And this might,' Ralph Nicholas appeared as if by magic. He was holding an envelope in his hands. 'Sorry, I've been away so long. As you know I went to London to see about an ancient right of way which runs through the woods. The original documents disappeared from the safe at Hopesay Manor, and there was a cryptic note in the file about Blackstock Farm belonging to the Nicholas family. So I've been investigating and I turned up more than I bargained for. My uncle Zach had lodged certain documents with the family solicitor, and it appeared they'd gone missing too. Luckily Uncle Zach was a wise old bird and he'd stored another copy elsewhere.'

'I wonder who could have taken them?' said Pippa, puzzled.

'Yes, I wonder,' said Ralph, as a black car could be seen entering the field from the other end. Pippa could just make out Luke Nicholas, who got out and was obsequiously pandering to a figure clad in wellies, souwester and hunting hat, sporting a pair of binoculars round his neck. Could it be? It *was*. Felix Macintyre.

'So what are these documents?' asked Pippa, as they watched Luke and Felix struggle across the muddy field.

'Proof that the Nicholas family gave this land over to the Blackstock family, until such time as it was no longer required. When the final farming member of the family dies, it reverts to us. The family own the house and gardens, but this part of the fields and woods, apparently belongs to me.'

'Does Felix know this?' asked Pippa.

'Not yet,' said Ralph, 'but I am looking forward to telling him.'

Felix Macintyre strode up to Ralph extending a hand.

'Well hello there. Where do I find these magnificent birds I've been hearing so much about? I gather they do exist after all. Your damned nephew told me they didn't.'

'First things first,' said Ralph. 'I believe you and your diggers are trespassing on my land.'

'*Your* land?' Felix looked astonished.

'Afraid so, old chap,' said Ralph.

'But Luke told me he'd got the deal sewn up,' said Felix.

'Well my nephew has been known to make mistakes in the past,' said Ralph, 'and I believe he might have accidentally lost these papers.' He showed them to Felix. 'I think you'll find everything in order here.'

'Apparently so,' said Felix after he flicked through them. 'Luke!' he roared, but as if by magic, Luke had disappeared.

# My broken brain

*I'm so done with this diary-keeping. 12am*

I've been writing this damned diary for the best part of a year, and it's got me nowhere.

Because I'm the biggest idiot in the world.

I wanted to tell Pippa how I really felt. How badly I've got things wrong. How I wish I could get her back. So what do I do instead?

Idiot, idiot, idiot.

Give her the impression that I'm not single any more. Why the fuck did I do that? To stop her feeling sorry for me? To make her worry about me less? After all she's getting on with her life, I didn't want her to think I'm not getting on with mine.

All I've done is given Pippa the chance to be independent of me, and made her think I still want to be independent of her.

Well done, Holliday. Even by your standards, that's spectacularly inept . . .

*December*

# Chapter Thirty-Four

'This is fantastic!' said Cat, as she joined Pippa and Marianne at the Town Square for the annual putting up of the Christmas tree and turning on of the Christmas lights. The place was milling with people drinking mulled wine and browsing in the Christmas market stalls. The word had quickly spread about the woods being saved, and the whole event had turned into a great big party.

'And so was the Winter Wonderland,' she continued, 'Lou Lou loved it.'

'The twins have not stopped talking about Santa's reindeer,' confirmed Marianne.

Cat and Marianne had visited Pippa's Winter Wonderland that afternoon. She'd done a grand job of turning the hay barn into Santa's grotto, and the children had been entranced as, to the sound of 'Jingle Bells', Santa in the form of Ralph Nicholas had turned up on a sleigh driven by four reindeer. The reindeer had been such a hit, the presents Santa gave out had been immaterial. It had been a thoroughly magical afternoon, and Pippa had told them she had bookings up till Christmas and was hoping to make even more money than she had at Halloween.

'I'm so glad,' said Pippa. 'It's all turned out rather well, hasn't it? Diana certainly seems to think so.'

Diana Carew was rather drunkenly sitting on a bale of straw regaling some rather baffled teenagers with her account of being arrested; in her account she'd practically single-handedly stopped the diggers coming in by lying flat on the ground in front of them.

'Funny I don't remember that bit,' grinned Marianne.

Batty Jack had a stall selling the first of his turkeys, or his 'heroines' as he put it. 'Without them the battle of the woods would have been lost for sure.'

Even the Yummy Mummies seemed reasonably happy. Felix Macintyre had found an old manor house five miles away going to rack and ruin, and it looked like he might be planning to put his new complex there instead. He had become quite a character in the town, and was often spotted in the woods birdwatching.

While Jenny Ingles, also rather tipsy, confided in Cat that, 'I only went along with the idea of the hotel because Tom thought it would get him a job, but he's managed to find work in Shrewsbury now, and it's much better paid. So we're saving for a house and looking to buy in the New Year.'

'And the woods are definitely safe?' Cat asked Pippa, sipping at her mulled wine.

She and Noel had just come back from a fractious weekend at Kay's, and had missed most of the excitement. When they got to Kay's after the last dramatic phone call it turned out Angela had got the wrong end of the stick. She'd spent the day with Kay, and had a little snooze after lunch, at which point Kay had popped to the shops without telling her, so it was all a storm in a teacup. But Noel had insisted on having a family meeting for Angela to tell them what *she* wanted.

After much wrangling, it had been agreed that Angela

would look for a warden-assisted flat (of which there were plenty) in Hope Christmas. Kay, it turned out had been under the mistaken impression that her mother wanted to be at home all the time, and it had driven her mad, whilst Angela was frustrated because she didn't know anyone in the area and couldn't get out unless Kay drove her places. In Hope Christmas, she'd be able to walk. On top of all that, Kay had discovered her husband Dave had been having an affair ('I'm not at all surprised,' Noel had snorted unsympathetically). 'I just can't cope with Mum too,' she'd wailed rather dramatically given that the situation was entirely one of her own making. As family rows go, it had been a humdinger, but Cat was hoping once the dust settled, her sister-in-law would calm down and accept that she and Noel weren't trying to muscle in, and just wanted to make sure that Angela was happy.

'Yup,' said Pippa with a grin, 'Felix Macintyre is going to build his hotel complex, but a few miles away in a more suitable spot. Here he's come up with a scheme similar to something they've done before: planning affordable holiday chalets, in keeping with the environment, for people who want to walk and see the local wildlife. Given that he doesn't own as much of the land as he thought, it's scaled down too. And he's so thrilled about the merlins, he's even talking about buying a place of his own here. Though knowing him, he'll have to be dissuaded from building some monstrosity on top of the hills. Who'd have thought?'

'Brilliant,' said Cat, 'I'm so pleased.'

'And,' continued, Pippa, 'when Ralph told him about my plans for the farm, he's prepared to give me some backing, so I can finance my new ideas without worrying so much about the bank loans, if I give over some land for camping overspill. So I can afford to go bigger than I thought I could.'

'Woo hoo!' said Cat. 'This gets better and better. I feel this Christmas is going to be a brilliant one.'

'Me too,' said Pippa. 'The Winter Wonderland tickets are going through the roof. It's succeeded beyond my wildest dreams.'

'I'm really glad,' said Cat. 'Things seem to be looking up all round. My little Christmas programmes apparently are a huge hit on the internet. Mind you, that's probably because everyone loves Lou Lou so much.'

'Way to go,' said Pippa, 'so you're not so old and past it after all.'

'Apparently not,' said Cat.

She felt a warm festive glow settle over her as the crowd jostled around them. Christmas was coming and all would be well.


Pippa sat at the kitchen table, looking through the books at the figures from Winter Wonderland, which were very pleasing. Thanks to Felix's input, Pippa was able to afford some staff to run things, so she and the boys could have a break. The Halloween Spooktacular had been fun but exhausting, and it wasn't as though all the other jobs on the farm had gone away.

She'd also spoken to her bank manager, who was more than happy to give her a mortgage when he saw the figures on the table. It was time to move on, and in the New Year, she could buy Dan out, she could afford to employ a farm manager, and Dan could get his new job and start planning a future with his new girlfriend. From where she'd been at the start of the year, her feelings about Dan aside, it felt like a miracle. So why did she feel so sad? Since

Richard, she'd been determined to be a strong single woman, and she was.

*What's the point in being strong if you're lonely?* a voice said. *And you miss him, even now.* Two years since they'd split. Maybe she was never going to be over Dan.

Willing herself out of her despondency, Pippa decided she needed some fresh air.

'I'm just popping out for a walk,' she told Nathan and George who were ensconced in front of the fire in the lounge, watching TV, while Lucy sat in her chair in the corner.

'Look after Lucy for me.'

'More like me looking after them,' typed Lucy grinning.

'Whatever,' said Pippa, giving her daughter a kiss. 'All be good now.'

Donning her wellies, a coat, scarf, woolly hat and a thick pair of gloves, she set off. It was a cold and crisp day, with a hint of snow in the air. Without realising it, she found herself wandering down a path she rarely used these days. It was the one that took her to the place she and Dan used to call theirs. Where they'd got together, had family picnics . . . and finally called it a day. Even now, she wasn't entirely sure why Dan had made that decision, but it was what he wanted. Somehow, after the accident, he didn't feel they could be together, whereas it had made Pippa want to be with him more.

She did a double take as she came to the riverbank. A familiar figure was sitting there . . . alone.

Dan turned to face her with a look so melancholy, she wanted to run into his arms, but that wasn't allowed. Not anymore.

'What are you doing here?' they said simultaneously.

\* \* \*

The sky was growing dark and cloudy with the promise of snow. Gabriel had been out all afternoon, trying to get the pregnant ewes inside. Though many of the farmers let their animals lamb in the fields, Gabriel preferred to keep them indoors. It was more work in terms of keeping everything clean, but it was easier than scouring the hillsides for missing sheep.

Marianne had fetched the children from nursery, and been glad she wasn't working today. Gabriel was still being moody with her, and she worried about what it meant. She couldn't believe that he was so stupid as to think anything was going on with Luke – particularly as the latter had turned on his tail and left Hope Christmas again – but he was still sulking about something. She couldn't get through to him.

Eventually, Gabriel came in looking exhausted.

'Did you get them all?' said Marianne.

'There's one missing,' said Gabriel, 'and I'm worried she's about to lamb. Yesterday she was very restless, and she wasn't where I last saw her.'

'What are you going to do?' asked Marianne, knowing full well what Gabriel would do – Gabriel the shepherd would never let one of his flock go. That was one of the reasons she loved him so much.

'Find her of course,' said Gabriel.

Marianne suddenly came to a decision. She didn't want to spend another few hours alone with the children, fretting about Gabriel. At least if they were together, he'd have to talk.

'Not on your own, you won't,' she said. 'It will be dark soon and the weather looks as though it's on the turn.'

The louring clouds were looking heavy and ominous.

'Sit there for five minutes, have something to eat and a

cup of tea, and I'll organise a babysitter and come and help you.'

'But—' said Gabriel.

'But nothing,' said Marianne.

Ten minutes and several stressful phone calls later, she ushered Eve through the door. Gabriel looked surprised, so Marianne said, 'Your mum wasn't available, ok? Eve wants to help.'

'Eve!' the twins looked delighted to see her and threw themselves on her. Marianne was pleased to note the pleasure on Eve's face, and she loved her children for their lack of discrimination. *They* loved Eve for who and what she was. Maybe grown ups should learn from them.

'Right, Gabe,' she said, once they were ready and heading down the lane to the field where they kept the sheep, 'where do you think this missing sheep's gone then?'

Gabe whistled for Patch, and they set off up one of the sheep paths.

'She was somewhere up this path last time I saw her,' he said.

Marianne pulled her scarf around her, and tucked her hand into her gloves, and she followed Gabe out into the twilight.

## Chapter Thirty-Five

'I came here to think,' said Dan. He looked put out to see her, and it made Pippa feel melancholy. Time was when they couldn't bear to be apart. Time was when this was their favourite place in the world.

'About?' asked Pippa.

'Life,' said Dan, 'and how it turns out.'

'Not how you expect usually,' said Pippa, with a sigh.

'No,' said Dan a little sadly. 'Why are you here?'

'I needed to clear my head,' said Pippa.

'Oh,' said Dan, 'I thought you had everything sussed. The farm's sorted, the woods are saved, you're doing fine on your own . . .'

'What?' said Pippa. 'What on earth makes you think that?'

'You,' said Dan. 'You ditched Richard and have managed brilliantly on your own. You're so capable and clever, you're clearly better off on your own.'

'I never said that,' replied Pippa sadly. 'Anyway, you're doing better than me. At least you've got Andrea.'

'Andrea?' Dan said, looking confused.

'Andrea? Your new girlfriend?' said Pippa, herself confused now. Unless . . . She looked at Dan suspiciously. 'Does Andrea actually exist?'

Dan looked a little sheepish.

'Um . . .'

'Why on earth did you make up a girlfriend?'

'Why do you think?' asked Dan.

'Dan, I honestly haven't a clue,' said Pippa. 'I haven't understood a single decision of yours, or known what was going on in your head for the last two years. Certainly not where matters of the heart are concerned.'

'I was jealous that you were coping so well and I wasn't,' admitted Dan. 'I thought you might stop feeling sorry for me, if you thought I was attached.'

'What?' said Pippa, sometimes he was so dense it made her want to thump him. 'Did you have a bang on the head? Oh, sorry, you did, didn't you? You are daft.'

'I am,' said Dan.

'And incredibly stupid,' said Pippa. 'You can't see what's right in front of you.'

'I can't?' said Dan.

'No,' said Pippa, and this time she felt sad. 'It's never been about Richard. I thought for a while it might be, but I was kidding myself. I know you felt you couldn't be the husband I needed after the accident, and I know we're divorced now and I'm buying you out, but it's always been about you. Dan Holliday, wherever you are, whatever you do, I will never stop loving you. I've tried, and I can't. There, I've said it. I'm sorry if it upsets you, but it's how I feel.'

There was a huge silence and Pippa felt incredibly stupid. What had she done? Time after time, Dan had made it perfectly plain, that he wasn't interested anymore. And she'd just laid her soul bare.

'Oh Pippa,' Dan said, 'I've been such a bloody idiot.'

Suddenly arms were wrapping themselves around her, pulling her in.

'Oh god,' he said, 'I've missed you so much. I thought

I'd bring you down, that you were better off without me. But this year, seeing you getting on with your life, and seeing how little you needed me, it's been torture.'

'Did you think I wanted to get on without you?' demanded Pippa through tears that wouldn't stop falling. 'You bastard, Dan, you bloody bastard. All I've ever wanted is you. I could have coped with anything with you beside me. But trying to save the farm alone – it's been hideous.'

Suddenly she was furious with him, and she couldn't help herself from raining blows on his chest. How dare he put her through all this, how dare he?

'How could you, Dan? As if the accident wasn't bad enough, you had to bloody well leave me, when I needed you most.'

She sobbed, and pulled herself away from him.

'Pippa,' began Dan.

'Don't,' said Pippa, 'just leave me alone,' and she stumbled away. She didn't care where she went, she just had to get away . . .

It had started to snow as they walked up the well-worn sheep path that took them to Gabriel's top field.

'With any luck, she'll have found the shelter up there,' said Gabriel. 'I hope so, I really don't like the idea of her giving birth out on the hill.'

He'd barely spoken to her since they'd left the house. Marianne had been quite glad of the silence. She wasn't sure she had the energy for a big debate. The day before Christmas Eve and they were out rescuing sheep. Should they be rescuing their marriage too?

They trudged slowly up the path in the gathering twilight. Gabriel calling out softly to the sheep. There were very few sounds on the hillside, the cawing of crows and the faint murmur of the brook were barely all they heard, and the snow seemed to be muffling them anyway.

'What if we don't find her?' said Marianne.

They were both used to these paths, but it was getting dark quickly, and a bitter wind was whipping up. From experience, Marianne knew how quickly a blizzard could blow up here. She didn't want them to get trapped in the dark.

Gabriel paused and looked around him. Conditions were definitely worsening.

'We'll give it half an hour,' he promised. 'And then we'll turn back.'

In the event they didn't need to. Within ten minutes, they had reached the sheep shelter, and Gabriel ran forward as they heard a faint bleating sound.

'Thank god,' said Gabriel, and ran to the ewe's side.

'Is she ok?' asked Marianne in alarm. The ewe didn't look happy, she was panting heavily and her eyes were rolling in a very distressing manner.

'She's very weak,' said Gabriel, looking anxious. He felt her tummy. 'I think she's ready to give birth. Let me feel.'

He reached inside the ewe and looking grim said, 'Damn, there are two of them, but the legs are the wrong way round. This is going to be tricky . . .'

He rooted around in his bag, and found some rope.

'Remember how to do this?' he said, with a grin Marianne hadn't seen for a long time.

'I do,' she said, vividly remembering the time they'd helped deliver twin lambs, many moons ago. She shivered. That time one of the lambs had died. She hoped that wasn't an omen, 'Come on, hand me the rope.'

The snowstorm was raging all around them, but Marianne

was scarcely aware of the cold as they worked on oblivious. Nothing mattered except getting the babies out safe. All her energies and focus went on that.

It seemed to take a worryingly long time, but eventually the first baby slid out relatively easily, and was soon suckling on his mother, but the second one was more reluctant. Gabriel tied the rope around its legs, but twice it slipped away. Gabriel looked grim, and Marianne feared the worst, not again, please no. It had been so horrible the last time this had happened. Please let them be able to save this lamb.

'Nearly there,' said Gabriel. 'I've got the legs. One two three . . .'

With a lurch backwards, Marianne pulled the rope, and they both tumbled to the ground. Gabriel stood up holding a tiny bundle in his arms. Within minutes, it too was suckling from its mother. Gabriel and Marianne kneeled back in the straw in satisfaction, watching them.

'Way to go, Mrs North,' said Gabriel.

'I think it was all your doing,' said Marianne.

'I couldn't have done it without you, though,' said Gabriel.

'I suppose not,' Marianne smiled.

'In fact, I can't do most things without you,' said Gabriel. 'I'm sorry, Marianne, I've been crap these last few months. Can you forgive me?'

He looked so sincere, Marianne wanted to hug him, but she was still angry with him for what he'd put her through.

'I'm not sure I can forgive you for being a total pillock,' she said. 'Watch my lips, there is and never has been anything going on between me and Luke Nicholas, I hope you'll believe me now.'

'I believe you,' said Gabriel. 'I was so angry about everything, it was an easy accusation to make.'

'Maybe you're forgiven just this once,' she said, leaning over and kissing him on the cheek.

'And about Steven,' he said. 'I was wrong and you were right. I know it's not relevant now, as Eve's leaving, but he is old enough to make his own mind up about things. I should listen to him more.'

'You should,' agreed Marianne, giving him another kiss. Gabriel, *her* kind compassionate Gabe, was back and that was all that mattered.

The ewe moaned suddenly and Gabriel leant over and felt her. She was shivering all over.

'Is she ok?' asked Marianne.

'I don't think so,' said Gabriel, looking worried. 'Oh god we'll never get the vet up here in this, and we can't carry her down the hill.'

In the event, they didn't need to, as the poor thing gave a shudder and died.

'Damn, damn, damn!' said Gabriel. He hated losing sheep, and took it terribly personally.

Marianne looked out at the weather, which had worsened. She touched his arm softly. 'You can't do any more for her,' she said. 'I don't mean to sound callous, but we need to get the babies back.'

'Yes, we should,' said Gabriel. 'We'll have to leave her here for now.'

They moved the ewe into the corner of the shelter, and then picking the babies up, they tucked a lamb each inside their coats, and got up to go.

Marianne felt hers all wriggly and warm close to her skin. Despite the sadness of the moment, it gave her a warm glowing feeling. There was nothing nicer and cosier than holding a newborn lamb in your arms. It gave her hope that there was always a bright future on the horizon.

'Come on, Marianne,' said Gabriel. 'Let's go home.'

'Mum, how could you!' Mel was fuming, she'd been up in her room on the phone for hours and her eyes were streaming red.

'How could I what?' said Cat in surprise. Where had this come from? It was a long time since Mel had been so angry with her.

'Do that bloody TV programme online?' said Mel.

'What's wrong with it?' asked Cat, feeling bemused.

'You never told me Lou Lou was going to be in it,' she said.

'I'm sure I told you,' said Cat.

'But not that she was going to be an internet sensation,' said Mel. 'Did you know it's gone viral?'

'Yes I'd heard but—' Cat looked at her daughter. 'Wait a minute. What is the problem here exactly? Is it a boy?'

'Yes it's a boy,' spat Mel. 'A boy who thought I was Melanie Carpenter, an A level student, and has just discovered I'm Mel Tinsall, daughter of Cat Tinsall and mother to Louise Tinsall.'

'You've got a boyfriend who doesn't know about Lou Lou?' said Cat in disbelief.

'Not anymore, I haven't!' said Mel. 'Thanks a bunch.' She grabbed her car keys, slammed the front door and left the house in a hurry.

'Mel!' Cat shouted. 'At least put a coat on!'

The weather was looking decidedly iffy. It was the day before Christmas Eve, and snow was predicted.

'Mummy?' Lou Lou came tottering into the kitchen.

'She's gone out, poppet,' said Cat, trying to be cheerful

but feeling quite worried. She wondered whether she should send James after Mel, but decided to give her half an hour's grace to calm down.

The half an hour nearly up, the doorbell rang, much to Cat's relief.

'Mel!' she said, flinging the door open with delight. 'Oh.'

Standing on the doorstep was a young man, looking very awkward and embarrassed.

'Er, hello?' said Cat, wondering who the hell he was.

'Hi,' said the boy, 'you must be Mrs Tinsall – Melanie's mum?'

'And you are?'

'Will Harris,' the boy introduced himself. 'Is Melanie in?'

'No, she's not,' said Cat. 'And I'm not sure when she'll be back.'

'That may be my fault,' said the boy. 'I think I overreacted a tad.'

'If you mean you just found out who Mel really is, no I don't think you did,' said Cat. 'I'll try and ring her to let her know you're here.'

'She's not answering my texts,' said Will miserably.

Just then the phone rang.

'Mel?' said Cat eagerly.

'Mum?' said Mel. 'I've got a bit lost, and it's dark and snowing, and the car won't start. And I don't know where I am.'

# Chapter Thirty-Six

'It's ok, Mrs Tinsall, I'll go and find her. I've got GPS on my phone,' said Will.

'Yes but you don't know the roads around here,' said Cat. 'I'll come with you.'

'James,' she said, 'you're in charge. Can you ring your dad and let him know what's happening. I'll call you when I have any news. Come on, Will. The sooner we're out there, the better.'

She followed Will out to his car, as the snow swirled round them in thick angry flakes. This was a horrible night to be out. Mel hadn't got a proper coat with her, she wouldn't have anything to eat or drink. Cat felt sick to the pit of the stomach. She hoped her daughter had the sense to stay in the car. She'd freeze to death outside.

As Will headed out of town towards the road that wound up to the top of the hill, Cat rang Mel again.

'Mel, have you any idea where you might be? Which direction did you drive in?'

Mel sobbed and said, 'I drove up to the top of the hill to look at the view,' – immensely sensible as it was getting dark – 'and then it started snowing and I must have taken a wrong turn . . .'

'Right, go this way,' Cat instructed Will to take the road that led to the top of the hills.

'Any idea where you took the wrong turn?' said Cat to silence. Bugger, she'd lost the signal. She rang back twice, to no avail, while Will skittered dangerously on the road.

'Go easy,' she said, 'it can be lethal up here.'

She was about to try Mel again, when her phone rang.

'Mel, thank god,' she said, 'I lost the signal. Are there any landmarks you recognise?'

'I don't know,' sobbed Mel, 'I skidded and the car's in a ditch.'

She sounded completely hysterical and it was all Cat could do not to join her. Mel's car was in a ditch?

'But you're not hurt,' she said, forcing herself to stay calm.

'No-oo,' sobbed Mel, 'just cold and frightened.'

'Take a deep breath, and stay calm,' said Cat, 'can you remember anything that might help us?'

'Wait, I think there was a crossroads,' said Mel.

Crossroads? *Crossroads?*

Bingo! Suddenly Cat knew where Mel meant, but the road up the hill was slippery and it was slow going.

'Be very very careful,' she said to Will, 'you need to go this way.'

It was nearly half an hour before they found themselves on the top of the huge stretch of hills. Cat tried to rack her brains as to how far away the crossroads was.

Will was proving a bit of a find. He seemed the rugged outdoor type, and completely unfazed about the situation they found themselves in.

'So you and Mel?' Cat was driven with curiosity to ask, now that she felt a little less anxious.

'She's not mentioned me?' said Will, looking hurt.

371

'Well to be fair, it doesn't sound like she really mentioned us,' said Cat, 'let's just say I think she was trying to keep her two lives separate.'

'We've been seeing each other for a couple of months,' said Will.

'And?' said Cat.

'And I saw your TV programme. I recognised you from one time when you came to pick Melanie up from college. I had no idea you were famous or that Melanie had written a book.'

'Or had a daughter,' added Cat.

'Or that,' said Will. He sighed. 'I didn't handle it well.'

'I'm not entirely surprised,' said Cat. 'She is silly, she should have told you.'

There was a pause, and then Cat said, 'But Mel has had a hard time of it. Her previous boyfriend treated her very badly. Don't be too tough on her.'

'That's why I'm here,' said Will. 'To say sorry, and see if we can't give it another go.'

Well, I like *you*, thought Cat.

They were coming up to the crossroads Mel had mentioned, and Cat started to feel anxious again. Which fork would she have taken?

Their first attempt was a mistake and Will nearly reversed into a ditch, but then they took the second fork, and halfway down the road, half covered in snow, was the forlorn sight of Mel's little Ka.

Will parked up and got out of the car. Cat followed at a distance, not wanting to get in the way. Mel opened the door to her car and looked at him in shock.

'Will?' she said

'Oh Melanie,' he said, 'I am so sorry,' and they threw their arms around each other.

Cat looked on in relief. Her daughter was safe, and had apparently regained a boyfriend. All was well with the world.

'Do you fancy Christmas at ours?' she said.

Pippa strode off in a fury, vaguely aware that it was getting dark, and maybe she should turn back. But she was so mixed up and angry, she didn't care. After *all* that Dan had put her through in the last couple of years, *now* he had to tell her how he felt. Now, when they'd been divorced for the best part of a year, and she was finally making a life for herself. He was a, 'Pig!' Pippa shouted suddenly to the snowy wasteland around her. 'Imbecile! Idiot! Bastard!' She let out a long stream of invective and frustration. Why, why, why? Why did he have to say all this now?

*But you're pleased, really*, a little voice in her head said, *just a little bit*. No, Pippa's fury answered her, I'm livid. *But he still loves you*, the voice persisted. It seemed to have taken on an annoying sing song tone. 'Not listening,' Pippa said out loud, as she strode onwards. It was dark now, very dark, and the snow which had been falling steadily all afternoon was piling up in drifts. This was stupid. She ought to get home, where she'd left the boys in charge of Lucy. It was unfair on them to be out so long.

She turned round to strike back down the path she'd come up, only to realise it had vanished completely. The snow was so heavy now, the path was totally hidden. Oh crap. This was stupid, and dangerous. She was fairly near the top of the hill, it made more sense to keep climbing upwards, that way she could find her way to the road which went across the top of the hills and led back down to Hope Christmas. With any luck there might be someone as idiotic as her out in their car, and she could follow the sounds of their engine.

It was hard going in the snow. Luckily she'd come out in wellies, but her feet were soon freezing, and her gloves wet through from where she'd scrabbled at the snow. She was puffed out, and ridiculously feeling quite hot, considering she was in the middle of a snowstorm. Cursing herself for getting into this idiotic position, she nearly wept with relief when she could just make out the sound of a motorbike in the distance. Pulling herself up the last steep bit, she managed to get to the top of the hill, and a few hundred yards away to her relief, she saw that there was someone on a motorbike, who'd paused on the road.

It wasn't just any someone, it was Michael Nicholas, sitting astride his motorbike, looking as if he didn't have a care in the world.

'Well you're a sight for sore eyes,' said Pippa, 'I was worried I'd lost the road.'

'Luckily you've found it again,' said Michael. 'If you hop on the back, I'll make sure you get down safely.'

So, feeling slightly surreal, Pippa got on the back of Michael's bike and he negotiated his way carefully down the road. She should have felt terrified, with the road being so hazardous, but somehow she didn't; she felt safe and contented, as though everything would be well.

Michael deposited her at the bottom of the lane.

'I expect you know the way from here,' he said. 'You'll be ok, now, Pippa. Everything's going to be fine.'

Pippa walked down the lane feeling a little bemused. As she got to the gate, to her surprise, she found Dan leaning against it, waiting for her as if it were the most natural thing in the world.

'You,' she said, remembering she was angry. 'I'm not talking to *you*.'

Then she looked around her. She'd left him way back in

the fields, and Michael had brought her home on his bike. How had Dan got there so quickly?

'How did you get here?'

'Ralph Nicholas showed me a shortcut, across Blackstock Farm which I'd never seen before,' said Dan. 'He seemed to think you'd be coming in this direction.'

Ralph and Michael helping them both? What a strange coincidence.

'Look, Pippa, I'm so sorry. For everything I've put you through. You're right, I've been ridiculously unfair to you. Ever since that bloody injury, it's like I haven't been able to think straight. But for the first time, now I am.'

The injury – that's where all this had started – Dan falling out of that tree. Pippa thought back to that awful day in hospital, when she thought she'd lost him forever.

'Oh Dan,' she said. 'We've wasted so much time.'

'But there's one thing I'm not muddled about, not anymore,' said Dan. 'And that's you. I pushed you away because I was afraid. I thought I'd ruin your life by staying. I was afraid you'd grow to resent me. But I'm too selfish, Pippa. I'm sorry. I can't do it anymore. I miss you and love you too much to ever want to be without you again.'

'Oh Dan,' said Pippa. 'You idiot. Please, just come home.'

# My Broken Brain

So we've come full circle, and ended where we began. And I've learnt a valuable lesson.

I might be broken. I might not be the person I used to be. But I still love the people I used to love, and they still love me.

I look at Pippa and the children every day and feel blessed that we've come through this storm. I was mad to ever think I could manage without them. To think that because I'd changed they wouldn't accept me anymore.

Life isn't the way it was. But we've all come through this stronger. And whatever the future holds, I know it will be fine.

Because Pippa and I are together again. And I'm back where I belong. And nothing will ever take me away from here ever again.

# *Epilogue*

'More mulled wine for you two lovebirds?' Cat came up to Dan and Pippa proffering a jug of hot spiced wine. She and Noel had decided to have an impromptu party for Christmas Eve, and the whole village seemed to have turned out. Diana Carew was there, hot footing it from the nativity play, which she had taken over from Marianne this year, about which there had already been complaints.

'Oh god,' Marianne had confided in Cat, who had had to endure watching the twins as mice in a play that had gone on forever, 'I'm going to be back doing it again next year aren't I?'

Pippa and Dan meantime were attached to each other like limpets. They appeared not to have let go of one another since they'd arrived back home the previous day. Cat was so pleased for them, it was like the balance of the universe righting itself now Pippa and Dan were an item again.

And Marianne and Gabriel seemed to have sorted out their differences too. Eve was coming for Christmas lunch, and when she discovered that Gabriel had reconsidered the situation with Steven, had changed her mind and agreed to stay in Hope Christmas. Steven would be moving in with her after Christmas.

'It's going to be a wrench,' Marianne said, 'but it's definitely the right thing to do, and Gabe agrees with me now, which is great.'

As for her own family, well it looked like they'd gained an extra member. It turned out Will had a complicated family situation and was going to be alone for Christmas, so Cat had asked him to stay with them instead. He'd hit it off instantly with James, who appeared pleased to have a surrogate brother. And Noel too seemed pleased of the extra male company. Lou Lou was a little unsure what to make of the new arrival, but Cat was hoping as she was little enough, she'd soon come round.

All in all, it felt like a very happy Christmas. A perfect one, in fact.

'Anything I can do?' asked Angela.

'Enjoy yourself,' said Cat. 'Go on it's Christmas.'

'I still think Mum would be better off near me,' Kay was arguing with Noel, but Cat could tell her heart wasn't in it.

'When's Santa coming?' asked Lou Lou. Since she'd visited Santa at Pippa's she'd been asking the same question every day. 'Want Santa now!'

'Time for bed,' said Mel, picking her daughter up and carrying her up the stairs. 'Come on, sweetie. When you wake up, Santa will be here.'

Lou Lou was already asleep by the time Cat had popped up to see how Mel was getting on.

'Shall we sort her stocking out now?' whispered Mel, who had been even more excited about planning what to put in Lou Lou's stocking than Cat was – it had always been Cat's favourite part of Christmas when the children were small, and it was lovely to have the ritual back.

'Ok,' whispered Cat, 'but let's not put it back in her room

till we go to bed, otherwise she might wake up at ten o'clock and think Santa's been.'

Giggling together, they crept out of Lou Lou's room with the stocking and went to the cupboard in Cat's bedroom where she had hidden the presents for years.

'You do know we worked out your hiding place ages ago, don't you?' said Mel, as she stuffed some chocolate coins in the bottom of the stocking.

'No, I didn't,' said Cat. 'Don't tell me you always found out what your presents were before the big day.'

'There was one year when James found his Playstation,' said Mel, 'but usually you'd wrapped them before we got to them.'

'I'm glad to hear it,' said Cat, 'I'd hate to think I'd ruined your Christmases.'

'You could never do that,' said Mel, 'we've always had the best Christmases ever.'

She gave her mum a hug, and Cat felt a lovely warm tingly feeling. Her family was growing up, but some things would always stay precious and perfect.

'And this one is going to be the best yet,' said Cat. 'Come on that's us done, let's go down and join the party.'

And join the party they did. Everyone was in cheerful mood, the mulled wine was flowing, and the chatter constant. Cat looked round her with satisfaction, as the Christmas lights sparkled on the Christmas tree. Her favourite time of year, with all her favourite people. Life didn't get better than this.

The doorbell rang and in walked Ralph and Michael Nicholas, to the delight of all.

'Our guests of honour,' said Cat, with a smile. 'I think we all owe you both something this year.'

'Which is what we're here for,' said Ralph, giving a very small bow.

'Let's raise our glasses,' said Noel. 'To families, friendship and love.'

'And a very happy Christmas to us all,' said Cat. 'A perfect one, in fact.'